As the Crow Flies

CRAIG JOHNSON

AS THE CROW FLIES

VIKING

VIKING
Published by the Penguin Group
Penguin Group (USA) Inc., 375 Hudson Street,
New York, New York 10014, U.S.A.
Penguin Group (Canada), 90 Eglinton Avenue East, Suite 700,
Toronto, Ontario, Canada M4P 2Y3
(a division of Pearson Penguin Canada Inc.)
Penguin Books Ltd, 80 Strand, London WC2R 0RL, England
Penguin Ireland, 25 St. Stephen's Green, Dublin 2, Ireland
(a division of Penguin Books Ltd)
Penguin Books Australia Ltd, 250 Camberwell Road, Camberwell,
Victoria 3124, Australia
(a division of Pearson Australia Group Pty Ltd)
Penguin Books India Pvt Ltd, 11 Community Centre, Panchsheel Park,
New Delhi – 110 017, India
Penguin Group (NZ), 67 Apollo Drive, Rosedale, Auckland 0632,
New Zealand (a division of Pearson New Zealand Ltd)
Penguin Books (South Africa) (Pty) Ltd, 24 Sturdee Avenue,
Rosebank, Johannesburg 2196, South Africa

Penguin Books Ltd, Registered Offices:
80 Strand, London WC2R 0RL, England

First published in 2012 by Viking Penguin,
a member of Penguin Group (USA) Inc.
1   3   5   7   9   10   8   6   4   2

Publisher's Note
This is a work of fiction. Names, characters, places, and incidents either are the product of the
author's imagination or are used fictitiously, and any resemblance to actual persons, living or dead,
business establishments, events, or locales is entirely coincidental.

LIBRARY OF CONGRESS CATALOGING-IN-PUBLICATION DATA

Johnson, Craig——.
As the crow flies / Craig Johnson.
p. cm.
ISBN 978-0-670-02351-6
1. Longmire, Walt (Fictitious character)—Fiction.   2. Sheriffs—Fiction.   3. Homicide
investigation—Fiction.   4. Native Americans—Fiction.   5. Indian reservations—Fiction.   6. Northern
Cheyenne Indian Reservation (Mont.)   7. Montana—Fiction.   I. Title.
PS3610.O325A8 2012
813'.6—dc22   2011040961

Printed in the United States of America
Set in Dante MT Std
Designed by Alissa Amell

ALWAYS LEARNING   PEARSON

For Marcus Red Thunder, who like Henry knows which way the wind blows

The Indians survived our open intention of wiping them out, and since the tide turned they have even weathered our good intentions toward them, which can be much more deadly.

—John Steinbeck, *America and Americans*

ACKNOWLEDGMENTS

People always ask me if I catch grief about using the politically incorrect term "Indian" in my books rather than the currently acceptable phrase "Native American." Most of my interaction has been with members of the Cheyenne and Crow tribes, who generally laugh when I try to use the more sensitive term. They ask me where, exactly, I was born—hence, my being a "Native American," too. I've been fortunate enough to spend time over the years with these magnificent people, and I can honestly say that I enjoy their company above all others.

Everybody knows that you never enter unknown territory without an Indian scout and in this go-round it was my good buddy Claude Rowland, with many trips to the Tribal Offices, Birney (both Red and White), and a few to the café in Ashland. Many thanks to Cheyenne Tribal Police Chief Algin Young for giving me an insider's view of his extremely difficult but ultimately satisfying job on the Rez. Big thanks to Linnie Birdchief for her time behind a badge and being the inspiration for Lolo Long (especially the eyebrows). As always, a hardy thanks to Leroy Whiteman for the porch talks and keeping me straight on the red road. Thank you to my good friend Charles Little Old Man for the stories and to Rosalie Bird Woman for the education on Sweet Medicine. Thanks with all my heart to Lonnie Little Bird for the campfire (say hey to Melissa for me). Thanks to Tiger

Scalpcane and Don "Porkchop" Shoulderblade for the prayers—they must be working.

A debt of deep gratitude is owed to the Ashland Ranger District for the use of the Whitetail Cabin and their valiant attempt at trying to keep me politically correct. To the Jimtown Bar, a great place to have a conversation and a couple of cold ones—just don't look for the beer can mountain that used to be there (even though I did my part in trying to rebuild it). Thanks to Eli Yoder and Yoder's World Famous Boots just north of Ashland, Montana—I'm proudly wearing a pair!

The usual ten little Indians get their fair share: Kathryn Court, Tara Singh, Maureen Donnelly, Ben Petrone, Gabrielle Gantz, Barbara Campo, Gail Hochman, Greer Shephard, John Coveny, Hunt Baldwin, Chris Donahue, Tiffany Ward, and Susan Fain (okay, so it's thirteen).

For the fall not winter, spring not summer, cool not cold that is my inspiration in all things, my wife Judy.

1

"I wanna know what Katrina Walks Nice did to get kicked out of a joint like this for sixty-one days."

I began questioning the makeup of the negotiation team I'd brought with me to convince the chief of the Northern Cheyenne tribe that he should allow my daughter to be married at Crazy Head Springs. "Don't call the White Buffalo a joint; it's the nerve center of the reservation."

My undersheriff, Victoria Moretti, shook her head. "It's a fucking convenience store." She smiled, enjoying the muckraking. "She must've done something pretty shitty to get eighty-sixed out of here for two months." Vic gestured toward the white plastic board above the cash register where all the reservation offenders who had been tagged with bad-check writing, shoplifting, and other unsavory behaviors were cataloged for everyone to see—sort of a twenty-first-century pillorying.

My eyes skimmed past the board, and I watched the crows circle above Lame Deer as the rain struck the surface of Route 212. It was the main line on the Rez, and the road that truckers used to avoid the scales on the interstate. Before 212 had been widened and properly graded, it had been known as Scalp Alley for the number of traveling unfortunates who had met their demise on the composite scoria/asphalt strip and for the roadside crosses that ran like chain lightning from the Black Hills to the Little Bighorn.

As my good friend Henry Standing Bear says, on the Rez, even the roads are red.

I was trying to pay attention, but I kept being distracted by the crows plying the thermals of the high plains sky; it was raining in the distance, but the sun appeared to be overtaking the clouds—a sharp contrast of blue and charcoal that my mother used to say was caused by the devil beating his wife.

"She must've stolen the cash register."

My attention was forced back inside and under cover, and I twisted the ring on my pinkie. My wife, Martha, had given it back to me before she died so that I could give it to Cady whenever she got married.

I looked up—the negotiations weren't going well. It would appear that Dull Knife College had suddenly scheduled a Cheyenne language immersion class at Crazy Head Springs on the day of the wedding. We had reserved the spot well in advance, but the vagaries of the tribal council were well known and now we were floundering. The old Indian across from me nodded his head in all seriousness. I was negotiating with the chief of the Northern Cheyenne nation, and he was one tough customer.

"That librarian over at the college is mean. I don't like to mess with her; she's got that Indian Alzheimer's. Um hmm, yes, it is so."

I trailed my eyes from Lonnie Little Bird to the rain-slick surface of the asphalt—Lame Deer's main street being washed clean of all our sins. "What's that mean, Lonnie?"

"That's where you forget everything but the grudges."

I smiled in spite of myself and took a deep breath, slowly letting the air out to calm my nerves, as I continued to twirl the ring on my finger. "Cady's really got her heart set on Crazy Head

Springs, Lonnie, and it's way too late to change the date from the end of July."

He glanced out the window, his dark eyes following my gray ones. "Maybe you should go talk to that librarian over at the college. You're a large man—she'll listen to you. You could show her your gun." He glanced down at the red and black chief's blanket that covered his wheelchair. "She don't pay no attention to an old, legless Indian."

Henry Standing Bear, my daughter's wedding planner, who had made the arrangements that were now being rapidly unraveled, sipped his coffee and quietly listened.

"But you're the chief, Lonnie."

"Oh, you know that don't mean much unless somebody wants a government contract for beef or needs a ribbon cut."

Up until this year, Lonnie's official contribution to the tribal government had been limited to falling asleep in council. A month ago, when the previous tribal leader had been found guilty of siphoning off money to a private account belonging to his daughter, an emergency meeting had been held; since Lonnie had again fallen asleep, and therefore was unable to defend himself, he was unanimously voted in as the new chief.

"She's in charge of all the books over there and she's full blood—that's pretty much the worst of both worlds."

A heavyset man with long hair and a gray top hat with an eagle feather in it stopped by the table and rapped his knuckles on the surface. "Mornin', Chief."

Lonnie sighed. "I wish you wouldn't call me that, Herbert."

Herbert His Good Horse, the morning drive announcer on the low-power FM station KRZZ, smiled and turned to the rest of us in the crowded booth. "Do you know the story about the three Indian women who died at the same time?"

Herbert was a mainstay on the Rez, where almost everyone

tuned in to 94.7 FM just to hear the outrageous jokes he told between songs.

Lonnie responded for the table. "Nope."

"St. Peter was sitting on his throne at the gates of heaven—"

"Is this a true story, Herbert?"

He nodded his head vigorously, the eagle feather stuck in the band of his hat bobbing up and down like a crest on his head. "It's from one of those priests over at St. Labre, and those Catholics, they sometimes tell the truth."

Vic barked a laugh. "Fuckin' A." She raised an empty coffee cup to get Brandon White Buffalo's attention in hopes of a round of refills, but the big Crow Indian was attending to another customer.

Herbert His Good Horse produced an elongated cigar from his silk brocade vest along with a cutter. "One of the women was Lakota, one was Crow, and the other was full-blood Cheyenne. St. Peter looked at them and said that they were heathens and there wasn't anything he could do to let them into the white man's heaven, but that he was curious because they had all three died at the same time. He asked the first one, the Lakota woman, if she had anything to say, and she said she didn't know anything about the rules but she had always lived her life attempting to seek a balance in the red and black roads. St. Peter listened and was impressed by the spirituality of the woman and told her she could go in after all."

Lonnie smiled and nodded as Herbert repocketed the cutter and produced a chopped-down, brass Zippo lighter, the one that he had carried in the seventies in Vietnam. "St. Peter leaned down to the Crow woman and asked her if she had anything she wanted to say, and she told him that to her, there was a spirit in the air, the land, the water, and all the creatures that populated mother earth and that she had spent her life attempting to be respectful of all these things. St. Peter was so impressed that he waved her into the white man's heaven, too."

Lonnie sipped his coffee, and Henry, smiling, glanced at me.

"Then St. Peter turned on his throne and looked at the Cheyenne woman. He asked her, 'Do you have anything you'd like to say?' The Cheyenne woman nodded and said—'Yeah, what are you doing in my chair?'"

Lonnie laughed so hard, rolling his head from side to side with his mouth hanging open, that no sound came out. After a while he began slapping Henry on the leg; I suppose just because the Bear had both of his and because he was also Cheyenne. "Um hmm, yes, it is so."

Herbert, who had recovered from laughing at his own joke, lit his cigar, rapped the table, and signed off with his signature slogan—"Stay calm, have courage . . ."

The entire booth responded with the rest: "And wait for signs."

Henry, probably glad for the interruption, put his own cold coffee on the table, smiled indulgently, and watched the disc jockey stroll away. It really wasn't the Bear's fault that our site had been suddenly appropriated at the last minute; as he'd explained to me, clearing all the events of all the organizations on the reservation was akin to herding prairie chickens.

I stared down at the platinum ring with the smallish diamond that was between two inset chips. "What's the librarian's name, Lonnie?"

At the mention of our collective obstruction, the laughter died away in his throat. "Oh, it's my sister Arbutis. Umm hmm, yes, it is so."

Henry raised a hand and massaged the bridge of his nose with a powerful thumb and forefinger. "*Ahh-he*', I had forgotten."

I knew Arbutis Little Bird—more as Lonnie's daughter's aunt

than as his sister. Melissa, with whom I'd been involved in a complicated case a couple of years ago, was now away in Bozeman playing point guard for Montana State. The news couldn't have been worse for our cause—Arbutis was a steely-eyed, iron-bottomed gunboat of a woman whose natural response to everything was an absolute negative that brooked no discussion.

I looked back out the window where the crows had disappeared and the rain appeared to be winning the battle. We were doomed.

"Henry, have you thought about taking him down to Painted Warrior? That's a pretty fine spot, um hmm, um hmm. There are crows all over the bottom land, and they circle the cliffs up where the warrior's war paint streaks the rocks. Yes, it is so."

The Bear released his nose. "Near Red Birney?"

They both smiled, and Lonnie nodded. "Yeah, definitely not White Birney."

In a perverseness of geography, there were two towns by the name of Birney just on and just off the Rez. To the Indians they will forever be referred to as Red Birney and White Birney, but to the politically correct Caucasians the names had been transmogrified to Birney Day (for the day school), and Birney Post (for the post office). Like most things on the Rez, it was complicated.

"You can take the ridge road, but you'll need a four-wheel-drive if it really decides to rain. If I was you, I'd take 4 down to the windmill at Tie Creek, and then go up the dirt track till you get to the spotter road to your right—that'll take you straight over to the base of the cliffs."

A spotter road was the name the locals called roads used to spotlight and poach deer on the Rez. I was already losing faith. "Lonnie, Cady's really got her heart set on Crazy Head Springs, and the wedding is in two weeks."

He nodded again and then became somber in respect for the gravity of my situation. "Well then, maybe you should go on over to the library, but take your gun, Walter. Umm hmm, yes, it is so."

Vic stopped at the counter to buy some chewing gum and was having a conversation with Brandon White Buffalo—probably something to do with Katrina Walks Nice.

Henry was rolling Lonnie out the door and into the stunningly mixed-up summer afternoon, the ozone hanging in the air like baskets. The Cheyenne Nation, thinking it might be wise to explore other avenues, looked back at me. "Would you like to go take a look at Painted Warrior?"

I made a face, thinking about how I was going to break the news to Cady. "Well, I really don't want to go over to the library and tangle with Arbutis Little Bird, I can tell you that much."

"It is possible I can do that later. Do you have your gun? I may have to borrow it."

I slapped the small of my back, where my duty sidearm rested simply from habit. "All I've got is my .45, and I don't think that'd bring down Arbutis." I pushed open the door and started toward Henry's truck, which I truly despised. I'd loaned the Bullet to Vic so that she could go ahead to Billings, where she would be taking a flight to Omaha later that day for a training seminar on police public relations. That left me with Lonnie, Henry, and Rezdawg, the most pernicious vehicle on the North American continent.

Vic made her way past, reading my mind. "You're sure you don't need your truck?"

"I'll be fine."

She placed a fist on her belt and stood there, hipshot.

"I'm still trying to figure out why it is you volunteered to go to Omaha."

"Somebody's gotta do it."

"Yep, but Saizarbitoria could've gone—Frymire or Double-Tough."

She shrugged and turned her head.

"This doesn't have anything to do with the upcoming nuptials, does it?"

She stubbed the toe of a ballistic boot on the asphalt of the parking lot. "Mom's going to be here the day after tomorrow." She looked to the distance, at nothing particular. "I'm not good at this shit. I'll be back right before the wedding, but I think I'll just avoid the run-up to the three-ring circus—if you don't mind." She hit the button on my remote, and the lights blipped on my truck.

"Okay, but I assume you're not taking Dog."

She responded by opening the door, and we watched as more than a hundred and fifty pounds of assorted canine lineage vaulted from the front seat and circled around to the '63 three-quarter-ton beast, first going to Lonnie. The Northern Cheyenne chief reached his wrinkled hands out the door and around Dog's head, running a thumb over the bullet furrow and holding him as if giving a blessing. "*Ha-ay*, big rascal."

I went around the back and lowered Rezdawg's tailgate, pinching my fingers in the chains in the process. I waited till Dog noticed me and came around. He looked at the derelict truck and promptly sat.

"Vic needs the Bullet. Come on, we both get to suffer."

He jumped in the bed and I closed the tailgate twice because, of course, the first time it didn't line up.

Vic rolled down the driver's-side window of my truck. "You're going to be all right up here playing cowboy with the Indians?"

I joined her at the door. "I think so." We both watched as Henry put Lonnie's blanket over his lap, folded up the chief's wheelchair, and placed it in the bed with Dog. "I've got a good scout."

"Uh huh." She hit the ignition and fired up the V-10 and then sat there, rumbling. "I'll call you from Nebraska." She thought about it and pulled the three-quarter-ton down into gear. "Fuck it, what else is there to do?"

It was only a mile up the road to Lonnie's place, which was good because that was about the distance that Rezdawg could make without breaking down.

In the numerous conversations I'd had with Henry concerning his pickup, I'd asked him why, as meticulous as he was with every other aspect of his life—his house, his business, his car—why it was that he didn't get his piece-of-crap truck really fixed. His answer, as we'd waited by the side of the road for another of Rezdawg's rest periods to pass, was that the truck was a holy relic of his life and that replacing parts would alter its spirit. I retorted that it seemed to me that the junk pile's spirit was in need of a little repair, but he'd ignored me like he always did.

I'd also pointed out that the thing didn't have its original gas, tires, or oil, but that hadn't gotten me anywhere, either.

I rolled the chief up the incline to his picture-perfect home. Lonnie had had some wilder days when he was younger and had played baseball and drunk on a professional level until losing his legs to diabetes. He was still under parole with a cadre of sisters, headed by the formidable Arbutis, and had to negotiate with his sisters for visitation rights whenever Melissa, the point guard, came home, but he complained that that was less and less.

"She has lots of friends up there in Bozeman. I can see why it is she'd rather stay there than come home and watch stories with me." The stories Lonnie referred to were the soap operas he watched religiously and reported on as if the characters were actual friends. "But it just makes me love her more when she does come home—um hmm, yes, it is so."

I paused on the porch so Lonnie could collect his mail from a box attached to the house; most residents on the Rez had post office boxes and didn't get this kind of attention to delivery, but Lonnie was special.

"They toy with our hearts, these daughters of ours—don't they, lawman?"

"Yes, they do."

He patted my hand in reassurance. "Don't worry; we'll get your daughter's wedding sorted out."

"Thanks, Lonnie."

I started to roll him into the house, but his hands fastened around the chrome runners of his wheelchair. "I think I will stay out here and watch the rain; maybe listen to some baseball. The Rockies are at home and playing the Phillies this afternoon."

I looked at the sky with its patchwork of sun and storm clouds—the devil must be beating his wife indeed. I bet I was the only one who used that phrase anymore.

I adjusted Lonnie's chair so that he could look northwest and watch the rain come in or not, whatever its choice. The laden clouds were reflected in Lonnie's thick glasses and joined with the tiny rainbows that had a tendency to magically appear there, confirming the impression that Lonnie was a pot of gold.

"The devil must be beating his wife. Um hmm, yes, it is so."

A damp Dog joined us on the bench seat as we headed back toward town, and I continued to spin the ring on my finger as I aired an elbow out the passenger-side window that only partially rolled down. "It's not your fault."

The Cheyenne Nation ignored me and stared out the cracked windshield.

"Look, whatever happens, she'll forgive you—just not me."

The Bear nodded and then moved on to one of our other myriad problems. "We have maxed out the Western 8 motel in Ashland."

There were no other motels for about fifty miles.

He shifted gears, and I listened to them grind. "There is my home."

"I don't want you to have to do that."

"It would be an honor."

If you hung around with the Cheyenne long enough, you learned when not to argue with their generosity. "Thank you." I stretched my hand across Dog's broad head and scratched behind both ears, something he enjoyed as though it was a religious experience. "Strange weather."

Henry didn't say anything but glanced at the ring on my pinkie. I tried to change the subject. "Why do you suppose the old-timers used to say that the devil must be beating his wife?"

He spoke over the aged engine as he made third, breezed through the stop sign at the corner of one of Lame Deer's few intersections, and headed south on Bureau of Indian Affairs Route 4, the rumble strips sounding like war drums underneath us. "It is a universal folkloric phrase." He threw Rezdawg into fourth, and we tooled back through the main part of town past the White Buffalo Sinclair Station, the Big Store IGA, which Henry says stands for Indians Grab Anything, and the tribal government buildings. "The Italian version is the same as ours but the French one is *Le diable se marie avec sa fille,* or the devil becomes his daughter's husband."

I stopped petting Dog, threw my arm over the back seat, and looked out the rear window. "Perverts."

"The German proverb is *Wenn's regnet und die Sonne scheint, so schlägt der Teufel seine Großmutter: er lacht und sie weint,* which means that the devil is beating his grandmother: he laughs and she cries."

A black Yukon with a heavy grille guard and Montana plates had started following us in town and was a little close to Rezdawg's back bumper, at which point I noticed that there was an understated halogen emergency light flashing red on the dash.

"There are similar phrases in Hungary and Holland."

"Have you been hanging around Jules Beldon?" The emergency lights in the vehicle behind us were definitely signaling us to pull over. "Hey, Henry?"

Unaware that some sort of official vehicle was dogging us, or more likely ignoring the summons, he continued to navigate our way out of town. "The Polish say that when the sun is shining and the rain is raining that the devil is making butter."

I fully turned in the seat to get a better look. "Henry . . ."

The GMC made an aggressive move and started to pull up beside us; the Yukon's engine surged, and the Bear finally noticed it.

"The Russians call it a blind rain; somewhat depressing but still poetic." He waited a moment for the SUV to go around and when it didn't, he pulled Rezdawg over to the gravel between the reflector posts at the side of the road. "Either way, the devil gets the blame for everything."

I watched as the Yukon, in direct violation of standard police procedure, pulled slanted in front of us as if we might make a run for it, which, considering it was Rezdawg, made the situation that much funnier. There were no markings on the vehicle, and I watched as the driver's-side door was jerked open and a very tall, athletic-looking woman with dark hair got out.

Resting a hand on the roof of the GMC, she concentrated her Oakley reflective sunglasses on us. She stood there for a second, then slammed the door and, ignoring the few cars that swerved to avoid her, started around the rear of her vehicle. She had high, wide cheekbones and a strong jaw that balanced the features framed in the blue-black hair that was braided to her elbows. Late twenties, she was wearing black jeans, a Tribal Police uniform shirt, black ropers, and a matching gun belt with a very large caliber Smith & Wesson N-Frame revolver banging against her hip.

She looked like one of those ultimate warriors who can step out on the sidewalk and run a marathon at the drop of a war bonnet.

"License and registration."

Henry didn't move, just continued to look at her. I didn't blame him.

She made the statement again, this time with a little more force, separating the words as she spoke. "License. And. Registration."

Henry glanced at me and then pulled the naked, cardboard sun visor down, the vinyl covering having disintegrated and shed like snakeskin long ago. The registration and insurance card fluttered onto his lap like a shot bird. He leaned up on one side and pulled his wallet from his back pocket and removed his license, adding it to the collection he handed her. "What is the problem, Officer?"

She studied the collection of documents and then gestured toward the black Yukon. "Do you see that vehicle?"

Henry made a production of lowering his Wayfarers and placing the flat palm of his hand above his eyes like some B-movie Indian spotting a wagon train. "Yes, I think I do."

The next statement had even more heat in it. "That is an *official vehicle*, and when it indicates for you to pull over—you pull over." She glanced down at the license and studied it for a moment. "I know you, Mr. Henry Standing Bear."

He studied her in an indifferent manner. "And I have heard of you, Ms. Lolo Long."

I noticed that this time when he called her by name, he did not proffer the title of officer.

Her chin came out as she locked eyes with him—something not too many people would or could do. "And what have you heard?"

"I have heard that you are the tightest . . ."

I interrupted, sensing that what the Cheyenne Nation was about to say wasn't likely to help our situation. "Why didn't you hit your siren?"

A long moment passed as she shifted her gaze from Henry, past Dog, to me. She lowered her own sunglasses to get a better look into the gloom of the cab, and her jasper-colored eyes leveled on me like the twin-bore of a battleship turret. "Excuse me, but was I speaking to you?"

I shrugged a shoulder and smiled inwardly at her resemblance to Vic. "Well, I guess it's none of my business, but there are no markings on that vehicle and this thing sits awfully high and as close as you were I had to really look to see your emergency lights—if you'd have just hit your . . ."

She threw an arm up on the door sill and interrupted me. "You know, Mister . . . ?" She left the statement hanging there like her arm.

"Longmire."

She shook her head ever so slightly, as if my name was an annoyance in itself. "That first part, the one about this not being any of your business?" She pointed a no-nonsense fingernail in the air, as if pinning my words, like bugs in a collection. "I liked that; let's stick with that one." The iridescent glasses came back up, and she turned to face Henry. "I know a lot of people around here consider you to be something kind of special, but that doesn't exclude you from the rules of the road." She raised a hand, gesturing back toward town. "That sign back there at the intersection says stop, not pause, not hesitate—stop is what it says, and whenever I'm around you better damn well stop."

I watched as she took his cards and disappeared back toward the Yukon, her wrist-thick braid held fast by a beaded barrette bobbing in counterpoint to her strut and the slap of the revolver.

The Bear looked bored and supported his chin with a fist and placed an elbow out the window. "So, when did you start wearing a pinkie ring?"

I stopped twirling it. "It belonged to my great-grandmother."

"The witch?"

I sighed at the Bear's knowledge of my family history. "She wasn't a witch; she was just one of those herb doctors." He nodded, but I could tell he didn't agree. "Martha wore it but gave it back to me to give it to Cady when she got married. The problem is that Michael already got her an engagement ring so I don't know what to do with it."

He mumbled into his fist. "Give it to her."

"People are weird about that kind of thing sometimes."

"Just give it to her." He reached out and smoothed a piece of duct tape that held the instrument panel to the dash. "Is that why you are wearing it, to remind you?"

"Kind of. I lost it a while back and then discovered it in a little cedar box I've got on my dresser. I thought maybe if I kept it on my finger I wouldn't lose it again."

The Bear didn't say anything but looked back at the Yukon. I could still see the adhesive where the sticker price had been on the inside of the window—and ventured a question. "Who's Ms. Lolo Long?"

"The new tribal police chief, an appointment from the last tribal chief."

I nodded. "The indicted one."

"Yes—the one whom Lonnie replaced." He pursed his lips and pointed them toward the Yukon, where it looked as if Officer Long was in the act of writing a lengthy ticket. "Iraqi war vet; I do not know what she did over there, but she came back wired tight like a Montana-made mandolin. I guess the old chief was trying to make up for his tenure and thought he was doing everybody a favor by installing a by-the-book police chief, but so far as I can tell, all she has done is made the lives of everyone miserable."

I watched as she opened the door and approached, the hi-tech sunglasses now secured in her breast pocket. "Including yours?"

He smiled the close-lipped smile. "Lately."

Officer Long stopped at the door and handed Henry his papers along with an aluminum clipboard and pen. "I've cited you for failure to stop at the intersection, failure to respond to an official vehicle, and the fact that you have no brake lights." She glanced down the dented, mottled-green length of Rezdawg and then back to the Bear. "I'm sure I could find plenty of other violations attached to this particular vehicle, but seeing as how this is our first official meeting, I thought I'd take it easy on you."

The Cheyenne Nation looked at me, but I didn't say anything and continued to pet Dog. The beast looked at Lolo Long with expectation, all smiles and wagging tail.

Traitor.

"You have thirty days to respond in the mail or in person at the law enforcement and detention center—you know where that is?"

"You mean the jail?" Henry smiled. "I do."

"I bet you do."

Henry signed the ticket and handed it back to her.

"Do you understand the violations as they have been explained to you?"

"Yes."

She pulled the space-age sunglasses from her pocket and dramatically placed them over the opaque chalcedony eyes, ripped his copy of the ticket from the clipboard, and handed it to him. "Have a nice day."

He continued to smile, pushed his old-school Ray-Bans over his eyes again in response, and handed me the $262 ticket as she started to turn and go. "Here, file this in the glove box—under chicken shit."

She paused for only an instant and slightly turned her head.

I watched as she took a breath and tasted in her mouth the words she wanted to say. I half expected her to draw the big .44, but instead she hitched her thumbs in her gun belt, held that last look, and then walked off, punishing the roadway with the heels of her boots.

It was the most professional thing she'd done during the entire interaction.

She started the SUV, did a tire-smoking reentrance to BIA 4, and continued south with a full head of steam.

Henry yawned, placed his license back in his wallet, and flipped it onto the dash. "I do not think that I ever have had brake lights."

The lower ridge that leads to Painted Warrior cliff runs for about a mile north and west from Red Birney, and the only way to the site is from along the ridge or back up through the dirt roads below. I doubted that Cady and Michael would want to be married on a cliff, but Henry assured me that the area at the base was as picturesque as it was dramatic.

He was right.

We'd followed Lonnie's instructions and eased Rezdawg off the road between the grass-covered hills that ringed the base of the cliffs and a large sedimentary rock cairn. We climbed steadily until we reached a saddle and a scattering of large boulders and parked at the top of a small ridge, just as wisps of steam were floating out from under Rezdawg's hood.

There was a thick-bodied mule deer a little off to our right, heading down toward Tie Creek, and I allowed her a substantial lead before opening the door and letting Dog out to patrol the area. He immediately went to where the doe had been standing and watched impatiently as she bounded through the scrub pine and clamored over the rocks toward the base of the cliffs.

"You never would've caught her anyhow."

He turned to look at me as I closed the door and joined Henry, who was leaning on the homemade, Day-Glo orange grille guard and partial steam bath at the front of the truck. "What do you think?"

It was just the way Lonnie had described it. I had heard of the site and might've even been here when I was a kid, but I guess I'd never really seen it. Framed by a box canyon below, the Painted Warrior raised his face from the ridge and looked toward the sky. As with cloud images, you had to look at the thing for a while before you saw it, but he was there. The features reminded me of another friend, Virgil White Buffalo, all the way down to the deep furrows that indented the rock visage's face. The majority was a khaki-colored stone, but there were a few massive streaks of war paint, the rocks stained by the deposits of scoria that ran vertically down the giant's face—hence the name, Painted Warrior.

It was a straight-up climb of about two hundred feet to the base of the ridge where the sheer cliff began.

The Bear tripped the latch, lifted Rezdawg's hood, and watched as a ghostly cloud of steam trailed away in the breeze. I wondered if it too would turn into something recognizable. Henry was gently working the radiator cap off with a red shop rag he'd retrieved from the cab. "When I was young, we used to hunt deer here; just run them up through the canyon and have somebody waiting at the ridge."

I looked around at the surrounding saddle studded with Krummholz pines, stunted by the altitude and atmospheric conditions. If you didn't know any better, you wouldn't think that the diminutive trees were actually hundreds of years old. Reflecting the sun that peeked through the assembled thunderheads were small outcroppings of rocks that surrounded the ridge like a wreath. "Is this the spot Lonnie was thinking of?"

"Here, or possibly just past the creek." He finally loosened the cap enough for a gurgling release and antifreeze dribbled down the radiator.

I glanced back at the panoramic display. "Where the opening in the rock walls leads toward the cliff?"

He rested the cap on the inner fender and turned to look along with me. "Yes." He glanced back at the steam continuing to roil from Rezdawg. "Would you like to hike over there and see it?"

"I guess I'd better. I just wish I'd brought a camera so that I could send Cady pictures."

"I have one in the truck." He wiped his hands on the rag, which he returned to the cab, and came back with a medium-sized bag with a strap that he threw over his shoulder. "I also have two bottles of water. I am prepared."

Tie Creek was at the base of the ridge, but it was summer and the water was only ankle deep. We forded the stream by walking on the rounded stones—Dog just splashed through—and continued among the trees to the next hill. There was a clearer view of the lower cliffs reflecting the bright sunlight that cascaded down in beams like some biblical illustration, the cliffs surrounding the bottom of the more impressive rocks above, and I had to admit that the whole area was pretty breathtaking.

I stopped at the top of the hill to catch my breath and stared up at something that had reflected near the top of Painted Warrior. I stood there and took in a few lungfuls, wondering what it was I thought I'd seen. I'd had quite the adventure in the Cloud Peak Wilderness Area only two months earlier, and the effects were still lingering. The Cheyenne Nation was watching me.

"Thought I saw something up there."

He turned and looked. "Where?"

"Near the top; something flashed."

His keen eyes played across the uppermost ridge. "I do not see anything."

I nodded. "Probably just a reflection off some quartz or an old beer can. Speaking of, can we get a beer after this?"

His eyes scanned the ridge. "Sure." He checked his wristwatch. "We can go up to the Jimtown Bar and get a drink before the professionals show up. We might not even get into a fight."

"In the meantime, can I have one of those bottles of water?"

He slung the bag from his shoulder, unzipped one of the compartments, and handed me a bottle, the condensation slick on the outside.

I sipped my water, slipped my hat off of my head, and wiped the sweat from inside the band. "Is that professional courtesy, when you visit somebody else's bar?"

He nodded and then squatted down and began pulling a large camera body and lens from the bag. "You bet." Having assembled the camera, he popped off the cap and pointed the lens toward me.

I held my hat up to block the shot. "Just the surroundings, please—not the inhabitants." Dog sat beside me and looked at Henry. "Take a picture of him; he doesn't seem to mind."

"Your daughter would like a photo of you, I'm sure, and since we are in the position of negotiating our way out of disaster . . ."

I put my hat back on my head. "All right, but then you have to let me take one of you for her."

He raised the camera and directed it toward me. "I am like Dog—I do not mind; I am photogenic."

When I laughed, he took the picture.

I held my hand out for the camera, and he gave it to me without argument. I turned it around and looked at the multitude of dials and buttons. "I'm used to the IPH cameras. . . ." I looked up at him. "You know, Idiot Push Here."

He took it and set the focus on automatic, then handed it back to me. "There, just push the big button on the top."

I raised the expensive device and looked through the viewer. "Thanks."

The Painted Warrior background made for an interesting effect, with one native face mirroring the other. I watched with my one eye as the autofocus first defined the features of the Cheyenne Nation and then the sandstone cliffs behind him, searching for whatever my wandering hand chose to photograph.

He repeated patiently through his close-lipped smile, "The large button on the top."

"Okay." I readjusted my aim, but the automatic function on the camera continued to focus on the cliffs just over the Bear's shoulder—almost as if the Painted Warrior was demanding a photograph of itself. "Damn."

It was right as I went ahead and pushed the button that I could see something scrambling at the top, above the giant Indian's forehead, and then plummet from the face.

I yanked the camera down just as a high-pitched wail carried through the canyon walls, and someone fell in an awkward position, almost as if holding something. Henry turned quickly and we watched, helpless.

The body struck a cornice once on the way down, then splayed from the side of the cliff and landed at the bottom where the grass-covered slope rose to meet the rocks. The liquid thump of the body striking the ground was horrific, and we continued to watch as whoever it was rolled down the hillside with a cascading jumble of scree and tumbling rock.

We were both running, the Cheyenne Nation ahead of me and moving at an astounding pace. Dog followed as we thundered down the hillside between the rock walls and back up the other side.

It was so surreal that I couldn't believe it had actually happened, but the adrenaline dumping high octane into my bloodstream and the Bear's reaction told me that it must've been true.

By the time I got to the last hill leading to the base of the cliffs, I could see Henry looking from side to side, trying to find where the person that had fallen might be. There was a copse of juniper to the left, and I watched as he started and then ran toward it. I was there in an instant, and what I saw was like some surrealistic painting. I felt as if the world had been pulled out from under me, too.

Her right leg was contorted to the extreme with her foot up above her shoulder, and there were deep lacerations on one side of her body. The eyes were unfocused as she stared at the rocks above, and her head lunged involuntarily, the brain attempting to send signals through the broken spine.

Henry kneeled beside her and cupped the side of her head in his hands, attempting to provide some kind of support without adjusting her. "Do not move."

A breath escaped her lips as a fresh flow of tears drained down her cheeks. She gulped air into her bleeding mouth three times, then turned her head toward the Bear's hand—and died.

I kneeled beside him and looked at her, reached up to her throat, and placed my fingers where her pulse had been. "Do you know her?"

He lowered her head and brushed back his hair with bloody fingers, the smears trailing from the corner of his eye to the clamped jaw like macabre Kabuki makeup. "No."

Dog began barking behind us, and I yelled at him, "Shut up!"

Henry and I must've had the same thought at precisely the same time, because we both looked up simultaneously. From this angle, we couldn't see anything at the top of the cliff—only a few pebbles that rained down on us that must've become dislodged during her fall.

I went ahead and yelled, "Hey, is there anybody up there?" My voice echoed off the rocks above and below, along with Dog's incessant barking. "Shut up!"

I threw my head back and yelled louder this time. "Hey, is there anybody up there?" I took a deep breath and shouted again, "We've got a woman who's fallen!"

Nothing, just Dog's continued barking.

I turned and saw him standing down the hillside. "I said, shut up!"

The big beast's head rose and cocked in a quizzical cant. After a moment, the huge muzzle dipped and nosed at something—and it was only when he gently pawed at the blanketed bundle in front of him in the high stalks of buffalo grass that I finally saw the tiny hand and heard a baby cry.

2

It was a boy. I kept dipping my little finger into the water bottle so that he could drink the drops; I wasn't much of an expert, but I estimated his age at about six months. He'd stopped crying and, amazingly enough, seemed to have survived the fall with not much visible damage.

He'd had help.

In a perversity of timing and luck, we'd once again blown through the intersection of BIA 4 and state Route 212 in Lame Deer just as the rear end of a black Yukon headed east.

When we got to the Indian Health Services building on the north end of town, Henry slid Rezdawg into the parking lot with a ferocity of which I hadn't thought the vehicle capable. Under the canopy of the entrance, I handed the child off to the Cheyenne Nation, pretty sure that he was more adept at negotiating the bureaucracy of federal health care than I.

I watched as he held the child close to his chest and rushed into the eleven-year-old building with the alacrity of the All-American running back he'd been at Cal in the sixties—before Vietnam had changed his life and him.

There was a story about Henry's first days at Berkeley. It seemed that four California boys from Stockton had taken it upon themselves to give Geronimo a haircut during the two-a-day practices, but after three broken fingers, a broken nose, a dislocated shoulder, and a concussion, they'd decided to go seek entertainment elsewhere.

Dog followed Henry inside at a clip, unwilling to leave the child's side; only fair, since he'd been the one to find him.

I circled around the truck and climbed in to move it away from the emergency entrance, but my smile faded as the truck's engine stumbled and died as soon as I closed the driver's door behind me. "Oh, you . . ." I ground the starter and pulled the choke out just the tiniest bit, but the cantankerous V-8 only grumbled and ignored my efforts. Figuring I'd just shove the piece of crap out of the way, I slipped the truck into neutral and threw open the door to start pushing.

When I brought my face up, there was a black Yukon nudged right against the back bumper and, more important, a very irate tribal police chief Lolo Long staring me in the chin.

"Hands on the vehicle."

"Look . . ."

I didn't get anymore out because when I started to continue speaking, she shoved my shoulder and trapped my right hand in a reverse wristlock that threw me against the scaly side of Rezdawg's bed. It was a good move and expertly executed, but I was a lot heavier and turned just a little to let her know I still could. "Officer, if you'll just listen . . ."

She put a lot more pressure in the wristlock, and the position of my arm forced me back toward the truck. My immediate response would have been to back pivot and deliver a roundhouse elbow into the side of her head, but I was hoping we weren't at that point just yet. "We've got an emergency."

She frisked me with her free hand under my arms and down my back. "Stop talking."

I could feel the weight of Rezdawg shift beneath me as the front tires edged toward the slight drop-off where the emergency area had been repaved. "We've got a child in there who might be hurt and a dead woman at the base of Painted Warrior cliff."

"I said shut up." Her hand froze at the middle of my back. "What's this?"

I sighed. "It's my duty sidearm, a Colt 1911, both cocked and locked, and I'd appreciate it if you'd handle it with a little care."

She fumbled with my canvas jacket, unsnapped the pancake holster, and yanked the semiautomatic from the small of my back, still holding me against the ever-so-slightly moving truck. "You know that carrying a concealed weapon onto semiautonomous federal lands or reservations is illegal unless you happen to be of tribal descent—and you just don't look like Chief Cleans His Bore Regularly." She spun me around and stuffed my Colt in the back of her jeans, then pulled her S&W. "You're under arrest."

"Oh, come on."

She leveled the .44 at my chest and tossed me her cuffs. "Put those on."

I could feel the truck behind me as it picked up just a little bit of momentum, rolling off the asphalt patchwork and starting toward the great, wide parking lot.

I snapped one of the cuffs on a wrist and turned to watch Rezdawg gain a little speed, Lolo Long's eyes now looking past me at the unpiloted three-quarter-ton as it continued to slip away.

Her face now took on a little panic. "You . . . you need to stop that vehicle."

"Sorry, I've been arrested."

She kept the Magnum on me but started moving past, undecided as to whether her responsibilities lay with her prisoner or the unbridled truck. "I said stop that vehicle."

I shrugged and held up my cuffed hand, the other end rattling against my forearm. "Nothing I can do."

Rezdawg was now in a full advance toward the car-filled parking lot, and Officer Long suddenly made the lunge to catch it, racing across the distance at an impressive speed—a heck of a lot faster than I would've been able to accomplish. She holstered her weapon and grabbed the door handle, but, as I would have anticipated, the latch didn't appear to work. She punched at the button and yanked mightily at the handle, even placed a boot against the bed and pulled as she hopped on one foot, pogo-style, all to no avail.

I leaned to the side and tried to judge the trajectory as the ugliest truck on the high plains took one of the loveliest, if irritating, law enforcement officers for a ride. It looked to me as if the point of impact was going to be a maroon '86 Cadillac parked at the end of the row.

Never a fan of spectacle, I turned and walked through the automatic sliding glass doors with one last glance at Lolo Long as she scrambled through the open window of the rolling Rezdawg.

Henry was standing at the reception desk talking urgently to a very large woman, but he raised his face at the sound of my boots on the tile floor. "Trouble finding a place to park?"

"No, no trouble at all." I glanced around. "Where's Dog?"

The Cheyenne Nation smiled. "In the examination room; we tried to hold him back but he gave every indication that he was going to eat all of us alive if we separated him from that child."

I nodded, leaned against the counter, and looked at the heavyset Native woman a little younger than Henry and I. "Hello." I extended a hand, suddenly remembering that it had a handcuff dangling from it. I decided to play it like being cuffed was nothing new for me. "Walt Longmire."

She looked a little uncertain. "The sheriff from Absaroka County?"

"Yes, Ma'am."

"Hazel Long."

"Good to meet you, Hazel." I paused. "Are you related to Chief Long?"

She glanced at the cuffs again. "Lo is my daughter, yes."

"Hmm." I glanced at Henry as he stared at my hand. "What?"

He closed his eyes and cleared the expression from his face. "We need to contact the authorities."

"Oddly enough, they've been contacted." I threaded the office key chain from my jacket pocket and used the ever-present universal cuff key that dangled from the ring to extricate myself, allowing the hardware to fall onto the counter. "Or, rather, they've contacted us."

He looked past me and down the hallway, and I could just about bet what was coming. "I believe she is about to make contact again."

Long grabbed my shoulder and yanked at me, half-pulling me around to face her. She was sweating, and I was momentarily entranced by the beads of perspiration at the base of her throat. "You are still under arrest." Her face was now about six inches from my own. "And you're going to pay for the damages to the cars in the parking lot."

Cars, plural. I guess Rezdawg had gotten more than one. Good for her.

"I was and still am under arrest, and therefore not responsible for the vehicle in question." She straightened, a little surprised. "I'm pretty knowledgeable about vehicular codes, along with concealed-carry laws within federal jurisdiction."

"Lo?"

It took a second for her to disengage from her primary target, but when she realized that it was her mother speaking to her, she locked on her. "Excuse me?"

The large woman started to stand. "Lo, there's been an . . ."

She snapped back in the way that only family can. "Is this official business? Because I am engaged in arresting this man and unless you have something pertinent to say concerning . . ."

"Lolo Louise Long, stop acting like an ass. There's been an accident. A child is hurt, and a dead woman, who is going to be a major part of your official business, is lying at the base of Painted Warrior cliff." She took a deep breath and shot air from her nostrils like a bull. "And, by the way, may I introduce you to Sheriff Walt Longmire of Absaroka County, Wyoming."

"You're still under arrest."

"Okay." I braced a hand against the dash as we swerved down BIA 4 at about a hundred miles an hour. "Can I have my gun back?"

"No."

I glanced past the elongated hood of the Yukon as we passed another unsuspecting motorist. "You might want to turn on your siren."

She said nothing and continued slicing the wheel.

"Seriously, if you . . ."

She fairly screamed it. "I don't know where the switch is!"

I gave her my best double take, but fortunately her attention stayed on the road.

Reaching across to the upper center console, I flipped down a small door and pulled a switch, flooding the surrounding area with the blooping noise of the hi-tech siren.

She flashed the amber eyes at me. "Thanks."

I nodded and thought about how I was getting myself involved with a federal investigation on reservation land. I'd thought about asking Henry to go with her but came to the conclusion that I was probably a little less of an adversary. The Bear looked just as happy to stay at the hospital with the child, Dog, and no Lolo Long. "Are you new to this?"

"What?"

"Law enforcement; I assume that this isn't what you did over in Iraq, huh?"

The response was more than a little defensive. "No, it wasn't."

"What did you do over there?"

"None of your business." She glanced at me, a sliver of jasper at the corner of one eye. "You serve?"

"I did."

"Union or Confederate?"

More and more like Vic. I went ahead and smiled; it was funny. "See, up until now you've kept that rapier wit sheathed."

The radio interrupted with a call from the Montana Highway Patrol, informing us that the FBI investigator would meet us on scene and would be bringing a team along with him; standard procedure on the Rez. Officer Long plucked the mic from the dash and rogered the call.

She hung it back up. "I know you. I mean, I know of you." She glanced at me again. "You were involved with the Melissa Little Bird rape case a few years ago."

I pulled the shoulder belt away from me with my thumb, my chest suddenly feeling a little tight. "Yep, I was."

"That was a cluster."

My chest got even tighter. "Yep."

She started to drive more steadily, braking before and accelerating into the curves, although our speed was still way over the limit. "There were a lot of rumors swirling around when those boys started showing up dead."

"Uh huh."

"One theory was that it was that buddy of yours, Standing Bear."

I didn't say anything.

"Another was that you were the one doing it."

I still didn't say anything.

"You caught somebody, didn't you?"

It took a moment, but I found words in my mouth. "We stopped the shootings, if that's what you mean." She rocketed past a windmill on the side of the road. "You're going to want to take a left at the next dirt cutoff."

She dutifully slowed the SUV and made the turn at a reasonable speed but accelerated again, still bouncing us against the seat belts. I indicated the spotter road, and she took it as I reached across and turned the dial, putting the GMC in four-wheel-drive, her glance letting me know I'd overstepped my boundaries. "I'll operate the vehicle from here on out, if you don't mind."

We got to the ridge and parked and, pulling a crime scene pack from behind her seat, she followed me as I retraced the path to the base of the cliffs. Our approach spooked a coyote, and we could hear the buzzing of the flies before we got there.

Chief Long was to my right as we got closer to the small stand of juniper trees, and I could see that the young woman's naked leg was still sticking up at an odd angle beside her face.

I turned to look at Officer Long, but she had stopped and, staring at the dead woman, was simply standing in the grass.

I waited a moment and then took a step back, blocking her view. "You know her?"

She looked surprised and then nodded in a distracted way, a traumatized look I'd seen before. "Yeah, yeah I do."

"Gimme the case."

She blinked once and then looked up at me. "No, I . . . no."

"Gimme the case and go sit by the creek; if I need you, I'll call."

She didn't move, even after I took the pack from her loose hand.

"Go."

She stood there for a bit longer and then turned and walked down the hill.

I moved back to the dead woman and set the case down without actually looking at her. There was a charade I played with myself in these situations, a falsehood that allowed me to do the job—telling myself that it was only an exercise. This woman was not dead to me, not yet. That part would start soon enough: the ferocious desire to find out who she was, why this happened and, if it was a factor, who did it.

Was it an accident, a suicide, or a homicide?

I put away my sunglasses and raised my face, getting a clear look at the cliff and watching the clouds race over in bleached streaks, leftovers from the storm that had hovered near Lame Deer. There was another crime scene up there where the majority of the questions would probably be answered, but that could wait.

I judged the distance and did a quick calculation of the physics, which were not unlike the deceleration and impact forces found in automobile accidents in which the occupants neglect to wear seat belts. In the tenth to twelfth second of free fall, terminal velocity is obtained—terminal velocity being one hundred and ten miles an hour. She wouldn't have made that, but she'd gone fast enough. There would be fractured bones and lacerated damage to internal organs as well as to the head and spine. She had told me that in those last few seconds—I only wish she could've told me more.

I felt the falsehood of ritual flow over me, insulating me from the lingering results of death, humanity's ultimate adversary. I unzipped the crime scene case and was immediately faced with another adversary, a camera. All these years and I still hadn't mastered the art of anything except the IPH model.

This reminded me that we had left Henry's camera on the ridge near where we had parked the Yukon, and I made the mental note to pick it up on the way back to the vehicle. The camera from the kit was large-bodied like Henry's but of a simpler design, which I appreciated. I switched it on and began the photographic procedure of shooting the entire scene—the relationship area, distance of fall, and the point where she had struck the cornice.

When I began photographing her, I noticed that there were

bruises on her face and arms, some of them older than those caused by her fall. There were also scratches on the backs of her arms that looked like they might've been inflicted by someone grabbing her with great force, maybe a week ago.

The devil must be beating his wife.

I continued photographing.

The fingernails on her left hand were bloody and bent back, some even missing, but other than this and the indications of abuse, she appeared to have been a normal, healthy young woman. I noticed that there was even a small purse still trapped under her arm as I covered her with the plastic sheet from the case.

I was tempted to move her and go through the purse, but I assumed the Montana authorities would just as soon do it themselves, making sure to use special care not to disturb any trace evidence. It seemed odd that she had decided to walk the air with her child. I thought that, at that horrible moment when I'd seen her fall, her only concern had been something in her arms. I finished up and put the camera away. My work would be preliminary in comparison to the crime lab that would soon be here from either Hardin or Billings.

Besides, I had other resources.

I walked down the hill to the creek and found Chief Long tossing small pebbles into a pool a little downstream. A small, brown trout had risen from the depths but then disappeared under my shadow. "How you doing, troop?"

She turned, sheltering her eyes with a hand, and looked at me. "What'd you just call me?"

I crouched down beside her and watched the lazy water coat the rocks so that she wouldn't be self-conscious about her red-ringed and still-damp eyes. "Troop. It's a term my old boss used to use on me when I was starting out; I use it with my deputies."

"Well, don't use it with me." She took a breath and tossed another pebble; this time the fish ignored it.

"We're pretty much done down here."

She looked at a simple Luminox wristwatch, the kind that Spec Ops used. "What the hell is taking them so long?"

I raised my eyes and looked at what now seemed desolate surroundings; as unlikely as it was that Cady would have gone for this site before, it was surely out of the question now. "Hopefully they didn't get lost."

"Yeah."

"Looks like it's still going to rain." I studied her, judging whether now was a good time and figuring the basics wouldn't hurt. "What's her name?"

She didn't move, and her voice might as well have been coming from the trees or the cliffs above. "Audrey Plain Feather; she was half Crow."

Audrey. "And the child's name—the boy?"

"Adrian."

I nodded to myself and looked up the slope; there was a more manageable route to the west, an area where the ridge fell back— it would be easier to make the grade, especially at an angle. "I'm going up."

"I'll go with you."

I placed a hand on her shoulder. "Somebody's going to have to stay here and wait for the crime scene folks."

She shrugged off my hand and stood, partially pulling the radio from her belt. "I've got this, and I figure they'll be able to get close on their own. I can spot them on the main road easier from up on the ridge anyway."

"Well then, can you do me a favor?"

"Depends."

I sighed. "It's going to take me a lot longer to get up this cliff than you, so I want a head start." I smiled, but she didn't smile back. "On the next ridge over there and toward the saddle?" I pointed to the area across the creek. "There's another camera sitting in the grass where Henry and I dropped it when we saw Audrey fall; would you mind going to get it and bringing it with you or putting it in your vehicle?"

She took a second to respond. "All right."

I looked up at the gathering gloom and then called after her. "You're sure you want to go up there?"

"Yes." She turned back and opened an ear stem of her sunglasses with her teeth, then carefully navigated them onto her face. "Besides, you're still under arrest. Now get moving—I don't want to have to wait for you."

She started up the hill, her broad back and strong legs aiding her climb effortlessly.

"Yes, ma'am."

The grade was indeed easier up to the right, and there was a gully to the left with trees in it to lean against; the older you get the more important things like that become.

The ground was soft where the earth had sloughed from the ridge above, and after a while I gathered a rhythm that seemed familiar and similar to the one that had carried me up Cloud Peak only two months ago. The thought of that adventure brought a chill, even though the ambient temperature lingered around ninety.

I removed my hat and took a breather about three-quarters of the way up. From this height I could see Lonnie's crows harassing an eagle that was lazily circling in patterns along the valley. The crows probably had nests nearby and were protecting their young, or just getting their exercise before the thunderheads massed and we had a real frog strangler.

I inhaled and started up again still using the smaller trees as walking sticks, finally getting to the depression at the ridge. When I did, I looked to the right and could see Lolo Long making mincemeat of the more difficult direct route.

I would've yelled to her, but I didn't have the breath.

There was a two-track dirt road that stretched in both directions just a little bit back from the precipice, so I turned right and worked my way along the ridge. After a few minutes, I noticed that the grass was flat and there were tread marks in the dirt; I stopped and kneeled down to look—someone had driven up here and back out and not long ago. My eyes followed the tracks where the vehicle had parked, made a two-point turn, and then gone out the way it had come. The depressions were deeper where the vehicle had sat for a period of time—there were even two small oil leaks with matching soot marks from where what I was assuming was a truck had been parked.

After a couple of hundred yards the grade leveled and the rounded surface of the rock fell away to the cliffs—a dangerous place. Lolo Long, looking out into the distance with her hands on her hips, stood about ten feet from the edge.

"Hey, Chief."

"What?"

"Somebody drove a four-wheel-drive up here and not too long ago. There are two patches of differential fluid, and the tires are wide and the duel exhausts are set close—I'd say a Jeep, something like that."

She turned to look at me. "How do you know where the exhaust was?"

I pointed. "The two soot marks from where it was restarted." I stood. "They're going to need a ring job before too long." Something further back on the trail caught my eye, and I walked over to where it was lodged among the taller stalks of Johnson grass; it was a plastic bag, the kind you find at any grocery or convenience store. "Did she have a vehicle like that?"

Her lips tightened into a line, and the muscles in her jaw worked. "No, the guy she was shacking up with, Adrian's father, does."

I pulled the blue plastic sack from the weeds. It was full of crushed beer cans, a couple of empty chip bags, and some candy wrappers. There was a receipt in the bottom of the bag, soggy from the remnants draining from the containers.

I pulled the receipt out and held it up. Across the top were the words WHITE BUFFALO SINCLAIR and listed below were the items that were in the used bag, with the exception of the beer and a pack of cigarettes, as well as thirty-two dollars' worth of regular gasoline; the date was today at 11:22 A.M.

Chief Long approached, and I handed the sack to her, along with the receipt; she read it, withdrew a couple of evidence bags, and carefully placed the slip of paper inside one, the blue plastic into the other.

I took out the camera and began taking pictures again, sucked in a breath, and trudged along to the precipice.

The surface was a loose scrabble of sedentary shale that looked like shattered terra-cotta in a wild cathedral floor; the footing was unstable, and a few lizards scrambled like ball bearings over the hard surface. I moved toward the edge and kneeled down to look at the disturbed rock shelves at the point where the woman had fallen. The wind picked up a little, nudging me from behind, as I allowed my eyes to drift toward the clouds again, some of them trailing low enough to almost reach out and touch.

The crows and the eagle continued to flirt with them, pinwheeling and passing away from each other, circling, and using the rising thermals and gusts of wind for lift.

There was a rapid movement that pulled me from my trance—a little pygmy rattler swiveled from a small outcropping to my left—probably after the lizards. I picked up a small rock and tossed it toward him to let him know he should keep going away from us, and he obliged by disappearing.

I could see where Audrey had gone over the edge, and where she'd desperately attempted to hold back the inevitable with one hand—must have been the one that was missing fingernails. There was another area of disturbance in the rocks right in front of me, possibly where she had tripped or possibly where there could've been some sort of struggle.

I shot a look back at Chief Long and pointed to the edge. "Do you see that?"

She stood her ten feet back and made no effort to move. "What?"

"The marks in the rocks."

She glanced over my shoulder. "Yeah."

"You can see it better from over here."

She adjusted the strap of the crime scene bag on her shoulder. "I can see fine."

I took another series of shots, the rocks crumbling and shifting under my boots. Catching my balance, I took the few steps back to where she stood like a pole. "You okay?"

"Yes." It was a quick answer and was meant to cut off any more conversation on the subject—the kind of response I'd learned to ignore.

"What's up?"

She gave me the full kaleidoscope eyes, and I felt like I'd been kicked.

"I don't like heights."

I gazed back at the cliff and gestured toward it. "Well, it's only natural, considering . . ."

"That's not it."

I tipped my hat back and studied her; she really was beautiful, and I could see the complexity of conflicting thoughts as they played across her face. I raised a hand toward her. "What then?"

She swallowed and retreated from the edge and my touch. "I . . . I have this urge to jump."

Shrugging a shoulder, I stepped past her toward the main part of the grass-covered trail. "That's normal, too. It can be categorized as a risk impulse; it's the subjective aspect of our natures that makes rodeo riders strap themselves to Brahma bulls or skydivers jump out of perfectly good airplanes. Freud called that kind of risk-taking behavior the 'death drive' and associated it with gambling, sex and, well, a lot of other things."

She stayed put and kept looking for signs in the passing clouds. "He connected everything with sex, didn't he?"

"Pretty much."

She turned and looked at me as her radio crackled. She lifted it out of her belt and looked at the road below. "Roger that, unit 1. We're at the top, but we'll be right down."

I walked back toward the cliff and could see a white Yukon, a black Expedition, and a highway patrol cruiser. "Looks like they didn't get lost after all."

"Yeah." She didn't move after reholstering the two-way.

"You want to go down and meet them?"

She nodded and reset her jaw. "Are we through up here?"

"With the limited resources we have, yes."

She still didn't move, and I could tell there was a lot more she wanted to say. "Look . . ."

I waited, but she didn't say anything else. Then she cleared her throat and coughed up a few words. "I'm . . . I'm new to this stuff, but I don't feel like being railroaded by the . . . I mean, maybe I'm a lousy cop, but I'd like to find out on my own." She stopped and turned to look at me. "Before we go down there, I'd like to make sure we're on the same page."

"Meaning?"

"I know more about this case than you or they do; I know the people involved, and I'm not buying it." Her eyes came down to the edge of the cliff and studied the surface—fractured and dangerous. "It's not that high."

"Most suicides are from approximately five hundred feet—high enough to kill, but low enough to not last too long." The wind gusted, and I was reminded that this was no longer a good place. "You're not buying what?"

Lolo Long stood there like a sentinel. "There's no way a woman walks out to the edge of a cliff like this with her child in her arms."

Bingo.

I smiled and studied her in a professorial manner. "Maybe you're not such a lousy cop after all."

Her eyes flared and she looked directly at me, and I thought for a moment that she might try and throw me off the cliff. She took a step and turned to the right toward the direct path down, then called over her shoulder. "There's another reason."

I followed along behind her. "Reason for what?"

I barely heard the words as they drifted back with the breeze that continued to stiffen. "For jumping: just to have it all over with."

The Feds were already setting up camp on the same ridge where we'd parked, and a blond-haired young man, who looked like one of the agents, and a highway patrolman were the first to reach us. The FBI agent, in a short-sleeved shirt, held out a hand to me.

"Bo Benth. It's a pleasure to meet you, Sheriff. I've heard and read a lot about you."

I shook his hand and introduced Lolo. "This is Chief Long." I went ahead and threw in the next, just so there wouldn't be any confusion. "She'll be the primary investigator."

Agent Benth smiled as Long studied her ropers. He glanced up at the cliff. "We understood it was pretty cut and dry."

"No, actually, it's not. There's a survivor, and a friend of mine and I actually witnessed the fall. Chief Long and I have already done the preliminary crime scene work, here and above."

He looked at the gathering thunderclouds building over the cliffs. "Good, 'cause I've got a feeling we're about to get pissed on." They started past toward the deceased. "As to whose responsibility this is, you can take that up with the new agent in charge."

"Where's he?"

Benth threw a thumb over his shoulder and gave me a strange smirk. "Trying to get reception on his mobile back in the vehicle. You're gonna love him."

As we walked down the hill, Officer Long hooked her thumbs into the pockets of her jeans. "Great."

"What?"

"A new AIC; just what I need."

I nodded. "Did you know the last one?"

"Only over the phone; I was lucky." She glanced back at Painted Warrior. "I guess my luck ran out."

We passed a few more crime lab infantry, but not my good friend Bill McDermott, who must've been working another part of the state.

The white Fed Yukon, which was the AIC vehicle, was parked the farthest away, and a tall man with a goatee and wild-looking hair dressed in a pink shirt and blue blazer hung an arm over the sill of the open door. He held his cell phone at the other arm's length and was looking at it with an expression of disgust, his sunglasses perched on his forehead.

Lolo Long glanced back at me. "I'll handle it this time."

The federal agent tossed the mobile into the backseat of the Yukon. "Is there any cell reception in fucking Montana?" He glanced at me. "I mean, I know there isn't any in fucking Wyoming, but fucking Montana, too?"

He turned to study Chief Long. "Hey, things are looking up."

Long ignored the remark, adjusted the crime scene pack strap on her shoulder, and held out her hand. "Lolo Long, Cheyenne tribal chief of police. I'm the primary investigator on this case."

He kicked his face sideways and smirked with even more enthusiasm than had the younger agent—evidently it was a bureau thing. He looked at her hand but didn't shake it. "You don't say?"

She was showing remarkable patience and ignored that remark, too—but her voice was now carrying that edge. "I am intimate with the subjects involved and have information that may lead to an early arrest."

He shook his head as if to clear it, glanced at me, and then back to her. "Early arrest, huh?"

She took a breath and finally lowered the hand. "Sheriff Longmire and I—"

He interrupted her carefully planned speech and glanced at me again with a more than knowing look. "Uh huh?"

She stumbled but then regained her footing; she was getting angrier. "We . . . I have reason to believe that this may be more than a simple case of misadventure."

"You do?"

Full on angry now. "Yes."

He took the sunglasses off his forehead, tossed them after the phone, and massaged the sockets of his eyes on either side of his elongated nose with thumb and forefinger. "Sounds like I don't have a thing to worry about." He raised his face—and this time it was a grin, the kind hyenas have—then reached out a fist and actually punched her shoulder; then he spoke in the singsong pattern of bad TV. "Well, how 'bout I introduce myself—Cliff Cly of the FBI."

3

"You could've told me that you knew him."

She banked the turns at ninety, and I was beginning to think that this was just the way Lolo Long drove, kind of like A. J. Foyt.

"And when was I supposed to have done that?"

"You could've jumped in at any time."

I braced a hand against the dash and checked my seat belt. "You said you wanted to handle it, in a tone of voice, I might add, which told me that I must've done a bad job previously." She didn't say anything. "You got what you wanted; you're the primary investigator on the case."

"No, you got what I wanted." She shot a look at me. "What makes you so cozy with the FBI that they just roll over and ask you to scratch their bellies?"

I took my hat off and rested it on my lap. "Not the entire FBI, just that one agent. And, as point of fact, I'm the one who patched up his belly."

Her voice took on the melodic quality that his had, but with more of an edge. "So how do you know 'Cliff Cly of the FBI'?"

I grimaced at the thought. "Well, first I broke his jaw."

"You what?"

"It's a long story."

She nodded her head. "We've got plenty of time—you're still under arrest."

I sighed and thought about a horse that had been trapped on the Battlement . . . and the woman who loved her. "He was working on a case we were both involved with, ended up gutshot down on the Powder River, and I was lucky enough to get him help."

"By breaking his jaw."

"That came earlier."

She took another curve as the V-8 in the GMC strained under her foot. "Lucky enough to help him, huh?"

"Yep."

"So, you're a lucky guy?"

We shot through another straightaway and barely missed a logging truck going in the other direction.

"Sometimes. Hey, speaking of—do you mind if we proceed somewhat under the speed of sound? My daughter's getting married next week, and I'd like to be there to see the wedding."

She let off the accelerator just a little, and I eased back in my seat. "Do you mind telling me why it is that you are so angry when you're dealing with people?"

"What are you talking about?"

"The way you spoke to Agent Cly and—"

"Did you hear the way he was with me?" Her knuckles bunched on the steering wheel.

"I did."

"Well, then, you know why." Her head bobbed in time with the words that she bit off. "He. Pissed. Me. Off."

"You'll excuse me for saying so since I've only known you for about six hours, but that doesn't seem particularly difficult to do." She shut down again and just stared through the windshield. "All I'm saying is that being angry with him didn't help your situation."

"So your suggestion is that I should've broken his jaw?"

I smiled and thought, that's what you usually get for moralizing. "Not exactly."

"Yeah, well, I'm a police chief, not a sheriff, so I don't have to be a politician—I don't need the votes."

I returned my own gaze to the windshield. It was now righteously pouring down rain. "Votes notwithstanding, you keep going at it the way you are now and you won't be a chief for very long." We drove in silence, the emergency sirens echoing off the surrounding hills the only sound. "His jurisdiction supersedes yours, and generally when you argue with the federal government, you lose."

She turned her lovely Cheyenne face to regard me. "Tell me all about that."

I shook my head and tried to enjoy the ride. "Do you mind telling me where it is we're going?"

"To see a man about a Jeep."

After a hard left on 212, we rocketed a couple of miles west to a cutoff that had a few signs, one of which read WELCOME TO MUDDY CUSTER, HE'OVONEHE-O 'HE 'E. "What does that mean?"

"Muddy Custer?"

"No, the Cheyenne part."

She shrugged. "Where they gather."

We circled a development where all the houses were exactly the same design but painted in assorted vibrant colors.

She saw me looking. "Remixes. Every summer Ace Hardware comes down here and has a tailgate sale."

She pulled into a driveway where an old Volkswagen minibus, bright yellow with the words OLD SKOOL written down the side, was sitting on blocks, and in front of that a midseventies Jeep CJ-5 with a partial convertible top.

I watched the rain pelting the canvas. "Somebody we know?"

"I do."

I looked up through the rain that was battering the windshield and thought about how wet we were about to become.

We both got out and, as I tugged my summer palm-leaf hat down tight, I looked past the rivulets of rain dripping from the brim to examine the Jeep's twin exhaust tips. I stooped to look at the matching differential drips rainbowing on the concrete surface of the driveway. When I stood, she was already around the other vehicle and headed for the porch to our right with her sidearm drawn.

I spoke loudly, so as to be heard above the sheets of rain. "I don't suppose I could have my gun back?"

She ignored me, and I watched as a curtain in the window to the left of the front door slipped back in place.

Chief Long stepped up and pounded on the frame of the screen, then turned to look at me as I joined her on the step below. "Hopefully, he's really drunk and passed out—what we don't want is him just a little drunk."

I crossed my arms and tried to make a smaller target for the downpour. "Because?"

She pounded on the aluminum door again, the saturated portions of her uniform making provocative patterns. "Then he's dangerous."

I thought I could hear somebody moving around in the small house. "What if he's sober?"

"Then I've got the wrong house." She reached out, pulled the screen door aside, and banged on the door itself a half-dozen times with the butt of the revolver. "C'mon, you Indian taco, I know you're home!"

I joined her on the porch under the remains of a metal awning that sifted the downpour into interesting streams that were hard to avoid, but it was better cover than nothing. "I'm assuming, and only assuming, mind you, that his real name isn't Indian Taco."

"Last Bull, but he's part Mexican." She drummed on the door again, leaving horseshoe-shaped indentations on the cheap, interior-grade surface. "Clarence, I know you're in there—your shitty Jeep is sitting out here leaking onto the driveway!"

It sounded like someone knocked a bottle off a table inside, and I waited as Long pounded some more. After a moment the door opened about four inches and a red, bleary eye looked past the security chain while the smell of alcohol and vomit breathed out.

"What?" His voice was deep and slurred, and it looked as if the chief had gotten the condition she'd hoped for.

"Open the door."

The eye seemed to consider it. "Wh . . . Why?"

"Because I said . . ." Her response was cut short when she noticed he had slipped the barrel of what appeared to be a shotgun into the opening.

His movements were slow, and he fumbled with the chain as he repeatedly attempted to undo it with the weapon stuffed under his arm; from my perspective, I could see that the breech was jacked and the thing was unloaded. I started to mention this to Long, but she had already reared a foot back.

"Chief, wait. . . ."

Her foot hit the door—from personal experience I knew what the cheap, single-ply doors did in these kinds of situations—and she booted a round hole in it about ten inches in diameter, admitting her foot into the house but little else.

Clarence Last Bull dropped the shotgun and, predictably, ran—as best he could.

I reached over and grabbed Long by the collar of her wet uniform shirt and yanked her back to the side in an attempt to get her free from the door. As we fell backward alongside the concrete steps into some grandfather sage, she elbowed me, scrambled off, and charged toward the doorway.

"Wait a minute!"

She continued to ignore me and splashed up the steps with the long barrel of her .44 leveled, careful this time to kick the more structurally rigid side.

I decided it was time to cut Clarence off at the pass.

There was a sidewalk that led to the back of the house and, after rounding the corner, I slapped open a cyclone fence to find a concrete stoop not unlike the one in the front. There was a wooden-handled garden rake leaning against the painted siding, and I grabbed it. Last Bull was pretty intent on getting to the dirt that constituted the yard, which kept him from noticing the rake handle I slipped between his legs.

Fortunately for him, he cleared the concrete steps; unfortunately, he then hit the largest puddle in the yard face first.

I had dropped the landscaping tool and started toward him when Lolo Long blew through the rear screen door and pitched herself on top of Last Bull just as he had started to get up.

He was tall but skinny and incredibly inebriated, which gave the chief the upper hand. The air had gone out of him and now they were both covered in mud. He flipped her to the side, but she wrapped her legs around the trunk of his body and pulled him over after her. He tried to reach a feeble hand back, but she struck him a nasty blow to the head with the revolver, and he slumped still.

She pushed him over and lay there breathing, looking up at me from the detonation of drops that struck the puddle surrounding her. She wiped her mouth with the back of her hand. "Thanks for the help."

"It was nothing."

She kicked at the dead weight of his body, and when his face slumped into the murky water, she holstered the Smith and cuffed his hands behind his back.

I looped a hand under one of Clarence Last Bull's arms and dragged him away from the puddle before he drowned.

It was dry in the Cheyenne Tribal Police Law Enforcement and Detention Center, and the environs were as comfy as could be expected; of course, I couldn't speak for the man snoring fitfully in the holding cell with a blanket over his head. A stolid-looking patrolman with a pockmarked face, who was gently humming a tune to himself and eating portions of an apple that he carved with a yellow-handled pocketknife, was watching me.

I twirled the tiny ring on my little finger, glad that it hadn't fallen off in the backyard melee. "Can I have a piece?"

He cut off another eighth, shoved it in his mouth, and looked at me, his expression as blank as the walls that surrounded us.

I leaned back in the chair that Long had told me to sit in and glanced around the empty office at the couple of other tables pushed against the bare walls. After placing the suspect in the holding cell, the chief had deposited me with the quiet man and had repaired to the locker room in the back. From the sound of it, she was taking a shower as the sphinx guarded me. I guess I was still under arrest.

"So, you barked too much and they cut your vocal cords?"

I looked out the vertical window next to Long's desk and watched the wind rock the trees and plaster rain against the double-paned glass. You can learn a lot about a person by examining her desk, even if there's not anything on it. Chief Long's was completely vacant, except for an old, push-button line phone and one manila folder.

"Hey, do you mind if I make a phone call?"

He sighed deeply and continued to hum.

I waited for him to say something, but he didn't. After a while, I started dropping my attempts at social graces and surrendered to the exhaustion I felt. I leaned back in my chair and pulled my hat down partially over my face.

It was that way sometimes with the Cheyenne—conversation simply wasn't required and silence was very often a sign of respect; however, even though I knew he wasn't attempting to make me feel unwelcome, he wasn't exactly knocking himself out to become my newfound pal, either.

Nothing happened for a while; then, from under the brim of my hat, I saw Lolo Long walk in our general direction. She sat in a chair beside the deputy, but they didn't look at each other, preferring to sit at an angle with their eyes centered on an area roughly midwall.

As far as I could tell, the two danced around subjects—one providing a counterpoint to the other's silences with singular responses and small sounds that I'm sure carried their own meanings of verbal sustenance. They were not whispering but were still respectful of my supposed sleep, and the consonants sounded like small, bright birds in faraway trees, the vowels like a lullaby.

His chair squeaked and he closed a door, and then she moved to my left.

I tipped my hat back up and opened my eyes. Her hair was still wet from her shower, and she had changed uniforms.

"I don't think your staff likes me."

She studied the folder that had been on her desk, shrugged, and kept reading. "He's probably just pissed off because we've got his half-brother in the holding cell, but Charles says only about three words a week anyway, so who knows."

"Every family has a black sheep; some have two." I looked around at the half-dozen empty desks that were shoved against the wall. "Where are the rest of your personnel?"

She gestured with a distracted hand and continued to study the file. "I fired them."

I turned and looked at her, expecting more but not getting it. "Excuse me?"

She shrugged. "I fired Charles, too, but he keeps showing up;

he hasn't been paid in two weeks. I don't know if he understands that he's been fired. He lacks imagination, and I have to admit that it's a trait that's growing on me." Her eyes came up. "I don't like people with imagination."

"I'm sorry to hear that." I nodded toward the sleeping man through the doorway. "That the file on the lodger?"

She looked back at the folder, and about a minute passed. "No, it's the file on you."

"I've got a file?"

She closed it. "As of today."

"So, am I still under arrest?"

"Yes. No. . . ." She tossed the file on her desk. "Maybe."

"Do you mind if I ask for what?"

She puffed a breath out with her lips. "Reasonable suspicion, which covers being friends with Henry Standing Bear."

There was a lot going on there, kind of like a nascent volcano. "What, exactly, is it you've got against Henry?"

Her eyes flared, which reaffirmed my concern. "He thinks he's above the law, and I don't like that."

I smiled. "Maybe not above, but certainly beyond." I stood, looking down at the phone on her desk. "I'd like to make a phone call."

She splayed a hand and pulled a wave of the damp, raven-colored hair past her shoulder. "I already made all your calls. You're spending the night at the tribal chief's house, and I'm going to drop you off." She leaned back in her chair, stretched out her arms, and left her fingertips on the edge of her desk like a kid testing her reach. "But right now I thought I'd buy you dinner."

The Charging Horse Casino is a strange-looking building tucked away along the main road of the Northern Cheyenne Reservation, and if it weren't the largest gaming facility on the high plains and covered in neon, you might miss it.

A thickset man a little older than me with a salt and pepper ponytail and a weathered face met us and opened the door of the casino. "Hello, Chief."

Lolo Long didn't respond but continued in.

I nodded to the man, who gave me the slightest smile, and then continued on to catch up with her. "Somebody you know?"

"Ex–police chief."

"Oh."

Most of the building was taken up by the five-hundred-seat bingo hall in the back, but the three-a-week sessions didn't start till tomorrow night, so the place was pretty much empty except for the professionals who were scattered around the slots and poker machines. We were seated in front of one of the diamond-shaped windows in the farthest corner of the restaurant, where we could watch the late light flare with a horizontal glow just before dying out.

"Is this your usual seat?"

She looked around. "They try to keep me away from the patrons."

I nodded and sat there, waiting; it was her party, so I figured I'd let her swing at the piñata, which gave me plenty of time to study the sickle-shaped scar that started under her right cheekbone, circled around the orbit of her eye, and disappeared into her dark eyebrow.

The waitress, a middle-aged Cheyenne woman, quietly approached with water and menus. We ordered, and the waitress came back with a pitcher of iced tea. I nodded, and she filled up two glasses, then left, giving Lolo Long time for the window and herself.

She turned back to me. "So, how did I do today?"

I felt like I'd just hit a pothole. "Excuse me?"

"On the job—how did I do?" Her eyes went to the surface of the table. "Look, I know you've been doing this stuff for a long time. A long time. I thought you might have some opinions."

"It's really not any of my business, but I think maybe you should give the badge back."

It took a moment for her to work up a response. "I know I didn't do everything exactly right today."

"Well, you didn't do much right today." I glanced around to make sure that no one was in earshot and continued. "With all due respect, Specialist, I don't know what your specialty was, but it wasn't law enforcement."

She didn't move.

I felt bad about saying it, but she'd introduced the subject and I was beginning to think that it might be my only opportunity. I tried to soften my voice. "I'm sorry to be the one, but I have to tell you this before you get yourself or somebody else killed."

The muscles bunched in her throat. "Well, what did I do wrong?"

I glanced around in an attempt to get a handle on the subject. "Let's just use the altercation with Last Bull as an example: with any kind of decent public defender, he'll walk."

"He had a shotgun."

"An empty one that he did not brandish toward us in any way. If you'd been paying attention rather than trying to gain admittance to a residence where you had no warrant—"

"I know him; he's a drunk and dangerous."

"Which makes it even worse. You approached the house with your sidearm drawn. I don't care how dangerous he is or isn't— you offered him up a written invitation to resist. He is a potential suspect—the operative word there is *potential*—and should be treated with at least a tiny bit of respect." She started to interrupt again, but I wouldn't let her. "What if you're wrong? What if he's a guy who just lost a loved one and his child and that's all? What then?"

She was angry. "I'll do something like apologize."

"That would be interesting since I haven't seen anything approximating an apology for anything since I've met you today."

She folded her arms, then unfolded them and started to take

a drink of her tea or maybe throw it in my face. "Apologies are a sign of weakness."

I sat there looking at her, making sure I'd heard what I'd thought I'd heard as the waitress arrived with our food—she stood a little to the side to avoid the bloodshed.

I went ahead and finished my statement. "Apologies are a sign of having some semblance of an idea of what's going on around you and not being a cocksure idiot." I should've stopped there, but the rest needed to be said. "Excuse me for saying so, but you don't have the training or, from what I can see, the temperament for the job."

Her eyes stayed steady with mine. She took a deep breath and then stood by the table. The only sounds were the air-conditioning and the noisome jangling of the slot machines.

Again she reminded me of Vic, but without the top-notch training that the Philadelphia Police Academy had provided, or the five years of street duty, or the field commendations that the Terror had hung on her bathroom wall. It was possible that Lolo Long could become a capable officer, but she would never last that long. She would end up dead on a frontage road or bleeding her life away on a patch of threadbare indoor/outdoor carpeting.

Without another word, she turned and stalked out, taking the time only to flip one of the waiting plates from the waitress's hand. It cascaded in a graceful arc over the startled woman's shoulder and crashed onto the tile floor with a clatter, bits of broken china and chipotle steak going everywhere.

I dropped my head and sighed. I knew I'd been going too far, but I hadn't considered how "too far" I'd gone and, considering the recent conversation, I figured the waitress wasn't likely to get an apology.

The poor woman was still standing there with the other plate in her hand, so I took it from her. "I'm assuming that mine is the one on the floor, so I'll take the fried chicken." I held my other hand out to her. "Walt Longmire."

She nodded and shook my fingers. "I know." She looked through the window as Chief Long lunged the Yukon out of the parking lot. "She used to be such a nice girl before."

Setting the plate on the table, I gestured toward the mess. "Do you need some help cleaning that up?"

"No." She smiled. "I can get it—you eat."

It was at this point, according to Officer Long, that I betrayed a weakness. "I'm sorry."

The woman braided her weakness with mine. "I'm sorry, too."

I sat and began eating the chicken with my fingers; other than the waitress, I was the only one there. I pulled a few more napkins from the dispenser as she returned with a dustpan, broom, a spray bottle, and paper towels. "My name is Loraine Two Two."

"It's nice to meet you, Loraine."

She made quick work of the mess. "I heard it was Audrey Plain Feather who fell off a cliff and died today."

I gave the chicken a momentary rest. "That moccasin telegraph never sleeps, does it?"

"I worked with her over at Human Services." She smiled but then it faded. "They said the child, Adrian, was with her when she fell."

I took a breath and thought about my nonofficial connection to the case. "He's over at the hospital, but I think he's going to be fine."

Loraine stood but averted her eyes from mine. "It's a troubled family."

I nodded, still holding a leg in my hands. "That's what I hear."

"The man, Clarence; he was paying attention to my daughter Inez, a year ago."

"Really?" I wasn't sure of what else to say.

"Yes." Loraine Two Two turned to go, but her voice carried over her shoulder. "She was thirteen."

It was about two miles up the road to Lonnie Little Bird's house, and I was once again regretting the loss of my truck as I trudged up Route 212, the thunder still resonating off the flat surfaces of the distant plateaus.

With my current luck, it was likely to rain again before I got there.

It was also likely that Clarence Last Bull had killed Audrey, but the final word on that would have to wait until Chief Long got the preliminary report from the Montana Crime Lab and the FBI tomorrow morning. It wouldn't have all the details, but it would be enough to get the slow-moving wheels of justice started on their uphill journey.

Rudimentary math and tonight's revelation told me that Clarence was having a little on the side, and the fact that it was with a thirteen-year-old girl didn't exactly endear him to me. I still had doubts, but then I wasn't sure what a man did after pushing his wife and child from a cliff. Would you just get in your car and drive home drunk? If you were trying to make it look as if it were an accident, you would contact 911 and stay there. It just didn't make sense, and in my line of work the things that didn't make sense often led you to the things that did.

I reminded myself once more that this wasn't my case. Twirling the ring on my little finger, I again remembered that I had a daughter who was getting married in a matter of weeks.

I could hear a vehicle approaching from the rear, and just for fun I threw a thumb out to see if I could get a lift. The thought struck me that it might've been Lolo Long in a fit of conscience, deciding to give me a ride after all. Yep, right, and it could also have been Chief High Bear wanting to show me the ledger drawings that he had painted in the roster book he'd taken from the first sergeant of the Seventh Cavalry.

I turned to look back—by the sound, the vehicle was awfully close—and when I did, it seemed to be bearing down on me. It was an older truck with some kind of hopped-up engine and Cherry Bomb mufflers. I stood there for a moment, thinking that the driver hadn't seen me and would momentarily turn the wheel and go by, but instead the truck continued on a course straight toward where I stood.

I ran across the shoulder and down the hill by the side of the road, passed by a signpost for Route 212, clawed my way up the slight embankment to a barbed-wire fence, and threw myself over into the wet grass. The jacked-up pickup followed me into the ditch and swerved just past, slapping a few posts and shooting sparks from the barbs on the wire that attempted to bury themselves into the sheet metal. The truck slid sideways as it struggled to get back up the hill and onto the highway, then drifted to a slower speed as the driver tried to get purchase.

It was about then that I noticed the elk tied to the hood.

I really started missing my gun.

Soaking wet from the rough landing, I stretched the old three-strand wire, scrambled back over, and started after the half-ton as it slid sideways some more, the bald tires unable to get a grip. There were brake lights and headlights but no license plate on what looked like an old, red Chevrolet.

The driver was sawing at the wheel in an attempt to escape a return trip into the ditch, but all I could see was a mantle of long, dark hair.

I was having trouble getting up the grade in my slick-soled boots but got to the edge of the road and ran along the white line. The Chevy wasn't making particularly good time going down the road sideways, but it didn't seem as if I was catching up.

The wide tires on the rear finally got to the gravel, and I watched as the vehicle squirreled to the right, the elk swaying on the hood.

My second and third winds were giving out as I watched, but the driver corrected again and shot ahead east toward Ashland with a roar like a top-fuel dragster. Forcing the air in and out of my lungs, I stopped and placed my hands on my knees, the V-8 echoing off the hillsides and disappearing around the far turn a mile away. "Good God. . . ."

I swallowed and stayed bent over until my blood pressure and adrenaline level approximated normal but kept my eyes on the road just in case the crazed driver decided to turn around and take another pass at me. After a while, the only sound other than me breathing was the cry of a few night birds and the croaking of some of the frogs in the ditch. I finally stood, pulled in two lungfuls of air, and coughed.

It was the time of the evening that was playing with night, and I walked up the road a few steps until I noticed something odd on the gravel. It was a carved piece of buffalo horn about the size of three of my fingers, with a smoothed tip, a piece of rawhide tied in a loop toward the end. There were a few holes drilled into the thing and a larger opening about a quarter down the length.

I popped it in my shirt pocket and glanced up the road—it was still a couple of hundred yards to the cutoff to Lonnie's place.

I knocked and shuffled my feet on the welcome mat of the tidy house—I wasn't sure if the chief was awake or not. I glanced down the concrete ramp that led to the front door and was glad it was a warm night; if worse came to worse, I could always sleep on the hanging swing on Lonnie's porch.

I knocked again and could hear someone rustling around inside; after a moment, the door opened, revealing the chief in his wheelchair. He looked up at me through blurry eyes but with a grin. "*Ha'ahe*, lawman. They said you were sleeping over, but I'd given up on you. Um hmm, yes, it is so."

I opened the screen door and followed Lonnie along the hall-way, where there were numerous photographs of him in his major-league ball-playing days and ones of his daughter in jingle-dress dance outfits and playing basketball.

I sat at the table in the kitchen as Lonnie examined my soaked, mud-covered clothes and the torn jeans where the voracious barbed wire had gotten me in my leap over the fence. "Rough night?"

I took a deep breath and wished Lonnie still drank, but he had given that up in a successful attempt at getting his daughter from the clutches of his sisters. "Somebody tried to run me over."

"Where?

I jerked a thumb past my shoulder. "Walking, right out here on 212."

"What were you doing walking?"

"Oh, I had a difference of opinion with your police chief." I tried to deflect the conversation. "Hey, Lonnie, do you have any of that really good root beer?" I knew the chief kept a single can of Rainier in his refrigerator as a token to alcoholic temptation, but I wasn't going to ask for that.

"Um hmm, yes." He wheeled over to the fridge and opened the door.

"You don't know anybody with an early-seventies pickup, Chevy, red or maroon, with a loud exhaust, do you?"

He returned to the table with two cans and parked his knees next to mine. "That sounds like a couple of trucks I know."

The can made a soft hissing sound as I opened it. "Can you make me a list?" I knew from experience that Lonnie liked making lists.

He had put on his glasses, and the reflection in them made it hard to see his eyes. It took a while for him to answer. "Yes. Is there something going on?"

"A woman and her child fell off Painted Warrior this after-noon." I tried to think if it was this afternoon, my body telling me it had been three days ago. I stretched my eyes to try and keep them open and took a sip of the pop. "Anyway, I helped that police chief of yours today, and I can't think of another reason in the world why somebody would want to make roadkill out of me." I felt in my shirt and pulled out the carved object I'd found, tossing it on the table between us. "Any idea what that is?"

He put his can down and picked it up. He studied it for a moment and then blew into it, moving his fingers over the holes to make a trilling sound just at the height of human audibility. He lowered it and looked at me. "It's an elk whistle made out of buffalo horn—the old type." He looked at it again in admiration. "This is a good one. Um hmm."

The root beer tasted good, and I could feel some of the knots in my shoulders and neck starting to release. "You know who made that one?"

He turned the flutelike whistle over in his hands. "No, but I can find out."

"Add it to the list."

We smiled at each other, but then his faded like an eclipse. "What was the woman's name?"

"Audrey Plain Feather."

"I know this woman, her family." He looked up. "She is dead?"

"Yes."

He nodded. "And the child?"

"Alive, and being checked at the hospital."

He reached out a hand and patted my arm. "Thank you for looking into this thing, Walter."

"Oh, I'm not—"

"It is good that you are a friend to the people."

Before I could answer, there was a knock at the front door. Lonnie's expression was one of mild surprise. He held up a single bony finger to keep me from responding. "I am popular tonight. Yes, it is so."

He wheeled the chair around the table, and when I started to stand, he sat me back down with a quick movement of the palm of his hand. He disappeared down the hall, and I listened as he opened the door. There was a brief, but fierce, conversation in Cheyenne. I figured it was Henry, who had come to pick me up, but as I listened to the tone of the conversation, it became obvious that somebody was receiving a royal dressing-down.

After a few moments, Lolo Long entered and stood by the wall in the hallway. Lonnie rolled by her and went straight to the refrigerator again; without saying a word, he placed another can of root beer on the table. As he passed by me on his way back to the hall, he stopped to address the room as a whole. "I am going to bed, but I'm sure that you two professionals have a great deal to discuss. Um hmm, yes, it is so."

The kitchen was quiet; the tribal chief of the Northern Cheyenne Nation, having spoken, had rolled to his bed in his portable throne.

Her arms were crossed, and her hair hung down over her face like a shroud. She lifted her head slowly, her voice a murmur. "I'm sorry."

I folded, like I always do in the face of female conciliation, and gestured toward her root beer and the only available chair. "Have a seat."

She did and then looked at everything in the place but me. "They're going to try and take my case."

I took a sip of my own soda and waited.

"The guy you know, the agent, he called and said that the Medical Examiner's report showed enough reasonable findings to consider this a homicide, so they are going to proceed with their own investigation."

Nodding, I waited for her to say more, but she didn't. "That's pretty much standard procedure with the bureau." I leaned forward in my chair and rested my elbows on the table. "Maybe you should let them have it."

I got the eyes. "No."

"Why?"

She took a slug of her root beer and absentmindedly played with the whistle. "She was a friend." Lolo held the whistle up to her face and studied it. "We had a house in Billings together once when we were both going to school. We had hopes, and I was kind of a mentor. She got pregnant. . . ." She sighed in exasperation. "And came back here—I went in the military."

I did some quick math. "Adrian's only . . ."

"It was before him, another pregnancy that ended up being a miscarriage, but she came back here anyway." Long glanced around the room in an attempt to find the words that must've been lying around somewhere. "Look, Sheriff, I want justice."

"Whose justice?"

The eyes again, but I was getting eyeproof.

"Help me."

I leaned back in my chair, took a breath, and thought about the soon-to-be-married greatest legal mind of our time. "I can't."

"You can. I've seen them with you; they're afraid of you."

That made me laugh. "They're not afraid of me."

"Well, they respect you, and the new AIC owes you his life."

I narrowed my own eyes at her. "And what does that have to do with you?"

She set the buffalo horn back in its place, folded her hands on the table, then reached over and lifted the corner of the place mat. She looked at the floor and then lowered the mat back to the surface and smoothed it with her fingers. "I know you think I don't know what I'm doing."

I smiled. "You don't know what you're doing."

She nodded very slightly in agreement, and her voice was losing its energy. "And you may not even like me." I didn't say anything. "But you could teach me." Her voice was almost a whisper. "Please."

4

I was drinking my coffee and watching the swirl of light foam that formed a riptide against the far side of the cup, crashed against the edge, and then split to circle around and rejoin with one another where they started. I would look at anything to avoid watching Clarence Last Bull cry.

Long had offered him coffee, offered him donuts, and even offered to let him go to the bathroom, but all Last Bull said was that he wanted to die.

I wanted to die just watching him.

The chief went so far as to get a box of tissues from God knows where, then placed it on his lap over the inert hands that draped between his legs.

I pushed the folding chair that I had been sitting on against the wall and went to the hallway with the man's file under my arm, Long following me. We stood there, the chief with her arms folded and me sipping my coffee.

Her voice was gruff, but I could see that she was a little shaken. "How long is this going to take?"

I dropped my head and took a deep breath. "As long as it takes."

We waited there like that for a good ten minutes, neither of us saying anything, just listening. It got suddenly quiet, and I could hear him stirring in the cell.

I raised my head, leaned a little to the side, and peered back through the opening at the end of the hall—he was slumped on the bunk and had his arms wrapped around his lanky legs, as if trying to keep them from running away.

My legs carried me back into the room, and I could feel Lolo behind me as I tossed my empty cup in the trash can by the door.

He looked up. "You're sure it's her?"

I nodded and kept my eyes on him. "I'm the one who got to her first; me and a good friend." I glanced at Lolo. "Chief Long here ID'd her right away."

He snorted, "Chief Long."

I made the next statement definitive. "Yes, Chief Long."

His eyes locked with mine, and we played stare-down for a good four seconds before he looked at the floor again.

"But you're sure it's her? I mean there could've . . ."

"No." I had to shut this avenue down quickly, or we'd lose him to misplaced hope. "The identification she had with her is unquestionable."

"I wanna see her." He used the palms of his hands to rub his eyes.

"I'm sure that can be arranged with the ME's office, but first I'd like to ask you some questions?"

"I wanna see my son. Where is he?"

I pulled the chair that I had pushed against the wall across the floor, placed it beside the bars, and sat. "He's at health services, and we'll take you there as soon as we go over some things."

He stood and looked down at me. "What the hell is there to go over?"

"Clarence, do you always answer the door with your shot-gun?" I took his file from under my arm and began studying it without looking at him. "I think you should sit down so that we can get this done as quickly as possible—then you can see Adrian."

He stood there for a few seconds, then backed to the bunk and slowly lowered himself piece by piece.

My eyes came up and focused on his face. He was young, close to Chief Long's age, and as I had discovered from the file in my hands, he too had been in the military. "Army, 2-583—Second Battalion, 583rd Forward Support Group." I glanced back at the file. "Food specialist?"

The words spilled from him rote and lifeless. "I'm a certified chef; I won the Thirty-fourth Armed Forces Culinary Arts Competition at Fort Lee, Virginia."

I nodded. "Is that what you do now—cook?"

He placed a hand alongside his head. "Till I got laid off over at the casino."

I studied him. "Is that your chipotle steak recipe that I almost had last night?"

He looked a little puzzled, and I was pretty sure it was the first time he'd escaped his thoughts. "Almost had?"

"Yeah." I glanced back at Chief Long standing in the doorway, again with her arms crossed and suddenly finding the wall of singular interest. I turned back to him. "Clarence, I need you to tell me the story of what happened yesterday afternoon. I need you to tell me what happened in detail so that we don't miss anything."

"There isn't anything to tell."

I continued as if he hadn't spoken. "I need to know everything, because if I guess right, the FBI is going to sweep in here later and try to scoop you away—and I need all my questions answered before they do that."

"They think I did it?"

"Possibly."

For the second time, his eyes lifted to mine. "Do you think I did it?"

"No, I don't, but right now I need to hear the story about yesterday afternoon."

He sucked in his breath like I'd hit him, and he slowly began to speak. "We were going on a picnic as a celebration; I got a job over in Red Lodge as a sous chef." He barked a laugh without much humor in it. "The job was advertised as a Sioux chef, S-I-O-U-X—you know, they misspelled it. I told them I was part Cheyenne, part Mexican, and part Sioux, and I think it's what got me the job. I was going to go there next week, then move them over there next month." He shook his head, and the tears simmered in his eyes again. "I guess that's gone to shit now."

"When did you head out to Painted Warrior?"

"I stopped in at the White Buffalo and got something to drink—pop and stuff, around lunchtime."

"Eleven twenty-two?"

His eyes widened just a little. "Um, yeah. I guess so."

This part checked out with the receipt we'd found; it didn't, however, account for the beer cans and the fact that he'd been drunk when Chief Long and I had arrested him. "Clarence, did you go anywhere else?"

"No."

My old boss, Lucian Connally, had taught me a long time ago that if you already know the answer, you don't ask the question twice—and once you'd asked it, you waited, forever if need be.

He cleared his throat. "I, um . . . I got some beer at Jimtown when they opened. I mean, it was a celebration."

"Okay."

"We drove out there, and I parked the Jeep. I was afraid it was going to rain, so I put the top up while she and Ado played there in the grass."

"Not out by the rocks."

"No." He looked at me again. "Hell no."

"Then what?"

There was a pause, a short one, but a pause nonetheless. "Well, we were fighting."

"About?"

The pause was longer, and this time I looked at him. "Inez Two Two?"

He froze, and I stood in an attempt to display the fact that I was not behind bars and could walk out of the room at any time. "Clarence, up until now you haven't been completely honest with me, and if you don't start, I'm going to personally hand you over to the FBI."

"No."

I placed my hands in my pockets and leaned my back against the wall beside Chief Long. He stood and walked over to the bars, hanging his thin arms between them; for a sous chef, he must not have been sampling a great deal of his wares.

"We were arguing about the job and moving. She wanted to go over there at the same time as me, but I wanted to get things ready. I rented an apartment over a bookstore from a guy named Gary. I just wanted the place to be nice." He quickly added. "You can check all this."

"We will. What happened after the argument?"

"Look, I don't want you to get the wrong idea—that it was some huge, shitstorm fight; it was just the same argument we've been having for over a year now." He studied me. "You married?"

"Widower."

He looked contrite, an appearance I was not particularly unacquainted with from people looking at me through bars. "I'm sorry, but you know what I mean about living with a woman?"

I smiled, just to let him know that the conversation might not be going as poorly as he thought. "Martha's been dead about six years now, and there are disagreements we're still having."

He nodded at me, and his eyes filled with tears again. "We kept arguing, and I drank beer; I don't know, I guess I fell asleep."

"You don't know, or you fell asleep?"

"I fell asleep." He glanced back and forth between me and the chief. "I know it sounds lame, but that's what happened. I swear to God."

"Then what?"

"I woke up, and they were gone."

"Did you look for them?"

"Yeah, I looked all over the place but they weren't there. I figured she'd gotten all pissed off and had taken Ado and walked home."

"Did you look over the cliff?"

He looked genuinely surprised. "No—I mean, it never occurred to me."

"What'd you do then?"

"I got in the Jeep and started home—thinkin' I'd pick them up on the way, but I never found them."

"Do you have any idea what time it was when you left?"

"No. Why, is that important?"

"Maybe." I paused for a moment, a conversational indication that we were changing gears from him to the wide world. "Clarence, do you have any idea who might have some kind of grudge against you or your family?"

The thought hadn't dawned on him. "You think somebody did this to her?"

"It's possible, and it's up to us to investigate all the possibilities. Now, can you think of anyone?"

"Against me, yeah." He stared at the speckled white tiles on the floor. "But Audrey and Ado, no."

"No enemies she might've had—family members, people she worked with?"

"No. Her parents are dead, and the only family is a sister of hers in Billings."

"What about where she worked? Any difficulties there?"

"No. I mean, not that I know of."

"Where did she work?"

The chief's voice rose from behind me. "Human Services, over in the tribal building."

"No arguments with anybody lately?"

"Only me."

I checked my Colt, worked the slide mechanism, reinserted the round into the clip, and slapped it back in the stag-handled grips that Cady had given me one Christmas. "Does this mean that I'm no longer a suspect?" I carefully placed it in the pancake holster at my back.

Chief Long shrugged. "You're low on the list."

We stood there in the hallway of the Native Health Services building while Chief Long's mother accompanied Clarence Last Bull in to see his son. "So, do I charge him?"

"That's up to you. Do you think he's a flight risk?"

"No."

"Do you think he did it?"

"No."

I shrugged. "Neither do I, but there might be a problem with his story."

"What's that?"

"Henry and I were at the base of that cliff when Audrey fell, so if Clarence was up there, why didn't he hear me yelling at him, and why didn't we hear his Jeep start up and drive off?"

"He was drunk, and we didn't get up there until hours later."

"Well, maybe."

"What other explanation is there?"

"I'm not sure, but it's important to keep inconsistencies in mind."

She nodded and hooked her thumbs in her duty belt. "He started opening up after he found out you were a widower; that was slick."

I rested against the wall and tipped my hat back. "It wasn't slick, it was heartfelt." Wondering if Lolo Long was a lost cause as a student, I turned my head and looked down the hall. "There is a common humanity in all of us, and if you need something from somebody, you'd better understand that—it makes the job easier. Clarence might be guilty and we need to be aware because we are in the suspicion business, but he's also a man who just lost someone who was very close to him."

I pushed off and circled behind the reception desk to a coffeepot and a tray of mismatched mugs. She watched me.

"I'm separated, in case you were wondering."

"I wasn't."

She fought with herself for a moment and then pointed to the .45 at my back. "Not to change the subject, but do you mind if I ask why you wear that antique, anyway?"

I poured myself a cup. "It's what I got used to in the service." I thought about it. "It's a failing to have a favorite, but there it is. Being overly familiar with a weapon is as much a fault as not knowing it at all." I rapidly listed the 1911's shortcomings. "Heavy, hard to aim, slow rate of fire—there's a cult of weapons which blinds you to their weaknesses, but it's what I'm used to." I sipped my coffee and gestured toward her large-frame Smith in return. "Unless things have changed a great deal, I'm thinking that's not what they had you carrying in Iraq."

"No, they gave me a 9mm and I hated it."

"And you like that .44?"

"Yes."

I sipped some more of my coffee. "I'll ask you again when you have back problems here in about ten years." I tried not to sound like Lucian. "It makes you stand funny; you're compensating for the weight of that thing."

"You're just saying that because I'm a woman."

I shook my head, gesturing at my six-and-a-half-foot frame. "You don't see me carrying one, do you?"

She patted the revolver. "I like the weight."

"No, you don't, or you wouldn't have to use a two-handed stance every time you pull it. I can guarantee that there will be times in your law-enforcement career when you will have more things to do with that other hand than aim." I sighed. "You're not up against body-armor-equipped assailants."

She countered with a little heat in her voice. "Drugs, adrenaline—those are all factors."

"Maybe, but nowhere near as large a factor as just plain missing, which is what you're going to do with *Dirty Harry* there." I gestured toward the pot with my empty mug, but she shook her head in a full snit, so I only recaffeinated myself. "I'm going to give you a little piece of information that most people don't know; 50 percent of police shot in the country on an annual basis shoot themselves. I'm not talking about suicide, but about officers who accidentally fire into their off-hand while drawing or into the strong-side leg while reholstering. Another 30 percent are shot by other cops, and 10 percent after that get shot by people who take their weapons away from them." I lifted the mug to my lips. "And that's the uniformed, trained portion—don't get me started on the common populace."

I was coming on strong and figured she'd had about enough, but she only stood there with a hand on her revolver like I might try and take it away. After a while she crossed her arms and changed the subject again. "I heard you talking about an important piece of information we're in possession of that the FBI doesn't know about?"

I continued sipping my coffee. "While Clarence was in custody last night, somebody tried to kill me."

She stepped in close with a little more urgency in her voice. "What?"

"You don't know anybody who drives a maroon '70 Chevy half-ton with Cherry Bomb mufflers, do you?"

"What happened?"

"Somebody tried to run me over on 212 as I did the walk of shame to Lonnie's last night."

She thought about it. "Maybe it was just some pissed-off Indian who saw a cowboy walking along the side of the road."

"There seemed to be a lot more intention in the act."

"You get a plate?"

"No, there wasn't one. Besides, I was trying to get away before being turned into a hood ornament." She looked up at me, and I repeated. "Maroon '70 Chevy half-ton, Cherry Bomb mufflers."

I watched as she retreated to the parking lot, her Yukon, and the two-way radio, in that order, and then thought about all the people who were probably angry with me right now. There was a phone at the nurse's station, and I figured Chief Long's mother wouldn't mind if I made a few phone calls.

I punched in the number for my office and waited.

"Absaroka County Sheriff's Office."

"Well, as it happens, this is the Absaroka County sheriff."

She fumbled with the receiver, the fancy one with the little neck cradle she used for extenuating circumstances; I probably led the league in extenuating circumstances. "Boy, mister, are you in trouble."

I sighed and whispered my daughter's name so that she might not hear me close to two thousand miles away. "Cady?"

"Oh, yes, and I wouldn't want to be you about now." There was a rustling of papers, and she spoke to someone else about getting Saizarbitoria, the Basque percentage of my staff, to do a little paper serving. "I don't have time for you, but your under-sheriff is on the other line; would you like me to patch her through?"

"Sure."

The next voice was full of Philadelphia-ese—where "good luck with that" translated as "go fuck yourself."

"Have you been abducted by the Indians?"

I smiled at Victoria Moretti's tone. "Kind of. I'm in the process of giving sheriff lessons."

"What?"

"It's a long story; there's been some drama up here on the Rez."

"There's always drama with you; you're like a traveling troupe." She sighed. "So, are we in the first, second, or third act?"

I thought about it. "Hard to tell; Henry and I saw a woman fall off a cliff up here, and we're in the process of finding out who might've done it."

"Isaac Newton?"

"She was carrying a child—boy, about six months." There was no flippant repartee for that. "The boy is in the hospital and appears to be all right, but I've got a new chief of tribal police up here who is getting crowded by the bureau."

You could almost hear her teeth grind.

"How's Omaha?"

"It's still in Nebraska."

Ruby must have finished dispatching and got on the line again. "You know you've got an entire list of people who are trying to get hold of you, Walter?"

"I figured."

"Lana Baroja called about the cake design, Rosalie Little Thunder from Rapid City called about the dress, the management for Jalan Crossland called and wants to know if there will be electricity at the site of the reception. . . ."

I made a sound in the back of my throat. "I don't know the answers to any of those questions."

"Who does?"

"How about Cady?"

Vic chuckled. "I gotta go."

There was a click as Ruby continued. "Cady's called eight times in the last two days. Would you like me to call her for you and patch you in?"

I was quick to respond to that. "No."

"I thought not." She was trying to hold her temper. "Walter, we have a growing situation on our hands and you're not helping."

"What about Henry—have you talked to him? I thought he was the wedding planner."

Her voice became even more forceful. "He is organizing the tribal portion of the wedding; the rest is up to you. Speaking of, how is the tribal portion of the preparations going?"

I thought about how little progress I'd been making for Cady's wedding; I glanced at the receiver and thought about where I could go and hide when Hazel Long returned and smiled at me. "Ruby, excuse me for a minute." I held the phone on my shoulder. "Hazel, could you loan me a pen and paper?"

She nodded and placed both on the upper counter between us. "Thanks."

I noticed that Chief Long had returned from the parking lot and joined Clarence as they stood a little away from each other in the doorway across the hall, Lolo's eyes giving me an exasperated high sign.

I continued to hold the phone against myself as if I were attempting to smother it and looked down at what seemed to be the only friendly eyes in the hospital. "Hey Hazel, can I ask you a really big favor?" She smiled, and I could've kissed her. "I've got an angry dispatcher by the name of Ruby on the other end of this line who has an entire list of angry people who want to yell at me. Is there any way I could get you to write that list down?"

She held out her capable hands, and I deposited my life's problems into them. As I turned around, I almost bumped into Lolo, who had walked over with Last Bull. "What's up?"

"I'm going to take Clarence home and then make a run to Rabbit Town over on the other side of the Rez, and I think you'd better come along."

I glanced back toward the room they had come from. "Is Dog in with Adrian?"

"Yeah." She gestured toward her mother, who was still scribbling away. "Mom put food and water and even a bed in there, but he hasn't touched any of it. Do you want to look in on the two of them before we go?"

I cracked the door open and could see Dog's large head rise up from the other side of the bed. I whispered, "Just because you're on guard doesn't mean you have to go without food and water, you know?" He wagged once and then settled in again as I studied the sleeping child, who seemed to be resting comfortably. The little body was so small, and I thought about what Henry had said one time about the world being hard on little things. Adrian Plain Feather had overcome some pretty spectacular odds so far, and who knew, maybe he'd be all right.

I closed the door and crossed back to the group, joining Chief Long as she studied me. "You don't really think that dog understands what you're saying, do you?"

"Yes, I do."

The automatic doors swooshed aside, and we were suddenly confronted with the Federal Bureau of Investigation, complete with a smiling Cliff Cly and a phalanx of two other federal agents. The AIC straightened the folder under his arm. "How's the kid?"

I shrugged. "Still not talking."

"I hate using the rubber hose on infants, but you gotta get results." He folded his arms. "Am I mistaken or are you not only out of your jurisdiction but in the wrong state?"

"You are not mistaken. I'm in Montana because Cady's getting married up here next week and I'm making arrangements."

He looked genuinely surprised, but with Cly you never knew.

"This the daughter I talked to on the phone at the bar in Absalom?"

"Yep."

He levitated his eyebrows, a look which expressed a loss of options. "Damn, I was hoping to meet her before she got hitched."

I leaned into him, the brim of my hat about two inches from his forehead. "I would not let you anywhere near my daughter— even on a bet."

He smiled a becoming smile and stuck a hand out to Last Bull. "Really sorry about your loss, Clarence." He glanced back at me for a second. "You're in good hands, and I'm sure we'll find who did this."

He then pulled a thick manila envelope from under his arm and held it out to me. "Full ME's report; I thought you might need it." He watched as I shifted my eyes to Chief Long and pivoted his arm as if he'd meant to hand it to her all along. "There you go, Chief. I would've put it on your desk back at the office, but I didn't want to clutter things up."

After we'd dropped Clarence off, she drove up the hill from Lame Deer on 212 at a regular speed for once. "Do you want to explain to me what just happened?"

I was studying the file on my lap. "I would say that the federal government just ceded jurisdiction on this case to the tribal police."

"Obviously they don't think he did it."

"I'd guess not."

She settled back in the seat and upped the air-conditioning. "How did you know about Inez Two Two?"

"Her mother told me."

"Who?"

"Her mother, the waitress at the casino you slapped the dish away from last night."

"Oh."

"See, if you're nice to people they tell you things."

We drove along in silence for a while.

"Is fooling around with thirteen-year-olds indicative of Clarence's character?"

She thought about it. "I guess."

I read the white placards on the fence posts that warned passing motorists to not shoot the prairie dogs because the Department of Wildlife and Parks was conducting an experiment.

"He . . . I knew him before he enlisted—real ladies' man. They say he was in a mortar shell raid that did some damage to his private parts. I don't know if that's what happened to him over there, but whatever it was, it messed him up. Anyway, he came back and he and Audrey hit a rough patch and he meets this kid, Inez, down at the White Buffalo."

She placed an elbow on the driver's-side doorsill and ran her fingers into the thick mane of her hair. I was struck by her monochromatic beauty—the jet-black hair, the jasper-colored eyes, and the sunset-colored skin.

"So pretty soon they're an item, but Audrey, who is pregnant at the time, mind you . . ."

"I guess Clarence wasn't messed up too badly."

"Yeah, well, she gets wind of this little tryst and catches Inez at the IGA and about beats the shit out of her."

"This Audrey was pretty tough."

"Yeah." The hand disengaged with the hair. "Was."

"Maybe we should go talk to Inez Two Two."

She nodded. "Maybe. Look, I really don't like Clarence, and I've never liked the way he treated Audrey, but I don't think he pushed her and Ado off a cliff."

I continued to watch the scenery pass.

"Why did you ask about Audrey's work?"

I shrugged. "Home and the office—those are usually the places of conflict; people spend most of their lives at one place or the other. What kind of position did she have at Human Services?"

"Secretary, receptionist, or something—I mean, she was the first face you saw when you came in the door—well, along with Herbert His Good Horse and Loraine Two Two." She put her finger in her mouth.

"Something?"

"Oh, I was just thinking about the sign they have on the wall beside her desk about how if you use strong language or raise your voice you will be physically ejected from the building."

That was interesting. "What, exactly, does Human Services do that they have to worry enough about abusive behavior to post a sign like that?"

"They're in charge of the federal support checks, and when the money runs out toward the end of the month, the natives get restless."

"So Audrey could have enemies through work."

"Indirectly, I suppose." She passed a slow-moving truck hauling a trailer with about five tons of small-bale hay. "I mean, it wasn't like she was the one who wrote the checks or anything—she just handed them out."

I nodded and repeated her words back to her. "But she was the first face you saw when you came through the door."

She rolled her eyes. "All right, when we get through in Rabbit Town we'll head back to Lame Deer and have a talk with Herbert."

"The disc jockey?"

"The bit he does for KRZZ is a second income. His Honorable

Herbert His Good Horse is Audrey's boss; nothing goes on at tribal HQ without his knowing about it."

I raised a fist. "Stay calm, have courage—"

She smirked. "And wait for signs."

The trees were all stunted on the highlands of the Cheyenne Reservation. After the Baby Dean fire swept across the ridges and carried sixty thousand acres of Ponderosa pine with it, the remains were sold at salvage, including the three trailer-loads of logs Henry Standing Bear brought down to my place that had built my house.

Her voice interrupted my wandering thoughts. "What I'm trying to figure out is why he didn't respond when you and the Bear yelled?"

I found it interesting that she'd just mentioned Henry in such a personal way but decided not to remark. "He says he was drunk, woke up, and they were gone. There are more than a couple of scenarios—maybe he was passed out and didn't hear us, another is that they did as he suspected and left."

"How do you explain both she and Adrian falling off the cliff then?"

"They came back after Clarence drove home, or somebody brought them back."

She shook her head. "Did you see any other tracks?"

"No, but just because I didn't see them doesn't mean they weren't there."

She didn't answer.

I leaned back in the seat, determined to enjoy the ride. "Do you mind telling me who we're going to see?"

"Fella by the name of Small Song."

"Artie Small Song?"

She nodded. "Yeah, you know him?"

"Unfortunately."

"He's got the only '71 red GMC registered on the Rez. Closest thing I could find to your Chevy." She studied me. "How do you know him?" She watched as I pulled the Colt from my back, dropping the clip and reinserting it back in the grip. "You're not going to shoot yourself, are you?"

I had to smile. "If it's the only way out of this chickenshit outfit." I holstered the Colt. "Are we going to the mother's place or the dental hygienist he's been shacking up with?"

She flicked some jasper shards at me. "And might I ask how it is that you are so intimate with Artie Small Song's personal life?"

"We liked him for the Little Bird case."

She concentrated on the road, for which I was thankful. "The only address I've got is the mother out on Otter Creek Road. Did you read his file?"

"I didn't have time; why?"

I twisted my wife's engagement ring on my little finger. "He's what my undersheriff, Vic, would call a bad motor scooter."

Lolo glanced at my finger. "Priors?"

I let go of the ring and draped my hand out the window. "Beaucoup, and he has a tendency to be well-armed—really, really well-armed."

She smiled as she accelerated, slapping a hand on her overloaded holster. "Maybe you'll be glad I've got this .44 after all."

I looked out at the burnt husks of dead trees, like black veins in the crystal-blue sky. "I doubt it."

5

I'd been to Artie's mother's house before—it was up one of the fingerling canyons that ran down to Otter Creek—and it reminded me a little of the departed Geo Stewart's junkyard back in Durant. The rusted vehicles trailed all the way down to the main road toward the more populated areas of the unincorporated Rabbit Town. I don't know why Rabbit Town is called Rabbit Town other than there might've been rabbits there at one time, but I hadn't seen any so far today.

So far, no '71 GMC either.

The further we went up the hill, the older the cars and trucks got, and we finally parked somewhere around 1939. It was hot, but there was a trickle of smoke whispering from the tiny cabin lodged into the hillside just like there was when I had visited the winter before last.

That time, I had remained in Henry's truck as he'd asked the old woman about her son, but this time I was there officially. I hoisted myself out of the Yukon and looked at the place, especially the windows, since Artie was known to be in possession of ballistic oddities like FAL .308s, MAC-10s, and even an M-50—I knew because I'd been through his closet or the dental hygienist's at least. "Hold up."

Lolo Long, who was already winding her way toward the cabin, looked back and immediately placed a hand on her colossal sidearm.

I pointed up—the smoke was actually coming more from the back—so I took the route around the corner of the house toward the hillside. Chief Long followed as I carefully picked my way around a rotting roll of mustard-yellow carpeting and the wire remnant of a bedspring. "Do you know his mother?"

Once again, her tone was defensive. "No."

I studied the nearest window and could see the rags stuffed around the casing, as much for insulation against the heat as the cold. "Just for the record, I don't expect you to know everybody on the Rez."

"Thanks."

"Now, do you mind if I do the talking?"

She gestured an after-you-my-dear-Alphonse and brought up the rear.

There was quite an operation going on out back, where an elderly woman was scooping preburned charcoal with a number two shovel and spreading it evenly in a pit lined with heavy stones and tinfoil. Tipped to the side was a rack made from sheep wire and rebar, which held a good-sized doe elk that had been butterflied and then stretched onto the contraption.

She froze when she saw me but then rose and rested her chin on the back of her gnarled hands, her cataract-impaired eyes staying right with mine.

"Mrs. Small Song?"

She didn't answer, but the milky eyes clicked to my right like the buttons on a rattlesnake's tail as she took in Chief Long's uniform.

I walked closer and pointed toward the complicated arrangement. "Open-pit elk cooking; I haven't seen that in quite a while. My mother used to do it." I extended a hand. "My name is—"

"I know your name, lawman." She turned her head and shot a prodigious stream of tobacco onto one of the forty-pound rocks, where it sizzled. The old woman then glanced past as Long joined me, but then her eyes clicked back the way they had before. "Looking for my son?"

I conceded the fact. "Say, does he still have that '71 GMC?"

She kept her gaze on me, and I was just as glad the cataracts were there to guard me against what was most certainly the evil eye. "You wanna buy a truck, lawman?"

I smiled. "Never can tell."

She took her time before answering and poked at the coals with the wood-handled shovel, its point worn down so that it looked indented. "Got plenty out front."

"I need one that runs." I looked through the window as if Artie might be inside. "Is he around?"

"No."

I nodded and kneeled down by the rocks to stick a finger into her gallon water jug of marinade, pausing to look up at her. "May I?" She nodded with a curt jutting of her chin. It tasted pretty wonderful. "Pineapple?"

"Commodity juice; all they had this month."

I ran my tongue around my mouth as I looked at the door, propped open with a kitchen chair, and the windows, which were curtained with all different calicos. I looked back at the elk's body, where I could see where the death shot had pierced one side and then continued on through the other, taking a lot of meat with it. I went ahead talking about the marinade. "Sage, garlic . . ."

She interrupted, impatient with my novice tongue. "Cider vinegar and beer—lots of beer."

I stood and looked down at all four-foot-ten of her, wrapped in a shawl and dressed in a full-length, layered skirt despite the 90-degree weather and the fire. She looked as if she should've been beside a sheep wagon telling fortunes and finding penta-grams in people's hands. "Maybe that's why I like it."

She cocked her head, regarding me. "You are the lawman from the *Ahsanta* mountains."

"I am."

"They say you're a good man, *Ahsanta*." She shifted her weight. "You know I had three sons?"

"No, ma'am."

"One was killed in the Vietnam. My second son, the one you hunt, never showed no interest in the white man's army—he's the smart one. My grandson, Nate, the one that works at the talking box, the boy of my son up in Deer Lodge."

I smiled. "The radio station?"

"Yes. He was going to fight in this war they have now; I don't know which one." She shifted the handle in her hands and rested it beside her face. "I told him no, that he couldn't join the white man's army, that they would only get him killed." She studied me. "You in the white man's army, *Ahsanta*?"

"I was."

She nodded, mostly to herself. "Only the white man survives the white man's army."

I glanced at Lolo. "Chief Long here was in the white man's army."

"*Se-senovoto ema'etao'o.*"

I saw Long stiffen, but she said nothing, and it was possible she was learning.

"Why you hunt my boy?"

I figured I'd just level with her. "Last night, he tried to run me over with his truck."

She stared at me through the clouds in her eyes, then her jaw dropped and she began breathing a convulsive laugh that pulsed her tiny back like a bicycle pump. "Maybe he doesn't like you, *Ahsanta*."

I shrugged. "Maybe, but I've never really met him, so I can't imagine what it is he's got against me."

"He doesn't like the ones make him sleep inside." She continued to study me, but she was making up her mind about something. Finally, she spoke. "Was here last night."

"Your son?"

"Who we talking about?"

She had a point. "What time?"

"Night time."

"Could you be a little more specific?"

She adjusted something in her mouth, and I thought she was going to spit again, but instead, she swallowed. "Don't own a clock."

I slipped a hand over my mouth to pull down the corners and keep myself from smiling. "Did he stay the night?"

"Nope, can't sleep inside no more. Told you—you people did that to him."

I glanced back at the holes in the deer and could see where someone had slit the butts and shoulders and removed the membrane from the rib cage. It was a professional job—Artie most certainly had been there last night. "Mrs. Small Song, I'm not here to arrest your son for anything; I'd just like to talk to him."

She motioned with the shovel handle, rocking it toward Chief Long. "What does *Se-senovoto ema'etao'o* want?"

I glanced over my shoulder as if I'd just remembered the young woman who was peering into the scrub pine and juniper bushes on the ridge above us. "She just wants to talk to Artie, too."

She nodded her head but continued watching the coals, glowing red around the edges, and it was impossible to tell what she might've been thinking. For a moment, I thought she'd forgotten we were still there, but then she spat on the rocks again. "I tell him you was here, whenever he come back."

"We'd appreciate that, Mrs. Small Song." I turned and started toward the corner of the house with Lolo in tow.

We were halfway down the path when she grabbed my arm and tried to yank me around. I kept walking, but when we got to the level, she stepped in front of me. "That's it?"

"Keep your voice down and get in the truck."

She looked a little startled and then followed me to the Yukon, where we opened the doors and slid in. "He's there?"

"I don't know, and that's the part I don't like." I gestured toward the ignition switch. "He's been there, and he's going to be there again, and I'm thinking it would be nice if we weren't quite so conspicuous on the next visit."

"Okay, Great-White-Detective, so how did you know he had been there?"

"Well, the elk, for one—that old woman didn't break up that five-hundred-pound animal and rack it herself; besides, I pride myself on knowing what an M-50 can do to living tissue."

"The very-out-of-season elk?"

"Yep, so all we have to do is wait for the prodigal and well-armed son to return."

She started the SUV and pulled it into gear. "What are we going to do, go sit up on a hill and wait till he decides to come back?"

I pulled my pocket watch from my jeans and looked at the dial. "That elk should be done in about seven hours." I tossed a forefinger down the red dirt road. "Let's go talk to Herbert His Good Horse, and we'll wander back around here come dark." I put on my seat belt. "So, what does *Se-senovoto ema'etao'o* mean?"

She roared the Yukon down the hill. "Red snake."

The tribal office buildings are a sprawling compound of warrens representing the different factions of tribal government, and there were a lot of them. The original building had burned down in the sixties and then again in the eighties. I remembered the controversy when it had been announced just what the new building was going to cost. Now it was just a question of when it was going to burn down again.

Long parked next to the concrete steps, and we climbed up and then through the double glass doors. Human Services was immediately to the right, but Chief Long continued walking down the polished surface of the hallway toward the center of the building.

I stood there for a second, looking at the sign above the vestibule that read HUMAN SERVICES, and then shrugged and followed after her.

I noticed a young Cheyenne, tall and lean in a black T-shirt, who was seated at a metal desk across from a stairwell at the midpoint of the building. He looked to be around seventeen and stood as we approached. "Hey, Chief."

She ignored him and signed the register, then handed the pen, attached to the desk with a piece of cotton twine, to me. "Sign in."

The young man stood, and I thought he looked slightly familiar. His voice was overly obsequious. "Can I help you, Chief?"

Without looking at him, she spoke in a low voice. "What is your desk doing in the middle of the hallway instead of down by the entrance?"

He gave me a look of animated incredulity and then glanced down both directions of the main hall. "You know, Chief, I did a reconnoiter and discovered that there are eight entrances to the building. I thought maybe I'd split the difference." He glanced at me again, and his eyes were playful. "It also gives me a clear view of the girls in accounting, right across from here."

Without answering him, she turned and started back down the hall.

He looked at the sign-in book and then at me. I stood there with the pen, glanced down the hall at Lolo Long, and then back to the young man with the smiling, jasper eyes.

"Hey, Sheriff. Nice to meet you."

I nodded and started after her, coming to a complete stop only two strides away.

There was a glass case like the kind that usually holds photographs and trophies in high schools. There on the third shelf was an 8×10 photograph of Lolo Long in her battle fatigues, steely-eyed, disciplined, and without the scar. There was also a photo of Clarence Last Bull being awarded the armed forces prize for his culinary skills, and a large silver trophy. It was almost as if it was a program for the current investigation.

My eyes came back to Lolo Long.

The young man joined me at the wall case and pointed at a toy vehicle complete with little machine guns alongside a very real Bronze Star Medal with Valor. "They gave her that one for hauling all the bodies out of the Humvee—even the dead ones." He shot a look down the hall to make sure the coast was clear. "When she got home she was so loaded up with antidepressant, antianxiety, and antipanic medicine that everybody started calling her 'Anti.' Have you driven with her?"

"Yep."

"Jesus, wear your seat belt and a helmet if you've got one." He leaned in. "I swear to God she still thinks she's in Iraq and that there are bombs and RPGs all along the roads. That's why she drives so fast, trying to outrun 'em."

"Are you coming?" We both glanced up to find the top half of the chief hanging out from the vestibule. "Or have the girls in accounting caught your attention, too, Sheriff?"

He yelled down the hall to her. "Hey, can I have a gun?"

She yelled back, "No," and then disappeared.

"You've got one, and so does he!" He stuck out his hand. "Barrett Long."

I shook it. "Little brother?"

"Yeah."

Human Services was a three-office complex with a communal area and a reception desk that barred the way to the inner sanctum, along with the sign in bold print that Lolo had mentioned. When I got there, Chief Long was staring at the photographs on the desk, from the kind of photo packages taken at discount stores. There was one of Audrey holding Adrian, another of Clarence with a chef's hat and white coat holding a casserole. There were a few more of Ado, smiling at the camera in confusion, and a piece of paper with tiny multicolored handprints.

"You guys know why the chicken crossed the road?"

We turned, and there was KRZZ's morning drive man, still wearing his top hat with the feather, and beside him in a wheelchair a younger man with two of the most powerful looking arms I'd ever seen. "For the indigenous Indian—because it is the chicken's inherent right."

"Herb?"

"For the old Indian—the chicken was escaping from residential school."

"Herb."

"Rez Indian—what's a chicken?"

She gave up and just stood there.

"BIA Indian—the chicken crossed the road because CFR 133, section 242, gives them the authority to do so under Department of the Interior regulations; they wrote a grant and we funded it. We are very proud of that chicken."

The young man in the wheelchair turned and looked at us. "You'll have to excuse my uncle—he's retarded."

Herbert glanced down at his nephew and smiled. "That's not politically correct." He turned back to us with a sigh. "Sorry, I was attempting to lighten the mood. I guess it's official, then." He looked at us. "We heard that Audrey met with an accident."

Lolo gestured toward me. "This is Sheriff Longmire; he's helping me with the investigation."

"We've met." He gestured toward the young man with no legs. "The one who doesn't think I'm funny is my nephew, Karl Red Fox."

I extended a hand and thought for a moment that he was going to pinch it off. "Hi'ya."

Herbert looked back at Lolo. "Investigation?"

I nodded and noticed a few more people in the adjoining

offices, including Loraine Two Two, quickly dodging back into their own rooms. I threw a hand toward Herbert's doorway. "We'd like to have a few words with you if we could?"

"Sure."

He glanced at Karl, who nodded. "I'll roll out and talk with Barrett about the girls in accounting." He popped a wheelie and rode it into the hallway.

Herbert led us inside, carefully closing the door of the windowless room behind him. We chose a few straight chairs, and he rounded his desk. His face and his expression were flat with the exhaustion that goes along with public service, but there was also a deep-seated concern. It was an expression I saw in the mirror every morning. "So, it wasn't an accident."

"We're thinking not."

He sat and shared his sadness with us. "So, how can I help you?"

I waited as Lolo asked the inevitable. "We were wondering if you knew of anybody who might wish Audrey ill or might want to do her harm."

"You mean to the point of . . . ?"

He seemed dismissive of the idea, so I softened the angle of the conversation. "We're not absolutely sure that that's the case, but we're going to follow up on all the possibilities."

I glanced at the framed photos Herbert had on his desk—there was one of Audrey, one of the Two Two mother and daughter, and of course, one of Karl—I was beginning to get worried that the entire tribal government was related. There was also a poster of Karl in the wheelchair with his arms raised in triumph as he crossed a finish line with a ribbon stretched across his chest.

I nodded toward the poster. "Where was that taken?"

He smiled as he took a cigar from his shirt pocket along with the clipper and lighter. "At the Oita International Wheelchair Marathon in Japan." He turned to look at us. "Lolo knows, but he lost his legs in a car crash; he was drinking. We've got a problem in the family. You really think somebody killed Audrey?"

Lolo answered. "Can you think of anybody?"

He shook his head and then clipped the end of his cigar, gesturing toward us. "Would either of you care for one? It's the only vice I allow myself anymore."

We looked at each other and then back to him. "No, thanks."

He leaned forward and lit the cigar with the cut-down Zippo I'd noticed yesterday, then switched on a fan mounted in the wall above his head. "No windows, but I've got my own exhaust fan, so nobody complains." He studied me. "You were in Nam?"

I nodded. "Yep."

He turned to Lolo. "Hey, Chief, how many Vietnam vets does it take to screw in a lightbulb?"

She stared at him. "I don't know."

He pointed his cigar at her in an agitated fashion. "That's right, because you weren't there, man!"

We shared a smile as he slumped back in his chair and tossed the lighter onto the desk toward me. "Got that from a friend who was in Saigon in '67."

I picked up the tarnished, encrusted lighter. Across the front was SAIGON, 67–68, 101ST AIRBORNE, and on the back, WHEN THE POWER OF LOVE OVERCOMES THE LOVE OF POWER, THE WORLD SHALL KNOW PEACE.

I handed it back to him. "Thoreau?"

"Hendrix, Jimi." He sat there for a minute, puffing on his cigar. "We get the usual malcontents in here; people that are angry just because—and don't get me wrong, they've got a right to be angry. We only get so much support money and we go through a lot of it at the beginning of the month. People have problems, I mean real problems, and we're the ones with the money so they come here." He paused to take another puff, and you could see him going through a mental list of everybody who might've ever threatened the young woman. "I'm not sure I want to implicate anybody on just hearsay."

Long cleared her throat. "You'd rather whoever did this got away?"

He darted his eyes between us. "No."

"Then why don't you give us a few names to go on; just anybody that might come to mind."

Even though the door was closed, he lowered his voice. "Have you spoken with Clarence?"

Long started to speak, but I cut her off. "Why would we want to do that?"

He looked around as if his office might be bugged. "She would come in with marks on her arms and face sometimes, nothing big, just bruises. I tried to get her to talk about it, and she said that he hurt her, sometimes. I mean, I assume it was Clarence."

In my peripheral vision, I could see Lolo's jaw muscles tighten. "How often?"

He thought about it. "Once a month, I guess."

"Once a month?"

"Yes."

She spit out the next words. "Why didn't anybody report it?"

Herbert His Good Horse leaned across his desk and spoke in a slightly more aggressive tone, dashing some ashes off his cigar into the ceramic ashtray on his desk. "You know how hard it is to get these things investigated or to press charges when the victim refuses." He looked at me, imploring. "She didn't even want to talk to me about it."

I glanced at the chief. "We understand."

He leaned back in his chair. "I'm not accusing anybody, but . . ."

"Right." I waited a moment. "Is there anybody else you can think of?"

He gestured helplessly.

"Anybody who might have seemed particularly angry with Audrey—any kind of odd behavior on her part when somebody might've come in?" He didn't say anything, but I could tell my soundings had touched something. "Anybody?"

He sighed. "There were a few, now that I think about it—I mean, I don't know if this means anything. . . ."

Long produced a small notepad and pen. "Please."

Herbert stared at the journal and then slowly spoke. "There's an individual from the eastern part of the Rez, a man by the name of Small Song."

For the second time today, I completed the man's name. "*Artie* Small Song?"

"I hate to bring it up because his nephew, Nate, works with me up at KRZZ, but yes, that's him." The social worker nodded. "Artie was in here last week about his mother's Elder support checks—we would give them to him to give to her. She's a medicine woman out that way—big medicine. We were worried that she wasn't really getting her checks and discovered she hasn't for the last three months—so, this time we refused to give him her check. He was very angry."

Chief Long was attempting to catch my eye, but I ignored her. "I bet he was."

"I just remember him because Audrey read him the riot act and told him that he should be ashamed of himself." His eyes went to Lolo. "Your brother had to throw him out. I thought he was going to kill Barrett."

Chief Long started to close her notepad and stand. "Thank you, Herb."

I placed a hand on her arm and reseated her. "Are there any others you can think of?"

His eyes, once again, went back and forth between us. "There are a few others."

"Who?"

"Kelly Joe Burns down in Birney."

I assumed it was Red Birney, which was not too far from the incident.

"Birney Day." He quickly added.

Evidently political correctness was making headway on the Rez.

"Is that that white asshole meth-head Houdini who can run a hundred miles an hour I've been chasing for a month now?"

Herbert nodded his head. "There was also Louise Griffin, who got in a shouting match with her a couple of weeks back." He thought. "You know? No, none of these people would ever . . ."

"Not even Artie Small Song?" He glanced up at me but didn't say anything. "It's not your responsibility to make those choices, Herb; we're just relying on you to provide us with some names. It's up to us to move forward with the investigation."

He didn't seem completely comfortable with my assurances. "You're not going to mention my name; I mean, I have a small and deeply disturbed following on the radio."

"Not to worry." I glanced at the door. "Is there anybody here in the building, people she might've worked with?" I paused. "I noticed Loraine Two Two out there."

"Well, considering what happened, they weren't the best of friends." He laughed. "No, God no. Audrey was a saint around here; everyone loved her. Everyone. She came in on her day off to do extra work, baked cookies on Fridays—that's what makes this so hard to believe." He glanced up at the poster behind him. "She ran and worked out with Karl, getting him ready for his races." His words caught in his throat, and he placed a hand over his face. "Excuse me for just a moment."

Lolo tapped my arm. "I think we've taken up enough of your time here, Herb."

We stood, and I nodded to him in appreciation of his help. "Thank you."

His eyes shone like puddles in his face. "Hey, there was this Indian woman hitchhiking back to the Rez in the middle of the night and this white woman picks her up. The Indian woman says, 'Hey, thanks for picking me up. What are you doing out on the road this late?' The white woman points to a bottle in a brown paper bag sitting on the seat between them and says, 'I got this bottle of wine for my husband.' The Indian woman nodded, 'Good trade.'"

Lolo Long smiled and placed a hand on his shoulder as we turned and left.

In the hallway, Barrett and Karl were chatting up who I assumed was one of the girls from accounting, who beat a hasty retreat when she saw Lolo coming. "You had a wrestling match with Artie Small Song last week?"

Barrett crossed his arms—it must have been a family trait. "Huh?"

Chief Long flipped through the register and then turned the book around on the desk and shoved it toward her brother, a finger pinning the personage on the page. "Him."

The young man leaned forward and read the name as Karl nodded a hello to me and backed his chair out of the line of fire.

"Oh, yeah, that guy." Barrett looked up at his sister. "He had a screaming fit down the hall. Said he was going to come back in here with an atomic bomb and blow the place up."

"Did he threaten Audrey Plain Feather?"

"He threatened everybody on the planet." He looked at her thoughtfully. "Does that mean I can have a gun now?"

She turned and leafed through the rest of the book in a disinterested fashion. "No."

"If he comes back, I could shoot the nuke out of his hand."

The chief looked at me and then returned her eyes to the

register. "Why don't you tell my little brother about the 50 per-cent of cops that get shot?"

I shrugged.

Karl continued to study me and then spoke. "If you're going after Artie Small Song, you better take an army with you."

"That's what I had in mind."

He grinned at the floor. "Back before I lost my legs, some friends and me, we were out hunting one time and shot this whitetail deer up near Kelly Creek. When we got to it, that dude Small Song was already butchering it. This buddy of mine steps up and says, 'That's my deer.' He didn't even look at us, four of us, but stood there with that skinning knife just moving back and forth." He looked up at me for the first time. "Swaying, you know, like a snake before it strikes."

I smiled. "You let him keep the deer?"

Karl nodded with the self-assurance of someone who has barely escaped death, perhaps numerous times, and is wiser for it. "You bet your ass we did; the guy's a psycho." He shuddered dramatically.

It was dark, but from my vantage point I could still see the old woman lift the planks and check the pit-roasted elk underneath. The shower of sparks rose like a constellation of orange celestial bodies reaching out for their brethren above, lighting the face of the woman as though she was onstage.

I was lodged at the base of a Y-shaped pine, the fallen branches making for a pretty good hiding place, or so I thought until the medicine woman looked up the hillside and directly at me—even from this distance I could feel the weight of those opaque eyes.

She had pulled a rumpled CPO jacket around her shoulders and the shawl she had been wearing earlier was around her head to protect against the slight chill of the evening. She might not know exactly where I was, but she seemed to know that I was out there and that most likely I wasn't alone. There were other eyes than mine here and maybe the eyes of Artie Small Song to boot.

Almost an hour earlier I'd discovered the spot and had carefully made my way down the slope to where I now sat. I'd learned long ago that you needed to get comfortable at the beginning of things, because you wouldn't have the luxury later on.

I usually had plenty to occupy my mind in these situations, and tonight was no different. My daughter and the impending wedding loomed large, and I was beginning to question my motives for sitting in the woods. Was I just avoiding the oncoming disaster that was around the corner by stretching my jurisdictional responsibilities, or was I focusing on a situation and a fellow officer who needed my help? Was I just out here because it was the path of least resistance and the kind of thing I was used to doing?

I had to fight to keep from sighing.

My daughter would be here tomorrow and, so far, Henry and I had not accomplished many of our assigned duties, the most important being finding a place for her to get married. Henry had actually gone over and spoken with Arbutis about the situation, but when I'd asked him about the meeting, he'd closed his mouth and said nothing—not a good sign.

This was a nice spot. Maybe I could talk Cady into a stakeout marriage ceremony that included armed guests—I'm pretty sure the groom's side would have no problem with that since they were almost all cops anyway.

Not only was my daughter arriving tomorrow but so was Lena Moretti, Vic's mother and Cady's soon-to-be mother-in-law.

The wedding was in less than two weeks.

I could just stay here; chances are they'd never find me.

The medicine woman returned to the kitchen chair that she had stationed by the back door, turned her head, and spat. She brought a forefinger up and slid it across her lip where a little tobacco residue must have remained, then flicked the offending particle away.

Despite the distance, I could still make out the erosion-filled plains of her face. It was not unique in these situations that you start developing a feeling for the person you're watching, almost as if they become an extension of yourself. It always comes down to being able to sit quietly and wait. Most lose the ability, the honing of their skills dulled and rusting in the forgotten kitchen drawers of their minds, but it was part of my job and I could just go away without going away and become a part of the landscape.

I had all night, but Artie didn't. It was late, and she wasn't going to be able to leave the elk on there for much longer. How much did Artie Small Song care about this meat? How much did he care about feeding his mother?

The answer came slowly, almost glacially, as I became aware of something to my left—something in the dark, vertical shapes of the trees that hadn't been there before.

I waited, the sides of my eyes aching from being locked in one direction. Move first and die is the maxim that had been taught to me, the one I'd followed on the high plains, in Vietnam, and in every dire situation in my life.

I waited.

It was possible that we were staking out an innocent man, as innocent as somebody like Artie Small Song could be, but an ounce of prevention is always worth a pound of bloody results.

I could've sworn that I'd heard something behind me.

He would be at a much better vantage point to see me, front lit by the fire below. Had the old woman known from which direction he would come? Had she spoken with him? Did he know we were there? All these questions and a multitude of others attempted to dislodge me from my suddenly uncomfortable seat.

I waited.

A dark form melted into the trees to my right. I could make out a hand resting against the rough surface of the bark. The fingers flexed, no more than three feet from my head. I stopped breathing, thinking that he might hear me. Then he disappeared again, the fingers slipping away as if they'd never been there at all.

After a while I saw him again, a little further down the hill, his outline breaking with the stark form of the trees. The old woman was now looking directly at him and, consequently, me.

My eyes were momentarily drawn to the medicine woman as she took a step toward the fire pit. She gripped a knee and lowered herself so that she could move some of the boards, and another flurry of sparks rose into the night.

I could see where Artie Small Song stood, and I saw him pause for just a second before his head turned and the rifle in his hands swung around.

The Cheyenne Nation struck like a war lance, carrying the two of them down the hill, and all I could hear was grunting and heavy breathing as both combatants refused to give way to the slightest energy loss by crying out.

I threw myself from the relative comfort of my hiding place and stumbled down the hill in a striding attempt at speed, hoping I wouldn't simply land on my face. The men continued to crash through the trees, and I heard a resounding thump as they reached the flat at the back of the house. I glanced off a creeping pine, which diverted my direction a bit, and tripped a little in an attempt to keep my footing.

The old woman had uncovered the pit and was holding one of the boards in her hands. The fire was blinding after sitting out there in the dark for so long, and I'm pretty sure that's what she'd had in mind. Directly below me, the two men were struggling, one rolling on top of the other until they reached the rocks at the edge of the fire.

I was still a good thirty feet away when Mrs. Small Song swung the board in her hands and comically struck at the Bear in an attempt to get her son free. I landed on the two of them, receiving the majority of the medicine woman's pummeling as Lolo

Long joined us from around the side of the house, where we'd stationed her.

I was able to yank the rifle out of Artie's hands and tossed it to the side, somewhat surprised that it appeared to be a simple single-shot bolt-action .22.

His mother was screaming as the chief pulled her away from us; she was surprisingly spry, and it was all Lolo could do to hold on, finally resorting to wrapping her arms completely around the old lady and lifting her from the ground.

We dragged Artie to his feet. I'd seen pictures of Small Song but hadn't ever met him face to face. With all the stories I'd heard about him cleaning out bars, I'd assumed he was a bigger man, but he stood only about shoulder height.

Once I got my breath back, I gasped out a few words. "Lolo, are you all right?"

"Yeah." She sat on the kitchen chair with the old woman in her lap and continued to hold fast.

I looked at Henry. "How about you?"

The Bear nodded and felt the back of his head, where the medicine woman had landed a telling blow. "Yes."

Artie took the opportunity to elbow me and try and make a break for it, but Henry grabbed him with both hands and stood him up, locking an arm into his back. "He is an active little rascal, is he not?"

He tried to head-butt Henry, the man's hair flying away from his face as he looked defiantly first at me, then at Chief Long, and finally at the Cheyenne Nation.

"There is only one problem."

I glanced up from Artie's surprisingly youthful face. "What's that?"

Henry grabbed the young man's jaw and examined him like a horse he was intent on buying. "This is not Artie."

6

The elk was really good, and I thought it was awfully nice of the medicine woman to invite us to dinner considering we'd staked out her house and had all but beaten the crap out of Nate, Artie's nephew and the smallest of the Small Songs.

We'd helped them pull the elk from the pit—it seemed like the least we could do. Then one thing had led to another and, seated in more kitchen chairs liberated from inside, all of us ate elk and watched the fire in the pit. The old woman had tossed the boards in on top of the coals, and there was now a nice fire going as she retreated into the house for more potato salad.

Nate's mood had improved when Henry had produced a twelve-pack of Rainier. He smiled at all of us. "So, you thought I was Art?"

Henry shrugged, and I nodded with my mouth full.

"If I'd been Art, man, you never would've heard me." He returned his gaze to the Cheyenne Nation. "I used to hear about how you were really something; I guess you're getting old, huh?"

Henry sipped his beer, and if you looked closely you could see the barest trace of a smile at the corner of his mouth. "I caught you."

Defiance glowed in the kid's eyes, his ego still stinging from having been taken. "You'd never catch Art."

The Bear chewed his elk and said nothing.

I caught the boy's attention. "When's the last time you saw your uncle?"

"Yesterday."

"What was he up to?"

The kid gestured toward the meat on his plate. "Hunting."

Lolo Long's voice rose from by the door. "He know it's not elk season?"

"He doesn't care."

I sipped my beer. "Where was he hunting yesterday?"

The young man gestured with his fork in a vague direction. "South of here."

"Were you with him?"

"No, he hunts alone."

I nodded sage-like, fished the elk call from my pocket, and tossed it between his hiking boots. "Is that yours or his?"

Nate balanced his plate on one knee and picked up the carved bone. "Artie's—you can tell from the notch on the bottom; it's his signature." He looked back up. "Where did you get it?"

"Somebody tried to run me over in a '70s red GMC pickup last night."

He didn't say anything to that.

"Doesn't your uncle have a '71 GMC?"

"Yeah, man, but I had that truck last night." He stuffed the elk call in his shirt pocket. "I had a date, if it's any of your business."

"Do you always go out on dates with an elk tied to the hood?"

He looked a little uncertain. "Um . . . yeah."

Mrs. Small Song exited the cabin and stopped to place a dollop of potato salad on Chief Long's plate, paused to deposit more on Henry's, and then advanced on me.

"Then you were the one who tried to run me over last night?"

His eyes dropped to his lap. "Um, yeah."

The old woman paused and then gave me another portion as I continued talking to the kid. "Why?"

"I don't know."

"You don't know why you tried to run me over last night?"

He shrugged but stayed silent. He was obviously covering for his uncle—or for somebody—and wasn't very good at it. I thought about the man I'd been able to make out at the wheel of the truck and thought he'd been bigger than the kid. "Where's the truck now?"

"Art must have it—he lets me drive it over to work at the radio station, then he picks it up. I do the afternoon drive."

"KRZZ?"

"Yeah." He slipped into his on-air voice: "Nate Small Song with the big sound."

I raised a fist in concert with Henry and Lolo, and we all chanted together, "Stay calm, have courage, and wait for signs."

I ate a little bit, washing it down with the beer, giving him plenty of time to elaborate. I risked a glance up at the medicine woman, but she was looking off into the trees behind her house. I followed her clouded gaze and thought about how, even with her limited physical abilities, she was seeing far more than I was.

"I unloaded the elk and then parked the truck down the hill. It was gone this morning, so I figure Art took it."

I glanced at the Bear, who continued eating. "How did Artie get here? You say you got the truck from him last night; where did you do that?"

If it hadn't been for the seriousness of the subject, it would've been funny to see how fast the kid was trying to think. "Lame Deer."

I continued badgering him. "Where in Lame Deer?"

"Well, not really Lame Deer—at the bar in Jimtown."

It was actually a pretty good play; it would be difficult to get a straight answer out of anybody who was there as to whether they had seen Artie or what time that might've been. "So, Artie gave you the truck last night with this elk tied to the hood. Any idea what time that might've been?"

"Nope."

I watched as the old woman beside me placed a hand on my shoulder, carefully took the can of beer from my hand, and then turned and went back in the house. It was a simple gesture, and you might've thought that it was completely innocent but for the touch. The medicine woman had tried to translate something to me in that instant. I attempted to see her in the kitchen, but she had disappeared. I turned back to look at Nate. "But the truck was gone this morning?"

He nodded his head, thankful that I'd taken the "nope" on his timing. "Maybe he got a ride from somebody in the bar, man. Maybe he just hiked over."

I was a little incredulous. "That's thirty miles."

"He's been known to do it."

Henry's voice rose from where he sat, across from the fire. "In the dark?"

The kid smiled back at him. "Tracking in the dark scare you, old Bear?"

Staring into the fire, the Cheyenne Nation took another bite of elk and chewed. The kid, naive as he was, didn't know that Henry Standing Bear was the thing that scared the things in the dark.

Later, we helped collect the rest of the elk, clean up the site, and dampen the pit. The old woman was washing the dishes in a porcelain sink speckled with lead divots set in an equally battered metal kitchen cabinet.

It was as I was drying the mismatched discount-store plates that I took the time to take the place in; it reminded me of my grandparents' house. Low-slung and notched into the back of the hillside, the house had been constructed with hand-scribed logs puttied with the old Oregon cement.

Her voice was little more than a whisper. "*Ahsanta*, you're the one whose wife died?"

I was always surprised by the way the Indians referenced me through my deceased wife. "Yes, ma'am."

I could see three different types of wallpaper in the kitchen addition over which the upper cabinets were affixed. They were also metal but were the kind found in gas stations, complete with stickers advertising AUTOLITE, CRANE CAMS, and PUROLATOR OIL & AIR FILTERS.

"You like my cabinets?"

"I do."

"My son, he got them for me."

I wondered which gas station he'd stolen them from. "They're very nice."

Her eyes looked over the sink and out the window to where the others were killing the fire. "Because Artie is the way he is, he is blamed for things he hasn't done." She shrugged. "Because he is who he is, he gets away with some of the things he *has* done— it is the nature of things."

I smiled down at her. "I understand."

She looked up at me, and again it was as if her eyes were reflecting the clouds I couldn't see in the nighttime sky. "He didn't do this thing you think he has." Her knotted hands gripped the edge of the sink. "He done some bad things, I know, but nothing like this."

I nodded.

Her eyes stayed on mine. "You believe me?"

"I do, but you are his mother." She smiled a becoming smile for somebody with that much chewing tobacco in her teeth, but it faded a little when I asked the next question. "How is it you know why I'm looking for him, other than what I've told you?"

She nodded her head slowly. "I have a way with these things, powers that I use for the good of my family and my people." She gestured toward the wall. "And somebody called me this afternoon on the telephone."

She cackled a brief laugh, and I shook my head. "I don't suppose you'd like to tell me who it was that called you?"

She hung her own dishrag over the faucet. "Artie."

"He called you?"

Her smile faded completely now. "He said you were looking for him; that a woman was dead, but he didn't do nothing."

I rolled down the sleeves of my shirt and snapped the cuffs. "In all honesty, Mrs. Small Song, all we want to do is talk to him. He had an argument with a young woman over at Tribal Services last week—had words with her. This week she ends up dead and somebody tries to run me over with Artie's truck—I think that warrants a conversation, don't you?"

She said nothing for a while, and I started thinking that I should've known better than to confront an Elder, a medicine woman, and a traditional in such a way.

"After the claims settlement in 1963, my husband and me built this house from the logs of our old days house. My husband died not too long after that, and like so many do in great sorrow times, I took the religious road and became a peyote person. My oldest son was also religious, and he used to go to meetings with me. Five years later he died in the Vietnam, and I stopped going to meetings so much because it reminded me of him."

She paused for a moment and bent her head just a bit, her gaze landing on the base cabinet.

"I went and got baptized on the egg-dyeing day, but after a while somebody told one of the priests that I had been seen at a peyote meeting. One day at my confession, the black robe asked me if I was still praying to that dried-up old peyote and calling it God." She smiled. "I told him no, that I pray to God, but that I sometimes still use the peyote medicine for when I am sick. He said that the peyote was a church and that I could not go to two churches, so I stopped going to the black robe church." She continued to stare at me. "Do you go to the churches, *Ahsanta*?"

"No. My wife was the religious one in our family."

She nodded. "My religion became my own. I would go visit sick and hurt people—that's when people need religion, not just on Sunday mornings or Thursday nights. Some people got better after I visited with them and people started calling me a medicine woman, and after a while, I became one, I guess." She pushed off from the sink and turned to face me more directly. "I tell you these things because I have had a two-part vision about you, and I would like to talk to you about it."

I wondered what the old woman's motivations were. "About me?"

"Yes." She struggled with what she had to say but finally spoke. "There's someone who would speak to you, but I don't know who he is. He comes to me in my visions in a great bear shape; does this mean anything to you?"

I could feel the scouring of wing tips against the insides of my lungs. "Could be."

"You have other family?"

The next words came out carefully. "I do; a daughter, and she's expecting my first grandchild."

She worked the chew in her jaw as if the words were tough and needed tenderizing. "The bear-person tells me that you must keep your family close; that there are those who would harm them."

I thought about my experiences on the mountain a few months back, an adventure I wasn't sure I'd ever be over. I thought about Virgil and the bear headdress he'd been wearing the last time I'd seen him, and about how I still wasn't sure if he was alive or dead. I thought about his grandson, Owen, and how

I knew most certainly that he was dead. Virgil or Owen had delivered a pronouncement upon my future or that of those close to me, some warning of impending disaster that I had put out of my mind—until now.

"Where is your daughter, *Ahsanta*?"

"Philadelphia, but she'll be on her way here tomorrow."

Her head nodded as she thought. "That's good; it will be easier for you to keep an eye on them when they are here in the good country."

Boy howdy.

"What's the second part of the vision?"

"That you should come to church with me. Tonight." She nodded.

I leaned an arm on the kitchen sink and lowered my head to look at her a little more closely as Henry, Lolo, and Nate entered through the kitchen door. "Go to church with you tonight?"

"Yes, the bear-man says that you should do this."

I looked up and could see Henry looking at me, his eyes a little widened. I glanced back at the old woman and asked. "Which church?"

She grinned at me with the tobacco between her teeth.

There is a federal criminal penalty exemption for the religious use of peyote by members of the Native American Church. The consumption of the small, dried button cactus is older than the Controlled Substances Act by about five and a half thousand years.

Fair is fair.

I'd heard about the ceremony but had never taken part in the rituals, let alone in the mescaline-based substance itself. Henry said that he had been behind the moon four times and around the moon innumerable times; he also said that it was like driving on the highway, then rolling down your window and tossing your head out, which didn't sound like something I wanted to experience.

The Bear dropped us off at the trailhead and sat there in the driver's seat of Rezdawg. "I was not invited."

The medicine woman was waiting by the grille guard of the truck, her head bowed and her hands stuffed into the folds of her skirt.

I leaned an elbow on the door of the vehicle I hated more than any other and twisted the ring on my little finger. "That means you can't go?"

"No."

"Can I invite you?"

"No."

"Can I get her to invite you?"

"No."

I nodded and glanced back at the ninety-pound woman who was taking me hostage. I turned to the Cheyenne Nation and could see just the slightest smile on his otherwise stoic face, which was pressed against his fist.

"Chief Long is not going to report me to the DEA, is she?"

He shook his head. "She is going home and going to bed." He glanced at the watch on his wrist. "I was not invited there, either."

"She doesn't like you."

"No."

"Any idea why?"

"No."

"You're just a font of conversation tonight, aren't you?"

"Yes."

I sighed and looked at the old woman again. "Big medicine."

He shrugged. "It is a great honor to be invited."

"I don't want to have flashbacks."

"You will not have flashbacks."

"I don't want to start going to Grateful Dead concerts."

His eyes sharpened on mine, the twinkle there a little off-putting. "You definitely will not do that."

I nodded.

"Unless, of course, it is something you have always wanted to do." He lowered his hand and let it drop to the sill. "It amplifies the heart." He reached out and thumped a curled fist into the center of my chest. "And I know this vehicle; it is a good one."

I took a deep breath to steady my nerves. "Thanks."

"There is no guarantee that you will even be offered peyote—you may simply be there to observe."

I lowered my voice to a whisper. "I think there's more to this than a simple come-to-Jesus meeting."

The shards of obsidian glinted toward the corner of the truck, to where the medicine woman had moved off a few steps and was studying the trees the way she had before. "No doubt about it."

"Where are you going to be?"

His eyes returned to mine. "Close."

"Good." I stepped back. "Don't let me go off into the forest and follow the little animals, okay?"

He nodded and ground the starter on Rezdawg, which sputtered, coughed, and sat silent, the surrounding chirp of the crickets the only sound. "She only does this when you are around." He patted the dash and ran his fingers through the eagle feathers along with the medicine bag that hung from the truck's rearview mirror. I recognized the ritualized gesture. "Rezdawg knows you do not trust her."

"She's right."

He hit the starter again, but this time the motor caught, fumbled a little on the lobes of her cam, and then cleared her tailpipe of a little soot and ran relatively smooth. "She feels your distrust and it causes her pain. You should apologize."

"I've said it before and I'll say it again—I'm not apologizing to your crappy truck."

He jammed the aged three-quarter-ton into gear and pulled the steering wheel toward the road. "Good luck with the little animals."

I watched as the single dim taillight with a lack of brake lights bumped down the wallowed-out dirt road and disappeared over a rise. Sighing, I stuffed my hands in my jeans and turned to look at the old woman patiently waiting for me at the trailhead. "I guess it's time to go to church?"

She held out a hand, and I wasn't sure if it was for her or me.

I took the hand and started up the trail with her following a little behind; she was careful to walk in my footsteps. The trail was pretty well worn and she was still holding my hand, but I was amazed at how well the old girl navigated by the stars at night. The moon remained hidden, and I was just regretting having not brought a flashlight when I felt her tug at my hand.

I stopped and leaned down. "Something?"

She nodded and gestured with her left hand toward another branch of the trail I hadn't seen.

"That way?"

She nodded.

It was about the third time she did this that I started wishing I'd brought not only a flashlight but bread crumbs. I figured if I kept the logistics in my head, I'd be able to orient myself with two lefts, a right, and a left and still have a fighting chance of discovering the road if I had to.

We got to a flattened area in a small clearing where there was a powerful glow from a large teepee with a fire inside. It was family style, painted around the edge with a brownish reflection of the individuals ringing the inside perimeter; at the apex, where the light didn't reach, it was dark.

Mrs. Small Song's hand tightened in mine, and she began leading the way. In keeping with tradition, the opening of the teepee was facing east in order to welcome the rising sun, and these flaps were tied open. The old woman paused at the doorway and spoke in a strong voice to the assembled within. After a moment, a collection of voices responded and, still holding my hand, she stooped at the entrance.

I followed, ducking my head through the opening, and stood, a little hunched in line with the angle of the canvas, my hat in my hands. I glanced around at the all but three smiling faces and didn't recognize anybody. This was rare—I usually knew a percentage of folks in any Cheyenne gathering—but I guessed that these were highly religious people and it was possible that we'd never crossed each other's paths. Some stood and approached me, but the three ancients who did not smile stayed seated.

I finally recognized one of the participants. It was the same man who'd ushered Chief Long and me into the casino, the ex-chief of the tribal police; he patted my shoulder. "Longmire, it is wonderful to have you with us this evening." His hand touched his chest. "Albert Black Horse."

"Yep, I remember."

"I am to be your sponsor tonight. Is that all right with you?"

"Um, sure."

He misread my confusion, "You would rather have someone else?"

"No, no." Like an idiot, I patted his arm back. "I'm happy to be sponsored by you, Mr. Black Horse."

"Albert."

I patted some more. "Albert."

Others smiled as I glanced toward the three very old, very solemn men, all of them seated behind the fire and in front of a slight, crescent-shaped berm that half-circled the perimeter. "I guess not everyone is happy to have me here?"

Black Horse shook his head. "No, it isn't that they are unhappy to see you, but they have important sacred duties. The first is the Road Man; he is responsible for making sure that nothing interferes with the ceremony and that you are well taken care of—lives are in his hands, so he must take all of this very seriously." He gestured toward the men seated next to the Road Man, one of whom held a #6 or #7 Dutch oven with a skin stretched across the top. "This is the Drum Carrier; he is the advisor to the Road Man. The other is the Cedar Man, and it is his job to keep the air purified during the ceremony."

Someone spoke from behind me, and there was a palpable pause and a sudden silence. I turned to see who it was that had spoken and could see another man seated by the opening who was pointing toward my back and talking rather quickly in an animated fashion. I turned to look for Artie Small Song's mother, but she had already made herself comfortable across the perimeter.

All of a sudden, there was a great deal of discussion, and this time I was pretty sure it wasn't pleasant. Albert's grip tightened on my arm. "Are you wearing a weapon?"

I'd forgotten about my sidearm and was now aware of the cause of the fuss. "I am."

"You will have to take it off; it is strictly against the rules of the church."

"What should I do with it?"

He gestured toward the opening. "You will have to leave it outside."

I nodded, not so pleased with the idea of just leaving the Colt out there unguarded, but not wanting to be insulting by insisting that it would be dangerous if left unprotected.

Excusing myself with a strong nod to the assembly, I stepped outside, ejected the clip and piped round and placed them in my shirt pocket, and then unbuckled my belt, slipped it through the loops, wound it around the pancake holster, and carefully put the bundle in my hat. I put the lot of it a step away from the door against the canvas and then pulled a folded handkerchief from my shirt pocket and placed it over the Walt Longmire Collection. I'm not sure why I felt compelled to cover the whole thing with what looked like a shroud, but the idea of leaving the .45 laying there in plain sight just didn't sit well.

When I reentered, things had calmed down.

The man who had started the discussion nodded a tight-lipped response as Albert took my arm again. "He is the Fire Chief; he and the young man next to him will tend the fire all night, keeping it strong." He gestured toward an open spot along the wall and invited me to sit beside him. I did as instructed and watched as the conversation died away. After a few moments, the Road Man spoke to the Fire Chief, who closed the flaps.

As I sat there, the features of the old men became more recognizable to me.

I knew the man with the drum; he had been a friend of my father's—of course much younger at the time—and the reason I remembered him was that every time he saw me as a child he had given me a shiny wheat penny. James Woodenlegs.

The Cedar Man also began looking familiar, and I recognized him as Willis Weist, who had disappointed my mother; she had observed him going to as many as four white-person church services each Sunday. A confirmed Methodist, she'd finally asked him which one he liked the best, to which he had responded, "Pentecostal." My heartbroken mother asked why. He'd shrugged, "Because they have the best potluck dinners."

There were four big chiefs in the Cheyenne nation and three of them were here. The Old Man Chiefs were a kind of loose Council of Elders, of which I knew Lonnie Little Bird to be a member (Lonnie most likely purposefully avoiding the ceremony because of his close association with me). Like Lonnie, when asked if they were chiefs, they would deny being such; they must exemplify modesty, and you could bet that if a Cheyenne told you he was one, he was pulling your leg.

It was a life of service, which few could live up to and from which many resigned. The old joke was that if you wanted to know who was the real chief of the Northern Cheyenne, look for the guy with the empty wallet on the road standing beside a car that was out of gas. That would be the chief: broke from giving all his money away and broken down from running food from home to home and providing a sounding board to the people's miseries.

This is not to say that the Old Man Chiefs had no power— their word was final on any subject of contention because they had proven beyond question that they had the people's best interests at heart. Big Medicine.

A few more words passed among the three men, at which point the Fire Chief approached the Road Man and received a number of bundles that included sage, tobacco, and corn husks, and a dried, powdery substance of which I could only guess.

The Fire Chief passed the sage around the circle first, and I watched as the members drew the bundles across their limbs, the trunks of their bodies, and then their heads in an initial purification ceremony.

I did as I'd seen the others do and watched as Albert smiled a nod of approval, did the same, and then passed it on. When everyone had smudged themselves, the Fire Chief took out papers and a simple tobacco pouch which he passed to the others, who in turn scattered a little of the tobacco into one of the small sheets and rolled themselves a makeshift cigarette.

It had been a while since I'd tried to roll with fixings and attempted to remember how Hershel, the old cowboy back on the Powder River, had rolled his. I fumbled with the paper. Albert's patient hands took the assembly from me, deftly rolled the thing up, and licked the edge with spit that was like Super Glue.

"Thanks."

He nodded and handed it back to me as the Fire Chief stoked the flames and pulled a short log, about four inches in diameter, from the fire. He handed the smoldering stump off to the participant to his right, who lit his home-rolled cigarette and passed the "lighter" on to the next.

I was able to light my ceremonial smoke without assistance and carefully handed the glowing log to Albert.

The others were now talking in subdued voices, and I could make out from the tone that they were praying. The older man curved his shoulder into me and quietly spoke. "These are the prayers of smoke and are a way of clearing your intentions for the ceremony."

I nodded. "What if I'm not sure what my intentions are?"

He smiled, the wrinkles in his eyes joining with the ones around his mouth like the ripples in a pond. "Then you need to think about why it is you are here."

"I guess I'm concerned for my family."

Albert's eyes played around the circle. "A lot of people are here because they have concerns for their families, including the woman who brought you." He studied me. "You don't have to lend voice to these prayers; you may keep them to yourself if it's more comfortable for you."

I nodded and focused on the fire, trying to remember when I'd last prayed for anything. My mind went back to the spring before last, and a time in Philadelphia when I'd sat in a hospital at my daughter's side. I'd prayed then—like a theological car salesman, I'd made deals, counterdeals, and threatened the very heavens themselves if they didn't release my daughter from the swollen solitary confinement to which a terrible accident had sentenced her.

Thinking about my daughter and her daughter, I found my lips moving. The words weren't important, but the thoughts were of hope that their lives might be spared the kind of trials that mine had held; that somehow the prices that I had paid in losing my wife and numerous others would balance the bill in their favor. Just keep them safe was all I finally asked, just keep them safe from all the things out there that would do them harm, and if that was not possible, at least give me a crack at those things before they had to deal with them.

When I became aware of the teepee again, I realized that I was the only one in the circle speaking.

The Road Man raised an eyebrow at the Drum Carrier and they both nodded. *"Haho."*

The entire group chanted the one word back, me included.

The Fire Chief collected the butts from around the circle and carefully placed them alongside each other at one end of the crescent-shaped berm. It was then that I noticed a groove along the ridge of the altar and remembered Henry's remarks about "sitting behind the moon" and "traveling around the moon." I assumed the ridge was meant to represent the road itself.

The Fire Chief stoked the flames, and I watched as the sparks rose and ascended through the opening at the top of the teepee like lightning bugs attempting to escape into the cool dark of night.

When I looked down, there was a bowl being held under my nose that contained a powdered substance with clumps. I'd seen pictures of the stuff, but never seen it live and up close. I took the bowl and watched as the person next to me placed a spoonful of the powdered substance into his mouth and then handed me the ornate spoon with a carved bird on the handle.

I sat there, an individual whose experience with drugs had so far mostly been limited to those in pill form—aspirin, Benadryl, and the occasional Vicodin.

Staring at the powder, I took the spoon in my hand.

It wasn't so much that I was intimidated by the thought of taking a psychoactive drug that held me still; I'd known Henry my entire life and knew he wouldn't allow me to be involved with anything that might harm me in any way.

It was me.

The dried cactus is said to set the user on a reflective road for eight to ten hours, and I wasn't sure that I wanted to meet me there. It was all a question of letting go, of allowing myself the freedom to see who and what lay on the other side. My experiences on the mountain had prepared me, and in some ways superseded anything the peyote might provide, but—

There was no pressure from the faces surrounding me, just smiles and looks of reassurance. Even the Old Man Chiefs who sat on the back of the altar were specifically there for my protection.

Henry's words kept thrumming in the back of my head, "It is a great honor."

I looked around at the faces again. Taking a small amount of the powder onto the spoon, I slipped it into my mouth.

It tasted horrible, bitter and dry, and my first response was to spit it out, but I figured that would've been worse than not ingesting the stuff at all. The saliva in my mouth began reconstituting the powder and, if possible, it started tasting even worse. A moment later, the man to my right handed me a small cup and filled it with a dark liquid, steam rolling from the opening of an earthenware jug.

I studied the small cup with a blue and white stripe near the lip and especially the brewed contents, and figured it had to taste better than what was in my mouth.

I was wrong. It was worse.

Swallowing the contents, I fought back the urge to gag and quickly handed the jug and cup to Albert. If I was going to throw up, I preferred not to throw up on the sacred items. Taking a few deep breaths, I felt a little better.

I found myself looking at the people in the circle and thought about the honor that had been bestowed on me. I felt an odd familiarity with the light; the glow from the fire filled the teepee like the golden one that sets off the sunset on a high plains summer evening. We were well past that time of day, but I basked in its warmth as I looked at the Cheyenne circling the teepee, with their heads bobbing and their mouths uttering the sing-song rhythm of prayer.

Other than a mild sensation of nausea, I really wasn't feeling anything, but I'd heard that that wasn't an unusual response to the stuff I'd ingested. Just a slight stomach upset. I was beginning to think that my size and possibly a natural tolerance to the stuff were going to make the whole experience a bust. The nausea kicked in a little harder, and I belched; when I glanced at Albert, he was watching me and laughing.

I was thankful I'd had the elk dinner, in that it was probably dampening the effects of the peyote. On the other hand, I have to admit that I was a little disappointed; it was about then that I became aware of the grain in the knotholes in the teepee poles.

The tempo of the singing had quickened and was reinforced by the beat of the Drum Carrier, who had joined the chant. I listened to the music and allowed my eyes to rest on the Fire Chief as he stoked the coals of the central fire again, the flurry of sparks flying up and away as before in an attempt to join the stars.

The warmth of the fire reached out until I could feel the ends of my fingers and toes glowing of their own accord. It wasn't a bad feeling, and certainly not the kind of thing I'd expected from a form of mescaline, but my knowledge was limited to what I had read, not what I had experienced. It was a good feeling but certainly not earthshaking. Once again, I was a little disappointed.

At this point, I think I was trying to make something happen, hoping for anything.

I studied the patterns in the spire-like poles that supported the teepee, willing some faces to appear in the wood, but they stubbornly remained knotholes.

My thoughts circled around to my daughter, who would be arriving in less than fourteen hours, and I hoped that Henry was making more progress in the wedding preparations than I. It was possible that I was going to have to leave Chief Long to her own devices in attempting to solve the puzzle surrounding Audrey's death. I didn't like the thought of leaving the case unsolved but maybe it was all for the best.

It was about then that I lowered my face to look around.

And everyone was gone.

7

I blinked my eyes and stared around the interior of the teepee just to make sure what I was seeing was what I was seeing— nothing.

The dirt altar that had made up the center of the ceremony floor was still there, even the indented road of the moon, the cigarette butts, the drum. The peyote bowl, spoon, and jug of tea were all there, all of it untouched, as if the participants had suddenly been called from the teepee and had left me behind.

The fire was blazing away as if it had very recently been stoked, but everyone was gone.

I continued to breathe deeply and sat there waiting for I'm not sure what. I blinked a couple of times and started to get the feeling that I was being made the butt of a joke. I found it hard to believe that the Old Man Chiefs would just get up and head out, but evidently they had, leaving the white guy in here to think about things.

I started to think about standing up when I noticed something on the ground leading to where I sat. Leaning forward, I poked a thumb and forefinger into the dirt and picked up a piece of rough twine, the kind that merchants used to use to tie up brown paper packages. I remembered the stuff from my youth on spools in dry-goods stores but hadn't seen it in years. Where had that come from?

I picked up the end of the twine and watched as it traced its way across the floor, underneath the teepee flap, and out.

Leveraging myself into a standing position, I lumbered toward the center of the circle and stood there beside the fire with the piece of twine in my hand. It was strange, because the fire didn't appear to be putting out any heat. I did a half-circle in both directions just to make sure that I hadn't missed anything or anybody, but I was definitely alone.

I stood there for a moment and then noticed more strings lying on the ground, each one leading to where someone had been sitting, all of them disappearing under the flap.

I moved toward the door, kneeled down, and put the twine between my teeth—I could swear I could taste the peyote in the jute—so that I could have both hands free to open the flap. The job was made easier because the tips of my fingers were glowing. I pushed the flap away.

It was daylight outside, which explained everything—I must've fallen asleep, and the others had left me there in the relative safety of the teepee. I lowered myself into a three-point position and pushed my way through the opening.

I was no longer in the land of the Northern Cheyenne.

Sand dunes, strangely red, furled into the distance like rollers in an ocean. The sky was a pale blue, and there was moisture in the air as if the sun had just risen even though it stood at midday.

I took the twine out of my mouth and looked to the horizon, but I couldn't see anything except the wind-drifted sand. I turned back—the teepee was exactly as it had appeared last night, my hat with the sidearm inside still next to the door with the handkerchief draped over the top.

I was just about to reach over and pick up my things when the forgotten string in my hand gave a tug. Startled, I almost dropped it but then saw that it made a beeline over the nearest dune and disappeared. I glanced around and could see the other strings that had come from the teepee—they traced off in all directions, but none of them appeared to be moving.

The string yanked at me again, so I started following it, the sand potholing under my boots as I wound the twine around the flat of my palm.

The going was surprisingly easy, and I could see the perfect outline of the Bighorn Mountains with the brutish hump of Cloud Peak and the jagged molar of Black Tooth in the distance; but there was nothing else except the red desert and the frosted sky.

The twine tugged at me again, this time strong enough to pull my arm away from my body. I stood there looking at it and noticed that the line appeared to be heading toward the dominating marker of the mountains.

I set off again, the roll of twine getting larger around my palm as I walked up and down the gentle slope of the dunes, developing a rhythm not unlike that of the drums I'd heard last night. I'd even started to hum the chant in the back of my throat as I continued on.

I wasn't sure what was really happening but figured it had to have something to do with the peyote. I guessed this was what happened when you took the stuff. It wasn't entirely unpleasant, but I felt disassociated, as if I were outside myself and watching my actions from far away.

I stopped singing, but the song continued. I listened to make sure it wasn't some sort of echo, but the tune persisted without mine. Standing there at the point of one of the dunes, this one knife-edged by what must have been a powerful wind, I turned my head and could see what looked like a swale that curved like the crescent of a moon; at the top, an enormous black bear was hunched over and striking at something.

It was only when my hand was drawn from my side in sharp yanks that I realized he was pawing at the twine attached to my hand. I froze and then began backing down the opposite side of the dune, rapidly unwinding the string.

I felt the pull again and started untangling myself at a higher speed, when I heard someone speak to me in the standard Cheyenne, man-to-man expression.

"Ha'ahe!"

"Ha'ahe!" Having used up a good portion of my formal Cheyenne, I spoke again, this time in English. "Hey, I'm not sure where you are, but there's a bear over here, so I'd be careful."

"Is it a black bear or a white bear?"

I remembered that the Cheyenne old-timers used to refer to grizzlies as white bears and yelled back. "He's a black one, but as big as a grizzly."

The twine that I had unrolled in my scramble to get away began retracting at an incredible pace as if it were on a fishing reel, yanking me toward the summit of the dune where the gigantic bear towered on his hind legs.

"Good," the bear said. "For a moment I thought we were in trouble."

The bear sat next to the crescent dune and grunted to himself as he wove the twine between his enormous claws like a cat's cradle. "The line is connected to you."

I was still trying to get used to the idea of carrying on a conversation with a bear, but he was pleasant enough. I stared at him and figured that it was all a part of some kind of dream. His voice sounded familiar, but I kept getting distracted by the fact that it was a bear talking.

He grunted again. "Of course, it is only your line in the sense that you picked it up." His massive head turned toward me, and I was struck by the smallness of his eyes in the context of his enormous head, but the eyes seemed familiar, too. "Why did you choose this string?"

I shook my head, unsure. "It was the closest." I studied him for a moment as he played with it. "Do you mind telling me where I am?"

"What?"

"This place, do you think you could tell me where it is? I mean, I can see the mountains, but I've never seen sand dunes like this out in the Powder River country."

He nodded but said nothing.

"Are we in the Powder River country?"

He shrugged.

"I mean, from the angle of the mountains . . ."

He suddenly growled and shook his great head. "How should I know; I am a bear." He glanced around. "This place is not mine, it is yours." He nodded at the string, threaded through his claws, and I noticed that he did not hold the end of it, that the one end was wrapped around my hand but the other disappeared over the next dune. "Perhaps it is the one that interested you the most?"

"What?"

He sighed. "The string."

I answered carefully, aware that I might not want him agitated. "I suppose."

The furry hump shifted. "Have you considered what is on the other end?"

"Not really."

He smiled with close to fifty teeth, some of them exceedingly large, and I noticed that there were strands of gray in his fur. "This is the strength of your character, and you do not know?"

I looked down at the twine still wrapped around my palm

and closed my hand into a fist. "The strength of my character is string?"

"The strength of your character is in following this string." He adjusted his forelegs, and the twine sprung loose. Then he rolled onto his front legs and lifted himself up on his hind ones like a running back, turned toward the direction of the disappearing twine, and sniffed the air. "The string is like the bread crumbs in your mind, consumed until the mystery of this thing becomes a part of you. You have no choice but to follow it until it gives a secret up to you or reveals another mystery, both equally irresistible—it is your nature."

I stood and walked past him, taking up the string as I went and thinking about what he was saying. "What if I don't like what I find?"

His voice echoed through me. "There is always that chance."

I nodded. "This quest you are talking about is not why I'm here, you know."

He studied me but said nothing.

I took a deep breath and climbed up the side of the dune, pulling the twine out of the sand. "I don't have time to follow strings; I've got things to do. My daughter is getting married."

"Yes, she is."

I turned back to look at him, now only a couple of yards away. "And I'm standing in an imaginary desert with a talking bear."

He nodded but now refused to speak, his feelings hurt, I guess.

"What if I just let it go?"

This got a rise out of him. "You will not."

"But I could."

"It is possible, but what would become of the living thing that is on the other end—have you asked yourself that?" His wide head canted in a quizzical manner. "The mystery, the story of whatever is on the other end, would be lost forever."

I was traipsing around in my own head, both the conscious and the unconscious, and pretty sure that the events of late were all products of my mind, but they seemed so real that I was becoming distracted. He was watching me when I looked back up. "Have you ever heard of a fellow by the name of Virgil White Buffalo?"

His smile broadened. "I knew him well."

"I bet you did." I chewed the inside of my lip. "How about Henry Standing Bear?"

"I know him, too." He grinned, but I'm not sure if it was a smile or if he was just showing his teeth. "But not as well." He looked off into the distance, away from the mountains.

I had a feeling that our time together was coming to a close and I was sorry for that, in that I was enjoying his company, cantankerous as he was. I held up the hand with the twine wrapped around it. "So, you're saying that whatever I do I shouldn't let go of the string?"

He shrugged again.

"Well, what use is a talking bear if you're not going to carry on the conversation?"

The lips curled back, and he continued to smile.

I lifted my hand, clearing the string from the edge of the dune. "Are you coming?"

He shook his enormous head and finally spoke. "That is not *my* nature."

I nodded. "And if you don't mind my asking, what is your nature?"

He lowered himself to all fours and slowly ambled back in the direction from where I had come, pausing at the top of the dune to look over his shoulder. "To question."

The bear picked up his pace, and I was left there with the twine wrapped around my hand, trying to fight the feeling I was a puppet. I could follow him, I could stay, or I could go on. I stood there for a moment more, knowing there really wasn't a choice in all of this—the decision had been made when I'd picked up the end of twine in the teepee. As the Bear had said, our natures are our natures.

Kneeling down, I tried to get a general idea of the size of the bird that had made the tracks—something not too small but not too large either. The bird moved easily on the ground, which led me to believe that it was comfortable walking, and there are only a few of those.

There was a hop, however, and this time the bird's talons were buried deeper in the sand. There must have been some sort of threat, and I could see where the wing tips had brushed the ground and where the edges of the pinfeathers had swept the sand.

Bigger than I first thought—a large wingspread, two and a half feet at least.

There were no more tracks—it must have taken to the air— so I just followed the string. Sometimes you just had to follow blind. Beyond the next few dunes I saw an outline of a burned-up cottonwood, rising out of the sand like a grasping hand.

The tree stretched out a good hundred feet and was twice as high, with gigantic limbs and branches that reached up to the sun.

The tough bark was matte black and covered with soot, and I could see where my twine circled the trunk and then disappeared. I walked around it a few times until the string was freed from the main body and swung up into the high treetop.

I leaned back, trying to make out what held the twine, and raised my hand to block the sun. I sighed and pulled on the string a little, in the hope that whatever it was would reveal itself.

I'd just started tugging when she called down to me. "Do you mind not fucking doing that?"

I looked up through the scattering of branches breaking up the sky like shattered glass. "Sure." I looked for the source of the voice but still couldn't see anything. "Hey, could you help me? I'm not sure what it is I'm doing here and was wondering if you might know where we are or what it is I'm supposed to do?"

It was quiet for a moment. "Do you have the other end of the string?"

"I've got *a* string; I thought maybe you have the other end."

There was a sultry laugh. "Well, sort of . . ."

I stared up into the sun again. "If you come down here, maybe between the two of us we can figure this out."

"I can't."

I looked at the string. "Can't or won't?"

"Maybe you should come up here."

I stared at the sooty surface of the burnt tree. "You've got to be kidding."

It was quiet, so I figured that there wasn't any other option. Circling the trunk, I found a limb that was within reach and stuffed the twine in my mouth, still tasting the bitterness of the peyote, wrapped my hands around the heavy branch, and swung my boots up toward the trunk.

I wedged an ankle in the crook and pulled myself around, the soot and grime turning my clothes black.

"Well, hell." Taking the twine out of my mouth, I fed it back under the limb and checked the direction it took around the main body of the tree—under another branch and then up.

I rested a foot and tried to circle, the trunk being far too wide for me to reach around. Placing my boot on another branch, I continued climbing, following the string as it weaved its way through the tree.

Every once in a while I had to pull slightly on the twine, and when I did there was a small cry from above. "Oww."

"Sorry." I peered through the naked branches, and even

though there was no foliage, it was hard to see. I placed the roll of string under my arm and wiped the black from my hands onto my jeans as I leaned back on another stout limb. "How much further are you?"

"Quite a bit, actually."

"Can you see me?"

"Yeah."

I looked up. "How come I can't see you?"

"Well, I'm smaller, and you've still got a ways to go."

I sighed and traced the path of the string as it worked its way in and out of the assorted branches. "Straight up?"

"Yeah."

I lodged another foot in the crux of a limb and lifted my other leg, continuing to climb with the string in my mouth again. The trunk split at one point, and I could see where it peeled off to the west and straightened out toward the mountains. I was getting pretty high and could feel the tree creaking as it responded to my movements.

The string led me to the western route, but the branches were becoming sparser and I was afraid that if I traveled too much farther on the limb, it might break. I took a chance and glanced down, immediately regretting it. It was a good hundred feet to the sand below, and there were numerous back- and head-breaking limbs between. I swore to myself and wrapped my legs around a little tighter. "Maybe it's only a dream."

It was about then that I raised my eyes and saw her—a good-sized crow.

Farmers and ranchers don't care for the birds, but I've always thought that they are beautiful creatures. They are also capable of more than two hundred and fifty distinct calls, which did nothing to explain the very female human voice in which this one spoke to me.

"How you doin'?"

"I guess I'm all right."

I considered her predicament. From my perspective, I could see that the twine was wrapped around one of her legs, then her body, and finally had trapped one of her wings against the limb from which I now hung. "You mind if I ask how you got like this?"

Her dark head shifted, and a beadlike, tarnished gold eye drilled into me. "Isn't that just like a man to ask a fucking question like that."

"Sorry." I studied the distance between us and the diameter of the limb. "I'm not so sure I can get out there to where you are."

Her dark, feathered head shifted. "Don't you have a knife with you?"

I thought about the Case I carried back in the real world and figured it was probably still in my left back pocket. "I think I do."

"Then just cut the string."

I thought about it. "I don't think I'm supposed to do that."

"Why?"

"Well, a bear told me that I wasn't supposed to let go of the string and I'm guessing that includes cutting it."

The crow continued to look at me. "A bear."

"Yep."

She flapped the free wing and picked at her feathers with a pointed beak, gleaning them straight, finally turning to look at me. "You're fucking kidding."

I sighed, thinking about how I was now having a conversation with a profane crow nearly at the top of a burned out cottonwood tree. "That's my story, and I'm sticking to it."

"Well, then, you're going to have to come out here."

I looked down at the ground again. I'd heard that if you fell in your sleep it was okay, unless you hit, and then you supposedly died. It sounded like hooey—I'd probably heard it from my mother, who gave credence to those types of things.

I edged my way out. I was getting coated in the graphite-like soot, and the fine powder didn't make it any easier to hold on. I gripped the branch and pulled myself another arm's length before hearing a tremulous cracking noise somewhere back down the trunk.

The crow and I looked at each other, and she was the first to speak. "That was worrisome."

"Yep, and you've got wings."

"I'm also tied to the limb your lard-ass is resting on."

I glanced down. "I wouldn't exactly call it resting."

Trying to ignore the sound and fury of the splitting trunk, I took the twine in one hand and passed it under the limb a few times, finally freeing it enough to untangle the crow's body, which allowed her to get a talon onto the limb. "Can you pull the string enough to get your wing loose?"

She tried, but it was obvious she couldn't. "Why don't you just let go of the fucking string?"

"I told you, he told me not to do that."

"You usually take the advice of blathering bears?"

I sighed. "It's a habit, like trying to save cursing crows."

She cocked her head, and if it was possible, she smiled. "I need more slack."

More carefully this time, I slithered a little forward and was happy not to hear anymore disconcerting noises. I extended my arms and threw her a loop that trailed over her wing. She picked at it with her beak and was able to pull it partially loose, but I was going to have to get out there a little farther, perhaps a yard and a half from her.

The limb was getting narrower, and I was feeling a little tippy as it was. I grabbed the next arm's length and gently pulled myself out farther. There wasn't any sound, but I waited, just to make sure. I pitched the twine again and was rewarded with a loop that went past her wing this time with enough slack to allow her to scramble loose and hop up onto an adjacent branch that faced me.

"Thanks."

"You bet." I continued to look at her and noticed that the twine was loose but still attached in a bow to what appeared to be a bracelet wrapped around her leg. "The twine is tied to the bracelet?"

"Yeah."

I readjusted a little, the pressure of the limb against my chest becoming a little uncomfortable as I studied the silver chain just above her talon. "How did you get the bracelet caught on your leg?"

"It was shiny, and I liked it."

I studied it a little closer and noticed it had a medical symbol on it. "I guess we have to make a decision."

She cocked her head and with one quick movement hopped onto my arm. "Yeah."

"Can you pull it apart and free yourself?"

She shook her swarthy head, the feathers gleaming blue-black. "Nope—tried."

"So, if it gets done, I have to do it?"

She shrugged a winged shoulder, pumped up her breast in a provocative manner, extended her wings, and then refolded them; I could feel a slight sway in the limb beneath me.

"Maybe you're supposed to stay here."

She looked off toward the mountains. "And never fly again?"

"The bear said I wasn't supposed to let go of the string until I found the living thing attached, but he didn't actually say what it was I was supposed to do once I found you." Maybe it was all just a mass rationalization, but I figured not allowing birds to fly was a crime in any reality. "Hop up here on the branch where I can hopefully use both hands."

She did as I requested, landing with the encumbered talon closest in an attempt to make the job just the tiniest bit easier.

I loosened my grip and rested my wrists on the branch, trying to retain some sort of balance. I held the tab ends of the bow and laughed, mostly to myself. "Something's going to happen when I pull this apart."

"Yeah, I'll be free."

"No, something more than that; I've got a feeling."

She studied me. "Then don't do it."

"After all this?"

Her head movements took on a more animated quality, and I could tell she was a little annoyed with me. "I'm not fucking around; if you don't think you should do it or something bad is going to happen, don't."

I thought about what the bear had said about our natures; about how we did what we did because of who we were.

I pulled both strings.

There was a thunderous crack, the tree trunk split, and I slapped against the limb, causing it to fall even faster with my rebound. The crow exploded in a battering flush of wings, the feather tips swatting me as I was jarred sideways. I slipped to the side and attempted to grab hold of the falling limb—for what reason, I have no idea.

My face turned toward the chill of the sky, and I could see her frozen there with her wings fully extended, the tiny chain bracelet still hanging from her talon. I watched as she hammered the air with those black wings like two, massive blankets thrown into the wind, and then she flew toward the mountains like a razor—as straight as the crow flies.

I tried to get my eyes focused, but it was as if I was looking up from inside a well. I felt a jolt in the core of my body and found that I could move. Everything ached, and I wondered if I'd hit the ground and been knocked unconscious. My muscles were sore—even my rear-end hurt—but it was more the dull thrum of inactivity than the aftermath of impact.

I jerked a shoulder loose, followed by an arm, and then watched as my hand came up and rested on Albert Black Horse's shoulder. "Whew."

His face cracked into a wide grin. "We were worried about you."

I took a deep breath and blew the stale air from my lungs. Looking past him, I could see the entire group from inside the teepee had gathered around with concerned looks on their faces. "I think I need to stand up."

He placed a hand on my arm and carefully helped me get to my feet as the top of my head bumped the canvas and I leaned inward. "And go outside."

Albert nodded and ushered me toward the flap that was propped open with the lacings trailing down to the ground.

I stepped into the wooded clearing that I'd remembered from last night. It was morning, and a few members were preparing breakfast in a Dutch oven and a frying pan. An old, porcelain percolator squatted on a log by another campfire. Albert was beside me again and placed a hand on my back as I swayed a little in the clear, flat light of early morning. "You're all right?"

"I think so."

I took a few unsteady steps under Albert's careful inspection and placed a hand on the rooted part of the old, fallen tree. I cleared my throat and spoke to the large man who looked up at me with a cup in his hand. "I'd gladly kill somebody for a cup of that coffee."

He laughed, plucked another tin cup from the ground, twirled it by the handle like a gunfighter, and picked up the percolator without benefit of a pot holder. He poured me a cup and stood as he handed it to me. "How was your trip around the moon?"

"I am never doing that again." I looked around, just to make sure the desert of my dreams hadn't crept up on me. "How did I get back in the teepee?"

He looked puzzled. "You . . . never left."

I lifted the mug up, but a slight flip in my stomach caused me to pause. Glancing over to the opening, I could see my hat still laying there with the handkerchief draped over it. "I was in there the whole time?"

The Cheyenne Nation looked at Albert, still standing beside me, and the older man nodded. "You took the peyote, and it was the strangest thing we'd ever seen. You looked around for a bit, and then you just froze and stayed like that for . . ." He paused to look at his wristwatch and for some reason it reminded me of the bracelet around the crow's leg in my dream. "Coming up on ten hours."

"My ass feels like it's been sat on for ten years." I forced myself to sip the coffee, and it started tasting good. I glanced at the Bear, who looked a little tired. "You were out here all night?"

"I was."

I took another sip and approached vaguely human. "You must need a nap."

"I do, but we have errands to run."

I looked longingly at the bacon sizzling and popping in the frying pan and could imagine the golden biscuits rising in the Dutch oven. I sighed. "No breakfast?"

"Not unless you can talk Mrs. Small Song and Albert here into a breakfast sandwich to go."

I chewed the biscuit as we made the turn on the trail into the opening at the base of the hill where Lola, Henry's '59 Thunderbird convertible, sat like a chrome-bedecked spaceship. There was somebody I knew in the back, and he wagged his tail and stood with his forelegs on the sill to meet me face to muzzle.

I ruffled his ears. "Are you happy to see me, or are you just happy to see my biscuit?" He didn't answer, and I was just as pleased to be around an animal that didn't talk. I turned to the Cheyenne Nation as he slid in the front and slipped the key in the switch. I fed Dog the remainder of my breakfast. "We're traveling in style today."

He smiled and closed the driver's-side door. "We have to pick up Cady and Lena in Billings."

A major organ in my chest did a flip as I pulled out my pocket watch by the Indian Chief fob just to make sure we had enough time for what I had planned. "Oh, boy."

"Oh, yes."

I returned the watch to its pocket, straightened my hat, and placed my hands on the passenger-side door, resting my weight there. "I have failed miserably."

He barked a dwindling laugh. "We're making progress."

"That might not be the way they are going to see it."

I stood there like that, and he watched me readjust the pancake holster at my back and snap the safety strap on my .45, his face becoming even more serious as his eyes narrowed like the aperture of a scope.

He turned and placed a forearm on the steering wheel. "There is something else?"

I slid a hand across the gleaming, powder-blue surface of the vintage automobile the Bear had inherited from his father, the hand-buffed paint dancing stars of sunlight. "This is one beautiful car," I sighed. "And I'm about to utter something I never thought in my wildest dreams I'd ever say: can we trade Lola here for Rezdawg for just about an hour?"

I patted the chrome trim of the Thunderbird and glanced off in the direction of Painted Warrior, where Audrey Plain Feather had met her untimely demise. "We've got to do some four-wheeling."

I studied the rain-washed landscape—it must have poured here again during the night—and the edges of everything seemed more poignant, as if the country had redefined itself, imposed a sharper image onto the cliffs and the crowns of lodgepole pines that surrounded the valley.

The cliff was as Lolo Long and I had left it, with the exception of the CRIME SCENE DO NOT CROSS tape the FBI had strung between the trees and which we carefully pulled down and stepped over.

The Bear stopped. "This is illegal."

I looked at him as Dog went underneath. "I'm sorry, is this your first time?"

"I have always tried to lead a lawful life."

I cleared my throat and petted Dog. "Thank goodness; I'd hate to have seen what it would've been like if you hadn't shown a modicum of restraint."

He watched where he was placing his moccasins. "Virtue being my nature."

I thought about the talking bear. "I thought asking questions was your nature."

"What?"

"Nothing." I began looking around in a vague kind of way as he watched.

"What, exactly, are we looking for?"

"Something shiny."

He glanced up at the calypso-blue sky and breathed in deeply. "Can you be a little more specific?"

"You're going to laugh."

"I will not."

I nodded as I began searching the surrounding ground with Dog following me. "You will."

He raised a hand in solemn oath. "Indian Scout's honor."

"I happen to know you were never a Scout."

"Perhaps, but I have been an Indian my entire life—with the possible exception of a brief period in 1969."

"And what were you then?"

His head tilted, and he looked a great deal like the bear in my imagination. "I am still not sure."

I continued to look around at the edge of the cliff. "It was something the crow said in my dream."

"Vision."

"And something she was wearing."

He looked at me. "Wearing?"

"Yep."

He glanced around. "I am not sure I want to hear this part."

"It was a bracelet; one of those medical ones."

He paused for a moment. "On a crow."

"You said you wouldn't laugh."

He smiled instead. "Maybe the crow had a condition."

I glanced at him with a hard look, for all the good it was going to do, as he began looking in the branches. "Whooping cough; might have caught it from a crane."

"If you remember, I saw something reflecting up here from down below, and for some reason I've got it in my head that it's a bracelet." I stared at his Adam's apple. "Do you mind telling me why it is you're looking in the trees?"

He spoke in a pedantic tone. "Because that is where crows

live. They are drawn by shiny objects; if there was something up here, either on someone or left behind, the first thing a crow would do when it found it is take it to its nest." He lowered his face. "Now, if you had had a vision of talking prairie dogs . . ."

I joined him in studying the trees, and even Dog looked up. "All right."

He pointed skyward like the ghost of Christmas future, and his hand, tanned and powerful, extended from the rolled-at-the-cuff chambray shirt he wore. I followed his finger and rested my eyes on a twisted mass of branches and thick, seed-head grasses deep in one of the conifers.

"There."

I glanced down from the cliff to check the angle. "Gotta be it." I looked at the tree, which was a little to our right and almost at the edge. I indicated the lowest limb. "I don't suppose you'd like to . . . ?"

He glanced over the precipice. "Not really."

I looked up and sighed. "I already climbed one today, and that didn't end well; besides, I have to keep an eye on Dog." I placed a thumb through the beast's collar, just to emphasize my point.

He watched me for a moment more and then sauntered over to the trunk, and it was as if he levitated himself onto the thing. I watched as he effortlessly made his way up, his weight causing the pine to shudder but not crack.

He was almost to the nest when a large and very irate crow banked with the thermals rising at the face of the cliff and stalled for a moment before lighting about ten feet above his head.

"You've got company."

He leaned out and glanced up at the crow, which had begun screaming down at him.

I looked over the edge. "I think she might have young ones in that nest."

"Would you like to talk to her? You evidently have a knack."

"Very funny." I kept hold of Dog. "Don't let her knock you off."

"Thanks for the advice."

He started up again, and the crow flapped her wings and flew over me to circle the adjacent treetop. She planted herself in the pine next door and began cawing at Henry with a renewed ferocity.

He was just underneath the nest when three small heads appeared and, thinking the dinner bell must've rung, began calling back to their mother. "It is getting crowded up here."

"I think you should look on the side toward the cliff."

He shifted his position and went up a few more branches, the limbs getting closer and causing him more difficulty. "Your concern for my welfare is very touching." He was studying the bottom of the nest, and I saw him draw back. He smiled, shook his head, and pulled something from the bottom of the wad of intertwined material. He leaned out from the main trunk, holding on with only one hand, and tossed something through the air.

It shone and caught the rays of the sun as I held out a hand, barely capturing it before it hit the edge of the rock. I breathed a sigh of relief, stepped forward, and released Dog. "I wish you hadn't done that."

He was carefully descending, keeping time to the cacophony of crows but careful not to upset the nest anymore than he had to. "You always catch things."

I turned the item over in my hands—it was just like the one in my dream.

"Visions, they never lie." He was standing next to me now, examining the thin, stainless steel bracelet that lay in my palm.

The medications that were engraved across the broader section of the band were diazepam, tizanidine, baclofen, amitriptyline, oxybutynin, dantrolene, and pregabalin. "You ever hear of any of these?"

"Only diazepam; otherwise, no."

"Me neither." I flipped the thing over, and we both stared at the red caduceus insignia: two snakes intertwined. This was different from the one used by the American Medical Association, which had only one snake.

I held it out to Henry, who read my thoughts. "Caduceus; two winged snakes."

"Old."

"Yes, very."

I thought about it. "When did they stop using two snakes?"

"I am not sure."

"Well, I know a place where we can find out some answers to these questions." I glanced back into the tree where the mother crow was checking and tending to her still-squawking brood, and dropped the bracelet in my shirt pocket. "I must've seen it when we were up here and just forgot about it."

The Cheyenne Nation smiled as I held the FBI tape for him to step over. "Yes, that must have been it."

Rezdawg stalled out three times before we coasted into the Bear's driveway alongside Lola and traded the ugliest truck on the high plains for the Thunderbird, a more reliable and suitable ride for the trip to Billings.

The health center was on the way, and it was a quick drive, so we stopped there first; Lolo Long's cruiser was parked in front.

When we got inside, Henry stopped to look at Lolo, who, leaning with her elbows on the counter, was providing a remarkable, back-lit silhouette in the diffused light of the large window at the end of the hall. With one booted toe balancing on the tiled floor and the arched back I was once again reminded of just how breath-pausingly beautiful the tall woman was.

She was talking with her mother as we pulled up but turned to look at Henry and me with what could have almost passed for a smile. "So, while I've been working, you've been out getting a holy high?"

I waved at Hazel and turned back to her daughter. "It wasn't really my choice. Anything happening?"

"Artie Small Song, in a fit of remorse, hasn't turned himself in, if that's what you mean." She flipped a wave of her hair back, glanced at the Cheyenne Nation dismissively and then back to me. "Your buddy, the man who puts the 'Special' in Agent, Cliff Cly, left a message and wants to meet at noon."

I made a face. "Can't. I have to be in Billings in about an hour. My daughter and her future mother-in-law are landing from Philadelphia and I'd better be there to update them as to the ongoing preparations, or lack thereof." I tipped my hat back and thought about Cly. "He probably just wants an update; he's got people he has to answer to and reports he's got to write just like the rest of us."

She didn't seem convinced. "Uh huh."

I fished the bracelet from my pocket and turned to her mother for some relief from the jasper stare. "Mrs. Long, do you know when the AMA stopped using the two-snake caduceus in their insignia?"

Lolo answered. "In 1910; they thought it was inappropriate, witch-doctor symbolism—that, and when they discovered the double helix in 1953, everybody mistook the caduceus for DNA rather than snakes."

I smiled as it dawned on me. "You were a medic."

She actually smiled back. "Yeah."

I handed her the bracelet. "So this would be from 1910 or older?"

She studied the insignia. "But this isn't AMA."

"What is it then?"

"Army Medical Service Corps, or one of its ancestors; possibly the WWI Sanitary Corps." I was again attacked by jasper. "Where did you get this?"

"Painted Warrior."

Henry interrupted. "A little bird told him."

We both ignored him. "I'd seen something reflected in the trees, and we found it in a crow's nest."

She flipped it over in her hands. "It looks like it could've been up there since WWI." She paused. "No, it couldn't have." She handed the bracelet to her mother, who readjusted her glasses and stared at the engraving on the other side.

"These are modern medications." The older woman glanced up at me, and I was starting to see more of a resemblance between mother and daughter. "Heavy medications."

"What's that mean?"

She shook her head. "Diazepam is used to treat muscle spasms, seizures, and other side effects from alcohol addiction; the same with baclofen but it's more for control of spasms. Tizanidine is a muscle relaxant, and so is dantrolene. Oxybutynin is an anticholinergic used to relieve urinary and bladder difficulties, and pregabalin is a pain killer and an anticonvulsant." She handed the bracelet back to me. "Whoever is using these medications on a regular enough basis to put them on a medical bracelet is in enough trouble that they can hardly stand up, let alone push somebody off a cliff." She reached behind her and poured a couple of cups full of coffee and handed one to me and the other to the Bear. "But they might think about jumping themselves."

"So, a dead end on both counts?" I pocketed the thing and sipped my coffee, gesturing with the cup. "Thanks for this."

She smiled, and it was unreserved. "You both look like you need it."

I glanced at Henry, who appeared to be catching a second wind, and grunted an affirmative. "We had a late night." I patted my pocket. "Why would someone use an old bracelet like this for a medical ID?"

She shrugged. "We see it from time to time; people use whatever they've got here on the Rez. The first thing we do when people come through here is check every piece of jewelry they have on them. We had a guy one time whose allergies were engraved on a Howdy Doody bracelet."

Boy howdy.

"Can you do me a favor and check to see who in the health services records has prescriptions for all of these medications?"

"I'll need a warrant."

I appealed to a higher power and looked at her daughter. "Chief?"

Long looked at the head nurse. "Mom."

It was the three-syllable "Mom" I'd heard my daughter use on my wife for years, and a variation of the "Dad" that I would be hearing very soon.

Mrs. Long held out her hand for the bracelet. I deposited it in her palm and watched as she began writing the medications on a pad.

I turned to Lolo. "How's Adrian?"

"He'd be better if you brought back the dog; what's his name, anyway?"

I scored major points on the lack-of-imagination scale and told her. "I'll bring him in; he loves my daughter, but he takes up a lot of room." I gave Henry a look and started toward the car. "Lolo, any word from Clarence?"

"Nothing; why?"

"Don't you find it strange that he wouldn't be in to check on his son?"

She shook her head, the thick, loose hair mimicking her movements. "You mean if Adrian is really his?"

I stopped and turned. "What's that supposed to mean?"

"I've been asking around, and it would appear that Clarence indeed has some problems in that area, and besides, he's probably passed out somewhere. Anyway, I thought you didn't like him for this."

I slipped on my teaching hat as I turned to go. "Remember, *you're* in the business of liking everybody for this—until you find out who did it." Then I added, "*I'm* in the wedding business, until my daughter kills me, which should be in a little over an hour."

"I'm going to kill you."

I shifted to turn and look at the two beautiful women in the backseat of the Thunderbird, one family and one soon to be. "I'm sorry, Cady."

Lena Moretti kept her counsel but placed a hand on my daughter's knee in hopes of calming her.

"There's a case on the Rez that's kind of landed in my lap."

"A case." I could see the tears beginning to form in her gray eyes. "Unless I'm mistaken, Montana's not your jurisdiction."

"It's a homicide."

She turned her head, looked out the side window, and wiped her nearest eye with a swipe.

"A woman fell from a cliff with her child in her arms."

"I don't want to hear this; I really don't." Both hands came up this time, scrubbing the tears away. "I don't mean to come across as some self-centered bitch, but I just thought for a few days. I mean . . ."

Her mouth opened as she breathed and then turned her head toward Lena, the next words tumbling out. "Did I ever tell you about my college graduation? My dad couldn't make it because there was a case. My graduation from law school? There was another case." She sighed and smiled into her lap. "I can mark the progression of my life, every landmark—in cases." She looked up at me. "There's always a case, Dad."

There was a very long and uncomfortable silence in the car as we all listened to the tires on the interstate highway, rolling us into Little Big Horn country. She laughed a sad gasp, and it was far harder on me than the tears. I reached a hand out. "You're right."

Her eyes wouldn't meet mine and searched the floor mats at her sandaled feet. "I'm sorry."

"No, you're right." I cleared my throat in an attempt to stay steady. "If your mother were here, she'd kick me." This, at least, got a laugh. "I'll just gracefully back out of the case."

The eyes came up as she shook her head at me. "Daddy, you've never backed out of anything in your life, gracefully or otherwise."

The Cheyenne Nation grunted, and I gave him a quick look. "Well, maybe it's time I started." I took my hat off and rested it on my drawn knee. "They've pretty much figured out who did it, so it's just down to a manhunt at this point. They don't need me for that."

Cady took Lena Moretti's hand and held it, gently pounding her knee with both their fists. "It's okay."

I glanced out the side and noticed we were approaching Hardin and had taken the exit ramp for the Blue Cow Restaurant and Casino. Henry took the left at the overpass toward the Texaco station and the venerable café. "I have to get gas; is anybody else hungry?"

I smiled at Ray Bartlett, who was behind the counter, and he seated us by the window so the Bear could keep an eye on Lola and so we could enjoy the day. Wanda Pretty On Top came over and took our orders, and about a minute later, Cady excused herself.

Lena Moretti placed her hand on me this time, and I had to admit that it was a nice hand that I remembered from my adventures in Philadelphia no more than a year ago. "She'll be all right."

I nodded.

"She's just nervous."

I nodded some more.

"Christ, she's marrying my son—that's enough to throw a scare into any woman."

I laughed. "How's the family?"

The little curve came up at the corner of her lipsticked lips, sly and dangerous, just like her daughter's. "Mean as snakes, and they'll all be here in less than a week and a half." She crossed her legs and thanked Wanda for the collective iced teas she'd brought over. "How's the Terror?"

I thought about Vic. "Doing a public relations seminar in Omaha."

"Public relations? You've got to be kidding." She laughed. "So, she escaped?"

"Something like that."

Lena glanced at Henry. "This reservation thing: big case?"

"Well, maybe not the crime of the century, but it sure looks like a homicide."

"Aren't there Reservation police?"

Henry finally smiled. "Tons of them, federal, BIA, and tribal."

Her buckskin eyes shifted back to mine.

"Can't they take care of this?"

"It's complicated."

Her turn to smile. "It always is, isn't it?"

I explained about Chief Lolo Long in all its three-part harmony and found myself studying Lena Moretti more and more as I spoke.

"But there's a suspect?"

I nodded and tried to not get distracted by the shape of her neck. "A couple of them, but one has some truly antisocial tendencies."

"Such as?"

"A closet full of guns, and he pretty much threatens to kill everyone he comes in contact with."

"Sounds like wild, wild Westmoreland Street in Philadelphia."

Henry and I both laughed, and my eyes wandered toward the alcove where the bathrooms were located.

"Would you like me to go check on her?"

I scooted my chair out and stood. "I think that's my job—I'll just knock on the door and see if she's okay." I sipped my tea in preparation for the conversation to come and glanced at the Cheyenne Nation. "But, madam, I leave you in expert hands."

I walked toward the bathrooms, but Ray caught my eye and jerked his head toward the casino portion of the establishment. I nodded and walked into the windowless area where the electronic sounds of the numerous one-armed amputee machines drowned out everything else.

Cady was sitting at one of them, dropping quarters in and pulling the lever as if she were working on an assembly line. I watched her dispatch a good two dollars and two bits before crossing and sitting on the seat next to her.

She paused for a second and then went on playing, if you could call it that.

"I remember when your mother and I got married." I sighed. "Her parents didn't care for me all that much. She was kind of their princess, and I guess I wasn't their idea of prince charming. Then I lost my deferment. After the war, I got back and looked her up and we got in a whirl again. She wanted a big church wedding, but her father said he wasn't going to invest a big bunch of money in failure and that we'd be divorced in a year. I was working odd jobs, just trying to pay the rent on a little apartment south of town and have a little gas money. I'd heard Miles City was nice, so I threw your mother in a '66 Plymouth Belvedere and drove her up there for a long weekend. We got married by the justice of the peace and his wife played the wedding march on an accordion. It snowed like a bastard the whole time." I cleared my throat and laughed at the thought of it. "After a day, we were running out of food so your mother went off to the grocery store down the street with five dollars—all the money we had. She came back with two bottles of Coca-Cola, a package of bologna, a loaf of bread, and little jar of mustard—and change from a twenty."

Cady's hand paused on the lever.

"The man at the grocery store had mistaken the five for a twenty, and when he gave your mother the change, I guess she just nodded her head, stuffed that money down in her pocket as quick as she could, gathered up her things, and went out of that place like a shot."

I watched her swallow, and her hand slipped from the handle.

"For the rest of the weekend, she wouldn't walk on the same side of the street as that grocery store. I did, and I'd call over to her—Hey, Martha, Mrs. Longmire? How come you won't come over here and walk with me?"

There was a tiny sob of a laugh.

"When I got my first paycheck from the sheriff's department, she made me drive her up to Miles City so that she could pay that man back at the grocery store."

Her face turned toward me, and the tears were flowing freely, and I guess mine were, too.

"To my knowledge, that was the only illegal act your mother ever committed in her life."

We both laughed, and the greatest legal mind of our time launched from her stool and into my chest.

I held her there, wrapping my arms around her, and felt my hat flip off and fall to the floor as I rested my chin on the top of her red head. "I promised her that someday we'd have some kind of big wedding celebration, but we never got around to it; there was always something else that came up. About six months later the transmission went out in that Plymouth, the plumbing in the apartment froze up and the landlord wouldn't fix it, so we had to move; then she went and got herself pregnant."

Cady pulled her head away and looked up at me. "She did, huh?"

"Yep, and she had a girl so they could gang up on me." I pulled her back in and placed my chin back on the top of her head. "This daughter, she cried a lot at first, then she quieted down and didn't speak until she was two—no practice words, nothing—and began talking in full sentences, paragraphs, and pages; she has yet to stop." She tried to pull away, but I held her fast. "She kind of grew on me, and now she's the most important thing in my life, and I'm going to make sure that there will be a wedding here the likes of which she's never seen, in a little more than a week."

She sniffed again and grabbed my shirt. "It's okay."

"Hush."

She pulled away, and this time I let her. She clutched her hands in her lap and looked to me to be about ten, but maybe that was the way I would always see her. I was consistently surprised whenever she got off a plane and reentered my life. I always expected her to look like she did whenever she came back from the HF-Bar dude ranch where she would disappear from us each summer, and she would hit our cramped, little rental with the force of a teenage hurricane, generally with a retinue of broken adolescent male hearts in tow.

I looked into those gray eyes and could see the reflection of myself, a man who had mislaid some of the most prized moments in his daughter's life. I was ashamed of myself.

Pulling my handkerchief from my pocket, I handed it to her. "We'll get everything squared away. It's not like we haven't done anything, and we'll get all the details worked out."

She nodded and dabbed at her eyes. "I've got Lena with me, and she's a wonder."

"Yep, I know."

Her hand went self-consciously to her head and the scar along her hairline where the surgeons in Philadelphia had opened her skull to allow her brain enough room to swell, and I was momentarily reminded of Lolo Long's scar close to the same location. Cady's eyes drifted past me and over my shoulder, and I turned to find Lena Moretti standing a respectful distance away.

Her hands were stuffed in the pockets of her black linen slacks as she pivoted on one heel of a flat-soled shoe. "I'm sorry, but I think your food is getting cold."

By the time we topped the hill overlooking Lame Deer, regular conversation had been restored.

"Oh Daddy, I can't believe you did that."

I gave Henry the eye, but he remained silent. "It wasn't my choice."

"A peyote ceremony?"

"Well . . ." I glanced past the Cheyenne Nation's profile at the inordinate amount of unmarked and marked cars, along with a Mobile Task Force trailer emblazoned with the FBI's insignia, that were crowded into the small Tribal Police parking lot.

Henry finally spoke. "Uh oh."

We slowed at the stop sign, and the Bear and I looked at each other. Cady leaned up between us and glanced at the hubbub to our left, her natural Philadelphia lawyer tendencies getting the better of her. "What's happened there?"

"I'm not sure."

She looked at the Bear and then back to me. "Well, shouldn't we find out?"

I took a deep breath and gestured for the Cheyenne Nation to advance forward. "Not my job."

Henry didn't move, and someone honked an air horn behind us.

Cady leaned her face close to mine and pointed toward the clock in the ornate, chrome-slicked dash—it was almost three. "You can be a cop for another eighteen minutes."

"It's okay."

The horn behind us blasted again, and the Cheyenne Nation calmly slipped Lola into PARK, removed his lap belt, pulled the door handle, and stepped out.

I swiveled my head to get a look back, but Cady countered to block my view. "Henry and I can just go ahead over to Ashland and get you women into your motel room." There were noises coming from behind the car, including the opening and slamming of a door and loud voices. I redirected my attention to Lena, who was now looking out the back window. "And get you settled in."

Cady reached up and gripped my chin, redirecting my attention to her—a trick she'd adopted from her mother. "I'd rather you go over and get things settled than have you worry about this case, okay?"

There was suddenly no noise from the street. "I'm not going to worry about it."

Her eyebrows rose to the point where I thought they were going to fall off the back of her head as the Bear reentered the Thunderbird, sat, and reattached his seat belt.

I looked at him. "Sorry about the trouble."

He shrugged. "What trouble?" He gripped the wheel. "I am assuming we are making a stop at the jail to see what's going on?"

I shot a look at my daughter, who ricocheted it to the Cheyenne Nation, who, in turn, whipped the wheel to the left and blew across the intersection onto the street beside the full lot. I caught a glimpse of a large man behind us holding his nose in an attempt to stop it from bleeding while leaning against the fender of his eighteen wheeler. No problem—right.

Henry pulled up behind the Task Force trailer and parked as

we opened the doors, and I flipped the seat forward so that the Philadelphia contingency could join us in witnessing the spectacle.

Federal agents in flak jackets and full tactical gear were flying out of the adjoining buildings, jumping in the assorted cars, trucks, and SUVs, and making swift departures onto 212 and points beyond. Lolo Long and Cliff Cly were engaged in a heated conversation on the ramp of the Tribal Police Headquarters. Cady and Lena appeared to be enjoying the show. Henry and I looked at each other.

"Hopefully we'll be right back."

Cady waved and pointed at her wristwatch. "Fourteen minutes."

I bumped the Bear's shoulder. "Don't beat anybody else up, okay?"

We advanced on the ramp as Agent Cly broke from Long and stepped toward us, stopping when he saw me, extending a hand in admonition. "Don't even start."

"Have we missed something?"

"Well, hell, yeah." He looked over both our shoulders. "Nice car. Hey, is that your daughter?"

"Cliff, what's going on?"

He looked exasperated. "Listen, I wanted to let your little friend back there handle her end of the log, but its lumberjack time and we've got fugitives, okay?"

"What are you talking about?"

"That moron, Clarence Last Bull, was dealing out of his house and had a wire on his phone."

"What?"

"Yeah, I know; nobody knew, especially me. I mean, why would you check any of this with the fucking agent in charge, huh?" He pulled a pack of cigarettes from the inside pocket of his suit jacket and bit one between his teeth; I noticed that the stubble on his face was the exact length I'd seen days ago; he probably had an electric razor set to that length. "I swear to God my title should be Agent-Who-Doesn't-Know-What-the-Fuck-Is-Going-On." I could see Chief Long advancing as he lit the Marlboro and took a vicious inhale. "To make a long story short, we've got a tape on this asshole from an anonymous informant where Clarence is discussing with Artie Small Song how he wasn't going to pay him the money he owed him for pushing his wife and kid off the cliff."

"Oh, no."

"Oh, yeah. A very heated conversation that ends with an inordinately pissed-off Artie Small Song promising to turn Clarence Last Bull into the Native American equivalent of Jimmy Dean Hickory Smoked Sausage." He turned. "Did you know about this?!"

Chief Long had arrived. "No." She looked doubtful. "No."

Henry's voice cut through the emotion. "Where is Clarence Last Bull?"

The agent in charge removed the cigarette from his mouth. "That's a good question, and one we wish we had an answer to." He turned to the young Cheyenne woman. "Chief Long?"

"His Jeep is gone, but somebody spotted it in Birney." She added, before I could ask, "Red Birney."

I blew out a breath. "Has anybody seen or heard of the whereabouts of Artie?"

The chief and the AIC answered in unison. "No."

"What about the maroon truck?"

Lolo shook her head. "Up at KRZZ with the little nephew Nate."

The agent shrugged. "Well, that means the last of the Mohicans is perhaps afoot and possibly easier to capture."

The Cheyenne Nation pursed his lips. "Or not."

Cly glanced at Henry, and you could see that even he couldn't underestimate the Bear. "I gotta go, but you're all welcome to join in the great manhunt of eastern Montana."

I looked over my shoulder, where Cliff Cly's eyes kept wandering. "No, we've got a wedding to plan."

"Is that your wife, Sheriff?"

I sighed. "No, that is the mother of the groom and of my undersheriff, wife of the Chief of Detectives North, City of Philadelphia, and I'm sure that if you make a pass at her he will attempt to turn you into the FBI equivalent of Jimmy Dean Hickory Smoked Sausage."

He spoke as he passed us, going toward a Crown Victoria with a driver in attendance behind the wheel. "Philly's a tough town." He waved at Lena and Cady, and they waved back. "Never know till you ask."

I turned to look at Lolo Long, who was now conversing with someone by way of the radio attached to her collarbone. "You don't look happy."

She rogered the call and looked up at me. "Someone just punched a trucker out here on the highway." She fished her keys from her pocket, aimed the remote at the black SUV, and the vehicle chirped and blinked its lights. "Besides, what have I got to be happy about?"

"The investigative part of the case is over. Now all you have to do is capture the suspects, one of whom is apparently on foot." I glanced back at the women next to the vintage automobile, where Cady was pointing to her wrist. "Anyway, if I'm betting on who knows the territory best—my money's on you, Chief."

I started backing away with Henry following and she took a step after us. "So, that's it?"

I stopped. "Excuse me?"

She folded her arms and looked just as hard as the baking concrete on which she stood. "That's it?"

I stepped back toward her, Henry's hand on my arm. "There's nothing else to do, Chief. They got 'em red-handed."

"No pun intended." Henry glanced back at my daughter. "Come on, we need to go, for numerous reasons."

Long advanced another step after us. "You were there, you saw how he reacted; neither of us thought Clarence Last Bull did this." Her head began slowly shaking in disbelief. "You know that."

I made a beseeching gesture with my hands as the Bear continued to hold onto me. "It's the nature of the business, Lolo. Sometimes we're wrong."

"Yeah, right." Her head turned just a little, her hair moving with her, exposing the sickle-shaped scar. I stood there for a second more, and then watched as Lolo Long turned, walked back to her unit, and slammed the driver's-side door behind her.

She threw the car in gear and laid a strip of rubber on the roadside that would've made Mickey Thompson proud.

9

Standing in the dirt lot of the Western 8 motel in Ashland Henry and I leaned against the rear quarter panel of Lola, close to five hundred pounds of masculinity quaking before a hundred and thirty pounds of femininity. We tried not to look at each other as Cady stared at the less than a dozen units and pronounced them wanting.

"This sucks."

I pushed my hat back, pulled off my Ray-Bans, and glanced around at the rundown convenience store, the abandoned garages across the street, and the general dilapidation surrounding us. "We could maybe get some hanging baskets with flowers."

"Daddy."

I did what I always did in these types of situations and looked to my Indian if not so much Scout. "Help."

He thought hard. "There is the Whitetail Cabin in the Custer Forest, up near the Red Shale Campground."

She folded her arms and turned and looked at us. "What kind of services are there?"

He thought some more. "Porta-Potties."

Cady didn't say anything and began nosing a rock in the lot with the front of her turquoise flip-flop. "Are there any other motels?"

I glanced at the Bear, and he responded quickly, realizing what dire straits we were in. "Colstrip."

I turned and repeated the word to my daughter, as if she couldn't hear the Cheyenne Nation from only ten feet away. "Colstrip."

"How far is that?"

Unwilling to be the bearer of bad tidings, I looked at Henry. He shrugged. "About an hour."

Her eyes stayed steady on us. "What kind of motel?"

"I am not sure."

A voice rose from behind us as Lena Moretti arrived from the convenience store with a modified six-pack holder containing juices, sodas, and two bottles of Rainier beer. What a woman. She handed over the cardboard box as she read from the phone in her hand.

"The Super 8 Colstrip is conveniently located in the center of Colstrip, Montana, is AAA rated. Property features forty rooms, Super Start Breakfast, Wireless High Speed Internet, interior corridors, large vehicle parking, pets welcomed, guest laundry, fishing lake within short walking distance, and Subway restaurant is next door."

She slipped the two bottles of beer out and handed them to us. "Drink up, boys. I think you're going to need it."

Henry nodded solemnly as he twisted one open for me so that I wouldn't argue and then unscrewed the one for him, tapping the necks together. "It's 4:20 somewhere."

Lena's cell phone rang, and I recognized 'Donna è Mobile' from *Rigoletto* and smiled. She looked at the phone in her hand. "Hmm . . . not a number I recognize." She hit a button and held the device to her ear. "Hello?" A moment passed, and she grinned, holding the phone out. "It's for you."

I looked at her, rather puzzled, and held it up to my own ear. "Hello?"

"Are you still on the fucking Rez?"

"Um, yep."

I listened as my undersheriff repositioned herself somewhere in Omaha. "Do you know how many people are trying to find you?"

I glanced at Lena and, a little ways away, Cady. "Well, two of them found me."

"Good, then you're their problem now."

The phone went dead in my hand. I smiled and handed it back to Lena as Henry watched me. "Business."

After an embarrassing pause, Lena ran a hand through her almost black hair and continued. "There is also the Fort Union Inn with twenty rooms and within walking distance of downtown Colstrip, which I'm sure will be a comfort to the young Philadelphians, and the Lakeview Bed and Breakfast with nine rooms, more than half of which face the lake, which will be good for the Brahmans."

Cady took a fruit juice and unscrewed the top as she spoke to Lena. "You have the list?"

"In my head; we need seventy-three rooms in all." She immediately dialed the phone in her hands.

I thought about the chances of getting all the rooms during the height of tourist season but kept the thought to myself.

"Hi, is this the Super 8, Colstrip?"

She began walking away as Cady came in closer. "Next is the venue; what's the hang-up with that?"

"Arbutis Little Bird, the librarian over at the college."

Henry continued. "It would appear that the college is having a language immersion workshop at Crazy Head Springs on the date of your wedding. Lonnie, your father, and I have all tried to talk to her about it, but she is a battle-ax of a woman and is not giving any inches. We explained that we have had the date reserved now for months and that you have your heart set on the place, but nothing."

Cady's eyes sharpened, and she began walking back and forth almost as if she were deliberating in front of a jury, her flip-flops stirring up tiny clouds of dust as she paced. "And this Arbutis works at the library?"

"Yes."

"Will she be there today?"

"It's a Sunday, so I'm not sure. Cady . . ."

"I'll take care of it, Dad." She sipped her juice, and I took the time to study her, for the first time noticing the preperfection of her tan—not hiding the faintly visible Cheyenne turtle tattoo at her shoulder—her nails, and even the golden streaks in her otherwise auburn hair. Thank goodness she'd gained some weight back after the accident, and the rehab in the gym had transmogrified into a twice a day regimen. I was pretty sure my daughter was in the best shape she'd ever been in her life.

"You're beautiful."

Cady turned to flick her eyes at me. "Thanks, Dad." She looked embarrassed and quickly changed the subject. "Where is the list?"

"What?"

"The list you mentioned in the car; there's a list of questions that need answers?"

My voice fell. "Oh, hell."

"What?"

"I left it with Lolo Long's mother at Health Services."

She sighed. "Where's that?"

"Where we just left, Lame Deer."

"Then we have to go back."

Lena returned, sorted through the drinks, and took a Diet Coke for herself. "Thirty-seven rooms at the Super 8, all twenty at the Fort Union, and eight rooms available, including the suites, at the Lakeview B&B." Turning, she looked at the ten units of the Western 8 Motel and spread her arms like Moses discovering the promised land. "And rooms to spare." She chugged her pop and redeposited the bottle in the holder.

Cady looked at Lena. "I think we're going to want to go take a look at the rooms in Colstrip, and I want to talk to that librarian." She turned to Henry. "We need a car."

He spread his own arms. "Yours to command."

"Do you still have that shitty truck?"

He reacted as if he'd been smacked. "I do."

"Good, run us over to Lame Deer, drop us off, and then go get Rezdawg." She ran her hands along the glossy flanks of the Thunderbird's fins and grinned. "We're taking Lola."

We dropped the ladies off in downtown Lame Deer, where they were first going to attempt to take on Arbutis Little Bird. Then they would meet us at Health Services where they would abscond with Henry's pride and joy for a jaunt up to Colstrip to check out the lodgings.

I wished them luck in all of this, especially with the conversation with Lonnie's sister, and accompanied Henry so that I could drive the Thunderbird back to Lame Deer. I'd turned on the radio in Lola and was trying to drive the wedding complications from my mind by listening to Nate Small Song firing up the afternoon drive with, of all things, Gene Autry's *Sioux City Sue*. "Is this what they usually play on KRZZ?"

"The old people are the ones at home in the afternoons, so they play the classics; drumming and traditional in the mornings with a little rock thrown in, Cheyenne language programs around noon, then old cowboy and big band music for the shut-ins."

He waited a while before he spoke again, lazily drifting the big, square bird down BIA 4. "You do not think Clarence did it?"

"Well, evidently he hired Artie."

The Cheyenne Nation made a face.

"What?"

He considered his words and pushed his sunglasses up on his nose. "It takes a special kind of person to do this type of thing—to take money to kill a woman and child."

"You don't think Artie's capable?"

He adjusted the sun visor. "Capable, yes—willing, no."

"Have you ever met him?"

"I have." He settled in his seat. He smiled, and I figured I was going to get the story. "I met him when I was fifteen. It was during Crow Fair, and I was doing a little teenage teepee creeping. There was a girl I was infatuated with and she had some brothers. We stayed out a little late and when we got back the brothers were waiting for us; I fought all three, one at a time—Crow tradition. The Crow are good that way—the Lakota would wait with a half-dozen guys and they would all jump on you."

"What happened?"

He shrugged. "They went and got a friend, and it was Artie. I was pretty beat up, and I remember when I saw him that I thought this was probably going to be a good fight." He stretched his jaw muscles at the thought of it. "You remember when we used to play ball?"

We seemed to have changed conversations, but I answered. "Yep."

"You were a lineman so you know better than me, but do you remember lining up across from those guys who didn't have any imagination, nothing to distract them from the job at hand?"

I laughed and thought about Lolo Long's prejudice against imagination. "My father used to call it constructive stupidity; I got accused of it a lot in my teenage years."

He nodded. "Artie was like that, no imagination, utterly focused. I think he might never have outgrown that behavior."

"Who won?"

His face hardened as he thought. "It was kind of a draw."

We drove past the dirt road cutoff and the rumpled hills leading to the Painted Warrior's multicolored face, and my mind began playing the scenarios over in my head. If Clarence had been there, why did he hire Artie to do the deed? Why wouldn't he have been as far away from the actual killing as possible? Maybe they were both there—Clarence to get them to the cliff and Artie to push them over.

"So, you don't think either one of them did it?"

He smiled. "No, I do not think Artie did, and you do not think Clarence did."

"So, who did?"

"Someone who is highly motivated." He shifted in the seat and looked at me. "For the sake of your familial life, I am advising you to drop this."

We drove on, but my mind raced ahead. "We saw her die."

"Yes."

I nodded my head and turned my face back to the window. "It's not my case."

"No."

"We've got a wedding to help organize."

"Yes."

I turned the radio back up, and we drove in silence, until the words tumbled from my mouth. "But I'd like to hear those tapes. Would you like to hear those tapes?"

"Yes."

"I think we can arrange that, don't you?" I nodded my head some more. "I mean, it can't hurt to just listen to them. Right?"

"Yes."

I paused and then glanced at him. "Yes it can't hurt, or yes it can?"

He seemed to be considering the possibilities for a long time, and it was only when I was ready to ask again that he turned to look at me. "Yes."

I refused to drive Rezdawg but was happy enough to mosey along behind the patched-together vehicle in Lola. We parked in the lot at Health Services, and I noticed Henry nudged the three-quarter-ton's tire against one of the concrete curbs so that we wouldn't have a repeat demolition derby.

When we got inside, Hazel Long was once again at her station. The chief was nowhere to be seen, but her younger brother, Barrett, was, and considering how much his sister did not like the Cheyenne Nation, I was surprised by the smile with which he greeted Henry. "The Bear!"

His mother shushed him, but he stepped up to Henry and pumped his arm like a derrick. "My man." He smiled at me. "This your cowboy sidekick?"

I took off my sunglasses, seeing no reason to stay incognito. "That's me."

He placed a hand on the Cheyenne Nation's shoulder. "You ever hear about the U.S. Army Recruitment Expeditionary Basketball Tournament in Billings? It was a three-man and we were a man short, so the Bear here steps up in street shoes and scores nine three-pointers to win the tourney." He shook his right hand as if it were on fire. "Buuuuurn."

"Is your sister around?"

"Nope, she's out shakin' the bushes for Artie Small Song." He glanced back to Henry. "Hey, did you really punch a truck driver?"

I noticed the Bear had left his Wayfarers on—obviously he was still attempting anonymity.

I leaned against the counter. "Mrs. Long."

"Hazel."

I nodded. "About the list of drugs from the bracelet?"

"That's going to take a while; that patient file would be in the physical archives, and I haven't had a chance to get down there."

"Well, when you come up with that information you can give it to your daughter." I leaned in closer. "Hazel, did you by any chance save that list I had you copy down concerning my daughter's wedding?"

She looked surprised. "I gave it to her."

"Cady was already here?"

"They're still here. She said she wanted to see your dog, and I let them into Adrian's room."

I glanced at Henry. "I'll be right back."

I gently pushed open the door and could see Lena Moretti standing on one side of the crib and my daughter sitting in a chair with Dog's head in her lap, the baby clutching her forefinger as he slept.

Once again, she had tears in her eyes, and I watched as the trunk of her body shuddered with her breath. She looked up at me. "He's so small."

I joined them at the foot of the crib. "They start out that way."

Her eyes were drawn back to the sleeping child. "He's all right?"

"That's what the doctors say. A few bumps and scrapes, but evidently she was able to protect him from the bulk of the impact." I leaned over and looked down at the lone survivor.

"She died."

"Yep."

"But there's a father?"

"Yes, but he's been implicated. The FBI says they have tapes of him negotiating with another man about killing both mother and child."

Lena Moretti's voice sighed from the other side of the crib. "My God."

"It's all pretty sordid." I dropped my voice when I saw Adrian roll his head to one side. "We should probably get out of here."

Cady stood and then whispered. "What about Dog?"

"He doesn't really want to leave; he's the one that found him." The two women joined me at the foot of the crib. "We saw them fall and got to the woman, Audrey, as quickly as we could, but

Adrian here had rolled down the hill bundled up in a blanket and Dog found him."

I moved them toward the door, but Cady balked. "Wait a minute, did you say you saw them fall? You mean you were actually there?"

I cracked open the door, but she still didn't move. "We were researching another area for the wedding and happened to be below when they fell. I even had Henry's camera, which reminds me . . ."

Lena looked up. "What?"

"Nothing." I scooted the two of them out. "How did the meeting with Arbutis Little Bird go?"

"Umm," Cady answered, preoccupied. "She'll be there tomorrow morning, and we'll meet with her then."

"Well, Lonnie says to bring a gun."

Henry met us at the counter, and we moved as a group to the parking lot, where he dangled the keys above Cady's hand. He dropped, she caught, and we started moving to our neutral vehicles.

"Daddy?"

"Yep."

She steered me aside, placing her arm through mine and walking me away from both Henry and Lena. "What if I had something that would solve this woman's murder and I didn't use it. That'd be pretty bad, wouldn't it?"

"I suppose."

Unwilling to look me in the eye, she lowered her head, and I stood there staring at the strands of gold, auburn, and strawberry blonde, a combination that became more evident in the summertime. Her voice echoed against my chest. "What if I knew a way to make sure whoever killed Audrey Last Bull would be brought to justice?"

"I'd say that there's no such thing as a sure thing."

The eyes came up slow but sharp. "I would."

She rose up on tiptoes and kissed the grizzle on my chin, then pirouetted away with the keys dangling between her fingers. "Lena and I will spend the night up in Colstrip, but we'll meet you for lunch, here, tomorrow at noon."

I watched her sashay over to the Thunderbird, and the two of them climbed in, fired Lola up, and roared away like a high plains Thelma and Louise.

As I stood there watching them turn left and head north, the Cheyenne Nation rejoined me. "So, what just happened?"

I breathed a soft laugh. "Unless I'm mistaken, we just got put back on the case."

Henry drove us over to the Law Enforcement Center, but the place was vacant and the door was locked. Lolo Long's cell number was listed on the door as one of the emergency contact numbers, but I figured we'd just go do a little snooping on our own.

"What makes you think he is with Inez Two Two?"

"Inez's mother told me that Clarence was having an affair with her daughter a while back, and if Clarence is involved, then she might be a good place to start looking for him. If she doesn't know where he is, then she might have other ideas where we could look."

The Bear drove down Main Street and took a right toward the high school gym, which remained open on Saturdays and Sundays in conjunction with the Boys and Girls Club. We parked the ugliest truck on the high plains next to the outside basketball courts with their chain nets and cratered asphalt and walked in down the hall to the unlocked doors of the gym. I could see why the Bear had had no doubts as to Inez's whereabouts—the place was packed with young people. "So this is the place to see and be seen?"

The Cheyenne Nation snatched a worn ball from the rack just as a fat man with a whistle was about to yell at him.

"*Ha-ho*, Monty. Wassup?"

"Hey, you lookin' for a date, bad man?"

They shook hands and clutched each other's arms. Fortunately, Henry played youth basketball with Monty Farris, the coach, so there had been no trouble when the Bear asked if we could use one of the smaller, more private, half-court gyms to discuss things with the young woman.

"You realize, of course, that without jurisdiction she can just tell us to go jump in a lake."

Henry dribbled the ball and flipped it spinning in his hands, shrugged, and then began dribbling to the outside reaches of three-point land.

After about five minutes, a heavyset young woman opened the door and looked at us; she wore an oversized letterman's jacket despite the season, and a black straw cowboy hat decorated with a gold concho, the stampede strings slung to the back.

"Howdy."

She had the look of a whitetail that had just discovered two mountain lions at the watering hole.

I slipped off my own hat and stuck out my hand. "I'm Sheriff Longmire, and this is my friend, Henry Standing Bear."

She took my hand with a great deal of trepidation and allowed the door to slip shut behind her, the sudden sound in the empty gymnasium causing her to jump. I gestured toward one of the fold-out wooden bleachers. "Why don't you have a seat?"

She did, and I took the one beside her.

I waited a moment, but she just watched the Bear as he dribbled and strolled the arc. "I don't know where he is."

I waited a good long time and placed my hat on the bleachers brim up; I needed all the luck I could get. "And who's that?"

That got a glance. "Clarence."

Henry twirled the ball in his hands. "We understand you know him pretty well."

She glanced at him, and her voice became flirty. "I know you."

"Yes, but not in the same sense." The Bear's face remained immobile as he turned and effortlessly sank a thirty-footer. She looked at him and smiled as he retrieved the ball and dribbled back toward center court.

I shook my head at his prowess. "Can I ask you some questions, Inez?"

She took off her hat, which she placed brim down; evidently she didn't need any luck.

"When is the last time you saw Mr. Last Bull?"

She sniffed and took a pack of cigarettes from the pocket of her coat. "Can I smoke?"

I looked around the school property for emphasis. "I don't think so."

She stuffed the pack back in her jacket. "About a week ago."

I paused again. "Before the accident."

"Yeah."

"And where did you see him?"

The shrug was one I remembered my daughter perfecting at that age. "Where we always meet, at the Buffalo."

"The White Buffalo convenience store?"

She watched Henry some more and then spoke. "Yeah."

"Did you arrange a meeting there, or did you just run into each other?"

"Just ran . . . what you said."

I nodded and thought about what kind of chance Inez Two Two had in this world and was not overcome with confidence.

The Reservation schools were consistently ranked as the worst in the state. The pay scale for teachers wasn't bad, but the turnover rate was horrific and truancy was rampant; the student dropout point was around sixth grade and wasn't improving.

"I didn't know he had a kid." She continued to watch the Bear. "He told me he couldn't have kids." She called out. "I bet you can't do that again."

The Cheyenne Nation shrugged, turned from the top of the key, and drained another twenty-five-footer.

Even I was impressed. I looked back at her. "Inez, I doubt that anybody would blame you for the responsibility of that relationship. Clarence is a grown man, and I think it would've been his responsibility to know how old you were."

"I liked his Jeep."

Henry bounced the ball off the wall and slowly dribbled toward us.

"His car was cool." There was a trace of a sneer in the next part. "So we took a ride. That's how it all started."

I thought about it. "Did he ever take you to the cliffs at Painted Warrior?"

"Yeah, it was one of his favorite places." She made a face. "Or used to be."

Henry arrived and stood there flexing his fingers into the ball.

"What were some of his other favorite places?"

She thought about it. "He used to work for one of those Amish guys who'd fallen out with the others and lived down near Birney. The guy did handmade boots and had a cabin on the Tongue River near his place." The shrug again. "Clarence promised me a pair of boots, but I never got them."

"Do you happen to remember the boot maker's name?"

She laughed, and I could sense she was in the act of shutting down. "Stoltzfus, try and forget that one; but they had a falling out and I don't think Clarence was welcome there anymore."

"Anywhere else, places where you think he might go if people were looking for him?" I was losing hope. "Anywhere at all."

She actually smiled. "No."

The Bear interrupted. "Hey, Inez?" She took her time, turning to look up at him. "You know who the smartest man I know is?" The fingers laced around the ball and he palmed it, one-handed, in my direction. "Him." The Cheyenne Nation took a few steps back onto the court. "Now he may come on with the 'just-an-ol'-cowboy routine,' but when he does that it means the wagons are circling and pretty soon there is not going to be anywhere to go." He bounced the ball to her, and she caught it. "You and me, we are going to play a game of TALK; you win—you walk, I win—you tell us Clarence's hiding place. These are the rules—you shoot and miss, it is a letter for me. I have to match the shot to keep the letter. You shoot and make the shot, I will subtract a letter, two letters if I miss. That sound fair?"

She smiled and slipped off her coat, allowing it to fall to the floor. "You're on, Old Bear."

"I'll give you a couple of warm-ups."

I leaned back to watch and, spreading my arms, rested my shoulders on the next seat level.

Inez threw the ball back to the Bear. "Don't need 'em."

Evidently the hook had gone out with Kareem Abdul-Jabbar, because after Henry's graceful arc that hit nothing but net, Inez tossed a brick.

The Cheyenne Nation pivoted with a reverse layup and deposited the ball in the hoop. Again. He caught the ball and tossed it to her. "T. Reverse, left-handed."

Inez misjudged and bounced the ball off of the underside of the rim, almost crowning herself.

He went to the three-point line again, this time to the far end of the baseline, and sunk another. "A."

Inez took a deep breath and followed suit, and this time the ball rebounded off the rim.

He continued in his around-the-world venture and paused at the top of the key, raised his arms and, with his thick wrist, flicked the ball and swished another one. "L."

"Jesus." I whispered the word before I knew it.

She moved to the same spot, but you could see her enthusiasm was flagging. She shot again, and this time she made it. "Take that, Old Bear."

Henry gripped the ball and dribbled for a moment, possibly having pity on the kid, but it wasn't in him and he moved another thirty degrees along the perimeter, took a deep step into two-point territory, and drained another. "Back to A."

Inez moved to the spot and shot, but this time it jumped off the backboard over to me. I picked up the ball and stood, giving the Bear a good chest-to-chest pass.

Henry moved to the top of the key again and drained it. "L."

She slumped and slowly moved out to the spot to give the shot a try. "One step?"

"I'll give you two," he said, unsmiling.

It was the Cheyenne Nation's form of charity.

The young woman heaved the ball up to where it bounced off the rim twice and then kicked back off the backboard. He retrieved the ball and casually sunk another hook shot. "K."

He strolled over to her, slipped his arm around her shoulders, and brought her over to the bleachers, even going so far as to kiss the top of her head. "I guess we cannot call you Inez Two Two anymore."

She laughed in spite of herself and stooped to pick up her coat. After a moment she turned to look up at me, and I smiled.

"There was a fire lookout tower that he took me to down near Black's Pond. It was locked up, but he broke the clasp off and we spent the night there one time. Diamond Butte Lookout, I think."

Henry tucked the ball under his arm. "Anywhere else?"

"Not really; he was always looking for a place where we could, you know. . . ." She turned to me and then back to him. "When he could."

Henry asked. "Meaning?"

She glanced down and shrugged. "He had problems, down there."

I threw her a line. "Inez, do you know a man by the name of Artie Small Song?"

Her eyes widened just a bit. "I don't want anything to do with that guy; he's crazy."

"Do he and Clarence know each other?"

"I guess. They had a run-in one time."

"In all honesty, we're looking for both Clarence and Artie. Do you have any idea where Artie would be?"

The answer was hard and fast. "No."

"Is there any chance they would be together?"

"No."

"You make it sound like they don't like each other."

She looked at me, incredulous. "They don't; when I saw the two of them together they were screaming at each other and threatening to do things, kill each other and shit."

"And when was that?"

"About a month ago." She was silent for a while and then took a deep breath. "Can I go now?"

"Sure."

She took her hat and started for the door.

"Hey, Inez?" She stopped when she heard Henry's voice but didn't turn. "Be good, because I will be watching."

She nodded solemnly, but she didn't say anything as she opened the door and escaped.

Henry looked after her. "Rarely do you see the promise of a man in a boy, but you almost always see the threat of a woman in a girl—and sometimes the threat is not hollow."

"She's young."

"Not that young."

I tipped my hat back down. "Well, that was an interesting departure from the good-cop/bad-cop—the good-cowboy/bad-Indian."

He sighed. "Her family has a history of playing hand games. I knew I could count on her sportsmanship, if not her honor."

He easily evaded me when I attempted to slap the ball from under his arm.

"You never did have the guts to play in the paint, Henry."

He laughed.

The agent in charge was standing by Rezdawg when we got outside, along with two other agents, one still in the Crown Vic and the other examining Henry's truck, probably wondering if it ran.

"So, do I have to go talk to Inez Two Two, or have you done my work for me?"

I walked over and stopped, laying an arm on the bed of the truck. "I didn't know you guys worked on Sundays."

He slipped off his sunglasses, and we both looked around at the gorgeous day. "Neither rain, nor snow . . ."

"That's the postal service." I thought about it and quoted. "Neither snow, nor rain, nor heat, nor gloom of night stays these courageous couriers from the swift completion of their appointed rounds."

"Wow, I don't think I've ever heard the whole thing."

I nodded. "They stole it from Herodotus, about 500 B.C. during the Greek/Persian war—he said it about the Persian mounted postal couriers."

He shook his head in disbelief. "Are you sure you're a sheriff?"

I ignored the remark and joined him, tipping my hat back and absorbing the warmth of the sun. "Hey, you don't happen to have a copy of the phone recordings between Artie and Clarence on you, do you?"

He gave a small laugh. "Those recordings are FBI property."

"You don't have a copy?"

"I didn't say that."

"How 'bout we trade you what Inez said for a copy of the recording."

He lounged against the scaly surface of Henry's truck. "Not a good enough trade. I can always just go inside and question the girl myself."

"You might not get anything; she's tough." I gestured toward the Bear. "And you don't have an Indian scout."

Henry spun the basketball in his hands and glanced up at the outside hoop about thirty feet away. "I will play you for it."

The agent in charge's head came down, and he smiled at the Cheyenne Nation. "As much as I'd like to, I don't have time."

"Three letters."

Cliff Cly studied my friend for a moment, and then a broad grin spread across his face. He ceremoniously pushed away from the truck and then carefully took off his jacket, folded it, and placed it on the side of the bed and began loosening his tie. "I should probably warn you that I played JV ball at Rutgers."

Henry looked impressed. "Wow."

Rolling up the sleeves on his dress shirt, the FBI AIC paused. "Do I get to pick the three letters?"

The Bear dribbled the ball once, and then held it, his dark eyes studying the federal agent. "Funny, I was thinking A-I-M."

10

"Rutgers must have been really shitty that year."

He smiled to himself as we bumped along in Rezdawg, whose top speed today was, evidently, fifty-two miles an hour.

I held the CD in my hand and studied the broken AM radio with its cracked glass and missing buttons, the optic orange indicator frozen permanently at the bottom of the dial. "Have I told you lately just how much I hate this truck?" I sighed, and popped the CD back into its paper envelope. "What do you know about this Amish boot maker?"

"He makes really good boots."

"Other than that."

"He supposedly got into trouble for his tastes in women."

"He married an Indian?"

"He did. In many ways, Levi Stoltzfus is doing his part for the integration of the high plains races." He coaxed the truck off the rumble strip and back into the center of the lane with a movement that would've sent any other vehicle slashing into the opposite ditch. Rezdawg considered the movements of the steering wheel in Henry's hands as mild suggestions. "To his credit, he just loaded up his boot shop and moved on down the Tongue River to Birney."

"White Birney?"

"No, Red Birney; once you have gone red, you cannot get it out of your head."

We took a meandering right onto a dirt road just before the Tongue River and followed the dusty track for a good half mile before Henry urged Rezdawg to a stop, then threw the gearshift into reverse and backed up fifty yards with the transmission sounding as if it was going to fall out onto the roadway.

The truck stumbled to a stop, and the Bear pointed at a crooked ranch gate with words chiseled into the overhead log— STOLTZFUS WORLD FAMOUS BOOTS.

I pivoted to take in the empty road and hillsides and then turned to look back at my buddy. "Hard to be world famous 'round these parts."

"Give the people quality, and they will beat a path to your door."

I guessed. "F. W. Woolworth."

He shook his head.

"S. S. Kresge?"

He shook his head again at my listing of defunct five-and-dimes and spun the wheel several times to get the front tires to turn. "Actually, it was the Kinks."

The road was deeply rutted and wound around a tall knob of rocks to our right, then straightened into a washboard that leveled off into a low-slung building that must've been built around the same time as the original Small Song structure back in the forties. There was a house farther up the hill and a large garden where a Native woman was picking vegetables with two small children.

Henry parked near the shop; again he turned the wheels so that if Rezdawg decided to go on an unscheduled sojourn, it wouldn't be a long one.

There was a pinsized stream of antifreeze arcing from the radiator that I didn't see until I walked in front of the vehicle and it sprayed on me. I jumped away and wiped the excess down my jeans and clenched a fist as if to strike the grille guard. "I really hate this truck."

"Yes. So you have told me."

I dropped my fist and followed Henry toward the front porch when the woman called from the edge of some tacked-together sheep fence on the hill. "Are you here about your boots?"

The two children joined her and looked at me as if they'd never seen a grown man who had pissed himself.

I tipped my hat. "No, ma'am."

"Because if you are, they're not ready."

"Well, we're not really here about boots."

She continued as if she hadn't heard me. "He always sends a postcard when the boots are ready; did you get a postcard?"

"No, ma'am. We haven't ordered any boots."

She glanced at Henry and then back to me; it wasn't like we'd arrived in a reputable vehicle, so I could understand her concern. "Then what do you want?"

I gestured toward the Bear. "We'd like to speak to your husband, if we could. Are you Mrs. Stoltzfus?"

She pulled a bandana from her black hair and wiped her throat. "Yes, God help me."

"Is Levi around?"

She gave some quick instructions to the children, who looked disappointed but returned to work as their mother hiked up her skirt, climbed onto a wooden cross-step, and swung a leg over the fence. "Do we owe you money?"

"No."

She picked her way down the hillside, topped the porch risers, and walked over to where we were, her lace-up packers clapping the rough-cut wood like a xylophone. She'd been a beauty at one time, but age and hard work had worn her down; as Lucian would have said, you can't have 'em plow on Friday and dance on Saturday. "Doesn't make any difference, he's still not here." She glanced at the Cheyenne Nation. "I know you?"

Henry raised an eyebrow. "I do not know, do you?"

"You're Henry Standing Bear." She planted a provocative leg forward with a Mother Earth quality, and I immediately liked her. "I'm Erma Spotted Elk; you dated my sister."

The Bear nodded his head. "Erma, how is Dottie?"

"She's living in Seattle; she married some doctor and we never hear from her."

He folded his arms and leaned against one of the porch poles. "That is too bad." He looked past her to where the two children were working but continuing to sneak glances at us. "Yours?"

"Yah. They don't like to garden, but they like to eat." She turned to look at me, our heads about the same height with her standing on the porch. "You a cop?"

I smiled, but she didn't smile back. "Does it show?"

"Yah, especially with that hog-leg at the small of your back."

Henry's voice played around her. "Erma here has a varied past."

She laughed. "Varied. I like that." She dabbed at the sweat that was dripping into her eyes. "I lived down in Denver for a while, danced; got into some trouble. I developed a talent for a lot of things, including spotting cops."

I glanced up the hill. "And now you're Amish?"

Her head inclined a little, belaying the next statement. "Yah, I've seen the world out there, and you can have it. Everything is going to hell."

"Maybe."

She smiled and studied me. "You gonna fix it?"

I shrugged. "Doing my part."

"Which part involves my husband?"

Henry's voice was low, but it carried. "Clarence Last Bull."

She froze for just that brief instant, and if you hadn't been looking for it you might've missed it, but I had a couple of talents myself. She converted the freeze into a slow turn toward the Bear and then looked back to me. "You wanna buy a pair of boots?"

I looked at mine—they were a little worse for wear. "Not especially, but I'd really like to talk about Clarence Last Bull."

"That's too bad, 'cause I really want to sell a pair of boots." She turned, and the wide cotton skirt twirled as she clacked through the open doorway into the shop.

"Seems like the day for the barter system." I glanced at the Cheyenne Nation, and he nodded for me to pursue.

She was sitting in a wooden armchair and had propped her feet on another facing it. She studied me. I walked over, and she put her feet on the floor so I could sit, settling my hat over the embarrassing stain near my crotch. She motioned toward the floor, so I pulled off 50 percent of my footwear and handed it to her. Erma took my boot and examined it like a surgeon would a tumor.

"I'd like to know about Clarence Last Bull."

She examined the boot some more. "He used to work for my husband, but that was a while back." She ran her hand over the nap. "You like rough-outs? Because we only do regular leather."

Surprising me, she took my foot and propped it on the edge of her chair between her legs. "Clarence was really good; an artisan. He had an ability and flair, but what he didn't have was stick-to-itiveness; he'd show up and work a few days and then disappear. Levi finally got tired of it and told him to hit the road. I understand he joined the army and became a cook or something." She wrapped her strong hands around my foot. "Big feet."

I nodded. "When was the last time you saw him?"

There was that momentary pause and the flicker of eye movement that meant the truth had just flown in the doorway, inspected the place, and flown out. "Year ago." She looked down at my captured foot and leaned forward, her breasts on either side. "Fourteen."

"Thirteen."

I watched as she eased back and pulled a piece of paper from a sheaf on the rolltop desk. She placed the paper on the floor. "Stand on that."

I did as she instructed, placing my stocking foot on the sheet as she pulled a carpenter's pencil from the tomato can on the desk and traced around my foot, first at an angle underneath and then vertically. "I understand you have a cabin down by the river where he used to stay?"

"Yah, when he worked for us he used to bunk down there." She tapped my leg, and I stepped off the paper. "I need your other foot."

I pulled off the left boot and stood on another sheet. "Do you mind if we take a look in the cabin?"

She continued to regard me. "Yes, I do." She studied my foot again. "If you want to wait you can ask for my husband's opinion, but you might be here for a while."

I examined the tools and the dust on them. "Where is he?"

"Buying leather in Rapid."

I glanced up at the calendar and noticed it hadn't been changed over from June. "How well did you know Clarence?"

"Well enough."

"Did you know he was involved with Audrey Plain Feather?"

She paused and then continued around my heel. "I'd heard that."

"Did you hear that there had been an accident?"

She traced around my foot twice, just as she'd done before, and finally looked up at me. "What kind of accident?"

"His wife was pushed off a cliff; Painted Warrior, a couple of miles up the road."

She tapped my leg again, and I stepped off the paper and sat, bringing our faces a lot closer. She placed the two sheets together and tossed the pencil onto the overcrowded desk. "Pushed doesn't sound like much of an accident."

"No, it doesn't." I pulled my boots back on. "The added tragedy is that their little boy, Adrian, was in her arms when she fell."

Erma couldn't hide the fact that she was stricken with this bit of news. She wouldn't look at me anymore, instead choosing to look out one of the tiny panes in the casement window above the rolltop. The glow of the afternoon light was prismed by the windowpane and played off her features. I could see a young girl who had jumped the Rez and headed out for the big town to a place she wouldn't know anyone, least of all herself.

If it was a performance, it was a damn fine one.

She looked up the hill at her children and then finally turned to look at me. "That's horrible."

"Yes, it is." I waited a few moments and then tipped my hat back. "You're sure you haven't seen him in a year?"

"Just ropers, like the ones you've got on?"

"Yep."

She nodded and copied down my contact information, including the office address. "You're kind of out of your territory, aren't you?"

I didn't say anything, which is the most unsettling thing you can say.

She stood and placed a hand back on the worn edge of the old desk. "And you don't think the world is going to hell?"

I smiled. "Like I said—I'm just trying to slow it down a little bit."

She remained silent until I saw no more reason to stay and took a step toward the open door.

"We have an eight-page list. It'll be a year and a half."

I glanced down the rows of boots. "I'm pretty good at waiting."

The Bear took a few snap peas from a paper bag that he had liberated from the young farmers he had assisted on the hill while I had been ordering boots from their mother, and handed me one as he drove on through Birney Day proper. "So how did it go with Erma?"

I munched on the pea pod, crisp and delicious. "I ordered a pair of boots."

He nodded as he navigated the vintage truck down the road. "It is good that you are supporting the local economy."

"She knows something, but she didn't know about Audrey." I glanced out the window and watched the scenery flow by. "I think she's seen Clarence a lot more recently than a year ago."

"She saw him yesterday."

I turned to look at the Cheyenne Nation. "The kids?"

"Yes, they were very chatty." He took out another handful and handed me a few. "I thought it was very nice that they offered us this lunch."

I chewed on another. "And?"

He glanced at me. "Only the peas."

"About Clarence."

His eyes went back to the road as we recrossed the rumble strip. "He was here yesterday afternoon, and she gave him supplies."

"I assume we're now on our way to Diamond Butte Lookout?"

"We are."

I nodded and reached for more peas, but he slapped my hand and then took one for himself. "We have to ration our supplies."

I listened to him eat as we continued down the road. We came up on a skinny kid walking on the gravel beside the asphalt who was wearing only one shoe. Henry slowed, finally matching the speed of the child's pace, and being that I was on the passenger side, I went ahead and spoke to the young man. "Lose your shoe?"

He turned his head at my voice and looked at me. "No." His smile was wide and beatific. "Found one." His face brightened even more when he noticed the truck and, more important, the driver. Henry leaned on the brakes in an attempt to stop Rezdawg before it could run over the kid, who had bolted around the front and had pulled himself up on the grille guard. He stared at us from over the hood. "What'choo doin', Bear?"

The Cheyenne Nation laced his fingers over the wheel and placed his chin there. "Looking for somebody."

The kid smiled. "You're always lookin' for somebody—I'm just glad it ain't me!"

Henry smiled back at him and then gestured toward me, his partner in justice. "This is my friend, Walt Longmire." He reversed the gesture. "Walt, this is Wiggins Red Thunder, head of the Birney Road Irregulars."

The boy interrupted. "The Bear says you saved his life up on the mountain."

I laughed, glanced at Henry, and then tipped my hat. "Pleasure to meet you, Master Red Thunder."

He cocked his head and closed one eye to look at me. "What did you jus' call me?"

"Master. It's a formal address used for young men of undetermined age below thirteen."

He continued to study me. "I'm twelve."

"That would be under thirteen."

The grin broadened. *"Heeeeeeeeeeehe'e!"*

The Bear laughed. *"Evoohta?"*

Wiggins shot his eyes at me. *"Emasets'estahe."*

Henry nodded, but the young man continued to look at me, uncertain as to my motives.

"You want a ride, Master Red Thunder?"

The smile returned. "Yah, up here."

He turned and lodged his rear end between the top bar of the guard and the dented hood, facing forward and banging an open palm on the rusted green surface.

The Cheyenne Nation shouted, *"Tosa'e?"*

Our impromptu hood ornament pointed to the right down a dirt road leading to a cluster of small, shabby houses and a few trailers. Henry wrapped the wheel a few times, and we eased off the paved road and down the wallow of burnt-umber dirt.

"The Red Road?"

He gave me the horse-eye. "I have to check in with my homies."

With a little direction, we pulled between a couple of the houses and found two younger children, a boy and girl, who had propped up a john-boat with rocks and filled it with a nearby garden hose, making a homemade pool. I watched as they splashed each other and then waved ferociously at us as Rezdawg parked.

"I sometimes miss being that age."

"It was a good time, but now is a good time as well."

I smiled as I started to open the door. "That was a point I was trying to make to Erma, but I don't think she was buying."

He looked thoughtful for just a moment. "Perhaps her now is different from ours."

"Of that, I have no doubt."

We met Wiggins at the front of the truck, and I noticed the rolling piece of work hadn't pissed on the Indians. Rezdawg was obviously a racist.

Henry gestured toward the pair in the flooded boat. "Indian hot tub."

The girl cried out. "We're going to Alaska!"

We joined Wiggins and walked over. Henry dipped a hand in. "Warm; did you pee in this?"

They yowled with laughter until a man's voice sounded from one of the trailers. "You damn kids better fuckin' shut up out there!"

Henry looked left, and my eyes followed his to where a weathered blue '69 Dodge Power Wagon with a white replacement door that read COLSTRIP CONCRETE sat parked next to a crummy, olive-green single-wide. "Who is that?"

Wiggins frowned. "Kelly Joe Burns."

I remembered the conversation at Human Services. "Herbert His Good Horse mentioned this individual as one of the people who might have something against Audrey Plain Feather."

The Cheyenne Nation's eyes were slow to return but finally came back to us as he introduced me to the two other children. "Walt, this is Leslie S. Little Hawk and her sidekick, Charlie Shoulderblade."

I tipped my hat again. "Troops."

The Cheyenne Nation placed a closed hand over his chest. "What is our motto?"

Wiggins and the other two did the same with their smaller fists and shouted back, "To go everywhere, see everything, and overhear everyone!"

"*Epeva'e.*" He took a breath, but just as he was about to speak, a pale, bald, shirtless man threw open the door of the trailer and started off the porch toward us, pulling his belt from his pants with his head down.

"All right, God-damnit, I told you little fuckers that if you keep makin' a racket, I'll whip your asses."

Henry squared off quickly, lowered his arms, and waited.

The Kelly Joe Burns character was about ten feet away when he raised his head and saw what it was he was up against. Burns was thin with the obligatory tattoo of flames creeping up his neck, and he swung the belt from the buckle, but you could see his enthusiasm was waning. "You . . . you, you tell those fuckin' kids to keep it down."

"No, I do not think I will." Henry gestured toward the impromptu weapon in the man's hand. "And you better put your belt back on before you lose those pants."

Kelly Joe took a step back. "Fuck you!"

The Bear took a few, easy steps toward him.

I looked around the Cheyenne Nation and made eye contact

with the skinny guy, and saw no reason not to throw a scare into the probable drug dealer, who was a cliché walking. "Hey, is that your Dodge over there?"

He drew the belt back, and I wondered what it was going to taste like when Henry shoved the thing down his throat. "Who wants to know?"

"Sheriff Walt Longmire."

He looked confused for a moment, probably trying to remember who was sheriff of the adjoining county. "This is the Reservation; you've got no jurisdiction here."

I stepped up to the Bear's shoulder. "I'm working with Tribal Chief Long on a case."

He took another step back and then turned quickly to get to the steps of his trailer. "Yeah, well, I don't know anything about anything."

"Of that, I have no doubt."

Henry continued to follow him until the man barricaded himself behind the aluminum screen door. "You better get off of my property."

The Bear's voice was low. "You better not come after these children with anything but a smile. Do you understand me?" Kelly Joe slammed the inside door between them, and I waited the long moment it took for Henry to turn and walk back. "Do you think he took me seriously?"

"I do."

The Cheyenne Nation returned to the children, leaned his hands on the rails of the boat, and then dipped a finger in and tasted the water. "No pee pee."

They immediately began roaring with laughter again, Kelly Joe Burns forgotten.

Henry turned serious. "I am looking for a man; a man driving a yellow Jeep."

The three talked among themselves in Cheyenne, and then

Wiggins looked at me and back to Henry. "Les says she saw one go by last night."

The Bear pursed his lips. "What time?"

There was another flurry of Cheyenne, and I had to admit that I was impressed that the tykes were fluent in their native language; so few children were these days. Wiggins, the official spokesman, turned back to Henry. "'Bout nine-thirty—two men."

The Cheyenne Nation and I shot glances at each other before Henry spoke. "Two men?"

Wiggins questioned them again, focusing on the girl. "She says they were long-hairs, but she thought they were men; they had the top down, but it was a long way away."

"Which direction?"

The boy threw a thumb over his shoulder, southeast. "Off the Rez."

Henry nodded, thumped his chest with his fist, and extended it to bump with the smaller ones. *"Nestaevahosevoomatse."* His gaze drifted to the single-wide and Kelly Joe. "You have anymore trouble with him, you let me know." He turned, and I followed him toward Rezdawg as Wiggins called after us.

"Hey, when are you going to give me that truck of yours?"

He waved the kid away. "When I am through with it!"

We slammed the doors, and I listened as he ground the starter. On the fifth try, it caught and shuddered a cloud of bluish smoke that we had to back through.

"He can have it now as far as I'm concerned."

We turned south on 566 and took a right on Hanging Woman Drive, the washboard surface of the gravel road attempting to rattle loose the fillings in my teeth. "Two men."

The Bear nodded. "Two men."

"That's not good."

Henry shrugged. "For one of them at least."

I braced a hand against the dash in an attempt to augment the three-quarter-ton's lack of suspension. "You think it's Artie?"

"Who else would it be?"

"That's the sixty-four-thousand-dollar question now, isn't it?" I shook my head. "So they rolled through here last night, stopped at the boot maker's, and continued south, which means that it's possible that Erma knows who was with Clarence?"

"Stoltzfus's children said nothing about another man."

"Would they have told you?"

"Yes."

I smiled. "Don't tell me they're part of the Birney Road Irregulars?"

There was a pause. "They are now."

"That means that Clarence picked up the mystery man somewhere down here." I glanced out the open window at Hanging Woman Creek, which was little more than a dried-out trough. "How far are we from Painted Warrior?"

"As the crow flies?"

I looked out the window, sad for the Crow who hadn't flown straight.

"What?"

"Nothing."

He gave me a look. "From Birney, about four miles."

"Close."

"Yes."

I pulled my hat down over my eyes. "Wake me up when we get to the lookout."

Henry had stopped Rezdawg alongside the vault toilet on the dirt parking lot. I captured my hat before it fell to the floorboards and rubbed my eyes with one hand in an attempt to get them to focus.

Diamond Butte Lookout is situated precisely in the middle of nowhere. Just off the Rez and about a mile from Sonnette Road, near, appropriately, Diamond Butte, it was a two-story, thirty-foot masonry fire tower built on not so much of a butte as a hill. Diamond is the high point in the surrounding terrain and glowed gold in the horizontal light of the setting sun.

The point had first been used as a fire lookout after World War II, and the makeshift structure that was erected in 1956 was rebuilt in 1968 with its own tower. It was abandoned almost a decade ago when the Forest Service had discovered it was cheaper, easier, and more efficient to scout for fires with airplanes rather than manning lookouts all over the high plains. As far as I knew, Poker Jim Butte was the only surviving manned lookout in the area. This meant that the tower at Diamond Butte was up for grabs at the remarkably reasonable price of twenty-five bucks a night, firewood provided.

"This must be the place."

He looked around the parking lot. "No other vehicles."

"You see any Jeep tracks?"

He pointed to the left—the wide tires of the CJ-5 had left plainly visible tracks where it had pulled in, reversed, and then circled back out. "There."

"So, one of them got dropped off?"

The Cheyenne Nation nodded and pointed some more. "Yes, departed from the vehicle there."

"Pretty lonely spot." I glanced around, reaffirming the obvious as he peered through the blue tint at the top of the windshield. "What?"

He indicated the lookout. "Someone is still up there."

I crouched down and followed his line of sight; sure enough, an individual seemed framed in the corner window. "You think he didn't hear us pull up?" I found it hard to believe with Rezdawg's Swiss cheese muffler, but we had parked at such an angle that most of the truck was hidden behind the Forest Service facilities—maybe he was hard of hearing.

"Perhaps." I watched as he reached behind the seat and pulled out an old pair of Bell & Howell M19s from their case and focused them on the lookout. "He is armed."

I took the binoculars and had a look for myself. It was Clarence, and it looked as though he'd dragged a chair over to the southwestern corner of the main lookout and had a rifle barrel up near his face where the butt must've been resting on the floor between his legs; the weapon was short, maybe a .30-.30 carbine. I lowered the multi-green-colored optics and glanced at the Bear. "If you were being pursued by somebody and wanted an even chance, what would you do?"

"It poses an interesting problem; certainly he can see anyone coming from a long way off, but he also presents a regal target up there."

I looked through the 7×50s and sighed. "He had to see us coming; he's facing the road where we came up."

"Perhaps we are not who he is looking for."

I handed him back the vintage binoculars. "You think we should honk the horn?"

"It doesn't work."

"Of course it doesn't." I shook my head. "How about we just set fire to it?"

He ignored me and returned the Bell & Howells to the case behind the seat. "We should get out of the truck before it gets completely dark."

I glanced back at the tiny yellow bulb in the cab light fixture, which was missing its cover. "The interior light works?"

"Yes."

I gripped the bridge of my nose with my thumb and forefinger. "Of course it does; it's inconvenient, and that is most certainly the watchword for this piece of crap."

"You are hurting my truck's feelings."

I gently pulled the handle and slid out, watching as the bulb in the cab glowed feebly, a light noticeable from possibly six feet away. I met the Cheyenne Nation at the back of the truck, because I was trying to avoid getting sprayed on.

"Maybe he's drunk." I slipped my 1911 from the pancake holder and checked it—cocked and locked—snapping off the safety. "You have a weapon?"

I watched as he silently slipped the foot-long heirloom stag-handled Bowie knife from the small of his back, holding it high so that I could see the turquoise inlayed bear print in the bone.

"That should do, unless he spots you a couple hundred feet off."

He said nothing and disappeared around the corner in order to work his way toward the side of the butte where Clarence was facing, leaving me to take the easier unobserved trail.

There was a fence at the edge of the parking lot, and I watched as the last glimmers of the day lingered above the Bighorn Mountains as if the yolk of the sun had gotten hung up on Black Tooth.

I carefully opened the gate and stared at the narrow two-track that circled to my left and then made a run up the spine to the cabin's backside. Near the top I could see a utility wagon that must've been used to ferry supplies to the lonely lookout.

I was reminded of one of Henry's sayings that you could just about escape anything on the high plains—anything except yourself. You could go to a mountaintop or back yourself into a brick wall corner, but you could always count on being bushwhacked by yourself.

My eyes traced over the profile of the hillside, but the Bear had disappeared like he always did. Keeping an eye to the reflective surface of the windows that surrounded the structure on all sides, I walked carefully up the gravel path. There was an overhang on the fire tower, and I was concentrating on that when I saw something move down below.

Standing still, I waited and watched as the heavy metal door that provided the only access to the place swung back just a little. I waited, but it just hung there, about two-thirds open, and I half expected to receive a Winchester slug in the chest.

After a moment I noticed a soft breeze, something not uncommon in summer on the high plains when the light changed, and watched as the door slowly closed again. Ghosts.

Keeping my Colt aimed at the darkened doorway, I carefully made my way across to the safety fence that stood by the drop-off to the left of the walk that led to the bottom floor of the lookout. I heard the slightest creak of the boards in the room above. I swung around, slowed my breathing, and listened for another footstep, but there was nothing.

Swallowing, I went through the open doorway to my left and rolled the .45 around the empty room, only slightly illuminated by the square window on the other side. I checked behind the door and took a look at the clasp and lock hanging from the surface where it had been pried off with the tire iron that now lay on the gravel.

Inside there were some tools and a wall full of firewood, but nothing else except the wooden stairs that started up to a landing in the corner and then hugged another wall before dead-ending into a trapdoor where Clarence sat.

I crossed the patchwork rock floor, stopped at the base of the stairs, and looked up at the trap, which was slightly ajar.

There were no more sounds, so I carefully put my weight on the first step and wondered where the hell my Indian scout was. There was a slight sound, but I was pretty sure the only way you could've heard it was if you'd been in the room with me. I continued up, made the landing, and clutched the two-by-four railing in my free hand.

I could see a sliver of yellowish light at one edge of the trap that hadn't been there before, carefully fanned my finger over the floor's undersurface, and slowly pushed upward.

The trap faced the majority of the room, and I'd turned so that I was facing the corner where Clarence had been sitting. There was a table and a couple of chairs in the way, along with a propane stove and a few bunks. I stuck my head the rest of the way out but the table had a blanket draped over it, obscuring the view.

I soundlessly leaned the trapdoor back against the wall. Easing the rest of the way up the stairs, I could now see that one of the propane lamps on the far wall had been lit and gave out with an unrelenting hiss. I led with the Colt and looked over the table top where an empty bottle of Old Crow and two pint Mason jars were lying on their sides.

I could now see that there were two individuals in the corner, Last Bull in the chair still facing the dead sunset and another man leaning against the narrow facing between the windows, holding something and following Clarence's gaze.

"Those stairs are noisy."

I came the rest of the way up and could now see clearly that it was Henry, palming the great blade as it flashed in the propane light.

"How did you get here?"

"I pulled myself up on the walkway to the east."

I kept the .45 out and circled around the table. "He must be dead drunk."

The Cheyenne Nation turned to look at the man in the chair as I got there. The shirt at the center of his back was exploded with blood and the material was burned from the close proximity of the gun that had shot him.

The Bear's voice was resigned. "No, just dead."

11

"Sure, I can get you DNA testing on the glass—it'll take about nine weeks."

I sat on the lip of the trapdoor and stared at the can of beer the AIC had handed to me at the scene; Cliff Cly was certainly not the usual field agent for the Department of Justice. It was even a Rainier, my brand. "That's not the way it works on television."

He nodded and opened his own with the rest of the six-pack dangling from his fingers by the plastic loops. He sipped his beer as his crew went about their business, and the ME's office loaded Clarence up. "Yeah, have I told you what a pain in the ass all that TV stuff is for me?" He thought about it. "Other than I'd like to nail Kyra Sedgwick . . ."

"Do you think it's really a good idea to be drinking beer at a homicide investigation?"

He ignored me and sipped his some more. "Christ, somebody siphons gas out of somebody's car and the assholes want you to dust the garden hose for prints." Cly watched as they zipped the body bag. "Taxes, that's the other one I get. My taxes pay your salary; you need to find out who stole my cat." He laughed. "That's how I lost my first assignment, cherry, too. Georgetown—D.C." He shook his head. "How much crime goes on in Georgetown?" He thought about it. "Punishable crime, I mean. There was this spat of cat disappearances—I shit you not—and this senator's wife wanted Justice to look into it, so they sent me over to this mansion to talk to this woman who lost Fluffy. I get over there and make the mistake of joking with her that it's probably the Chinese restaurant down the street. Well, she believes me and starts asking questions like, 'Surely they just catch alley cats or strays and not domestic cats from the neighborhood?' So I laugh and tell her, 'Oh no, it's the domestic ones that they get because they're fat and stupid.'" He shook his head. "Jump-cut to promising young field agent in Absalom, Wyoming."

I smiled and set my unopened can on the floor beside me. "That would do it." Glancing over my shoulder, I looked back at Henry, who had grown more and more silent since the Feds had arrived. The Cheyenne Nation was seated on the windowsill in the darkness by the east wall. "What do you think?"

His voice rumbled back. "I guess we can take Clarence off the list."

Cly turned to look at him. "You think?"

There was a pause, and then Henry spoke again. "Reasoning says that whoever killed Audrey and attempted to kill Adrian must've killed Clarence."

The agent lowered his can. "Unless it was revenge."

"Possibly, but the only one who could've felt an emotion that strong is being zipped up in a bag right now. Someone killed the woman and attempted to kill the child, and then they killed the man."

Cliff made a face. "What makes you so sure it's the same person?"

Henry stood and walked over into the light of all the propane lanterns we'd lit; the place sounded like a snake pit. "Talk of killing is talk; killing is different."

The agent pulled a can from the plastic and held it out to the Bear, but Henry ignored him.

I figured I'd better speak up. "What he's saying is that there aren't that many actual killers on the Rez."

The agent continued to sip his beer. "You guys get anything out of the shoemaker?"

"Boot maker."

"Whatever."

I leveraged myself up and stood so as to make way for the med-ex team and the body. "He wasn't there, but I had an interesting conversation with his wife, who said that Clarence hadn't been there for about a year, but we discovered that he was evidently there last night."

"So I need to go sweat her?"

I smiled. "Good luck with that."

"Tough?"

"Like a Flying J truck stop steak."

We watched as they carefully turned the body and made their way down the stairs and into the darkness; but for the flashing blue lights in the parking lot that cast through the open doorway below, it was as if they were carrying Clarence into the grave.

I sighed. ".38?"

Cly nodded. "Sure looks like to me."

"Close. Somebody he knew."

"Yeah." The FBI man held the beer out to Henry again. "Sure you won't have one?"

Anyone who knew Henry Standing Bear would've been able to spot the storm clouds on the horizon, but Cliff Cly's experiences with him had been limited. Personally, I was just hoping I could stop the Cheyenne Nation from throwing the federal agent through the plateglass windows.

His voice was smooth, like the surface of the ocean with sharks underneath. "Agent, I am having a hard time believing that you are taking this investigation seriously." He leaned in. "Somebody has almost wiped out an entire Native family."

Cly's eyes searched the face of my best friend and stayed there as a strong moment passed. "Do you want me to call in the black helicopters? Because I can." He glanced at me. "I can make a phone call and have a hundred Ivy League graduates wandering around the Rez with their heads firmly planted up their asses, and the only thing they're going to do is make it harder for the guys that are probably going to really break this case." He extended a forefinger from the can and first punched the Bear in the chest with it, and then me. "Batman and Robin of the Badlands. You know everybody; you know everything—and besides, Sheriff, you're the one who wanted me to hand the baton over to the Indian Princess. I'm just waiting to share the credit so I can move on to another and better assignment."

He sipped the beer again, and I thought it was a remarkably gutsy performance in the face of impending Indian disaster.

Tapping the can with the same forefinger, he smiled. "And this? I just think better when I've had a beer—one beer." He extended the four-pack to Henry again. "How about you?"

The Cheyenne Nation didn't move but then abruptly snagged a can from the plastic loop, pulling it free and then tapping Cly on the chest with it in return. "I just want us to be clear."

The agent smiled a matinee idol smile. "We are." He spread his hands and glanced at me. "Okay, boys, so where's the next body gonna drop?"

Henry and I looked at each other, neither of us with an answer.

"Did you listen to the CD?"

I shook my head. "We are technologically deprived here in the Wild West."

He crushed his can and stuffed it in the pocket of his Windbreaker. "Let me know if you want me to dub it onto an eight-track, but in the meantime we'll keep looking for Public Enema Number One."

"Artie Small Song?"

He pointed a finger at me like a gun but held his fire.

"So who gets to be Batman?"

"You do; I have the legs for Robin."

I glanced around in vain for a clock in Rezdawg's dash as we drove on through the night. "I am worn out; what time is it?"

He glanced at his wrist as he eased the truck up Lonnie's drive and swung the vehicle in a circle pointed back toward the road before going up the hill. "Almost three. I'll drop you off here so that we don't wake up the chief."

"Why do you suppose Lonnie wants me to keep spending the night at his place?"

"He likes the company; I would imagine he gets lonely without his daughter." I thought about my daughter as he pulled Cly's can of beer from the seat next to him and handed it to me. "Here. As we both know, Lonnie only has the Beer of Temptation in the house."

I slid out of the truck, closed the door as quietly as she would allow, and spoke through the open window. "Two beers; I can have a party." He didn't say anything, and we listened to the crickets chirping in the velvety night. "You all right?"

"Just tired."

I nodded. "I thought that was going to be the second ass you were going to kick today."

The Bear shifted the truck into first, probably anxious to get home to his own bed. "Do not forget that we have a lunch appointment in nine hours."

"Right." I started off toward the back porch. "Get some rest."

He said nothing, and I watched as Rezdawg rumbled down the gravel drive, turned left onto 212, and slowly disappeared.

———————

I was about halfway up the hill when I saw another vehicle coming from the same direction that we'd traveled on 212 and watched as the Yukon signaled and drove up to where I stood.

The driver's-side window whirred down on the official vehicle, and Lolo Long looked at me. I leaned an elbow on the sill. "You pulling double duty?"

"My one-man staff, Charles, is following Nate Small Song."

I held up the two cans. "You want a beer?"

"No, thanks."

I nodded and blew a breath out, extending my cheeks. "Clarence is dead."

She gestured toward the radio. "I know." She reached up and turned the motor off. "I think the BIA called the family."

"Is there anybody besides Charles?"

She rolled a shoulder. "A few cousins, but nobody close." She watched me thinking.

"No offense, but should we consider adding Charles to our ever-narrowing list of suspects?"

She laughed. "I told you, he doesn't have enough imagination to carry on a conversation. Anyway, why would he kill his half-brother, sister-in-law, and nephew?"

"I thought maybe you'd have an idea about that."

She shook her head. "Nope, dead end."

There was a pause, and I could feel the exhaustion creeping into my marrow. I stood there for a moment more and then asked permission, since it seemed like she wanted to talk. "All right if I come around and sit down? I'm not so sure I can stand up for much longer."

She pushed her shooting bag and aluminum clipboard onto the floor with a certain panache, and I circled around, opened the door, and sat. She glanced up at the dome light. "It'll go out in a minute." Another pause filled the cab, and I thought for a second I was going to fall asleep. "If you were going to pursue the investigation after all, did it ever occur to you to let me know?"

"It was a spur of the moment kind of thing; we went and talked to Inez Two Two, who gave us a lead on two of the places where Clarence might've been—one he wasn't and, as it turned out, one he shall ever be."

"It's a lonely spot."

"Yes, it is."

I took the time to study her some more; mostly the muscles in her neck. She was tall with a broad-trunked body, but it was sexy the way she carried herself, like she was built for go. She took a deep breath, which gave me plenty of time to study the sickle-shaped scar, almost as if her face itself had been marked with the crescent of Islam.

She looked at me. "I don't sleep."

"Ever?" I looked out the window. "I didn't either until 1972."

"What happened in 1972?"

"I got tired."

She laughed a deep, throaty laugh.

"Later, I got married, had a kid; I guess it took my mind off of it."

"Been there, done that." She unbuckled her seat belt and turned a little to look at me as I stared at her. "You should see the look on your face right now."

"You have a child?"

She ran a hand over the leather-clad steering wheel. "He's with my husband in Billings."

"What's his name?"

"Cale Garber; ranch kid from up near Judith Gap. We met in school; I was already ROTC, so he knew he was marrying a soldier. . . ." The words trailed off.

"I meant your son."

"Danny."

"How old?"

"He's five." She smiled, but the joy was missing in it. We sat there for a long time before she felt the need to fill the silence. "Before my first deployment I went over to Radio Shack and bought one of those talking picture frames and put a photo of me in it. I was smiling." She cleared her throat and touched the scar on the side of her face. "Before I had this." She dropped her hand and picked at imaginary lint on her uniform pants. "I recorded this stupid message, you know . . . I love you; I love you so much—please don't forget about me! The frame had a motion detector, and every time they'd walk into the living room the thing would go off. I love you; I love you so much—please don't forget about me! It became a joke around the house; you know, a catchphrase."

I sat there staring at the elliptical scar and remained silent.

Her hand came back up and stayed at her temple. "We were in Sadr City when this thing went off, concave, like a dinner platter with something like sixty pounds of explosives underneath—made to go through a Hummer like it was lard." She turned her head to look at me, consequently hiding the scar. "It killed the driver, Garston, instantaneously; didn't even know what hit him. Took Van Holt apart and sliced off Kestner's legs. Stevenson got it in the chest and bled out fast. I mean, we'd been hit by EFPs before, even multiple arrays, but this thing, this one . . ." She placed her hand on the wheel again, but kept her eyes on me. "It sounded like something ripping—like the air was made of canvas."

She said the lines again, with the same singsong tune. "I love you; I love you so much—please don't forget about me!"

I continued to study her.

"Garston was dead, but his foot was still on the accelerator. The wheel turned, and we were suddenly doing this graceful arc into the desert. So there I was, Medical Specialist Lolo Long with my one eye full of blood—but with the other seeing the vivid blue of the sky and the straw color of the sand." She breathed, and I watched the muscles in her throat bunch as she swallowed. "It felt like that part went on forever; riding across the desert in a shape just like the scar on my face."

I watched as a tear welled in the nearest eye.

She chanted again, and I knew I was hearing the mantra that had kept Specialist Lolo Long alive in that crippled, still-moving Hummer. "I love you; I love you so much—please don't forget about me!" She laughed. "Sometime during my second deployment the battery ran out on that damn picture frame, and Cale said they didn't replace it because it had become such an annoyance, a reminder every day that I wasn't there." She took a deeper breath and blew it out between her lips, pushing the emotion away. "When I got home, I threw it in the garbage."

We sat there like that for a long time, and I pretended to study the dash as she wiped her eye. I waited a respectful amount of time before asking. "How often do you see him?"

"Twice, since I've been back." She wouldn't look at me. "My mother visits him, Barrett, too. . . ." I waited as she composed herself. "I'm just . . . I think that maybe I'm not cut out to be a mother."

Thinking I better redirect the conversation a little, I took my hat off and dropped it in my lap, rubbed my face with both hands, and then ran them through my hair. "I was in my office one day when my wife came in and sat in the chair across from my desk and told me she was pregnant." Her eyes came back to mine. "I'll never forget what she said next: people have been screwing this up for thousands of years; I guess it's our turn."

She laughed again, but this time there was a little more heart in it. "Thank you."

"You're welcome."

The crickets were chirping, and I could even hear a few frogs down in the barrow ditch. We both watched as a couple of bats made mincemeat out of the miller moths dodging patterns in the dusk-to-dawn light in Lonnie's driveway.

"I looked you up."

I smiled, thankful to be on safer ground, and put my hat back on. "I've got a file; you told me."

"I looked up your service record, too. You were the Sam Spade of USMC Investigators, huh?"

I nodded. "In a fitting tribute, there is an illustrious manila envelope in a file cabinet in the basement of the United States Marine Corps Archives in Quantico, Virginia, with my name in it, yes."

"Grunt."

"Hump." I figured we were done here, and I was going to have to start up the hill to Lonnie's while I still had the energy. I pulled the handle on the Yukon and stepped out, closed the door, and leaned in the window, knowing full well I was heading back out on thin ice. "When this is over, however it's over, you should go see your son. He loves you. He loves you so much—and you better not forget about him."

I walked the rest of the way up the hill with the two cans of beer in my hand. About halfway up I heard her start the engine, saw the GMC back down the gravel road and sweep onto 212, following its headlights and a full night of patrolling the Rez by a woman who could not sleep.

There were boxes stacked on Lonnie's back porch amid what looked like a bone yard—skulls, horns, and the like that the real chief procured for the numerous reservation artisans he knew. I pulled the key he'd given me from my jeans and had just started to put it in the lock when I felt the edge of a large knife at my throat, and the Colt at my back was unsnapped and professionally whisked away.

The blade disappeared, and I raised my hands to telegraph my intentions, which were none, and slowly turned. The individual who had unarmed me now sat in the darkness of the porch swing with our collective weapons in his lap.

I heard the safety go off on my sidearm, but his voice was soft. "Sit."

"Gladly." I glanced around. "Where?"

"Right there."

I lowered myself onto the concrete stoop and, looking up at my assailant, leaned my back against the exterior of Lonnie's house. I tipped my hat so I could get a better look at him, but he'd situated himself in the shadows so that the bug light that Lonnie had left on for my convenience illuminated only the few miller moths that circled it and me, but not him.

"You know who I am?"

"You're Deep Throat."

"What?"

"Nothing." I waited a moment. "I have an idea who you are."

The shadow of his head shifted as he studied me. "You need to stay away from my mother."

I glanced around to show him that I wasn't really in any position to argue. "Okay."

"And you need to stop chasing after me."

"That's going to be a little more difficult."

He started to speak, but I interrupted him. "You want a beer?" I lifted the two cans in my one hand. It seemed like all I'd done this evening was offer beer to Indians only to be turned down.

He held my .45 steady, and I was starting to get a little concerned, when he spoke. "Open it for me."

I pulled the tab and carefully handed it to him.

"Artie, why don't you give me back my gun. Unless you're

specifically here to kill me, I'm going to work on the assumption that you're here to tell me that you're innocent." I opened my own can, played at sipping my beer, and waited.

"I am innocent."

"Well, I'd be more likely to believe you if you weren't holding my own loaded gun on me with the safety off."

He sipped but kept the Colt pointed at my chest. After a moment, I heard the safety snap back on. "That better?"

I shrugged. "We can work in increments." I watched as he took a deep breath and his leather jacket creaked. I estimated him to be pretty good sized but rangy. "So, where have you been keeping yourself?"

"I have places."

"I bet you do; is Diamond Butte Lookout one of them?"

There was a pause, and he genuinely sounded confused. "No."

I studied him, but my eyes were having trouble adjusting since I was in the light. "So let me guess, you're here to tell me you didn't kill Audrey Plain Feather?"

He sat there without moving and then stuffed the can between his legs and rustled something from his shirt pocket. In the darkness I could just make out his mouthing a cigarette from a pack and one-handing a Bic lighter. There was a brief flash before he snapped it shut, and I got a pretty good glimpse of his face; lean like a coyote, with a do-rag and a goatee.

He took a deep drag on the cigarette. "I would never do something like that—push a woman off a cliff while she was holding her child? I would never do that."

"You've done some stuff."

He pulled the cigarette from his mouth and let it dangle in his fingers. "Nothing like that." It was quiet, and then he plucked the beer from between his legs and sipped. "Nothing like that."

"I guess you had a pretty big argument with her last week."

He nodded. "At Human Services?"

"Yep."

He laughed through his cigarette, and two plumes of smoke shot toward me. "Everybody argues at Human Services; it's what you do there."

"Evidently your argument made an impression."

He grunted. "They were trying to cut off my mother's dole checks."

Dole check—he must've gotten that term from her. "They said you were cashing them."

His voice got a little strained as he took another puff. "For her, not for me."

I waved my hand to indicate that it was neither here nor there to me. "Why did you try and run me over with your truck the other night?"

His voice sounded genuinely surprised again. "What?"

"Somebody in your '71 GMC tried to run me over right down here on the Red Road two nights ago."

"Wasn't me."

I pretended to sip my beer again. "Your nephew tried to take responsibility, but I don't believe him." It got quiet again. "I figure somebody lifted it after you loaned it to him up in Jimtown. Any idea who that could have been?"

"I don't know."

"For an innocent man, you don't seem to have a lot of answers for me, Artie."

"It wasn't me."

I set my still-full can down beside me and stretched out my legs, my boots almost reaching him. "I'll be honest with you; I really didn't think it was you who tried to run me over, for the simple reason that I can't imagine what it is you could've hoped to have gained."

He ventured an opinion. "Scare you off?"

"I don't think you're that stupid." His cigarette flared. "But, then there's the tape."

Another silence, and when he spoke his voice sounded more unsure than it had before. He took another drag. "What tape?"

"The one where Clarence Last Bull tried to chisel you out of the money he promised you for killing Audrey and Adrian."

He stood. "What?"

"I guess you're on that tape, too."

"No way. Get Clarence and let him look me in the face and say that."

"I'm afraid that's not possible—he's not talking to anyone." I decided to keep at least one hole-card hidden, in case he hadn't been the one who'd killed the man. "Have you had any contact with Clarence in the last few days?"

He slowly lowered himself back on the swing. "No, I hardly know the man."

"Knew." I glanced into the darkness. "Do you know a woman by the name of Erma Stoltzfus?"

He dropped his cigarette butt and nipped off another from the pack. "No."

Strangely enough, I believed him. "Well, Artie, I haven't listened to the tape, but if you're telling the truth then somebody's gone to a heck of a lot of trouble to make it look like you committed these murders."

"Then let's go get Clarence and get him to tell the truth." He grunted. "Gimme five minutes with him and he'll talk."

"I doubt it." He didn't say anything more, so I figured I'd level with him. "Clarence's dead, Artie. Somebody put a bullet into him at Diamond Butte Lookout."

He lit up, and I waited.

"Wasn't me."

"Is there anybody who can corroborate where you've been in the last forty-eight hours?"

"No."

"Do you own a .38 pistol?" Stupid question; I knew by experience that Artie owned every gun in the *Jane's Small Arms Catalog*, so the answer was predictable.

"Yes."

"Would you mind if we had a look at it?"

He said nothing.

"Artie, you've got to admit that it doesn't look good." I rubbed my tired eyes with a thumb and forefinger. "Except for one glaring fact that I can't see a single thing you could gain from killing these people."

"That's right."

I took a breath. "There is the argument."

He laughed again. "You're saying I killed this woman and her husband for a crummy subsidy check?"

"It doesn't sound all that convincing, does it?" I shrugged. "But there's the tape. As I said, I haven't heard it yet, but supposedly Clarence was going to give you quite a bit of money for killing his wife and child."

He shook his head, and I watched the end of the cigarette move back and forth like tracer fire as he mumbled from one side of his mouth. "Bullshit. I don't know him, and I never talked to him on the phone. Ever." The tip brightened with his inhale. "Must be somebody else, somebody who had something to gain."

I let the dust settle before making the next statement. "I think you should come in, Artie; turn yourself over to the authorities."

"No way. I've seen how that turns out; once they get their hands on an Indian, it'll be the right Indian—one-way trip to Deer Lodge."

"I can see how this would have a limited appeal, but how do you see it ending? It's a manhunt, Artie—you're the guy that we're going to have to catch and the more you run, the guiltier you look."

"We?"

"Me, Henry, Lolo Long, the Feds, everybody who stands behind a badge—we're all going to be looking for you."

"You'll never catch me, none of you." He shook his head. "I heard what you did to my little nephew; you tell Standing Bear I owe him one."

"I will."

"Seems to me, I owe you, too." Looking off to the right and his avenue of escape, he sipped his beer and rested my sidearm on his leg. "Drink your beer."

"Artie, you're also not stupid enough to do something to me. Turn yourself in."

He shook his head, and I listened as he clicked off the safety on my Colt again. "Can't do it. I done time and I can't do it again. Even short time—I just can't do it. Not for nothin', and I don't wanna braid horsehair key chains up in Deer Lodge for the next forty years."

He started to stand, and it was then that Artie became aware of another large knife with an eleven-inch homemade blade that had been silently and professionally placed at his throat. From the sudden glow of Artie's cigarette, I recognized the turquoise bear paw engraved in the bone.

"Do not worry about it; maybe they will let you do hat-bands as well."

12

"Took you long enough."

After having packing-taped Artie's hands behind his back with a roll he'd discovered on the porch, the Bear sat Artie on one of the kitchen chairs. "I decided I wanted my beer back."

I collected Lonnie's boom box from the living room where he used it to listen to KRZZ and baseball games and carried it in, setting it on the table. "How long were you out there?"

"Most of it. I saw somebody on the porch and figured it was too late for Lonnie, so I parked over at the casino and doubled back on foot. It seemed as if you were having a nice conversation with Chief Long, so I did not want to interrupt."

I shot him a look.

"Then I did not want to interrupt the wide-ranging conversation you were having with Artie."

I took the CD and pulled it from the paper sleeve that read OFFICIAL EVIDENCE—FBI. "He says he didn't do it."

The Bear watched as Artie stared at the surface of the table. "That is what most of the men in Deer Lodge say."

I hit the EJECT button, dropped the CD in, and glanced at the silent Small Song. "Well, since Artie isn't talking, let's see what he had to say." I punched the button, and we listened as there was a fumbling of a receiver, and then the conversation started; it sounded as if it had been picked up midway and had been recorded through a barrel of bourbon. Someone cleared his throat, and then the voice of Clarence Last Bull mumbled something that ended with, "So, do you think you can help me out with that thing?"

Artie's voice resounded through the phone lines—he sounded angry but it was still hard to hear him over the music playing loudly in the background. "I'll kill the bitch!"

Clarence's voice dropped, as if he were trying to get Artie to lower his. "Yeah, yeah, that thing that we talked about. I was just wondering how much?"

Artie's voice continued to rise. "Twelve hundred God-damned dollars!"

Clarence pleaded. "Hey, keep your voice down."

"Fuck you. Twelve hundred dollars is what I'm talking about!"

I glanced up at Artie, who continued to look at the surface of the table. Henry was watching him with an impassive expression on his face, and I was one of the few who knew that it was when the Cheyenne Nation appeared the least emotional that he was the most.

Artie: "I'll kill the whole family!"

Clarence: "Right, right. Look, Artie, we're going for a picnic up on the cliffs at Painted Warrior and I was thinking that would be a good time to do the job. You know what I mean?"

The receiver rattled again as Artie must have changed his position. "I don't give a shit!"

Clarence: "I know, I know. Look Artie, it's gotta seem like it's an accident or the whole thing is off."

There was a loud noise as if Artie had struck something on his end. "Fuck it, man!" There was a woman's voice in the background, but I couldn't make out who she was or what it was she was saying, but it sounded as if she was in the same heightened emotional state as Artie.

Clarence's voice rose a little now. "Artie, I need you to keep a lid on this stuff till we can get it planned out."

"Fuck yeah, man."

The two men hung up, and I reached over and hit the STOP button. I looked at the culprit. "That you, Artie?"

He said nothing.

I glanced at Henry. "That sounded like Artie to me."

The Bear stood, taking him by the arm. "We should go."

Artie didn't move.

The Cheyenne Nation used a little more force and Small Song rose slightly and then, wrapping his feet around the chair legs in protest, slumped in his seat, "I'm not going to jail."

I figured we were looking at a struggle but wasn't sure what it was that we could do to get Artie over to the Law Enforcement Center against his volition other than an epic wrestling match. I glanced at Henry, and the Bear looked at Artie and then reached to the small of his back and slowly drew the bone-handled Bowie knife, letting it drape down beside his thigh, clearly in Small Song's view.

Artie shrugged, and you could've cut the air in the room with, well, a knife. "Kill me; I ain't goin' to jail."

I wondered how Henry was going to play the bluff when he suddenly raised the butt end of the elk-bone handle and brought it down on the back of Artie's head with expert precision.

I watched as the man's forehead rebounded off the table, and he fell to the floor in a heap, unconscious.

I looked up at the Bear as he flipped the knife and gestured the business end toward me with a hard look. "Do not say anything."

I raised my hands but found my mouth opening of its own accord. "You . . ."

"Do not."

I glanced down at the captive, a not insubstantial lump on

the floor. "You couldn't have knocked him out a little closer to the truck?"

The only one on duty at Tribal Police Headquarters was the taciturn, unpaid-in-weeks patrolman Charles Last Bull. "How's it going, Chuck?"

He stared at us and glanced at Artie's dead weight hanging between the Cheyenne Nation and me.

"You mind if we come in?"

We struggled in the door—I backed my way past the front counter, the bulletproof glass, and continued on toward the closed door that entered the hallway. Charles caught up with us and produced a ring of keys that he used to allow us access to the holding cells. "I thought you were off for the night, Charles."

He said nothing and, swinging the door wide, unlocked the same cell where his brother had been held, whereupon we deposited Artie Small Song on the steel bunk anchored to the concrete wall. "Thanks."

We paused there for a moment as Henry produced the knife again and freed the prisoner's hands from the impromptu packing tape handcuffs, even taking the extra time to pull out the blanket at his feet and cover him up.

I glanced at Charles, who closed the door and returned the keys to his belt.

Henry stepped over to the small fridge in the commissary, stooped, and took a tray of ice cubes from the freezer compartment.

I patted Charles on his shoulder, which felt like a fifty-five-gallon drum filled with concrete. "Where's the chief?"

He stared at me for a full ten seconds but couldn't find a way not to respond to my direct question. "Sleep."

Henry placed the tray on the counter and took a plastic bag

from the shelf, filled it with some ice, and came back to the bars where we stood. The Bear gestured toward the door. "Open."

Charles regarded him through sloped eyelids. "This the man who killed my half-brother?"

The Bear said nothing but just stood there holding the bag of ice.

Charles's eyes returned to the breathing lump on the bunk and placed a hand on his sidearm. "The hell with him."

The expression on the Cheyenne Nation's face never changed, but he leaned a little forward so as to make eye contact with Charles.

I spoke again, if for no other reason than to keep Henry from decapitating Lolo Long's only staff. "You know, Chuck, he's already knocked one guy unconscious tonight."

I snatched the keys from the patrolman's belt and unlocked the door in one quick move, tossing the ring back to him before he could react badly; the Bear entered and placed the bag of ice under Artie's head. Charles had advanced and was now standing in the doorway as Henry started out. They stood there like that for a moment, chest to chest, and I was reminded of the bulls that had sometimes locked horns in the pastures on my father's ranch.

Slowly, the Cheyenne Nation raised a hand and spread his fingers over Charles's chest, pushing him until the man was forced to step back in an attempt to catch his balance.

I closed the cell and gestured toward Charles to lock it back up.

He did, as Henry and I moved into the hallway. "I'm not so sure it's a good idea to leave an unconscious Artie Small Song here with Charles Last Bull."

He nodded his head. "I will stay."

"No, I can sleep anywhere. You go on ahead home, and I'll crash here."

Charles joined us in the hallway, and I made the pronouncement. "I'm waiting in here till Chief Long checks in."

The patrolman shrugged and turned between us, facing Henry and looking into his face. Henry followed him toward the door but shot me a look with a dramatically raised eyebrow. "I will see you in the morning."

"I hope so."

I made a makeshift bed with a lineup of chairs and a few more blankets from the closet in the hallway. About halfway through the process, Charles came in and studied me as I attempted to get comfortable. "You don't have any extra pillows, do you?"

He continued to stare.

"Down would be nice—I'm not allergic."

He stood there for a moment more and then left.

Fighting a yawn, I mumbled mostly to myself, "Could you flip off the lights?"

The disgruntled patrolman did but left the one on in the hallway as I collapsed onto my front-row bed. I'd folded another blanket up for a pillow, scrunched it a little, and tilted my hat up to where I could keep an eye on Artie, who had begun snoring like a water buffalo. Henry must've done a job on him, seeing as how to knock somebody out you had to come within an ace of killing them. Whenever I thought of such things, I always remembered the dent in Lucian's head where his in-laws had tried to beat some sense into him; as far as I could tell, it hadn't worked—didn't think it would work in this case, either.

I thought about my transportation needs and figured I could get someone to drive my truck from the airport in Billings so I wouldn't have to rely on Rezdawg, which was like relying on the wind. Lolo Long probably wouldn't like the idea of an Absaroka

County Sheriff's vehicle driving around the Rez, but since I'd helped out with the investigation she might be a little more forgiving.

I yawned so deeply that I thought my jaw was going to dislocate and then pulled the grey blanket up to my chin. Maybe I was overtired, but I was having a hard time falling asleep; first I blamed it on the indelicate rhythm of Artie's snoring and then on the peyote, even though I knew that neither was what was plaguing me.

My mind kept racing through the events of the last few days, and how tidily things had worked out; perhaps too tidily. I thought about the conversation with Artie and how he had seemed genuinely surprised by Clarence Last Bull's murder. Was it possible that Artie had killed Audrey but not Clarence? But the man's vehement denial of the contract murder had been convincing, especially at the price of just over a thousand bucks. So in essence, I was lying here for good reason—to protect a man who I didn't think perpetrated either act.

That was about the size of it.

Maybe Clarence had killed his wife, but he certainly hadn't killed himself.

Then there was the tape. Why would the man attempt to hire Artie for the job and then turn around and do it himself? With all the bravado that Artie had shown in the phone conversation, it certainly seemed as if he had been ready to perform the deed. Maybe, and then again, maybe it's one thing to agree to do such a thing but another to look into the eyes of a young woman holding her child and push them off a cliff.

I thought about Clarence, and the response he'd had to Audrey's death and the attempt on his son, and how I didn't think he was guilty, either.

So everybody was innocent?

Some detective.

The pivotal point of evidence was the wiretapped conversation between Clarence and Artie, which had been an odd one. Clarence's voice had seemed normal enough, but Artie's heightened responses struck me as weird. Maybe he was drunk; maybe he was upset about the twelve hundred dollars.

And the woman in the background; who was she? What was she saying? I'd heard a word or two that I'd maybe understood—dome, dose? Maybe there was more going on between Clarence and Artie than we knew about.

I dozed off for a while and then repositioned my head—I thought I might've heard some noise from out in the lobby, but it was hard to tell over Artie's snoring. I'd just settled back into my folded blanket when I heard the door at the end of the hallway open and the dangling wind-chime noise of Charles's ring of keys.

I saw his shadow and spoke to him as I removed my hat from my face. "You find that feather pillow?"

The light switch was flipped on, and I have to admit that while I wasn't surprised to find Charles looking down at me, I was surprised to see Artie's nephew, Nate, with a small revolver jammed into the policeman's neck. He nudged the patrolman forward. "Open the door."

I started to sit up but kept one hand underneath the blanket at the small of my back. "Nate, what are you doing?"

"Shut up, man." He pushed Last Bull toward the holding cell.

I unsnapped the safety strap on my Colt and drew it from the holster as I sat the rest of the way up, still keeping it concealed. Bleary as I was, I gave him a good look to make sure he wasn't drunk or otherwise impaired. He wasn't, but he looked excited and pretty scared at the same time. I tried to sound as lifeless and bored as possible, which wasn't so much of a reach. "Nate, have you lost your mind?"

"Shut up!" He pushed Charles's shoulder. "Unlock it."

Charles looked at me.

I blinked my eyes. "Do you know what time it is?"

Nate pushed the patrolman again. "I said unlock it."

I didn't say anything more and watched as Charles flicked up the right key and turned it in the lock, swinging the cell door wide. Nate pushed the patrolman inside and held the revolver on him. Charles backed against the bars with his hands raised, the key ring still in his fingers.

"Nate, what are you gonna do? Take your uncle and run off into the wild? Every law enforcement agency on the high plains will be looking for you."

"Shut up!"

I yawned and wondered if I was ever going to get any sleep. "Does your grandmother know that you're here?"

He redirected the pistol at me; the hammer was not pulled back. "I told you to shut up, man!" His attention went to his uncle on the bunk, and I noticed he'd stuffed Charles's sidearm in the back of his jeans. "C'mon, Artie, I'm bustin' you out."

The elder Small Song did not move but continued snoring loud enough to rattle the only window on the far wall.

"C'mon, Artie!" He waited a moment and then reached out a hand to jostle the big man's shoulder; still no response. He looked at the ice pack Henry had placed at the nape of Artie's neck. "What did you guys do to him?"

I stood and now held the .45 behind my hat. "He's asleep—like everybody else except for you."

He gestured with the pistol. "Come on in here; you guys are going to help me carry him out."

I shrugged and shook my head at the youth, pretty sure that none of us were in imminent danger. I casually slipped my hat onto my head and made a show of stuffing my sidearm back into its holster. Quickly, I took a step forward, snatched the keys from

Charles's raised hand, slammed the door shut, and locked the cell. I tossed the key ring into the hallway where it struck with a jangle and slid to the far end of the tile floor.

Nate looked at me and raised the pistol higher. "What'd you just do?"

"I just locked you in the cell." I sat on one of the chairs and looked at him as Artie continued to snore.

He looked a little uncertain as to how to proceed from this point. "Fuck!" After a moment, his arm wavered and then redirected itself at Charles, who still stood against the bars with his arms raised. "I'll shoot him!"

"Go ahead, I don't care for him that much anyway." Charles turned his head and looked at me with his eyes a little rounded.

Nate swung the revolver back at my face. "I'll shoot you!"

I casually palmed the Colt from the small of my back and rested it on my knee. "You do, and I'll shoot you back."

He literally stamped a tennis shoe. "Fuck!"

I readjusted my bed, yawned again, and made a big show of stretching. "Here's the deal; you give me both guns, I unlock you, you go home, and we all get a good night's sleep." I holstered the Colt and stood. "How about it?"

"Fuck!"

"I need a different answer."

He glanced at his snoring uncle, at Charles, and then back to me. "How do I know I can trust you, man?"

I distended my cheeks with a hearty exhale. "You're kidding, right?" I stuck a hand through the bars and motioned for him to hand me the drawn gun.

He didn't move at first but then his grip relaxed on the revolver and it swung down, dangling from his index finger.

I studied it in hopes that it wasn't the same caliber as the one that had killed Clarence. It was, but I could tell it hadn't been fired in a long time. I gestured toward the semiautomatic in the waist-band of his jeans. "That one, too."

He handed them to me, and I stood there looking like I had just come from Bed, Bath and Pistols. "I'm going to go get the keys, and then I'll unlock you and you can get out of here—I'd be quick about it, because I've got a sneaking suspicion that Charles here is going to want to beat the hell out of you." I glanced at the big patrolman. "I got that right, Chuck?"

He nodded and grunted.

I retrieved the keys, came back, and unlocked the door, handed the ring and sidearm back to Charles as a more contrite Nate stood by the bars. When the young man attempted to follow the patrolman, I placed a hand on his chest.

"Hey, you said that . . ."

"After I ask you a few questions."

The sullenness returned in a flash. "And what if I don't want to answer?"

I gestured toward the big tribal policeman, who was holster-ing his weapon. "Then I stuff Charles back in here, lock the door again, and go take a walk for about five minutes." I glanced at the patrolman's pock-marked face. "That about how long it'll take, Chuckles?"

"Two." The large man had become remarkably more conver-sational.

I held up the revolver. "Where'd you get the gun?"

He grimaced. "Artie's locker at Gramma's house."

"I don't suppose you'd know where Artie's been since night before last?"

He nodded. "Eating the elk at the house."

I stuffed the revolver into my own jeans. "He came back after we left?"

"Yeah."

"He was there the whole time?"

"Yeah."

"Were you there the whole time?"

"No, I got work up at KRZZ."

I thought about it. "How did you get here?"

He shot a look at his sleeping uncle. "Artie's truck."

"The one you tried to run me over with?"

"Um, yeah."

"Nate, did you know that you say *um* every time you lie?"

"Um . . ."

I shook my head and thought about the sleep I was losing. "You're not the one who tried to run me over. I think that you're trying to cover for your uncle, but in all honesty I don't think he was behind the wheel either." I felt a sudden surge of exhaustion and leaned my head against the bars and closed my eyes. "I'm thinking that whoever stole Artie's truck at the bar was the one who tried to run me over, and that someone might have a connection to Audrey's and Clarence's deaths."

His attention, at least, was peaked. "You think?"

"I think." I opened my eyes and studied him. "Who else was at the Jimtown Bar that night?"

He made a face. "Everybody." He gestured. "He was there."

I glanced at the patrolman. "Charles?"

"Yeah."

"Who was there, Charles?"

He snorted. "Everybody."

I squeezed the bridge of my nose. "You know, I'm going to lock the both of you back in here in a minute."

Nate was the first to break. "Me and a buddy of mine—we were just sitting on the tailgate of the truck, but then a friend of ours came by and said he'd buy us a beer."

"Who?"

"Kelly Joe Burns."

That loser again. "Who else?"

"Herbert His Good Horse came in and grabbed a six-pack to go. We tried to cadge a few off of him, but he wouldn't give us any." He thought. "Louise Griffin was there with Inez Two Two."

I frowned. "She's underage."

"So?" He paused and then continued. "Besides, her mother— you know, Loraine, the one who works over at Human Services, came and dragged her out. Boy, was Inez pissed."

I gestured toward the snoring man. "Was your uncle there?"

"No."

"Anybody borrow your keys?"

He smirked. "It's a Rez-Ride, man. You don't need keys; it's got two little wires that stick out from under the dash, but you gotta turn on the headlights first."

"How many people would know that?"

"On the Rez? Everybody; half the cars around here don't have keys and the other half don't have forward gears." He smiled. "I had a Chevy Corsica that I drove in reverse for seven months. You had to hook up the wires on it, too."

"Speaking of hooking up, I've got another question—does Artie have a girlfriend?"

"What?"

I sighed and tapped my shirt pocket where I'd stored the CD. "There is a recording of your uncle talking to Clarence Last Bull on the phone, and there's a woman in the background with him. If I can find out who that woman is, maybe she can go to bat for your uncle."

The young man stared at me, and for the first time he relaxed. "You really don't think Artie did it, do you?"

"No, I don't."

He thought. "He was hittin' on some chick up on the Rocky Boy Reservation, but I think she got engaged or something."

"What about the dental hygienist from Billings?"

"Old news."

I stepped back and allowed him egress from the cell. "Oh well, it was a thought."

He stood there, looking at me. "How about I listen to the CD?"

"I don't have a player."

"We can go up to KRZZ or I've got one in Artie's truck."

I shook my head in disbelief. "You don't have a starter switch, but you've got a CD player?"

"I work at a radio station." He transitioned into his on-air voice. "Pumping the wattage into your li'l red cottage." He smiled, started for the hallway, and tried to get past Charles, who stepped in front of him.

The big man placed himself between Nate and the wide world. He leaned in. "You ever pull a gun on me again, you better use it."

"Okay." The kid's response was too quick for Charles's taste.

Charles had him up in the air and against the wall faster than I could've possibly reacted. He grabbed fistfuls of the young man's shirt and then slammed him against the concrete block.

It took both hands, but I wrenched one thumb away, reverse-wrist-locked the large man all the way down the hallway, and shoved him against the far door with a heavy thump. I held him there until he stopped struggling. "Knock it off."

He didn't respond verbally—no surprise there—and tried to throw his body against me.

I applied so much pressure that I was afraid I was going to dislocate his thumb. I repeated the words again and felt his body relax just a bit. I let him go and stepped back.

He turned quickly and squared off with me, his face red from the exertion. "Keep your hands off me."

I raised mine, just to indicate that I was done for now. "How about we all just keep our hands to ourselves?"

Charles raised a finger and pointed at Nate. "Get him out of my jail."

Nate and I were sitting in Artie's truck in the Tribal Police parking lot under the yellowish glow of the arc lights as the young man pulled on the light switch and then held the two wires together, causing the small-block to cough, sputter, and then rumble into a lopsided idle. "You gotta have the engine running to get the player to work."

I handed him the CD—he took it and slipped it into the slot in the dash. We listened to the whole recording three times. "I'm sorry, but it's not broken into tracks, so we have to listen to it all."

"That's all right."

He leaned in at the portion of the recording where the woman was speaking in the background and focused on what seemed to be the one discernable word. He swallowed and then hit the EJECT button and handed me the CD.

"Do you recognize the woman's voice?"

"No."

"Neither do I, but I probably wouldn't." I tipped my hat back and looked into the night, the streetlights of Lame Deer trailing away from 212 into the heart of darkness. "Well, it was worth a try."

"The word she says . . ."

"Yep. I still can't quite make it out; something about 'dome' or 'dose'?"

"Dole, she's saying dole. It's a word my grandmother uses."

I waited a moment. "You think that's your grandmother?"

"No, but that's the word the woman is using—dole."

My limitations loomed audible. "What about the music in the background?"

"The jukebox up at Jimtown is always playing." He shrugged

and slipped the truck into reverse. "I can take us to a place where we can hear everything that's on there."

I grabbed the open passenger door and held it. "I can't go anywhere."

He looked incredulous. "What, you're still under arrest?"

I looked past him and into the lighted windows of the Tribal Police Headquarters. "Do I have to remind you who Charles's half-brother is?"

He cleared his throat and rubbed his neck where the patrolman's grip still showed red. "Oh, man." He dipped his head and looked up the hill to the blinking light at the top of the radio tower. "KRZZ's got production studios that can do anything; slow the track down, pump up different levels." He looked at the wristwatch on the carabiner attached to his belt loop. "I gotta be up there in two hours anyway—why don't you meet me there?"

"I thought Herbert His Good Horse did morning drive."

"He does, but he also gets hung over and I get stuck pulling doubles." He shrugged. "That was mean. He takes care of his nephew, the one that's got no legs."

"I saw a poster of him winning some marathon in Japan."

"He's unreal."

I nodded. "If you're going to be up there all morning, I'll head to the radio station once Chief Long comes in and replaces Charles."

"Cool, man."

"Well, I'd better get back inside before Charles tries to drown your uncle in the toilet." I closed the door.

Nate tossed a worried look to the jail as I walked around the truck. "Hey, Nate?" I pulled the small revolver from my belt and tossed it into his lap through the open window. "No more of this Indian outlaw stuff, okay?"

He looked genuinely embarrassed. "Okay."

Inside, I found Charles reading the newspaper with his feet up on the counter, the black and white monitors showing the holding cell, the duty room, and the parking lot where Nate was turning around and pulling away.

I yawned and placed my elbows on the high counter. "I'm thinking you need to put a few hours into some sensitivity training seminars."

He was reading the *Billings Gazette* but looked up at me; predictably, he said nothing.

"Just for the record, I don't think Artie's the one who killed your brother, which means that the person that did do it is still out there and needs to be brought to justice. Have you got any ideas of who might've held a grudge against Clarence and his family?"

He folded the paper, placed it in his lap, and looked at me. "Everybody has enemies."

"Including you?"

He cocked his head. "Including me; it goes with the job."

"Anybody dislike you enough to go after your half-brother?"

He shrugged.

"How about Audrey and Adrian?" I stifled the yawn in my throat. "That's a lot of dislike."

He unfolded his paper and rustled it to straighten the pages.

"You know, generally you don't have to look very far for people who do things like this; it's usually friends, so-called, or family."

He continued to study his paper.

"It seems to me that somebody is looking to wipe out your entire family, Charles. And you don't seem to care."

The tribal policeman's voice rumbled over the *Billings Gazette*.

"I care enough that if you leave here for another five minutes, I'll go into that holding cell and do society a favor."

I waited a moment and then continued on like a wrecking ball. "You a killer, Charles?"

After a moment he released one side of the paper, lowered his hand to hit the button under the counter so that the door behind me buzzed in a persistent manner. He sat there with that expressionless look on his face and watched me.

I straightened up, took the two steps to the door, and yanked the thing open, his stare following me into the hallway. "Good to know, since we're looking for one."

13

I was having this dream where the talking animals were at it again—even Dog was having a go at me. It was only when he asked me the second time if I wanted coffee that I started thinking that things seemed suspicious.

Flapping my eyelids open and shut cleared a little of the bleariness and allowed me to focus. Lolo Long had pulled up another folding chair from the Law Enforcement Center's endless supply and was holding two cups from the White Buffalo convenience store, a manila folder under her arm again. "I understand we had an attempted jail break last night?"

I peeled the blanket back a little more. "As jail breaks go, it wasn't much." I sat up and looked out the small rectangular window at the sky, already worn to a lighter shade of blue. "It's mid-morning?"

"Say . . . you are a detective."

I slumped back onto my blanket-pillow. "Shoot me?"

"There is a member of my dwindled staff who would be happy to comply with that request, but in consolation, I bring you coffee and photographs."

I struggled up and thought my back was going to fragment like not-so-fine china. Groaning, I reached out and took the Styrofoam cup she proffered. Written on the side in a ridiculously perky font were the words FRESH BREWED. I undid the top and looked at the complex, frothy content with what looked like mouse droppings decorating the top. "What is this?"

She leaned forward, taking a look in mine, and then undid her own and traded cups with me. "Sorry. Mocha Chip Frappuccino."

"You're kidding."

She sipped what she called coffee and raised one of those samurai-sword eyebrows. "I take my comforts where I can." She handed me the envelope. "Here are the photos from Henry's camera that you guys took. There's not much there, but one thing jumped out at me."

I pulled out the prints and looked at them one at a time, finally looking up at her. "She wasn't facing forward when she went over."

"No." She sighed. "And as far as I know, nobody does a suicide holding their child and attempting a back flip." She waited a few moments. "There's nothing else that I can tell."

"Me either." I placed the photos back in the envelope, careful to close the metal tabs.

Long glanced at the still-snoring man in the holding cell. "You caught Artie."

"Henry caught Artie." I sipped my regular black coffee and watched as she made the same face she always did whenever I mentioned the Cheyenne Nation. "How come the cavalry hasn't shown up?"

"The Feds?"

"Yep."

"I don't think they know—no access to the moccasin telegraph."

I thought about it. "Let's keep it that way for a while, shall we?"

After I'd given her the rundown on last night's events, she stood and walked over to the bars. "Strange behavior for a guilty man."

"I was thinking the same thing. I mean if he was guilty, why would he care what I thought?" I stretched the remnants of my back. "We played the recording for him."

"What'd he say?"

"That he didn't do it."

She turned to look at me. "What do you think?"

"That he didn't do it."

She nodded her head in a defeated fashion. "Well, our only other suspect is dead."

"Inconvenient, isn't it?" I strained a little more coffee through my teeth. "Have you listened to the recording?"

"Your buddy, Cliff Cly, played it for me yesterday, but the sound isn't so good."

"You didn't happen to hear a woman in the background, did you?"

She turned her full attention to me, placing her broad back against the bars of the holding cell. "No. I mean, we were listening to Clarence and Artie; I don't think anybody paid much attention to anything else."

"Did you hear music in the background?"

"Kind of."

"Well, fortunately, I've got an expert in the field who says he can help us out."

"Who?"

"The jail breaker."

She looked dubious. "Nate?"

I gestured toward the snoring man. "He's got a vested interest."

"I can call my mother and have her bring in food and Artie-sit." She nodded and continued chewing her coffee. "As you know, we've got a shower here; would you like to use it?"

I ruffled my hand through my hat hair, I'm sure causing it to stand up at all angles. "Is that a hint?"

She did her best to suppress the grin caused by my appearance but failed miserably. "Could be."

I didn't have any clean clothes to change into, but Chief Long was kind enough to loan me a shirt from Tribal Police supplies with a nifty little patch set like hers but with the name PRETTY WEASEL printed on the pocket. "Is this my undercover name?"

She drove south on the gravel road leading to the radio station, the tail end of the Yukon swinging around behind us like a flat-track racer. "What?"

I braced a hand against the dash. "Nothing."

KRZZ's was not the most inspiring of buildings, but then most everything concerning radio rarely is. I'd done a brief semester as a freshman at KUSC, University of Southern California's student radio station, where I had been the worst DJ they'd ever heard. The programming in the early sixties was almost exclusively classical and didn't require a great deal of talk between the twenty minute tracks, but even I had to admit that I was horrible.

It looked to be a utilitarian building from the sixties with a slab roof and a wall of small-pane windows overlooking what there was of downtown Lame Deer. The white paint was peeling off the concrete block, and the front screen door was propped open with a cardboard box full of CDs that had been marked on the side with the plea, TAKE ME, I'M FREE! There was a battered Honda Civic in the parking lot as well as Artie's truck.

Lolo parked and we got out. I could hear music drifting through the open door, John Trudell's *Bone Days,* a stream of consciousness blues opus I recognized from hanging around Henry.

In the tubular-style font of the seventies were the words KRZZ, LOW POWER—HIGH REZ, the lettering also peeling like a second-day sunburn.

"Looks like Native radio's seen better days."

Inside there was a green carpet that showed the fiber grid underneath, and a surplus steel government desk where a pretty-enough young woman, who was a friend of Melissa Little Bird's, was working on a book full of Sudoku. She raised her head as we entered. "Can I help you?"

Lolo looked at the large poster behind the girl's head—it was a badly done offset print of four men dressed in period western costume with the words REGGAE COWBOYS, I SHOT THE SHERIFF in red. She glanced at me. "No offense."

"None taken." I thumbed my Tribal Police patch. "Anyway, Poppa's got a brand new bag."

The young woman was uncertain, looked at the two of us, and decided the only course was to repeat her request. "Can I help you?"

I smiled. "I'm sorry. Is Nate here?"

She rolled her eyes toward the inner sanctum and immediately went back to the puzzles as we turned and made our way into another room with a few more desks and a glass wall that gave a view of the "on-air studio," principally discerned by the large red light with white lettering that read ON AIR. Nate was standing in the middle, swaying to the Native beat-poet's words and the searing guitar accompaniment.

I stepped forward and knocked on the thick glass. The young man couldn't hear us with the headphones on, so I knocked a little louder, afraid that if I applied much more pressure the glass would most certainly fall out of the frame onto the floor.

Nate finally swayed around so that he was looking at us and immediately motioned that we should join him through the door he pointed to at the left.

KRZZ's studio was a world apart from the tawdry outer office where the receptionist sat—there were multiple computer screens, sound boards with about a hundred slide controls, and banks of

CD and computer inputs. The inside of the room was covered in acoustical foam and at the center was a stylish, air-cushioned chair. There was another window to the outside, but it was so plastered with Indian Power, AIM, Thunderchild, and New Day Four Dances Drum Group stickers that I doubted you could tell the weather by looking out of it.

"Welcome to the nerve center. Federal grants can go only to actual transmission equipment. Say what you want about Herbert His Good Horse, he knows how to write grants."

It was an impressive setup. "I guess."

"Hold on just a second." He reached up and, just as the song finished, swung the elevated mic in front of his face. "John Trudell, my brothers and sisters, just a human being trying to make it in a world that is rapidly losing its understanding of being human. It's ten o'clock in the AM, daytime for you Indians, and you're listening to KRZZ 94.7, Low Power—High Rez, the voice of the Northern Cheyenne Reservation. *Nestaevahosevoomatse!*"

He touched another button on the computer and a strong drum beat filled the studio with background singers chanting something I vaguely recognized. "Are they singing about Mighty Mouse?"

Nate smiled. "Yeah, a group called Black Lodge. It's a favorite of the kids down at the elementary school."

I pulled the CD out of my pocket, slipped it from the paper envelope, and handed it to him. "This isn't likely to make it on your top-ten list."

Lolo added, "Even with a bullet."

Nate put the CD in one of the players, punched a few buttons, and we listened to the beginning of the recording before realizing we were hearing it over the same speakers as the Mighty Mouse powwow song.

"Is that going out over the air?"

He rapidly hit a few more buttons and made a face. "Just a little."

"I don't know if this is a two-party consent state, but I'm pretty sure we could get sued for what just happened."

He shrugged. "We'll just keep it between ourselves."

"And a couple of thousand listeners?"

He adjusted the volume on another off-air track. "I think you're overestimating our listenership."

I glanced at the studio phone as the lights began blinking, not unlike the ones in my office that regularly plagued me. "Uh huh."

We ignored them and carefully listened to the recording again, but I couldn't make out anymore than I had before. Nate's fingers jigged on the computer keyboard, and then he hit a button on the CD player. "I downloaded it to the computer, so now we can manipulate it any way we want."

The Sudoku woman flung open the studio door. "Nate, did you just put some kind of crazy shit on the air? People are calling and want to hear the John Trudell song about Mighty Mouse again."

"Um, tell them it was a demo." He flicked his hand at her, and she disappeared. He hit a few more buttons and turned down the on-air volume, and we were once again listening to the hiring of a hit man.

We got to the portion where I thought I'd heard music; Nate's fingers tapped on the keyboard and isolated the track, bringing the background noise up and the primary voice down, allowing us to hear the melody of something.

"Do you recognize that song?"

He listened intently to the simple chord progression but shook his head. "No."

Lolo leaned in and propped an arm on the counter. "Play it again."

Nate did as he was told, and we listened to the music as he lifted the volume—a strong bass-baritone and a chicka-boom rhythm passed through the speakers.

"Jail was often his home
They'd let him raise the flag and lower it . . ."

The rest was lost in the background noise and angry voices.

"Johnny Cash—that's *The Ballad of Ira Hayes.*"

Nate looked at me. "Who?"

Lolo Long gently slapped him in the back of the head. "The Pima Indian who helped raise the flag at Iwo Jima." She glanced at me and gestured toward Nate. "This is what we fought for— you know that, right?"

"When was that?"

She looked at him. "Iwo Jima?"

"No, the song. When was it released?"

I thought about it. "Before I went to Vietnam, '64 I'd guess."

He made a face. "The sixties? No wonder I don't know it." He looked at the CD player as if it held the Dead Sea Scrolls. "Wow, man."

I glanced at the chief. "Well, we need to go up to the Jimtown Bar anyway. I don't think anybody's going to remember anything, but we've got to leg it out. I've got a couple of hours before Cady and Lena come back from Colstrip." I gestured toward the computer again. "Can you play the part with the woman's voice?" He did, but the only word that I could discern was the word dome/dose/dole.

Lolo Long had a strange look on her face. "Play it again."

Nate did as he was told and then played it again and again.

I leaned a little forward to get her attention as she stared at the blank screen. "Anything?"

She didn't hear me, or she was concentrating.

"Do you know who it is?"

Even Nate turned to look at her, but she shook her head. "No, I thought for a minute, but . . ."

"What?"

"Nothing."

I studied her. "You're sure?"

She straightened and stepped back from the counter. "Yeah."

I sighed and looked at Nate. "You?"

He shook his head. "Sorry, I wish I did. Believe me."

"I do." I patted him on the shoulder. "We're going to head up to Jimtown and ask around. Do you think you can keep manipulating the recording so that we can try and get more out of it?" I paused. "Without putting it on the air?"

He smiled and looked at the lights still blinking on the phone. "Hey, man, I may have produced a hit here."

Chief Long had been silent in the five miles up to the notorious drinking establishment; it had been a quick five miles, but five miles nonetheless.

She slid the Yukon to a stop in front of the steel-red posts sticking up in front of the Jimtown Bar's front door—likely there to keep the patrons from instituting an impromptu drive-through—and sat staring at the dash, the midday sun drying the irrigation water in the surrounding hay field with wisps of vapor trailing up from the ground.

"Something wrong?"

"I'm thinking."

"About?"

She looked at me as if I'd just fallen off the official sheriff's-only turnip truck. "I'm just wondering how complex this case is, you know?"

I nodded. "It usually is complicated when it concerns matters of the heart; things tend to get venal and earthy."

She pressed her lips together. "So you don't think it's a hidden gold mine or about nuclear weapons?"

I smiled. "No, I don't; I think it's something small, something personal, and probably something stupid." I waited a moment. "You got anything you want to tell me, Chief?"

She looked at me for a longer moment and then pulled the handle and threw open her door. "Not really."

The Jimtown bar itself isn't an impressive sight, but the beer can pile out back most certainly is. Documented by *National Geographic* and Guinness World Records as the largest beer can pile in the world, it dwarfed the actual bar, where the twin mottos, which appeared on the back of souvenir ball caps, had always been WHERE THE CAN OF WHUPASS IS ALWAYS OPEN, and FRIDAY NIGHT SPECIAL, SHOT, STABBED, OR RAPED. I got tired the way I always did when approaching such establishments and hoped that Luanne, the proprietor for the last few miraculously quiet years, was about.

I started to follow Long toward the door but paused when I saw an old, faded powder-blue Dodge with a white replacement door that read COLSTRIP CONCRETE and a phone number belying its age with only four numerals.

I stopped.

The moment must have lasted longer than I thought, as Lolo paused with her hand on the front door of the bar and looked at me. "Something wrong?"

I thought about repeating the conversation in reverse but decided her mood wasn't conducive. "I've seen that truck before."

"There are only a couple of thousand vehicles on the Rez, so I bet you have." She pushed the door open but instead of going inside turned to look at me. "Where?"

"Birney."

"Red or White?"

"I'll tell you later." I glanced at the truck one more time, then caught the heavy glass door and followed her into the interior gloom, lit only by the red neon spelling BAR in the small window. It was still well before opening time, but a familiar character sat on one of the massive log stools bolted to the concrete floor.

Thom Paine had been the unofficial mayor of Jimtown for as long as I could remember; half Cheyenne and half Crow, he was the perfect peacemaker for the just-off-the-Rez bar. He was a small man, so his best technique for breaking up beer brawls was to get the patrons to laugh with an unending stream of politically incorrect Native humor mostly borrowed from Herbert His Good Horse. He leapt off his stool as soon as he saw us. "*Haho!*"

Lolo held up a hand to stop the coming tirade as I wandered over to the jukebox at the far end of the bar. "Thom, is Luanne around?"

"No, she went to Billings for a hair appointment." His voice became more excited as he thought of a joke to tell. "I got this one off the morning show the other day—there were these two cowboys out ridin' and they came onto this Indian lying on his belly with his ear against the earth."

I thumbed through the machine's old-style tabs as Long's voice sounded dubious. "She left you in charge?"

"No, Nattie Tyminski is here, but she's in the bathroom." He continued with the joke as if she hadn't interrupted. "The one cowboy turns to the other and says, 'See that Indian, he can put his ear to the ground and hear things from miles away.'"

I got to the end of the song listings and then went back in the other direction just to make sure I hadn't missed it.

"About that time the Indian looks up at them and says, 'Covered wagon pulled by two oxen, one white, the other speckled, one man, one woman, three children and a black dog—wagon full of all family supplies.' The one cowboy looks at the other one and says, 'That's amazing.' The Indian continued, 'Yes, ran over me about a half-hour ago.'"

Lolo chuckled in spite of herself and glanced toward the two bathroom doors, one marked "SQUAWS," the other "BRAVES," that led toward the pool table past the jukebox where I stood. "Thom, sometimes . . ." And she finally laughed wholeheartedly.

His eyes almost disappeared in the folds around the sockets. "It makes me happy to see you laughing the way you used to, Little-Lo. You don't laugh enough anymore."

She gently placed a hand on his shoulder. "I guess it's the job, Thom." She took a deep breath and glanced over to me. "I've had some help with that lately, though."

I leaned against the jukebox and tipped my hat back in an aw-shucks manner. "No *Ballad of Ira Hayes*."

She let the hand slip from the mayor's shoulder and crossed to me. "No?"

"No." I glanced at Thom. "When's the last time they changed the music on this machine?"

He shook his head, looked at the floor, and then back to us. "Never that I know of."

"That means that Artie didn't call from here."

She studied me. "Then where?"

"Could've been anywhere: a cell phone in Artie's truck, a home stereo, or a radio station."

Thom watched us like we were a tennis match, but I cut him off before he could start in with the jokes again. "The key is the woman; if we know who the woman is then we know where the place might've been."

"And why are you telling me this?"

"Because I think you know who she is."

It was at that point that the Squaws bathroom door opened and two individuals of separate sexes exited. One was an obese woman with a modified beehive hairdo and way too much makeup; the other was a skinny white guy with a shaved head, a flame tattoo spiraling up his neck, and sunglasses, despite the gloom inside. The man held a brown plastic grocery sack and looked very surprised to see us.

I smiled. "Mr. Kelly Joe Burns—I see you have your belt on."

He paused there for a second, pushed Nattie Tyminski toward us, and then dodged behind the bar through the doorway toward the back. It took both of us to catch the screaming woman, who stumbled, fell halfway to the floor, wrapped one arm around me and the other around Chief Long's leg, and held on for dear life.

The chief was the first to disentangle, and she lithely leapt over the bar and through the back door. "Arrest her!"

After getting the woman to her feet, I handcuffed her to the refrigerator and went outside to take a quick look at the blue Dodge. I busied myself for a moment and then went to the right in the direction of the as-big-as-a-very-large-house giant pile of beer cans but couldn't see where Lolo and Burns might've gone.

I stopped by a Dumpster, which was made out of a couple of fifty-five-gallon drums sitting on a crumbling concrete pad next to the huge pile, and listened; it sounded like the cans were being stepped on and were sliding down the hill.

I approached the gigantic assembly and worked my way around the periphery—Lolo Long with her sidearm drawn was thirty feet above me and was panning the .44 around the area. She must've half-seen me and swung the big Smith toward my chest.

"Whoa, Chief!"

She raised the barrel of the revolver skyward. "Where is he?"

"You don't know?"

She slipped on the mountain of crushed aluminum and almost fell. "No, he disappeared."

I circled the base of the thing, held in check by the remnants of an old foundation, and figured that must've been how "the largest pile of beer cans in the world" had started; somebody had run a wheelbarrow out the back and dumped them into the place where a building must've been in the twenties, and the tradition had continued on into the twenty-first century. The smell of stale beer, even in the moderate heat of the morning, was sinus clearing.

"Where did you lose him?"

She screamed in frustration, finally forming words. "I followed him up over this trash heap, and when I got to this side, he was gone!" She took a step and then slid down and fell in a tumbling avalanche. "Damn it!"

I stood there watching the slipping cascade of cans. "Well, I guess there's only one thing to do." She stood back up and watched as I drew my Colt and raised my voice. "Throw a few shots into this pile and see what happens. If he's in there, I'll probably get him."

There was a wheelbarrow load that hadn't made it to the mountain proper, smaller and more scattered than would've hidden a man. I raised my .45, snapped off the safety, and pulled the trigger—a few cans flew into the air.

So did Kelly Joe Burns.

As I'd suspected, he'd slipped and fallen but had been smart enough to realize that the mountain of cans could provide a fine hiding place, at least before I threatened to shoot it.

If we'd thought Kelly Joe was fast before, we hadn't seen anything. The man practically levitated from the cans downgrade from where Chief Long sat and about a third of the way around the base from where I stood before remembering to throw the bag he held over the top of the pile.

We both yelled at him to stop, but we might as well have been talking to the wind in both solidity and velocity. As I circled the base, I pointed toward the spot where he'd been buried. "Get the bag!"

She stumbled and slid as I ran after the world's fastest non-Indian.

Back at USC, as an offensive tackle, I had been able to outrun any other two-hundred-and-fifty-pound man in Southern California for forty yards; we were now more than a couple of decades past that, I was coming up on my forty yard limit, and Kelly Joe Burns didn't weigh close to two hundred and fifty pounds.

He had run toward the road but had circled back to the front of the bar, and I could hear the sound of the Dodge's starter, grinding away.

I stopped at the edge of the asphalt and attempted to catch my breath by bending over and placing a hand on one of my knees for support as I pulled the coil wire from my shirt pocket and dangled it like a dead rat for him to see.

He looked at me, threw open the door, and ran across Route 39 just as an eighteen-wheeler bellowed down the road from Colstrip. The white cattle truck locked its brakes and blew its horn, and I watched as Kelly Joe slid underneath and came up on the other side.

"You've got to be kidding. . . ."

I skimmed around the rear end of the Freightliner full of unhappy cows when another horn sounded and caused my heart to skip like a warped record album. I was pretty sure I'd checked for oncoming traffic, but was surprised to find both of my hands, one still holding the .45, on the hood of a Baltic blue 1959 Thunderbird convertible.

The car had stopped, and my daughter and soon-to-be in-law stared at me with stunned looks on their faces. I coughed and held up one finger as I lurched off the stationary Ford into the barrow ditch after Kelly Joe.

Holstering the sidearm felt like the right thing to do in front of Cady and Lena, and besides, I figured I wasn't going to really have to shoot Burns. There was a well-worn trail at the base of the ditch beside a barbed-wire fence. I looked north, then started off south—my daughter kept pace with the Thunderbird in low gear and Lena, having folded her arms on the door sill, sat up on her knees to look down at me as if she were in a parade.

"What are you doing?"

I coughed again and struggled to get enough air to reply. "Chasing a drug dealer."

"I thought you were chasing a murderer."

I glanced around and jogged on. "This is kind of a side bet."

They accelerated and kept up, Cady driving, Lena talking. "Two felonies with one stone?"

"Something like that."

She turned and was talking to Cady. "The driver says to remind you that you have a luncheon in thirty minutes."

"I'll be there."

There was another brief conversation. "The driver says to tell you that we're taking it on faith that since you've holstered your weapon, your life is not imperiled?"

I was getting a little of my air back and responded, "He may run me to death, but he's not armed, if that's what you mean."

"You're sure you don't want our help? We do our best work from concours vintage automobiles."

I waved them on. "I bet."

They sped off, and I watched as the driver didn't spare the horses.

Good girl.

It was pretty much a straight shot along Rosebud Creek, so other than a few high stands of grass, I could see about a hundred yards heading south and left toward Lame Deer. I glanced out at the swathed fields to my right and could see all the way across that flat area as well. No one.

I stopped as I remembered something Henry had once told me—something about a culvert nicknamed the "time tunnel," which was somewhere in the area. It was reputedly filled with mattresses so that those who had imbibed and didn't want to run the risk of becoming the forgotten dead up on Route 39 could sleep it off. Dire stuff, but better than being roadkill.

I turned and looked north. I had automatically followed the flow of the traffic on my side of the road and started south, but what if the time tunnel was north? It was a crap shoot.

Standing there for a moment more, I made a decision, turned, and began trotting back up the path. After about three hundred yards, I came to a culvert and stopped. The grass was high and only a little water spilled from the corrugated pipe, which was almost as tall as a man.

I thought about the last time I'd climbed in one of these things and had almost been killed by a big Crow by the name of Virgil White Buffalo. I reached around to my back and felt for my venerable Maglite, but then remembered I wasn't wearing my duty belt.

Standing there, I could see that there was an uneven light at the end of the tunnel where it opened out on the other side. The smell of the place was less than inviting, but in I went, crouching down and once again pulling the Colt from the small of my back. "Kelly Joe, if you're there I want you to know I'm coming in!"

Nothing.

I kept a wide stance and trudged over the first mattress that smelled more disgusting when I stepped on it. I cleared my throat and tried to breathe shallowly, in hopes that the odor wouldn't overtake me before I got out.

Stepping to one side, I watched as some sort of snake slithered from under the mattress and continued on in the direction from where I'd come. I started talking to the animals again. "You're not the variety I'm looking for."

I turned and reached the halfway point, where one of the mattresses was bunched against another. Thinking that it was pretty much the only place where someone could hide in the confined space, and with a few more flashbacks to the other culvert down on Lone Bear Road, I put a foot on the mattress and pushed. Burns once again flung himself from cover and ricocheted down the culvert like a pinball. I thundered after him but tripped on the corner of a soggy sleeping bag and fell forward. I scrambled to get to my feet, but it was slippery and I knew in my heart of hearts that I was going to lose him.

God hates a quitter, so I staggered forward and watched as he got to the opening at the other end and the bright sunlight lit him up like a candle.

That was when the candle snuffer came down with a vengeance.

Lolo Long must've been waiting above the tunnel on the other side, and I watched with a great deal of satisfaction as she landed on Kelly Joe with all six feet of everything she had. She planted him face first in the mud with a knee at his back as she grabbed two fistfuls of his wifebeater T-shirt.

He struggled to get at her, but it was like a replay of the events at Clarence's house when she'd pig-wrestled him.

I staggered out into the light as she slapped her cuffs on Burns and dragged him to his feet, his entire body smeared with blackish mud.

"I want a lawyer."

She smacked the side of his head. "You're gonna see a lot of lawyers, trust me."

I took a couple of deep breaths and could smell the strong scent of stale beer coming off of her. "Did you find the bag?"

She smiled as she took the drug dealer's arm. "I did, and inside was about five hundred grams of methamphetamine in tiny, individual-serving baggies." I took his other arm, and we walked him up out of the ditch toward the Jimtown Bar parking lot. "That's almost a pound of Schedule II substance, and you know what that means, don't you Kelly Joe?"

She was happier than I'd ever seen her as she informed him of his Miranda rights. When she finished, Kelly Joe continued to say nothing so she turned to me. "I'm sorry it took so long and that I smell like an old brewery, but the cans covered up the bag when it hit on the other side of Mount Rainier and it took a while for me to find it."

"No big deal."

"Do you know how long I've been looking to get this rat?" She laughed, and I was glad I hadn't spoiled her moment in the sun. "Two months, and this is by far the biggest bust of my career."

I was happy for her; there's a camaraderie and euphoria that goes along with these situations, when you get the bad guy with so much evidence that there's no way an informed jury or sober judge will ever let them walk. It's a feeling that is amplified only by the fact that no one was hurt and that everybody, with the exception of the perp, got away clean—well, mostly clean.

My mind kept drifting back to the case at hand, though. I thought about the dead father, the injured child, and the woman we'd watched fall. I kept my mouth shut as she stuffed the drug dealer in the back of the Yukon and turned to look at me with her hands on her hips.

The smile, a million watts, only slightly dimmed. "Audrey."

I focused on the tribal police chief's face. "What?"

"On the recording; the woman's voice."

I waited.

"It's Audrey."

14

We had deposited Nattie Tyminski in the BIA jail, where there was a female docent. She would probably walk as we hadn't actually seen her in possession, but a little time behind bars wouldn't do her any harm.

We sat on the folding chairs in the Tribal Police Headquarters and stared at Kelly Joe—he sat on the bunk in the corner of the holding cell with his knees drawn up in protection. So far, Artie Small Song hadn't made any aggressive moves toward him, but the drug dealer was playing it safe; I didn't blame him—it was like being trapped in a Havahart with a pissed-off badger.

Artie's fingers were wrapped around the bars like the kind of vines that choked trees to death. "I don't have any idea."

"You must have had some kind of interaction with her."

"No, I didn't." He flung himself from the bars and started pacing back and forth, Kelly Joe's eyes tracking him like radar. "The only time I ever laid eyes on the woman was there at Human Services when I was trying to get my mother's support check."

"No other time?"

He turned the corner at the far end of the cell and started back past me. "Never."

"Not even on the phone?"

He stopped on the next pass. "Ever." He grabbed the bars

again, and Kelly Joe jumped. "And I wasn't at that bar that night! You ask and see if anybody remembers me being there."

"Your truck was there."

"My nephew was driving it."

"With your elk on the hood?" I got up and leaned an elbow between the bars and paid a glance to Burns. I would've been lying if I'd said I wasn't enjoying the drug dealer's discomfort. "Then where were you?"

"Hunting!" The spit flew from his lips, and his face moved near mine. "You had part of that elk; you saw it, did it seem fresh to you?"

I nodded. "It did."

"I went after another one; now let me out."

"It's not that easy, Artie. The Feds are convinced that you did it because of the recording, and we haven't come up with anything that counters that very impressive piece of evidence."

"That conversation never happened." He pushed off the bars. "I never spoke to her husband, what's his name?"

"His name was Clarence." Burns's voice rose from the back, and one look at him told you that he wished he'd kept his mouth shut, but he was Kelly Joe after all, and silence was not one of his strong suits.

"Clarence?"

I nodded.

"I had an argument with a guy named Clarence in the parking lot of the White Buffalo one time."

"About?"

"He left his stupid Jeep in front of the gas pump while he was serenading some teenager. I told him to move it or I was going to get all Crazy Horse on his ass."

I looked past Artie and raised my voice so that Kelly Joe would know I was speaking to him. "You ever have any dealings with Clarence Last Bull?"

He pulled at the collar of his T-shirt, feeling the heat from me and his tattoo, and then tried to cover it by resting his chin on his knees. "I'm not talking to you."

"Okay." I pushed off the bars, leaving a few fingers on the steel like I was loath to leave. "I can see how it is that you wouldn't want to bother to help Artie with his problems. Chief Long and I are going to walk out of here in about two minutes anyway, so you two are going to have plenty of time to talk about things and work it all out."

Artie Small Song turned to look at Kelly Joe Burns.

The drug dealer slowly raised himself up and stood on the bunk with his back against the concrete blocks. "Hey, hey, wait a minute. I want my own cell."

I kept my eyes on Burns but tossed my voice over to the chief. "Anything available?"

She shrugged. "Not just now—housekeeping might have something later."

I turned back to him. "Looks like you've got a roommate for a while."

His hands came out, attempting to hold the air between himself and Artie. "Look, it was purely business. Clarence dealt in bud—that was all. Sometimes he ran short, and I'd front him product. That's all."

"That doesn't make any sense, Kelly. Why would the Feds be interested? It's not exactly high on their substance abuse table."

The drug dealer continued to keep his eyes on Small Song. "How the hell should I know; go ask them. What the fuck—you think they're pals of mine?"

Lolo's voice sounded from the hallway where she now stood. "That's okay, white boy, they're gonna be."

I joined her, and we started out.

"Hey, wait a minute!"

I turned and looked back at him—Artie had moved closer to

Kelly Joe and was now standing in front of the corner bunk where you could hear his fists clinching, the sound like bark tightening.

"What?"

"I could make you a list of users."

Chief Long crossed her arms. "Oh, you and the Federales are going to get along."

Small Song leaned in closer to him. "You scumbag."

"Artie?"

He turned his head and looked at me. I suppressed the smile that was growing on my lips and gestured for Small Song to move. "Give him a little room, Artie." I waited until he stepped away. "How is that going to help us, Kelly Joe?"

He seemed relieved to have even the smallest amount of breathing room. "It would be all the people that Clarence had anything to do with."

I turned to Lolo. "You think we can trust Mr. Burns in your offices if we give him a pencil and paper to make a list?"

She looked at him. "If we handcuff him to the radiator."

I turned back to the drug dealer. "You right- or left-handed?"

I joined my family at the Law Enforcement Center parking lot as they sunbathed in Henry's convertible. The Cheyenne Nation leaned against the front fender and pointed at a mark on the hood of the '59 Thunderbird about a quarter of an inch in length. "You scratched my car."

"I'll buy you some rubbing compound or one of those bulldog hood ornaments with the eyes that bug out and light up."

He closed his eyes, canting his head toward the sun's rays like some Algonquin sunflower, as he always did. "I understand you arrested Kelly Joe Burns?"

"The chief did."

The Bear silently applauded. "Bravo."

I looked at Cady, who was applying suntan lotion to her feet. "How was your discussion with Arbutis Little Bird?"

"I made a deal with her. They won't reschedule, but I convinced them that we could combine the wedding with the language immersion retreat."

Lena adjusted her sunglasses. "I am beginning to think that your daughter could litigate ice from an Eskimo."

I walked the rest of the way around Lola and looked at the two exquisite women, replete with bikini tops and suntan oil, towels lying over the reclined seats of the T-Bird. "A Cheyenne language immersion retreat and your wedding—how are you going to manage that?"

"It's going to be traditional, performed entirely in Cheyenne." Cady tipped her Prada sunglasses up and looked at me with her frank, gray eyes. "We convinced her that it was a wonderful opportunity for the students to experience the Cheyenne language in a unique context."

I glanced at Lena, who had yet to move. "How does the Moretti contingency feel about that?"

The mother-in-law-to-be rolled her head toward me. *"He'ehe'e, na-tsehese-nestse."*

I shook my head and watched the traffic on 212. "The two of you wouldn't want to work on this homicide case, would you?"

Cady removed her glasses completely but shaded her eyes with a hand. "I thought you arrested somebody?"

"We did, but it's the wrong guy."

A smile pulled at the corner of her mouth. "What about the drug dealer?"

"He's in the office making a list of known associates of the deceased, but I don't think he did it either."

"Sounds like you've got more real work to do."

"Yep, but . . ."

"We don't need you."

I was a little hurt. "At all?"

She caught my tone of voice and sat up, turning in the seat and pulling herself onto the sill, clutching onto my shirt in a playful manner. "I always *need* you, but I don't need you this afternoon if you've got things to do." She looked at the shirt in her fingers, especially the name PRETTY WEASEL. "Did you hire on?"

"I just needed a clean shirt."

"It's not that clean." She studied me, with the smile she reserved for me playing on her lips. "Repeat after me—*Na-he-stonahanotse.*"

"What does it mean?"

She was more emphatic this time. "Repeat—*Na-he-stonahanotse.*"

"*Na-he-stonahanotse.*"

She nodded at my pronunciation. "Good, now try this one: *E-hestana.*"

"*E-hestana.*"

"Now put them together."

I thought. "*Na-he-stonahanotse. E-hestana.* Now, what did I just say?"

"This is my daughter; he may take her."

Maybe it was the sun, maybe it was the lack of sleep, but I felt my knees give just a little bit. I swallowed and could feel my eyes well and just hoped that she wouldn't notice, but of course she did.

Her eyes softened, and she placed her head against my chest. "I'm getting married, Daddy."

I laughed, but it was short and choked in my throat. "Yep, I guess it just hit me." She pulled her head back, and I swept a wave of the strawberry blonde hair away, just a little damp from the sunbathing.

"You won't have to worry about me so much."

"Right."

She continued to smile. "I'm settling down and having a baby; things get easy from here on out, right?"

I shook my head. "Oh, yeah."

"We're stealing the Bear and going to Billings for supplies, but we'll be back tonight with another Moretti."

"The groom?"

She smiled. "*He'ehe'e*—I asked him if he could come early and help, and besides, I kind of miss him. The rest of the family is staying in Denver till the last hour so we don't have to worry as much about the rooms, which, by the way, were okay. Michael, Lena, Henry, you—we're all having dinner."

I glanced at the Cheyenne Nation as if I didn't know. "At Chez Bear?"

Cady retrieved her sunglasses. "Actually at the Charging Horse Casino if we don't get going. Could you make us a reservation, just in case, Dad?" She glanced at the clock in the T-Bird's dash. "You have six hours to catch a killer."

Lena Moretti was looking at me again. "No pressure."

Cady kissed my grizzled face and lowered herself back down, put on her shirt, and stretched the seat belt across her lap.

Part of me wanted to go, but I knew I'd be more help to Chief Long. "I don't have a vehicle."

The Cheyenne Nation pushed off the fender of the Thunderbird and turned to stand over the passenger-side door, his gaze tracking first to Lena Moretti and then to his truck parked behind the car. "I'll leave you Rezdawg."

He fished the keys from his pocket and tossed them to me, assorted fetishes, feathers, and all.

I couldn't believe he actually bothered to take the keys out of the thing.

I studied the fob in my hand and then looked at the rusting hulk. The bunch of them wheeled out of the parking lot, made a right, and headed for the big city.

"Like I said, I don't have a vehicle."

When I walked back into the Tribal Police office, Lolo Long was on her way out. "What are you doing here?"

I shrugged. "Abandoned."

"Good, you can come to KRZZ with me; Nate called and said that he's got more for us."

"What about Charles, Artie, Kelly Joe, and the impending euthanasia?"

"Mom brought over lunch, and she'll stay till we get back." She pulled a slip of paper from her shirt pocket and handed it to me.

"What's this?"

"The list of people on the medications that were on the old bracelet you found. The database only goes back about twelve months, but she said she would check and see who might have had anything critical before that that would have led to that amount of medication." She gestured toward the waiting GMC. "To the radio station?"

I raised a fist. "Stay calm, have courage, and wait for signs."

With the chief driving, we were there in three minutes. The same vehicles were parked, with the addition of Herbert's Cherokee. "I guess the morning drive guy finally showed up for the afternoon shift."

Lolo led the way in, and the Sudoku gamer pointed toward the production studios beyond. Bill Miller's *Ghost Dance* hovered in the speakers, and I could see Herbert His Good Horse wearing his signature mottled-gray top hat with the leather studded band stuck with the large eagle feather. He was in the on-air studio and turned and waved at us, pointing past the offices to an area where we hadn't been before.

We turned the corner—Nate was sitting in a stripped-down studio about the size of a walk-in closet, his head resting in his hands as he listened intently, a pair of hi-tech headphones over his ears. Chief Long stepped up behind him and casually placed her hands on his shoulders, causing the young man to leap up and turn around.

Lolo raised her arms, and we watched as he slipped the headphones off. "Jeez, you guys scared the crap out of me."

"Sorry." She smiled. "What's up?"

He stepped past us and started around the corner. "Hold on, let me get Herbert."

We stood there looking at the rock-and-roll posters of artists I certainly didn't know, and after a moment Nate reappeared with Herbert in tow. Nate pushed past us, and Herbert stuffed the rest of the room with himself before closing the door on the clown-car studio.

Nate cleared his throat. "This is pretty important." He stuck his hands in his pockets and looked worried.

Herbert gestured toward the young man. "Tell 'em."

"This tape . . ." Nate paused. "It's produced."

I shot a glance at Lolo, but she looked as confused as me. "What do you mean *produced?*"

His eyes flitted around in a nervous way. "The Feds made this recording. These two guys aren't even talking to each other."

Chief Long leaned into him. "What?"

"I was listening to the amplified tape, and I kept hearing these little bumps—you know, sounds between the people speaking.

It's really well done, but it's dubbed." He gestured toward the equipment behind him. "This conversation's been patched together—the Feds made this up, man."

He half-turned and hit a few keys on the computer—and Artie Small Song's and Clarence Last Bull's voices exploded through the speakers. He immediately turned the volume down. "I edited it so that you can listen to the transition points between them talking."

I listened carefully to the amplified version—and he was right.

Lolo Long's eyes were wide as she turned to me. "I can hear it."

"Yep, so can I."

Nate punched some more keys, and the music in the background leapt forward. "There's something else."

I listened for a moment. "*Ira Hayes*, I know. We checked the jukebox up at Jimtown, and it's not there."

Nate shook his head. "No, not that. Listen."

We all did, but it was Lolo who asked. "What are we listening for?"

"The lyrics."

The chief and I looked at each other and then at Nate. He gave us an exasperated look. "They're repeated."

We listened to the portion about the flag and throwing a dog a bone and then listened to it again.

Lolo laughed. "It's the chorus."

Nate frowned. "No, it's not, and even if it was it wouldn't be repeated that soon. Somebody dubbed the music in so that it would drown out the edits, but they didn't realize they were repeating those lyrics."

I glanced at Herbert, who had had a lifetime of experience in the field. "What do you think?"

He nodded his head and looked sad. "The kid came and got

me, and I listened to it a bunch of times. He's right; somebody put this recording together."

"Why would they do that?"

Nate was almost vibrating with energy. "It's the federal government, man—this is the kind of shit they do."

As one of the two people in the room with a badge, I didn't really want to be that voice of reason, but it seemed like somebody should say it. "Nate, that's kind of crazy."

"What do you mean?"

"I mean that if Cliff Cly thought there was anything fishy about this tape . . ." I paused for a moment, thinking about the AIC's flexible attitude concerning any kind of rule, which had resulted in his being here on the Rez in the first place.

Lolo studied me. "What?"

I took a deep breath and tried to flush the wacky idea from my system. "It doesn't make any sense. Why would the FBI be after Artie?"

"They've been after my brother for years, man. He's a warrior, and they've been trying to keep him down." He pulled the CD from the player. "We should go to the newspapers and get them to expose this."

I reached out and took the CD. "No, we're going to go play this for Cliff Cly and see what he has to say."

Nate pegged the needles. "Are you crazy? Those are the guys that did this, man!"

"Maybe, maybe not. Anyway, if Cliff had anything to do with it, us confronting him will pretty much stop this stuff in its tracks. If he doesn't know about it, then maybe he can help us figure out who did it."

"They'll burn the radio station down, right Herb?"

Herbert shrugged. "They could—I mean stuff like that happens all the time."

I looked to Lolo for a little support, unsure of what I was

going to do if she joined in with the conspiracy theory. "Chief Long?"

She looked at both Nate and Herbert. "You guys watch a lot of Fox News, don't you?"

Nate waved her remark away. "I'm serious; the black helicopters are going to come along and sweep you guys away, and Herb and I are going to be sitting up here at ground zero." If he'd had room he would've paced. "Audrey knew something so they killed her; then they killed Clarence to shut him up, and now they wanna pin it all on Artie."

I interrupted the rant. "What could Audrey have known?"

"I don't know; something."

I sighed. "This all sounds pretty crazy, Nate."

"Fine, go talk to your buddies at the FBI and see what they say." He waved a hand in my face. "Been nice knowing you."

I looked at Herbert, but he seemed to be concentrating on the floor. I stepped past him and opened the door. "C'mon, Chief, let's go."

Long followed, and we started out, making it to the reception area before Nate caught my arm. "Hey, look, if something does happen to you guys, what should I do?"

"Stay away from the windows."

I'd meant it as a joke, but I don't think he got it.

"How well do you know this Cliff Cly?" She was powering her way down the gravel road, the big V-8 yowling in protest.

"Like I said, I dealt with him out on the Powder River. He's not the most ethical of the bureau guys I've dealt with, but he gets results."

"Do you think Artie is one of his results?"

I braced my hand on the padded dash and could see where I was wearing an impression into the leather. "Well, it was strangely convenient how that tape showed up to seal the deal just when we needed it, but it seems, well, awkward."

She roared the GMC onto the asphalt and laid a strip of rubber that must've been a good ten feet long. The people on the sidewalks of Lame Deer ignored the racing Yukon as if it going down Main Street at sixty miles an hour was a daily occurrence; come to think of it, it probably was.

"You think we should take this to the head office in Salt Lake?"

I shook my head. "Mike McGroder? No, we'll give Cliff a chance to hear it and see what he has to say. Do you have any idea where he might be?"

She pulled the mic from her dash and hit the button. "Base, this is unit 1—anybody there?"

Static. "Unit 1, this is base. Over."

"Charles, do you have any idea where the AIC might be?"

Static. "Yeah, he was just here—picked up both Kelly Joe and Artie Small Song. He said he was taking them to Hardin for protective custody."

She glanced at me. "How long ago?"

Static. "Maybe five minutes."

I reached up and clicked on the light and sirens as the warrior chief four-wheel-drifted through the main intersection of Lame Deer, barely missing a delivery van and a Ford Explorer. By the time we got to the big ridge overlooking the separate lands of the Cheyenne and Crow we were doing a hundred and twenty.

The muscles at the side of her jaw bunched. "That settles it."

"Not necessarily."

"Bullshit! He forged the tape, and now he's trying to seal it up tight by taking Artie." She flung the Yukon around a sweeping corner, and I was pretty sure the inside wheels were off the ground. I glanced up at the integral roll bar and was slightly reassured. "It has to be."

When we hit the straightaway above Busby, not to be confused with Birney, white or red, you could see the caravan of federal vehicles approaching the gigantic Moncure teepee that had once been a gift shop and tourist trap located beside the town's general store.

Lolo's foot sank deeper into the SUV's throat, and I watched as the orange needle wound higher. By the time we approached the string of one Yukon, one Suburban, and the Expedition, I'm pretty sure we were only hitting the high spots on 212.

The chief launched past the rear vehicle, and I could see the surprised looks on the faces of the Feds as she blew by the second one and slid past the leading vehicle with her antilock brakes most assuredly locked.

We were still hanging out into the forward lane, clouded in blue smoke when the thing finally stopped, and I was just glad the airbags hadn't deployed. I unsnapped my belt, pushed the door open, and stepped onto scoria-colored asphalt.

Cly was the first out of a vehicle, and he stepped toward us with a hand on the Sig-Sauer at his hip, motioning to the agent who had been driving to lower his weapon as he came out the driver's side. He smiled at my appearance. "Hey, nice shirt. You decide to go Native?" He opened his arms to encompass the Little Big Horn country. "Good place for it, Kemosabe."

Lolo Long came around the back side of her unit and pointed a finger at Cly. "Where are my prisoners?"

The agent looked as if he'd been smacked. "What?"

I kept an eye on the driver as he lowered his weapon but did not reholster, as three more field agents showed up from the other two vehicles. They looked like a preppy barbershop quartet.

Long had made it to the front of the Suburban and actually kicked the front bumper. "I said where are my prisoners? You can hand over Kelly Joe and Nattie to the DEA or whoever, but you have no right to take Artie Small Song." She glanced at the other agents, who were wisely keeping their distance, self-preservation being a core class at the academy.

Cliff glanced at me with an odd look on his face and then pushed his sunglasses up on his wavy locks. "You're running a skeleton staff in a concrete block; I thought I'd do you a favor."

"I don't need your favors."

He looked at me again, spoke slowly, and with the Midwestern accent that Wade Barsad had had, said. "O-key."

She circled around to stand in front of him, and I think he was glad the open door was between them. "I'm running a homicide investigation, and you're trying to run off with my chief witness."

The agent looked at me again. "I thought he was the chief suspect."

"He was until we listened more carefully to your bullshit tape."

I watched him closely, and you could be mistaken about which side of the coin it was that Cliff Cly of the FBI had been playing, but he seemed genuinely very confused. "What are you talking about?"

"The phone recording is crap, and you know it."

An eighteen-wheeler slowed at the phalanx of official vehicles, the air brakes blowing out like an angry mechanical bull. The operator hung out the window to look at the drama unfolding. Lolo Long was momentarily distracted and shouted at the truck driver. "What are you looking at; you want me to check your logs or something?!"

The truck sped up, and I stepped a little closer to the epicenter of the conflict, hoping the chief would remember I was on her side. "Why don't we pull these vehicles over to the other side of the road and get this all straightened out?"

Long looked at me for a moment and then marched past to navigate the GMC into the gravel lot surrounding the derelict tourist attraction.

The Feds followed suit, and Cly told a couple of his boys to go get the rest of the agents a few soft drinks from the general store three hundred feet back. They disappeared, but the eyes of the remaining agents in the assorted vehicles watched us like we were trying to steal their collective bones.

Which at least one of us was.

"Play it again."

Lolo hit the button, and we listened to the remastered CD for the second time.

The expression on his face didn't change, but he disengaged himself from the vehicle and stood there, dusting the toe of his dress shoe on the back of a pant leg. After a moment he walked across the crumbling concrete pad and peered into the Moncure teepee, raised a hand, and pushed open the flapping screen door, which was held to the structure by half a hinge. "So, you think the recording has been doctored?"

The chief and I stood by the grille guard of her unit and watched him. "You heard it—what do you think?"

He didn't say anything but stepped forward and disappeared into the shingled structure, his voice echoing in the emptiness. "I heard this thing was built by the WPA, but I think that might be bullshit."

We listened as the resonance of his footfalls circled the inside, the FBI men watching. I pushed off the SUV, followed Cliff's path, and found him standing in the center, looking up at the blue sky, which was approaching the zenith of afternoon heat.

Lolo followed, and we watched Cly slip off his navy blazer—he continued to look through the openings where the shingles and roof underlayment had let go. "Why would the WPA build something like this? I mean a dam, a trail, a retaining wall I can understand—but a giant wood teepee? That doesn't make much sense."

I tipped my hat back and wiped the sweat from my forehead. "What's going on, Cliff?"

He walked to the side of the building and put a hand on a support as thick as a telephone pole; the one he had chosen was cracked and would someday give way, taking the southern portion of the structure with it. "To be honest . . ."

Long interrupted. "That'd be nice."

He smiled the matinee-idol smile he'd probably been using since junior varsity. "I don't know."

"Bullshit." Lolo took a step toward him, her face suddenly lit by the cascading beams of sunshine blasting through the openings like head lights. "Bullshit."

He sighed. "Honest Injun." He looked at me and then licked his lips like he was looking for the words. "Look, the tape was forwarded from a source in the BIA." He gestured toward the CD still in the player in Lolo's vehicle. "They seemed really fired up about it. Now, I don't know how they got it, or who they might've gotten it from. . . ."

"Bullshit." Chief Long wasn't buying it. "It's just too convenient, Agent—just too convenient."

He shook his head. "I thought the same thing, but the BIA guys are the goods; on the up and up, really."

She folded her arms. "Well, that leaves you."

"Chief?"

The two of them turned to look at the field agent standing in the doorway to my right.

"I'm sorry to interrupt, Chief Cly, but I got you a Coke."

The AIC walked over and took the can, then dismissed the lesser agent with a curt nod. Cly turned to look at us, the soda dangling in his hand. "So let me get this straight, Chief Long—you're accusing me of all this?"

"Who would you accuse?"

He glanced at me and then back to her. "Look, I know I've got a somewhat checkered past, but do you really think I would do something like this?"

She didn't say anything, and I had just started to when he spoke.

"Ouch." He started to open the can but then didn't; instead he just stared at the pull tab. "That hurts, Chief."

He continued on through the battered screen door, carefully closing it for comic effect. Then he stuck a forefinger and pinkie in the sides of his mouth and blew out a whistle that loosened a few more shingles.

A chorus of doors opened in the Fed vehicles out front. "All right, people, listen up. As is the plight of the white man in Indian country, our wagons have been surrounded and we are going to give up our prisoners."

Lolo glanced at me and then back to him. "What does . . . ?"

"You want one; you get 'em all." The agents were smiling as they opened the rear doors and began unlocking the prisoners. It was all great fun.

I shook my head at him. "C'mon, Cly."

He ignored me, tucked the can of Coke under his arm, and clapped his hands. "Let's go, we've got lunch at Walkers Grill in Billings—the federal government is buying."

There were mild cheers as they walked Kelly Joe and Nattie in their traveling chains toward the chief's Yukon. They needed to make a little more effort into getting Artie Small Song from the Expedition, since he'd been heavily drugged.

"Thorazine."

Kelly Joe was the first to poke his head back out the door and ask. "Hey, what's going on?"

Cly shrugged. "You've been remanded from our responsibility, Mr. Burns. I guess they're going to take you back to Lame Deer." He turned to look at Lolo. "Are you taking them back to Lame Deer?"

She looked at him, defiant till the end. "Yes."

He made a big show of slapping his forehead. "Oh, wait, I forgot. With the amount of controlled substances these two had on them the charges were upped and they have to be transported to a federal facility and the closest one would be Hardin."

I stepped in close and looked down at Cly as they tried to get the limp and drooling Artie Small Song into the passenger side of the Yukon, Nattie having taken up more than her third of the bench seat. Finally, and with great enjoyment, the agents decided to just dump Artie in the rear cargo space.

Kelly Joe's voice sounded from inside. "Hey, can I get some of what you gave him?"

"Cliff . . ." He wouldn't meet my eyes and watched as his men closed the hatch on the drugged Artie. "This isn't right; we brought this to you."

He pointed a finger at me. "You know, Sheriff, I thought we had an understanding. I know you're pretty much a by-the-book guy and I'm not, but we're both on the same side and we get results." He started to say something else, then thought better of it, and started off again. He slid in the gravel, and his voice struck the hard, sun-baked ground. "I owe you my life, but I don't owe you my reputation." He handed the can to Lolo Long as he passed. "Here, Babe, have a Coke and a smile."

15

Lolo Long chugged her Coke and looked out the driver's-side window at me standing there in the Law Enforcement Center's parking lot, a place where I was making a habit of saying good-bye to beautiful women.

She pulled the pop can from her lips. "I figure I should enjoy it—it may be the last thing the federal government gives me." She considered the can. "Along with whatever communicable diseases Cly might have."

Kelly Joe and Nattie were still in the back, comfortably dozing in the Yukon's air-conditioning. "Two hours round-trip?"

"I can do it faster."

"Please don't." She laughed, and I placed my forearms on the sill and twirled the ring that was still on my little finger. "That'll put you back here this evening; come have dinner with us."

She shook her head. "I can't. I've got too much to think about, and besides, I've got to go find a killer."

I started to open my mouth, but she spoke quickly. "I know you didn't want any part of this from the beginning, but you helped me, and then I thought you were feeding me to the Feds when they came up with the tape, but you didn't. I really appreciate that and, whether you know it or not, I've learned a lot from you in the last week." She tightened her grip around my forearm where I'd rolled up my sleeves.

"I wasn't much help; as a matter of fact, I think I made the situation worse."

She shook her head. "No, you didn't." She averted her eyes to the windshield and the glare of the late-afternoon sun, her words taking on a note of finality. "You're probably right about me not being fit for this job, and I probably won't be able to keep it, but it was nice to get a taste of what it can be like." Her breath wavered in her throat. "I want to thank you for that."

I thought about how this was not how it was supposed to end, with her providing cab service for the Feds and me walking away. In a perfect cinematic world we would've captured the bad guys in spectacular fashion with explosions, car chases, and a parting kiss. She would've been played by Ava Gardner, and I would've been played by Robert Taylor.

I looked at her. "I was wrong."

She looked back at me, and I could feel her eyes on the side of my face.

"You're going to make a great cop if you stick to it." I turned back and tried not to let the sickle-shaped scar draw my attention like a tide. "Don't let them run you off your patch; you can do a lot of good here."

Her eyes stayed level, and there was no irony in her response. "Thanks." She patted my arm. "I'll see you around, Sheriff." She pulled the gear lever down. "Who knows, I might need a job."

I watched as the GMC whipped from the parking lot and headed out for the territories west. I was thinking about a lot of things and felt that strange feeling—like a thought that needed scratching, the one I couldn't reach—but the final thought before I started to wrestle with the starter on my nemesis was that I was hungry. The next thought was that I didn't have anybody to have delayed lunch with when it dawned on me that I did.

He was still waiting by the hospital bed when I came to get him, but his charge was fast asleep in the crib. His tail thumped the floor, and his mouth lolled open with an inviting smile.

Lolo's mother stood by me with a clipboard under her arm as we watched Adrian move once, place a tiny hand by his head, and relax again.

I spoke softly, like I was in church. "He's a quiet kid; the only time I ever heard him cry was when somebody threw him off a cliff."

She looked at me for a moment, possibly unused to cop humor, and then nodded. "I think he's cried three times since he's been here. At feeding time or changing his diapers, you come in and he's just looking around like he's taking in the place. Audrey used to bring him to work with her, and nobody complained because he was such a good little guy." She walked over to the crib and arranged the blanket, her hand lingering on the child. "I was out putting some things in my car and saw Lolo pulling out hell bent for leather, not that she drives any other way."

"She's headed for Hardin but said she'd be back later this evening. I think the federal agencies are going to pull the plug on our homicide investigation."

Hazel looked sad and answered in a low voice, our conversation taking on a conspiratorial quality. "That's not going to make Lo happy; she's really enjoyed working with you, and I don't think she's enjoyed much of anything else since she's gotten back."

"What's the story on her husband—Kyle is it? And her son?"

"Danny. Oh, I go see them up in Billings every other weekend."

I studied her. "And Lolo doesn't?"

"No. I'm not sure what to make of it, but I'm hoping that over time she'll work whatever it is out." The baby clutched Hazel's finger. "I've gotten to the age where I try and let people solve their own problems."

"What age is that, anyway?" My eyes returned to the orphan, and I was overwhelmed by the odds against the little guy. "Do you have any idea where Adrian's going to go?"

She sighed. "Not really. There's Audrey's sister, but . . . Herbert His Good Horse is the godfather, and he's been so sweet in coming in and checking on him, but I don't see him as the adoptive father type. I don't know. Maybe I'll see if I can get him."

My eyes came up from the baby to her face.

She caught my gaze. "I'm pretty good at raising children, even with Lo's present problems, just in case you haven't noticed."

"I have."

"Anyway, you better get out of here. Don't you have a wedding to plan?"

"Oh, the wedding juggernaut appears to be staggering forth on its own weight and took off toward Billings for supplies and the groom. My daughter arrived and took charge. I was released on my own recognizance." I laughed gently. "I've been finding myself in that position a lot lately."

She gently pulled her finger away from Adrian and joined me at the foot of the crib. "It must be hard with your wife gone."

"Yep, it is. All I can think about is how much Cady looks like Martha and all the things that Martha would've wanted to tell her. Hell, I can't remember to tell her all the things I want to tell her. Every time I look at her and realize what's happening, I just choke up."

Hazel gripped my arm and put on a voice tinged with brio. "Get a grip on yourself, man. It's only a wedding." She pulled a slip of paper from the clipboard under her arm. "I gave Lo a list of the individuals who were prescribed all or most of the medications that were listed on the medical bracelet you found, but I found a few more."

I looked at the piece of paper, and there were more than forty names on the list. "Brother." I scanned down the lines, my eye catching on Lonnie Little Bird. "Lonnie?"

"He went through a bad period when he lost his legs."

I continued reading—Running Wolf, Lone Bear, American Horse, Bear Comes Out, Big Hawk, Bobtail Horse, Buffalo Horn, Red Fox, Crazy Mule, Eagle Feathers, Elk Shoulder, Fire Crow, Little Coyote, Magpie, Old Mouse . . . but nothing from the menagerie struck me. I folded the piece of paper and placed it in my breast pocket. "Well, it was worth a try."

She pulled me toward the door. Smiling, I gestured toward the brute. "You mind if I take my dog to a late lunch?"

She went back to watching the baby. "Not at all, just have him back here by tonight; I sleep easier knowing he's in here with the little guy."

I patted my leg, and the monster rose from the floor rear-end first, stretching and yawning with a terrifying show of teeth. "C'mon, I'll buy you a cheeseburger."

He wagged, which I took as a yes.

When we got outside to Rezdawg, Dog sat on the concrete parking lot and looked at me. "I know, but it's all we've got." I opened the door, but he continued to look at me. "C'mon." With a look of resignation, he made the leap to the shower curtain–covered seat, the very picture of fallen dignity. I closed the door and went around and climbed in the driver's side. "Don't worry; I'll get our truck back. I promise."

I hit the starter and, predictably, nothing happened.

The GEN and OIL lights glowed feebly back at me, and I

looked at Dog in apology. "As much as you hate this truck, I hate it more."

I climbed out, unhooked the rubber straps behind the grille, pinched my finger into a blood blister with the hood latch, and finally got the thing open long enough for it to close onto the back of my head. I pushed it up again, with more effort and a little anger this time, reset my hat, and stood outside its jaws long enough to make sure the hood would stay up.

Relatively sure I wasn't going to get snapped again, I wiggled the corroded positive clamp on what had to be the original AUTOLITE STA-FUL battery and thought I'd be happy if the damn thing just STA-CHARGED. The greenish-white buildup on the lug fell away just enough for the worn bare part of the cable to turn and rub against the inner fender and shoot sparks around the engine bay, my hand held in an electrified death grip.

I yanked away and stood there holding my fingers and restrained myself from kicking the grille guard, sure if I did that it would release the parking brake and the three-quarter-ton would roll over me. Then I remembered it didn't have a parking brake and went ahead and kicked it.

When we pulled up to the Charging Horse Casino, which I had decided was as good for late lunch as anywhere, there was no shade in the parking lot, so, even if I wanted to leave Dog, which I didn't, I couldn't. He followed me up the concrete ramp to the door where an aged Cheyenne with an impressive ponytail and a black silk jacket with a security badge stopped us with an extended hand.

He looked at me for a moment but then let his hand fall. "Hello, Walt."

"Mr. Black Horse."

The older man, who had been my sponsor at the peyote meeting that seemed like years ago, dropped a hand down to Dog's level so that the beast could sniff at it and then lay a lick on him that covered the width of Albert's knuckles. "I'm afraid there are no dogs allowed in the casino."

"How about service dogs?"

Albert looked down at the behemoth.

"He outgrew his vest."

Albert smiled and scratched behind a red, brown, and black ear. "How about I let you take him into the Bingo Hall? There's nobody in there, and I can get Loraine to serve you at the back commissary window."

"Sounds like a deal."

He ushered us through the discordant music of the one-armed bandits and deposited us at the counter in the cavernous room in the rear. The place was as big as a gymnasium, complete with a scoreboard the size of a ballpark's, and what must've been a hundred event tables with folding chairs.

After a moment the gate rolled up, and Loraine Two Two smiled at me and even at Dog. "I see you took the precaution of eating almost alone this time?"

I laughed and looked down at the furry face. "Oh, he'll get his share. As a matter of fact, I was thinking that I'd order him up his own. They've been feeding him dry food over at the health center, and I figured he was about due a hamburger."

She looked concerned. "Was he hurt?"

"Nope, he's been standing guard over Adrian Last Bull."

Her eyes melted. "I'll see that he gets a double helping."

Albert Black Horse came around the corner and took a stool on the other side of Dog, then reached out and rubbed the beast's head. "The afternoon guy is here, so I thought I'd come back, rest my dogs, and eat my late lunch with you, if you don't mind?"

"Speaking for the both of us, we are delighted to have your

company." Turning back to Mrs. Two Two, I ordered up a double cheeseburger for me, a couple of patties for Dog, and anything Albert wanted, along with some iced teas.

"I'll take one of those Mexican salads. Watching my heart."

Loraine smiled and disappeared into the kitchen, and I stared at him. "You were the previous tribal chief of police?"

"I was, in the sixties and seventies, then was appointed interim for a short period up until a few months ago."

I nodded. "You were pretty good buddies with my old boss Lucian?"

"I was. How is he doing?"

"Busy as a one-legged man at an ass-kicking convention."

He extended his hand in a more formal manner this time, and I shook it. "I've known about you for years, Sheriff. You made a big impression on my people with your efforts in the Little Bird case."

"Thank you." I thought about it. "Correct me if I'm wrong, but wasn't Eddie Bailor the chief up here for the last eighteen years?"

"He was, and then I was the interim chief for a few months until they could find a suitable replacement." He reached down and ruffled Dog's hair. "I guess the previous Elder Chief decided I was too old to have the job on a permanent basis again."

"That would be the Elder Chief who gave Lolo Long the job?"

"Yes."

"The one who was indicted along with Bailor?"

He nodded with a sad smile. "Yes."

"How come you didn't stick on as a patrolman?"

"They had a full compliment of officers, and there were no openings."

Loraine brought us out a brace of iced teas; I thanked her and thumbed the straw into my mouth. "Well, that's certainly not the case now."

He continued to smile, but this time it took on a mischievous, foxlike look. "I heard she fired the entire department."

"She did."

He shrugged and smiled, shaking his head. "Probably for the best; they were a bunch of lazy bastards."

"You should go back."

He sipped his own tea. "To what?"

I pointed to my shirt, especially the name tag. "The job."

He studied me. "You join up?"

"Nope, I'm just on loan on a temporary basis." I watched him and could see the thought traveling around there bumping against the ceilings of his mind like a benevolent honeybee.

"No, I'm too old to be wrestling drunks and getting hit in the back of the head with wine bottles on domestic disturbances. Anyway, I got shot a while back; they patched me up, but . . . I think I lost my enthusiasm."

"She needs help."

A stillness overtook him, the stillness that only Natives can do—like a breeze of cedar smoke, it blows through their bodies and becomes a nontangible thing, almost as if they become completely invisible.

"She's going to be a good cop, but after this week I'm going to be gone and she could use a little guidance."

He broke the spell by speaking. "I don't know if I would make a very good patrolman—I was chief for so long." He glanced up at Loraine and then to me. "And I know it's wrong, but I've never worked for a woman."

Loraine stifled a laugh.

I squelched a little chuckle of my own. "Are you married, Albert?"

"Thirty-two years."

"Then don't worry about it."

He smiled some more. "Nobody wants an old broken-down Indian cop."

"Well, I don't know if you've noticed, but people aren't exactly knocking down the doors over at the Law Enforcement Center." I sipped my tea. "I'll give you a recommendation, if you need it."

He nodded some more. "She has a reputation."

"Yes, she does, and I'm sure we do, too."

He changed the direction, if not the subject. "How goes the investigation into the two deaths?"

I was reticent, but if he was willing to bring up the subject in front of Loraine, it was fine by me. "You already know about Clarence?"

"Moccasin telegraph."

"The Feds laid a trump card onto us with a recording of a conversation where Clarence Last Bull tries to hire Artie Small Song to kill his wife and child, but there's been some doubt cast on its validity."

"By who?"

"Nate Small Song and Herbert His Good Horse."

"They would know."

There was a cry from the kitchen, and Loraine left for a moment and then reentered, balancing three plates with rolls of silverware in her hands. "Who gets the half-cooked mound of ground beef?"

I glanced down. "Oh, you lucky Dog." I took the plate and watched as the brute froze. "You take off my hand, and I'm never bringing you gambling again." Sensing my tone of voice, he promptly sat. I lowered the plate as if I were submerging my hand into crocodile-infested waters; he waited and then dove in.

Albert and I began eating as Loraine disappeared into the kitchen only to come back with a pitcher of iced tea. I would've just as soon had the old police chief to myself to discuss the recent happenings, but I wasn't going to send her away. I'd had my say in trying to enlist the man and changed the subject. "What did you do in the interim, Albert, between service?"

He chewed his salad. "Worked construction, was a jack-leg electrician, plumber, you name it. I built most of the offices over at the tribal headquarters."

"It's an impressive building."

"State of the art, or was about ten years ago." He sipped his tea. "Back in the economic heyday, after 9/11, we got all this extra Patriot Act money and put in an entire audio/visual security system."

I thought about it. "Is it still in operation?"

He shook his head at his plate. "No. Most of the equipment wasn't kept up, and the added expense of having somebody in the security crow's nest just wasn't feasible. Now they just have a desk in the middle of the hallway."

"Barrett Long?"

Albert nodded. "He's a good kid, but boy he gives that sister of his hell."

I smiled. "He's a pistol."

Loraine's voice joined in with the hush of gossip. "He's also a rounder." She looked embarrassed. "He's a very handsome young man."

"Gets around, huh?"

She shrugged. "He was after my daughter for a while, but I put a stop to that."

I thought about Clarence but figured the best thing to do was let dead men lie.

"He was even flirting with Audrey Plain Feather when she and Clarence were having their problems."

Albert glanced up at her but remained silent.

She noticed his look and was immediately apologetic. "I don't mean anything. I mean, he's there in the building and flirts with everything in a skirt." She smiled in a nervous way. "He looks good in a black T-shirt." She stood there for a moment more, then refilled our glasses. "I'd better go check on the kitchen."

Albert watched her go, silently shook his head, and brought his eyes over to mine. "And you want me to get involved with all that again?"

I thought about how much of my six hours to break this case were gone and what I could do between now and dinner. "Maybe sooner than you suspect." I sipped my tea and rested the glass back in the perfect circle of condensation on the counter and then picked up my burger. "You wouldn't happen to have a set of old keys to Tribal Headquarters, would you, Albert?"

It wasn't easy to break into the Northern Cheyenne Tribal Headquarters since the damn thing was completely surrounded by roads, parking lots, and dusk-to-dawn lights. We'd parked Rezdawg at the rear of the building with an unhappy Dog sitting on the bench seat; it was going to be difficult enough to go about breaking and entering without being accompanied by a prairie grizzly.

Albert Black Horse sorted through a ring of keys that looked like a holiday wreath. "It's one of those square-head, do-not-duplicate ones; I always keep one of them."

I stood with my back to him in order to provide a blind and keep a lookout. "Wise decision." After a few moments, I asked. "Any luck?"

"I think Long might've changed the locks." There was a jostling. "Nope, got it."

I listened as the heavy security door swung wide, just as an aged Plymouth rolled by with about a hundred people in it. They stared at me, and I waved, figuring a bold crook is a successful crook. After they'd chugged around the swerve in the road, I turned and followed Albert.

"Something?"

I shook my head and carefully closed the metal door. "A war party in a minivan, but I think we're safe. What are they going to do, call the police?"

He nodded. "They could call the FBI."

"They're busy having dinner in Billings."

"The BIA?"

"There's that. Do you have any friends over there?"

He smiled with the one corner of his mouth. "A few, but not many—they're all from other tribes."

It was true, the BIA was staffed mostly with members of other tribes. I followed him through a hallway I didn't know existed, and we approached a stairwell. "The crow's nest is in the basement?"

"Yeah, more like a crow hole." Albert called over his shoulder as we went down the steps to open a second door. We turned right into another hallway that ran lengthways underneath the building with storage spaces and adjacent utility rooms. Albert reached over and flipped on the lights, bare bulbs hanging from conduit holes along the metalwork in the ceiling. "I don't think we have to worry about being seen down here."

He walked along the hallway with his shoulders stooped, stopping in front of a nondescript door with a small, wire-mesh window. It looked like there had been an identifying plaque on it, but all that was left was the adhesive where the sign had been.

Albert fumbled with more keys as I leaned against the concrete wall. "Sounds like Loraine Two Two doesn't care for Barrett Long."

"Loraine Two Two doesn't care for anybody who shows an interest in Inez, and that would be about half the tribe."

"The male half?"

"Pretty much, but that kid." He shook his head as he turned a key in the lock. "She's a tough one." He pushed the door open with a scraping sound from the hinges, noisy from lack of use. "Here we go."

He brushed a hand along the wall, and I heard a switch being flipped but it was unaccompanied by illumination.

"Damn it." I heard him shuffle closer to me. "Hold the door open, and I'll steal a bulb from the hallway."

I watched as he went out, licked his fingers, and reached up to untwist one of the bulbs, only to let it escape from his grip and pop on the concrete floor with a surprisingly loud sound. I glanced at the army of retreating lights. "Looks like there are plenty more to choose from."

He nodded, advanced on the next one, and was more careful this time. Cradling the bulb in his hand as he entered the room, he undid the old bulb, handed it to me, and screwed in the borrowed one. The room flashed into view and so did the dust and cobwebs of the abandoned security center. There was a single chair, a counter, and small monitors in a shelf system, along with a rack of recording decks that looked as if they might've never been used.

"Looks like you were right; nobody's been in this place in years."

"Do you mind if I ask what it is you are looking for?"

I took a few steps toward the rolling chair, placed the burnt-out bulb on the counter, and studied the monitors that studied me back like gigantic, myopic eyes. "Nothing, really, I was just thinking."

There was a portion of one of the audio recording decks where some of the dust had been wiped away, as if by accident. I reached behind it and nudged it forward—something brushed against the back of my hand. I caught a couple of cables. "Should these be unplugged?"

He shrugged. "They're just the usual RCA cables, stereo— one red and one white, and this place hasn't been used in years." He paused for a moment and then fingered the end where another Y-shaped cable joined the other two and combined them into one small, thin junction plug. "Hmm."

"What is it?"

He ignored me and leaned around the side in order to study the back and then turned with a puzzled look on his face. "It's disconnected from the junction box, but that's not the only funny part; that splicer on there is to connect the cables into a modern computer."

I fingered the cable end. "You didn't have anything like this back when you wired the place?"

"No, this is a USB connector." He glanced up at me. "You don't know a lot about computers, do you?"

"Next to nothing." I looked at the monitors. "Albert, are the audio and visual surveillance systems connected or separate?"

"Separate; we had a lot of money back then but not that much."

"Is every office in the building wired for sound?"

He shook his head. "No, just the communal areas."

"Like reception?"

"Yes."

I held up the cables. "Are these the ones connected to Human Services?"

"I don't know."

"Is there any way to find out?"

He shrugged. "Sure, there should be a location code on the junction box, and then we just need the code off of the mic at the reception desk." He leaned behind the rack and ran a hand up the wall to a large, open junction box in the ceiling. His eyes raced down the small black and white labels. "R-7."

I was about to speak when it sounded like one of the heavy metal doors to the stairs opened and, after a few seconds, closed. Albert and I froze, looking at each other and then toward the audio room door which we'd lodged open.

Albert looked more worried than me. "Should we close that door and turn off the light?"

"We're the good guys." I listened, but there weren't any more sounds. "But maybe we can catch a bad guy."

He nodded, went to the doorway, and peered around the corner, then turned back to me. "Should I go down the hall the other way and up those stairs, double back and come down behind them?"

I pulled the .45 from the small of my back. "Do you have a weapon?"

He reached under his black satin jacket and held out one of those antiquated, garage-door-opener style Tasers. "I have this."

I looked at the thing doubtfully. "Well, let's hope it's not a gunfight."

He nodded solemnly, went down the hall the other way, quickly made a right, and disappeared. I could hear him climb the stairs. As he moved away, I flipped off the switch in the security room.

Albert was gone for about a minute when the rest of the lights also went out.

I edged to the doorway and kneeled, placing my shoulder against the jamb. It sounded as if someone was moving to the left, the grit of the hard floor twisting underneath leather soles.

My eyes closed, because there wasn't anything to see there in the subterranean part of the rambling complex, and I wanted to give my ears all of my attention. Whoever was out there was out there in the dark along with me, and it was also possible that he didn't care for the thought of bullets ricocheting in the confined, concrete area any better than I did.

I heard the sound of footfalls again, but this time it was farther away, and I got the feeling that whoever it was, he had gotten to a certain point and was now retreating.

I edged farther into the hallway and listened. It wasn't as if he didn't know somebody was down here, and it wasn't as if he didn't know that I knew he was there. The big question was whether he was armed.

I clicked off the safety on the big Colt, the noise echoing through the darkness. There was no metallic mating call, so either they were unarmed or already in a position to fire.

I leaned out a little farther and could hear someone carefully retreat. I was momentarily distracted by an unpleasant smell but then slowly raised myself from the crouching position, stood, and listened to make sure I was hearing what I thought I was. Satisfied, I took a step and softly moved forward in the darkness on the balls of my cowboy boots. I got halfway down the hall and crunched the broken glass of the forgotten lightbulb.

Every muscle in my body seized as I waited for the incoming bullet.

After about forty seconds, I heard a slight sound and raised the Colt in my hand, aiming it toward the faint glow coming through the tiny window in the door leading to the stairwell where we'd descended.

In one flash of movement, the door was yanked open and somebody threw himself through the opening and let the door slam behind him.

I launched myself and ran down the hall as fast as my limited visibility would allow. I glanced off the wall, caught my balance, and turned right to claw at the handle with my free hand, finally getting some fingers wrapped around it and throwing it open.

Someone's boots pounded up the concrete steps, and I followed at full speed, making the landing in two strides. I raised the Colt and took aim at the individual who had his back to the door, his empty hands outstretched toward me. "Don't shoot!"

I looked at Barrett Long. "What the hell are you doing?"

He looked as if his heart might explode from his chest as one hand was placed over it, the other coming up to clutch his forehead. "What the hell are *you* doing?"

I lowered the .45 and held out an open hand in supplication. "Investigating."

His voice was hoarse and whistled in his throat in exasperation as he tried to catch his breath. "In the dark?"

"Sorry."

He looked around, possibly for his breath. "Jesus."

I holstered the Colt, more than a little relieved that most likely the possible shooting part of the evening was over. "I'm here with Albert Black Horse. I had an idea and wanted him to show me the old security room."

He breathed for a moment. "Why didn't you just ask me?"

"I didn't figure you were around."

"I wasn't actually, but I got a call from Karl Red Fox and some friends of mine who said they thought they might've seen somebody breaking into the building."

"That'd be us."

"Jesus." He took a few more deep breaths. "Is my sister with you?"

"No, she had to make a run to Hardin."

"So, who's with you again?"

"Albert Black Horse."

"The casino guy?"

"And retired police chief."

"Jesus."

"Let's go find him before he Tasers somebody."

The young man turned and pushed the bar on the heavy door, but it didn't budge. He paused for a second and then pushed on it again, this time with a great deal of force, but the thing didn't move. "Shit."

"What?"

He slammed an open palm against it, the echo filling the stairwell. "The damn thing must've locked when I came through."

I stepped next to him and tried pushing on the lever, but it still didn't move. "That's strange; this is a fire door, and they're supposed to always stay open out."

"The building's closed."

I shook my head. "Doesn't matter."

"It's no big deal—there are three more exits in the basement; we just have to go down and come up another stairwell."

I pushed off and started down the steps. "All right, but let's hurry; I don't want Albert to think that something's happened—I don't think his heart can take it."

Barrett clomped down the steps behind me as I opened the basement door and walked through, my hand still clutching it when I stopped and jammed the doorway with my bulk.

The young man ran into the back of me as I stood there. "Jesus." He stood still for a moment and then coughed. "Why'd you stop?"

I didn't move. "Do you smell that?"

"Yeah . . . Smells like fart." I ignored him, and he coughed again before leaning forward into the hallway. "What is that?"

I bent down, sniffing the air at a lower level. "Propane—a lot of it."

16

If the overwhelming smell of the compressed, three-carbon-alkane, one-and-a-half-times-heavier-than-air compound was now at waist height, there was enough propane in the substantial basement to choke us to death, if not blow us to the moon if ignited.

Barrett made a face. "Gas leak?"

"Either that or somebody drove a propane delivery truck into the basement and opened the hatch." I looked around. "Where are the other exits?"

He pressed himself against the door. "Four corner stairwells and two central on either side, but we should go back up and force this door open."

"It's a three-inch metal security door; if it's been locked on the outside then there's no way we're getting out."

"You think somebody locked it?"

"I don't know, but Albert Black Horse was down here with me and went upstairs to check the mic designation in the Human Services office, and he didn't come back."

Barrett stayed planted. "You've got your gun; you could shoot the lock."

I holstered my .45 and explained. "With the amount of propane flooding into this basement, discharging a weapon would most assuredly blow us to hell and not necessarily back." I did a few calculations. "Barrett, this basement is filling with propane, a highly flammable gas that sinks; pretty soon we're not going to be able to breathe because the oxygen it replaces will be gone. Now, that's the least of our problems, because if this gas reaches an ignition point like a pilot light or any kind of open flame, this entire basement is going to be like the ass end of a Saturn-V rocket."

I started off again but then turned and looked at him and then down the hallway at the lightbulb filaments. "Whatever you do, don't turn on any light switches or anything else for that matter."

"You think Albert did this to us?"

I sighed, coughed, and breathed in more of the gas as we made our way down the hallway where the smell was even greater. "I don't know, but somebody's killing people around here and one of the key elements for pinning it on Artie Small Song is that doctored recording. I've got a suspicion that Artie's side of that recording was made with the security mics in Human Services."

"The old security recording system?"

"You got it."

He'd caught up. "When he had that blowup with Audrey?"

"I'd avoid using the term blowup, considering our current situation."

He shook his head. "There aren't any fire sources down here; they're all up in the utility areas."

"That's not what concerns me."

"What, then?"

We arrived at the central stairwell. "I'll tell you if the doors at the top of these stairs are locked, too."

We hustled up the steps, and it was with a great deal of resignation that I pushed down on the latch. I pushed again, just to make sure, but there was only a little movement and the doors wouldn't open. "Damn."

Barrett stepped in as I peered through the small, rectangular windows and down at the bars on the other side, securely chained together with a heavy padlock. He shoved as hard as he could, but the two doors only budged open about an inch.

"Barrett, do they normally chain the security doors together when the building is closed?"

His eyes were widening a little as the realization of our predicament started settling in. "No, never. It's against the law." He went up on tiptoe again to look down at the heavy chains wrapped around the bars on the other side. "Jesus."

I nodded. "Like rats."

"We gotta get to another door."

"They're all going to be locked."

His hands slammed against the solid surface. "Then we gotta get this one open."

I looked up and could see that the doors were hinged from the other side. "Is there any way out of the basement other than the doors? Utility hatches, air ducts, dumbwaiters?"

"I don't know." He took a deep, polluted breath. "We're safe, right? I mean, if all the doors are locked then there's no way that anybody could light the gas."

"Sure they could; all you'd have to do is drill a hole in the floor and drop a match into the basement. Of course, they have to figure out how to get away before the explosion."

"Then why don't we just stay up here above the propane?"

"Because if that gas ignites, it's going to expand and take out every door in the place, probably with parts of us, and I don't mean gently."

"Then what are we going to do?"

I chewed on the inside of my cheek. "I'm trying to figure that out, if you'd stop asking questions." I thought back to the conversation I'd had with Albert about the sordid history of the structure. "Is this building sitting on top of the original tribal headquarters that burnt down twice?"

"Yeah, part of it."

"Do you have any idea how they used to heat that building back in the sixties and before?"

He shook his head but then pointed at it. "Duh, the one thing we have plenty of on the Rez—coal."

I nodded. "That means there's a coal chute back there some-where if it hasn't been filled in and sealed off."

I watched as he thought about it. "Like a cellar."

"Yep."

"It's there; I mean the doors are."

As we gingerly made our way down the steps and opened the door at the bottom, we could tell the limited airspace in the base-ment was filling with even more of the gas. "Same rules; don't flip any switches and stay clear of those lightbulbs—you break one and we're dead."

We ignored the stairwell doors at the southeastern corner of the building, and we could see where the poured concrete walls changed to block. By the time we got to the rear of the building, it had changed once again to a slip-form foundation with large rocks imbedded in the concrete.

There was a section of the wall with T-111 siding sealing off the opening. "Is this it?"

Barrett nodded his head. "Yeah, but don't you think it's sealed?"

"One way to find out." I pulled my Case XX from my pocket, slipped it between the thin sheath of wood, and pried loose a cor-ner, revealing the stud wall underneath. I placed a hand up to the opening. "I feel warm air."

I wrapped my fingers around the paneling and pulled it loose, yanking it with a little more urgency. "C'mon, help me."

"What if a nail scratches the concrete?"

"Let's try to make sure that that doesn't happen, shall we?"

Once we'd worked the plywood loose, we could see the facing

on the other side, along with the cobwebs where the wall had been undisturbed for decades. I pushed at the top and was able to smell the freshness of clean air, spread my fingers across the splintering wood, and forced it on top of the poured concrete they had used to fill the open space behind the wall. I braced a boot against one of the two-by-fours and lodged a shoulder in the opening just enough to give me the leverage I needed to pull the stud loose from the header. "It's been filled in, but there's room at the top where you might be able to squeeze through."

"What about you?"

I shook my head. "I'm too big, I'll never fit."

"What are you going to do?"

"Wait for you to come back and get me out of here." I laced my hands in a stirrup to give him a boost up. "C'mon, we're wasting time."

"What if I don't find a way?"

I smiled. "You will."

He placed his hiking boot into my hands, and I lifted him up to where he could flatten out and climb onto the surface of the concrete where there was about eighteen inches of space. "What if I can't get the cellar doors open; what if they're chained, too?"

"Are the doors old or new?"

"Old."

"Then break the wood."

I listened as he crawled through, carefully avoiding the nails, and slithered into the darkness. "I can see the light where the doors come together."

I waited and listened as he grunted with the strain of attempting to push them open. "They're locked or something but it gives, so let me give it a try with my legs." The sound of his exertions was accompanied by the noise of splintering wood, as a little more air broke through. "I got it, it broke the clasp, and I think I can make it. Where should I meet you?"

"The nearest stairwell to the left, the southeast corner. Find something to cut the chain or break the padlock." I thought about it. "And call your sister. Hell, call everybody."

"I thought this was a covert operation?"

"Not anymore."

He laughed, and I listened as he kicked more of the wood away.

"Anything else?"

"Find the propane tank and turn it off."

"Okay."

"And Barrett? Be careful."

"I will."

He didn't say anything else, and I could hear the pounding of his feet as he ran away.

I slumped against the wall. "And hurry."

The stairwell was now to my right at the corner of the building. I was looking forward to more oxygen than the hallway was providing. When I got to the corner, I thought for just a split second that I might've heard something. "Albert?" A cough, and I adjusted my eyes to the partial darkness. "Albert!"

There was a faint response, whispered and hoarse, from far down the hall, "Here."

The temptation to pull my sidearm was great but knowing that if I fired it the place would go off like a Roman candle in a fireworks trailer was enough to give me pause. I hustled down the hall—Albert lay in the doorway of the far stairwell and was trying to prop himself up. He was bleeding from a wound at the back of his head but not too badly.

I grabbed him and lifted him above the gas—it was something of a miracle that he hadn't choked to death already. "Albert, what happened?"

His head lolled a bit. "Stupid, got hit from behind."

I got him up on his feet when I noticed that he was missing one of his shoes. "They knocked your shoe off?"

He shook his head to clear it. "Lodged it in the doorway above so that we could get out."

I smiled. "Good man. C'mon, here we go."

Hoisting him up onto my hip, where I could grip under his arm and support most of his weight, I started us up the stairs. I looked at the exterior door and figured the first thing to do would be to get him to some fresh air; then I could decide if I was stupid enough to come back into the building. I stumbled toward it.

Albert coughed. "All the exterior doors are locked; there's a double-lock mechanism." He gestured toward his side. "They took my keys."

I turned and looked toward the interior of the building, where Albert's shoe was lodged in the door. It was like we were being herded. "Looks like we have to find another way out."

We limped our way across the concrete landing where I pulled open the door to the main part of the building, the wisps of propane gas following us; I was careful to kick Albert's shoe out of the way.

The lights were off in the main hallway, but the corner of the building where Human Services resided was lit up like Christmas.

I sighed. "Any ideas?"

He tried to stand, but I could feel that he still needed support. "We can try toward the back."

We turned and started down the main hallway that ran the length of the building. "Just out of curiosity, were the junction cords that had been tapped into from Human Services?"

"Yes."

"How many people know that that system exists?"

He stumbled in his attempt to get his feet underneath him.

"Hardly anybody. Nobody goes into that basement; you'd have to be an old-timer, like me."

I thought about old-timers, red foxes, and medical bracelets—and finally scratched that itch that had been bothering me. I turned to help Albert again and when I did, I saw a familiar outline silhouetted by the EXIT lights near the center of the building.

He was even wearing the hat and was leaning on the security desk, an unopened bottle of Wild Turkey sitting on top of the sign-in ledger.

I stopped and watched as he stepped into the center of the hallway and faced us, his hands clutched together. "Fancy meeting you here, Herbert."

He paused. "Hi, Sheriff." He pulled the unlit cigar from his mouth, and his voice was desolate and removed. "I thought I'd better clean up before you guys found out what I'd done." He exhausted a sad laugh and shook his head. "It's all so messed up."

"You killed her?"

The response was choked in his throat, crowded there along with his heart. "No. No, I didn't."

"She fell?"

"I was trying to talk to her, but she backed up and lost her balance. I tried to get to her, but she fell." His head jerked around in an attempt to find a way out of a place with no emotional exits. "I wouldn't have tried to kill my own child."

"So Adrian's yours?"

"Yes." He took a step forward, and I could see his face beneath the brim of the gray top hat, the eagle feather forward. It was at that moment I saw that he had put the cigar back in his mouth and was holding the old, combat-cut, brass-covered Zippo lighter in his hand.

I started to speak but coughed with a whiff of the heavy gas. "I don't suppose you'd like to take this conversation outside?"

He shook his head. "No." I took a couple of steps toward him, still supporting Albert, narrowing the forty feet between us.

He lifted the lighter toward the cigar. "I think you better stay there."

I stopped. "Did you kill Clarence Last Bull?"

He turned his head and looked at the door to the basement that he'd propped open to allow the gas to filter in. "He deserved it; he was a disease." He gestured with the cigar, pointing it at me like a gun. "He beat her. He beat her, and he hurt my child." There was a sob in his voice. "He slept with any woman who would have him. . . . The drugs around the place—it was horrible. My beautiful, strong son living in a place like that." He lowered the cigar but held the lighter next to his chest.

I waited a moment. "Are you planning on taking all of us with you?"

He nodded a curt nod. "That was the idea."

"Was?"

He cleared his throat. "I'm just . . . so tired of all of it." He looked down the hall. "Where's Barrett?"

"He got out through the old coal chute in the back."

"That's good; I wouldn't want him getting hurt."

I took another step and nodded toward the bottle of liquor on the desk. "So, it's just you, me, and Albert here to celebrate?"

I could see him swallow as he brought the cigar back up and glanced at the bottle. "I guess so."

I took a few more steps. "So you're going to kill off the only blood relative Adrian's got?"

He paused. "I don't see any other way out of this."

"There isn't any way out of this, but there's a way through it— you killed a man, and you're going to do time; I don't know how much because that isn't my decision, but you'll be alive and can tell your son what happened. You can tell him about his mother."

He nodded, but I could see his face tighten as he coughed. "She was a good woman." He stepped to the side and gestured with the cigar again, as if ushering us out of a movie theatre. "You might as well get out of here, Sheriff. The stairwell is unlocked. That way I can have a last drink and light my cigar."

I took a few steps closer. "You're sure that's what you want to do?"

He nodded his head some more, and I got within twenty feet of him before he stuffed the cigar in the corner of his mouth and flipped open the aged Zippo. "I'm sure."

I looked down and could see the old chief's eyes, dazed but watching us. "Albert?"

The eyes wobbled toward me. "Yes?"

"You think you can make it out of the building on your own?"

He nodded. "I think so, but . . ."

"You need to go. I'm just going to stay here for a minute and talk to Herbert." Even with his passive resistance, I ushered him through the side and watched as he carefully made his way toward the exterior door. He pushed on the bar, the door swung wide, and he turned to look at me.

I was thankful for the flood of clear air, but it didn't last long as the heavy door swung back and closed like a tomb.

Casually, Herbert lifted the lighter to the cigar, his thumb on the wheel of the thing; his only souvenir of a long-dead war. He didn't move but just stood there with his head dipped, ready to strike. "Tell my son that I loved him."

Keeping my intentions clear, I turned and folded my arms, leaning my back against the coolness of the corner of the wall behind me. I crossed my boots and stared down at the six feet between us as if I had all the time in the world. I brought my face up slowly to look into the one brown eye that was revealed under his hat with the one gray eye under the brim of mine.

He still didn't move but spoke out of the side of his mouth. "I'm not bluffing, Sheriff."

"I know that; I also know that as soon as this propane hits an ignition source like a water heater or a pilot light, it won't matter who's bluffing." I blew air through my nose in an attempt to drive some of the gas away. "You say you're tired and that you've had enough. Well, there's really only one way to end this in a respectable fashion—give me the lighter."

If I was going to make a grab for it, now would've been the time.

It was then that there was an incredible clatter behind Herbert from the other end of the hallway. I fully expected the building to go up, but it didn't, and we both stood there as I glanced out the window and saw Barrett Long's truck dragging the doors at the end of a tow strap.

I was right; he did figure it out.

I was just glad the sparks the metal doors were making on the surface of the parking lot were far away and receding.

Our attention was suddenly drawn to the other end of the hall where Lolo Long had thrown herself through the door and had swung both the beam of her Maglite and the barrel of that big revolver of hers toward us. "Freeze. Police!"

She was doing better.

Herbert backed against the desk and looked at me, his thumb still on the wheel of the Zippo.

I shouted as quickly as I could. "Don't shoot. The entire basement is full of propane; one shot and the whole place goes up."

She looked uncertain but continued down the hall toward us with her sidearm and flashlight still pointed toward Herbert. It was only when she was about twenty feet away that she noticed the cigar and, more important, the lighter in his hands.

"Holster the weapon, Lolo."

She ignored me and gestured at him with the barrel of the Smith. "Drop the lighter."

We stood there with her on one side of the stairwell opening, me on the other, and Herbert facing the creeping gas that continued to seep up from the basement.

"Chief, holster the weapon."

She looked at me for the briefest of seconds and then did as I'd asked.

I took a breath before speaking again, hoping it wasn't my last. "Herbert? I sure would hate to think that after all the places we've been and all the stuff we've been through, that it would all end like this."

After a moment, his eyes turned to mine.

I pushed off the wall and stuffed my hands in the pockets of my jeans. "You say you're tired. Well, I'm tired too." I watched as his eyes shifted, and he studied the lighter in his hands. "My daughter is getting married at Crazy Head Springs in a few days and I sure would like to be there for that, just like I'd think Chief Long here would like to go see her son up in Billings, and I imagine you'd like to be around for Adrian's first birthday whether it's through Plexiglas or not."

He didn't move, and I wondered for just the briefest of moments what it would be like to be flash fried in the instant it would take for him to roll the thumbwheel on the flint and spark the tiniest of flames in the lighter's windscreen. The alarms would clamor and most likely the building itself would be lifted off its foundation; the sprinklers would come on, but unlike the movies, reality would dictate water pressure—and the Tribal Headquarters of the Northern Cheyenne would burn again.

We would likely never know it or see it; instead, the force of ignition and instantaneous explosion would carry the three of us through the hallway, through the doors and staircase, and throw us out onto the lawn like pulverized, flame-broiled meat.

But I had faith in Herbert His Good Horse, the man who had brought so much laughter and good will to his fellow man. "Considering what it is you're thinking of doing, I have to tell you that I don't see much romance in death. We've seen too much of it." I sighed and continued, figuring that if I was going to die, I was at least going to have my say. "I've been in these situations before and can tell you that there's nothing romantic about it, nothing heroic—dead is just dead." I slowly pulled a single hand from my pocket and held it out to him, steady there between us, palm up. "What is it that Jimi Hendrix says about love?"

He kept his eyes on me but didn't move, the words on the lighter pouring out of him like music. "When the power of love overcomes the love of power, the world will know peace."

His thumb relaxed on the wheel of the lighter. "Hey, a Native American, First Nations Indigenous Person, and a white guy walk into a multicultural drinking establishment. . . ." He studied me with a broad smile. "You don't like that one? Neither do I. Okay, try this one—two Indians walk *out* of a bar . . ."

I waited for the punch line with my hand still extended.

His smile faded. "Hey . . . it could happen."

EPILOGUE

I stood there in my stiff dress clothes and tried not to scratch as I watched the traditional Cheyenne wedding ceremonial procession approach, replete with mounted retinue and my white-buckskin-clad daughter.

As father of the bride, I had been offered a traditional outfit of my own but was having enough trouble with my tuxedo jacket and tie. I stuffed a forefinger into the collar of my dress shirt and pulled it a little looser, trying not to feel like the butler to the Northern Cheyenne tribe.

After a moment, I shifted back to twirling my wife's engagement ring on my little finger and felt a sharp jab from an elbow. "Stop fidgeting."

I spoke to her in a low voice. "I can't help it; I think the last time I wore this was at the Wyoming Sheriff's Association Ball when I first got elected."

"I thought sheriffs didn't have balls?"

"Ha, ha." I looked down at my undersheriff and sister of the groom. She'd elected to come over to the bride's side because she liked us better. "I figured we'd lost you to Nebraska."

"Fuck that."

The formal procession drew near, and Cady was radiant.

"She looks great."

I smiled. "Yep, she does."

"It's nice that she's not showing."

I gave Victoria Moretti a look.

"I'm just sayin'." Her eye wandered. "Even my two-headed brother looks good."

I studied Michael, who was about to become my son-in-law. He looked a little dazed and confused, kind of the way that other guy did what seemed like a century ago. Granted, Martha and I hadn't had the pomp and circumstance; we'd had only that justice of the peace from Miles City and his wife playing the accordion, but it had been enough to galvanize our lives together.

Michael looked like he might run, but there were the three other Moretti brothers to chase him down, and the old man, Chief of Detectives North, who would likely just put a bullet in his leg and then charge the municipality of Philadelphia for his ammunition.

Lena Moretti was lovely, as usual, in a knee-length off-white dress; she was doing her best to look cool and unflappable as her high heels sank into the rich earth of Crazy Head Springs.

We had a motley bunch seated on our side of the aisle—my dispatcher, Ruby, with Dog; my old boss, Lucian; and a contingency of deputies—Saizarbitoria with Marie and Antonio, the Ferg and his wife, and Frymire, Double-Tough having volunteered to man the desk back at the office. Dorothy, who had made the wedding cake from one of Alphonse's old-world recipes, was seated next to Lucian, as were most of the field office of the FBI, including Agent in Charge Cliff Cly, and even a couple of Philadelphia Police Department detectives of our own, Katz and Gowder. Mary Barsad was there with Juana and Benjamin, and Omar and Lana and Bill and, of course, Doc Bloomfield.

The Cheyenne chief sat in his wheelchair with Melissa behind him and smiled over the pageantry of the approaching bride. His right-hand man, the Cheyenne Nation, stood a little closer to us on the ceremonial bed of white sage. I repeated to myself, over and over—*E-hestana Na-he-stonahanotse, E-hestana Na-he-stonaha-notse, E-hestana Na-he-stonahanotse.*

"Are you chanting to yourself?"

I hadn't realized I was mumbling. "I'm trying to remember how to say my line."

She shook her head and spoke from the side of her mouth. "Look, nobody's going to be paying any attention to you. All right?"

I nodded.

She changed the subject, probably hoping to divert my attention. "So, KRZZ is looking for a new morning drive guy?"

I watched as the black horse carrying my daughter crossed the clearing as the other maidens, including Dena Many Camps, followed on their own mounts in single file. "I guess so. It turned out the first child that Audrey miscarried was Clarence's, but when he was in Iraq he got hurt."

Vic leaned in. "So the one that went over the cliff with his mother?"

"Adrian."

"Adrian belonged to Herbert His Good Horse?"

"Yep. Audrey was leaving the Rez with Clarence and taking Adrian with her. I guess it was more than Herbert could stand; Adrian is the last living heir to the His Good Horse name."

"What about the nephew in the wheelchair?"

"Karl's name was different, Red Fox, and that's why it didn't ring any bells on the medication listing I got from Lolo Long's mother at Health Services—at least at first."

"And the bracelet belonged to Karl?"

"Yep, it belonged to his great-grandfather, who fought in France during WWI; then Herbert used it to put Karl's medication on when he lost his legs in the car crash. After a while, Karl was doing so well that Herbert started wearing the bracelet as a reminder. Audrey must've pulled it off of him when they were struggling."

"So, he was the one who tried to run over you on 212?"

"Yep."

"And Herbert made the tape from recordings at the Tribal Offices?"

"Yep, and just filled in the parts he needed Clarence to say by manipulating his own voice. He'd been worried about what Audrey was going to do and had been taping her for months."

"And used the Old Indian Trick of blaming it on the FBI?"

I shifted my weight. "Herbert was a source for the BIA and dropped the tape on them anonymously. The FBI would've figured it out with a little more analysis, but everybody was in a hurry to jail Artie."

"Well, they must not have taken it too badly since they're in attendance." She glanced at the collected law-enforcement and then over their heads where a small contingency of tribal security, two officers to be exact, stood watch. "Is that her?"

I rested my eyes on the tall woman with the broad shoulders, her hair loose for once, spreading down her back like a luxurious, blue-black shawl. I noticed she'd traded in the S&W for a Sig-Sauer P229 .40, complete with stylish rosewood grips. After a second, the jasper eyes turned and looked back at us, and I could've sworn she'd overheard our conversation from almost fifty feet away. The nearest eyebrow was arched, and her full lips were smiling.

My undersheriff turned her head to look at me. "I don't like her."

"Too bad; you have a lot in common."

"You think so?"

I turned and looked at her for a change. "I was giving sheriff lessons."

"I bet you were."

A familiar voice sounded from just behind us. "I hate to break up this lovely conversation, but would you mind going and helping your daughter off the horse so that she can get married?"

I glanced back at the Cheyenne Nation, master of ceremonies, my best friend, and the man who was going to actually be marrying my daughter to Michael Moretti. *"E-hestana Na-he-stonahanotse."*

He looked at me blankly.

"Right?"

He shrugged and nudged me with a strong hand. "Close enough."

Vic added, under her breath, "You're on."

I started the walk down the aisle between the two families, as Ruby, always able to read my moods, stretched a hand out to squeeze mine as I passed, in a token of reassurance.

There were rows of poles meandering across the meadow and leading into the forest at the head of the valley that led down to the springs. The staffs were festooned with Indian paintbrush and white and pale-blue ribbons, the Cheyenne traditional colors, and flittered in the slight breeze.

The scent of cedar, sage, and sweetgrass filtered through the air as I pulled up at the back of the crowd alongside the tribal police chief and sighed deeply.

She glanced at me, still wearing the smile. "I don't think your undersheriff likes me."

"No, I don't think she does." I glanced at Lolo Long. "You mind telling me something?"

"What?"

"What is it you've got against Henry?"

She looked uncomfortable, and I was almost sorry I'd asked. "Nothing big." She paused. "I had this huge crush on him when I was a kid, and he never gave me the time of day. He even dated my mom."

I glanced at her.

"There was a time when my mother was rather hot."

"I don't doubt it." I played with the ring on my little finger. "Where is your mother?"

"In Billings, making arrangements to adopt Adrian—there was no other time or she would be here. I'm supposed to go up there after the ceremony."

I leaned a little forward and watched as Albert Black Horse, in full Tribal Police uniform, did his best to ignore us and watch my daughter approach. "Well, you've got good help these days."

I listened as the Four Dances Drum Group beat in time to the horses walking down the pathway. *E-hestana Na-he-stonahanotse, E-hestana Na-he-stonahanotse, E-hestana Na-he-stonahanotse.*

"I might try and visit my son, while I'm up there."

I nodded my head, and then realized what she'd said and smiled back at her.

"Nothing big, just touching base. You know, get things started."

"I think that's a great idea."

She waited a moment before speaking again, and I could tell it was still hard for her. "If I haven't mentioned it . . ."

"You have."

She leaned a shoulder into my arm and bumped me—and that was enough.

The black mare made the last turn in the path, and I could now see that its mane was braided like Cady's hair. "You know, it was something you said that jogged my memory loose about the connection between Herbert and Karl and the bracelet. When you were getting ready to head off, you said something about the family stuff being more than you wanted to handle, and it got me thinking."

"You're being kind."

"I'm being honest." I took a breath and repeated my line, careful to not speak out loud this time.

"You'd be very proud of me, Walt; I wrote up a very nice report explaining to the DOJ that Special Agent Cly was instrumental in breaking the case and that I was looking forward to working with him in the future."

I nodded. "You're trying to get rid of him."

"Just as fast as paperwork can travel."

Breathing a laugh, I glanced back at the AIC, and he raised his eyebrows at me.

My attention was drawn to the sky as two large, dark birds circled each other, and I quietly prayed that they weren't turkey vultures. I looked at Lolo. "So, you're going to keep the job?"

There was a long pause as she thought about it. "For a while; see if it suits me."

I reached out and bumped the extra mags on her gunbelt with the back of my hand as I stepped forward. "It does."

Cady had pulled Wahoo Sue up to the assigned spot; she was an admirable horsewoman but working without a saddle or bridle was always a trick. I raised my hands up to her, took her by the waist, and gently lowered her to the ground.

She looked at me and grinned, and I don't think I'd ever seen her so beautiful. She spoke in a whisper as her hand crept up and stroked the big horse to quiet her. "So far, so good."

"Better than the wedding march on an accordion, I can tell you that." I took her hand, and we turned toward the altar, a little time to spare as the menfolk answered Henry's questions and got themselves together. "You look marvelous."

"Thank you; you look pretty spiffy yourself."

"Spiffy, huh?"

She hugged my arm. "Yeah."

"I seem to recall that as one of your mother's words."

"It was." She hugged my arm tighter, and we both took a deep breath. "I wish she was here."

"Me too." I cleared my throat and remembered the ring. "Um, I've got something to give you."

She glanced at me, a trace of annoyance in her voice. "Now?"

"Well, yep. Here in a couple of minutes, it'll be too late." I placed my fingers around the ring on my little finger and pulled. There was a slight panic when it felt as if I might not be able to get it over the knuckle, but, after the second try, it came free.

I handed it to my daughter.

She took it, staring at the smallish diamond surrounded by two chips, one on either side of the antique setting.

"It belonged to your great-great-grandmother. I gave it to your mother as an engagement ring when we got married, but she made me take it back for you when she . . . when . . ." I took another breath, knowing our time was running out. "Toward the end."

She looked up at me through the wayward strands of strawberry blonde, her eyes shining.

"She wanted you to have it."

She swallowed and slipped the ring onto the same finger as the engagement ring that Michael had given her, the dichotomy between the sizes of the two stones almost laughable.

"In 1863 that was a big diamond."

She laughed and cut the circulation off in my arm. "It's all going to be all right." Her clear, gray eyes came up to mine. "Right?"

"Right."

Henry Standing Bear gestured toward the small Longmire family, the fringe under the arm of his outstretched sleeve swaying with the light breeze. We started down the aisle and toward the waiting Morettis. For a second, I was reminded of something a friend had said, something on the mountain, something ominous—but I pushed that from my mind and looked up to see that the two birds I'd noticed were crows circling right above the meadow, the primaries of their wing tips spread like fingers as they rode the thermals that lifted them into the cloudless sky.

Maybe it was an omen, but I decided to take it as a good one. I'd heard that crows mate for life and are known to raise their young for as long as five years.

Sometimes you don't get that long.

I thought about Audrey Plain Feather and how her life hadn't turned out the way she'd hoped—maybe nobody's did.

My wife Martha's hadn't. Mine hadn't. Even Henry's hadn't.

Maybe Cady's would.

It's hopes like this that you cling to at major turning points in your life and, more important, the lives of your children. You keep going, and you hope for the best, and sometimes, maybe not very often, your hopes come true.

I took the luxury of watching the crows playing tag above our heads for a moment more, the graceful arc of their patterns intertwining in figure eights of infinity. That was probably our job here, to keep going and to do it with as much artistry and beauty as our hearts could bear.

Henry was talking to me when I lowered my face.

I hadn't caught what he'd said, and it wouldn't have made any difference if I had, because I wouldn't have understood it, but I looked down at the young woman on my arm, all my dreams and hopes bundled together in one achingly beautiful woman.

I turned to my friend and the world, and the words poured from me like a fervent prayer. *"E-hestana Na-he-stonahanotse."*